THE ANGELS ARE CRYING
2nd Edition

Richard D'Onofrio

THE ANGELS ARE CRYING
2nd Edition

DOUBLE DRAGON

Dedication

For Brenda:

My Inspiration;
My Collaborator;
My Muse;
My Mentor;
And The Love of My Life!

For the strongest person I know; I love you with all my
heart!

Chapter 1

Dozens of waiters dressed in tuxedos walked between the tables in the large, dimly lighted room. Workers transformed the company cafeteria into a surreal scene for the very special event. Black lights bathed the white walls with a purple glow. Symphony music played from speakers while fog machines covered the floor with a white mist. The waiters served drinks and appetizers to approximately five hundred guests seated at the tables. A single white candle on each table lighted the guest's faces while they watched a video on a huge plasma monitor. They were silent, intrigued, while watching scientists working in a nearby laboratory.

News reporters and film crews lined the walls of the room. Reporters documented the activities, while their crews recorded the activities in the cafeteria.

Peter Samulson, the president of Endeavor BioEngineering stood near a podium at the front of the cafeteria. He motioned to Raymond Jacobs, the company's Vice-President of Research and Development. "I'm going to make history today with my announcement."

"I agree." Ray smiled. "You're about to describe a great scientific achievement."

Peter gestured toward his guests. "I flew these investment bankers in from around the world. They represent billions in investment opportunities. I need them to invest their money in my company, so I can expand."

"Present the details of Osiris to them. When they see it in action, they'll know it's a money maker."

Peter motioned toward the monitor. "I need my brother to run the live demonstration without any problems."

"I read the text of his presentation. It's first rate. He'll impress these investors."

"They know we're onto something big. They need me to save their banks and portfolios, and their jobs. Banks and institutional investment firms need our help to make them money. Things change in just a few short years." Peter laughed while waving to people he recognized.

"Why do you say that?"

Peter greeted several institutional investment executives by name. "Some of these so called executives refused to give me funding when I started this company eight years ago. They're all neophytes compared to me."

"Maybe they were concerned you were asking for millions based only on theoretical ideas."

"They told me I was too young at thirty. They didn't like my strategy to market bio-engineered products developed by superior researchers."

"This company is best in class today. They were wrong about you, and the amazing capabilities of our research and development staffs."

"They're sheep, following the leader. Our sales are in the billions. I'm a multi-millionaire. They're here to get a piece of my action." Peter pounded his fist on the podium. "It's going to cost them

8

substantial amounts of money to be part of my history making achievement."

Ray realized Peter's anger was becoming uncontrollable again. He pointed at the monitor to change the subject. "Our preparations for the demo are right on schedule."

"They better be. I want this demonstration to portray my company as a world class organization."

The guests watched the scientists pull on rubber gloves and safety goggles. They moved around a long and tall clear glass trough to fill it with hundreds of empty plastic water and soda bottles. They placed plastic forks, spoons, knives, and cups on the bottles. Then they placed a layer of clean diapers on the bottles, and a large number of foam cups and plates.

An overhead spotlight suddenly highlighted Peter in the cafeteria. His long bleached blonde ponytail dangling on his custom tailored suit was a stark contrast to his shoulder length black hair. "Good afternoon, everyone. You're watching activity that is taking place in a laboratory sixty feet beneath our feet. You're about to watch a demonstration of my company's Model 276 Bacteria, otherwise known as Osiris. Our newly engineered bacterium has the potential to help solve the world's need for oil!"

The investors immediately became skeptical. Many expressed their concerns. One man laughed before he said, "Don't tell us you're converting grass into a fuel additive. That's an outdated concept, and will not make any of us money!"

"I'm wasting my time here, when I should be out looking at money making investments," an investor told his colleagues. "This is a dog and pony show, where both animals are old and tired."

Peter walked between the tables to be closer to his audience. "I invited you here to share the details of a new product that will change the world. It will produce hundreds of billions of dollars in revenue. If you're not interested, please get up and leave."

The man appeared embarrassed. "Maybe we all spoke too soon. Please continue with your presentation."

"Thank you all for allowing me to continue, uninterrupted." Peter concealed his contempt for the people in the cafeteria. "My bacteria will make millions for you, keep your shareholders happy, and save your plush jobs!"

An investment executive said, "That's what we're here to learn about. Give us the details." Others agreed.

Peter took a deep breath to calm himself. "When my researchers created Osiris, they considered the largest untapped resource in the world." Overhead projectors began displaying videos of towering piles of trash in landfills, onto the walls around the cafeteria. "That resource is the plastic and foam materials created from oil."

"I'm not investing millions in another trash to energy plant," a woman said, as she sat back on a chair. Many others vehemently agreed with her statement. "History has shown, they're not profitable, and we lose tens of millions of dollars each year."

"Trash to energy is old news. Converting that trash to fuel is the new solution!" Peter nodded to the group. "Nature will take thousands of years to biodegrade plastic and foam trash. Every piece of plastic and foam discarded by man remains buried in a landfill somewhere on this planet. That almost unlimited supply of plastic, and my Osiris bacteria, is what the world needs to fuel its cars."

"Create fuel from plastic? Absurd!" Someone shouted.

"I want to hear more." Another investor appeared intrigued by Peter's explanation. "Tell us how this process works."

"Simply put, Osiris converts ordinary plastic and foam waste into synthetic fuel."

Everyone appeared shocked after the explanation. They began talking, expressing their views to one another.

A man said, "Where will you find huge amounts of plastic to convert to fuel?"

"My bacteria will facilitate the need for everyone to recycle. Everyone will understand their efforts to save our planet, will also produce a cheap fuel for their vehicles."

"Can you retrieve the plastic trash buried in our landfills?" A woman said, while others around her shouted questions to Peter.

"I'm working with a major earth moving equipment producer. We're developing machines to burrow through landfills to retrieve plastic. So yes, we will have the technology to locate plastic in landfills."

"That is a marvelous idea," a man said. Others agreed in conversations with colleagues.

"The demand for my bacteria will outperform expectations when governments realize it will solve another problem. Removing the plastic from landfills will make space available for more trash.

"Waste disposal is a huge global crisis, because we're running out of landfills, and places to dump our trash," a woman said, while writing notes on a pad. "I'm already investing in trash compacting equipment."

Peter laughed before he said, "My company has the only solution that will make your venture capital companies, and banks, huge sums of revenue. Our nation will no longer bury plastic and foam products in landfills. My bacteria will remove bulky plastic waste, to free additional space in currently operating landfills. The bacteria will also reopen closed landfills for years to come, after removing the plastic buried in them."

"Do you have your marketing strategy we can review?" Someone said.

Other financial people began asking for more details about the bacteria and the profit projections over a several year period. The people in the room became excited, as they realized investment in Peter's company would make them money.

"I'll share that information with all of you. My financial projections show Model 276 will make my company the most profitable in the world, even during times of economic crisis."

A man rested his chin on his hand, while thinking. Then he said, "Helping the environment, while producing fuel, is an intriguing concept. This may make all of us heroes." He smiled as the group unanimously agreed with his comments, showing their growing enthusiasm.

A video of whales in the ocean flashed onto the walls. The scene changed to show miles of plastic bottles, plastic containers, and plastic trash, floating on seemingly endless blue ocean water. Music appropriate for a funeral accompanied the depressing graphic video.

Peter took a glass of water from a waiter. He sipped it, intentionally pausing to give the people time to view the vast array of plastic trash floating on the water. "This is a lesser known problem."

"Is that plastic garbage floating in our oceans?" A frowning man said. He listened as other people began shouting similar questions.

Peter raised his hands to quiet the group, so he could continue. "Two-hundred billion pounds of plastic products are produced each year. Ten percent ends up in the ocean, creating what we refer to as the Great Pacific Garbage Patch. One patch floats between California and Hawaii. It's twice the size of Texas. The second patch containing plastic garbage is west of Hawaii."

"That's appalling," a disgusted man said.

"I had no idea this problem is so extensive," an outraged woman said. "We're destroying our oceans."

"Imagine how the price of my company's stock will increase in value, after I announce Osiris will clean up the oceans, while creating precious fuel. The environmentalists will love me!"

As one man wrote notes on a napkin, he said, "How will you retrieve that plastic from the ocean?"

"Shipbuilders are designing vessels to harvest the plastic. Osiris will convert it to fuel at sea. Each time a ship docks, it will carry millions of gallons of cheaply produced fuel."

"Let's get back to basics," someone said. "How do you grow your bacteria?"

"We utilize a cheap nutrient solution to propagate the bacteria." Peter displayed a graphic on the walls. "It's nothing more than chicken soup."

The bankers studied the numbers. "No costs, other than storage and application. This bacterium has great potential." He smiled to others while realizing their skepticism was quickly turning to loud enthusiasm.

"Is the bacteria environmentally safe?"

"We've proved with extensive testing that the bacteria will not harm the environment." Peter noticed his technicians on the monitor were ready. "My brother Roger, the project's lead scientist is ready to demonstrate Osiris."

Roger lifted a microphone in the laboratory. He stepped to the glass trough. "Hello everyone. This test area represents the trash found in landfills. During this demonstration you'll watch how Osiris biodegrades the materials into a highly flammable liquid which can be used as an alternative fuel source."

"What happens to the bacteria when it's done biodegrading?" An impatient woman said as she looked at her watch.

14

Roger smiled after the interruption. He was two years younger than his brother, but was much more charismatic. "After Osiris completes the biodegrading process, it dies from a lack of nourishment. The cells remain in the created fuel, and are burned away harmlessly in an internal combustion engine."

Another scientist stepped to a control panel. "I'm Paul Jackson, one of the primary Osiris designers. I'll apply the Model 276 sample bacteria to the test area." A bluish green liquid began spraying onto items in the trough from small overhead tubes. The bacteria coated the plastic and foam products.

"Now you'll see my bacteria in action." Peter smiled as his guests intently watched the monitor.

"I see something happening," a surprised man said, "The plastic bottles appear to be collapsing."

"They're turning into a liquid," said a woman excitedly. In her excitement, she knocked over several nearby champagne glasses. "It's working! I can see it working!"

"The entire pile of trash is collapsing," said another amazed woman. "It's turning to liquid."

Thirty seconds later the last of the trash seemed to disappear. Roger said, "Thomas Goldberg will now demonstrate the combustible characteristics the fuel Osiris created, while biodegrading the plastic trash."

A short and overweight man removed a container filled with a bluish green liquid from under the trough. "You could put this fuel into your car right now, and use it to get home." He poured the liquid into a shallow clear glass container. Then he placed an electronic igniter into it. A large blue flame suddenly erupted from the container, when the fuel ignited explosively.

Peter raised his hands, symbolically calming everyone. "You are in no danger. That concludes our demonstration of Osiris. A revolutionary bacterium, that will help solve the world's energy and trash issues. The latest product from Endeavor BioEngineering."

"This might be the most important discovery in the past one hundred years," a young financial person said, as he entered a message into his cell phone.

Another man agreed. "I want to see your research data and financial projections. This company will be a large part of my investment portfolio tomorrow."

A door opened and Roger, Paul, and Thomas walked into the cafeteria. Peter's invited guests began congratulating them. They were surprised and pleased after the investors unexpectedly stood and began clapping.

Peter placed his hand on Roger's shoulder. "My brother has a Doctorate from Vanderbilt University. Together we form an unbeatable team!" He vigorously shook Roger's hand.

"Thank you." Roger nodded to the group. His boyish face, blonde hair, and alluring smile made him immediately likeable. He rolled up the sleeves of his white shirt.

Peter shook Paul's hand. "This is Paul Jackson. He graduated from Cal Tech. He's been a member of the Osiris project since its inception three years ago."

Paul waved to the clapping people. "Thanks." The periodic table symbols covering his tie signaled the group he was the technical member of the team.

Peter then said, "This is Thomas Goldberg. He's a graduate of MIT. He joined the project team less than a year ago."

"Hi ya'all. Glad to know yah." Thomas' artificial southern accent, and his red shirt and jeans, seemed to confuse the invited guests. He smiled self-consciously, after he heard them making unflattering remarks to one another related to his attire and presentation skills.

Peter said, "Now the development team leaders we'll explain the process that went into the development of our bacteria."

Roger began explaining the details contained in a PowerPoint presentation projected onto the walls of the cafeteria for the financial people. He explained the strategy employed to develop and test the bacteria.

Paul spoke next, reiterating Model 276 would benefit the world by reducing trash in landfills, while reducing the world's dependency for oil.

Thomas spoke last. He shocked Peter when he said, "This presentation is so boring. Let me show you how my recommendations helped Model 276 to evolve."

"What are you doing?" Roger watched Thomas open his own PowerPoint presentation. Rock music suddenly began blaring from the speakers, while various images of laboratories displayed on the wall.

Thomas smiled at the investors, confident he could impress them. "When I joined this company, the Osiris project was going nowhere. It was an over budget, failure. It was my brainchild, my ideas, which gave birth to a bacterium that can biodegrade plastic." He paused while watching people whispering to one another.

Peter was furious after the unexpected statements. "This is not part of my presentation."

"How did you accomplish that amazing feat, and save the project for Peter?" An investor said, while pointing at Thomas.

"I determined how to re-engineer a bacterium living deep in the earth stratum. It's the same bacterium that creates oil from decaying debris which is millions of years old." Thomas lifted a piece of cheese from a shocked man's plate, before he ate it. When a waiter passed by with a tray, he grasped a glass of champagne, before he drank from it.

An investor said, "Do I understand this correctly? You reversed the process that creates oil?"

"Yes I did. My ideas will biodegrade plastic into fuel." During the next thirty minutes, Thomas explained his theories, proposals, and efforts that fostered development of Osiris.

"Will you improve Osiris in the future so that it biodegrades rubber too?"

Thomas laughed at the question. "No, that would make the bacteria uncontainable and very dangerous. I'm pleased the bacteria in its present form, will help to save the world from an ecological disaster, and put gas in my car."

"This scientist is a genius," a man said after the detailed explanation. He clapped with his companions.

"He saved your project, Peter," another said, "You should double, no, triple his salary."

"This genius may have singlehandedly saved our planet with his groundbreaking ideas," another finance person said. That remark brought cheers and clapping from the group.

Peter frowned as he said, "The Osiris development team will now take your questions."

The group responded to questions for three hours. News camera operators filmed the discussion in the cafeteria, as reporters documented notes using their electronic devices.

Peter eventually concluded the meeting, when he said, "Ladies and gentlemen, I want to thank you for your participation. I hope you consider Endeavor Biological Engineering a sound investment option, with the promise of high return on your investments."

An investor speaking to his partners on his cell phone said, "When do you envision the first full production test of Osiris?"

Peter noticed other institutional investors were already on the phone, buying Endeavor stock. He became ecstatic. He realized he had their interest. "I plan to conduct a test within ninety days."

"Why are you waiting so long? Why can't we have the test conducted sooner, so we can see the results in a real world setting?"

Peter motioned to a tall man in the cafeteria. "Let me introduce John Harrison, from the Environmental Protection Agency. I'll let him explain the holdup."

Harrison, a tall black man, stepped to the podium. "My agency is coordinating the first outside of the lab test of Osiris. Our job is to ensure the bacteria will not adversely affect or influence people, or the environment. When we're satisfied the bacteria is safe, we'll approve the test."

"What is your opinion of Osiris? Will it help resolve some of our environmental problems?" An investor asked. He wanted information while on the phone buying huge amounts of the company stock.

"We're very impressed with the bacteria, and the safeguards the company instituted during the development. We've worked very closely with Endeavor throughout the development process, and we already see it as safe."

A bank investment officer on his cell phone speaking to his colleagues frantically said, "I want you guys to buy half a million shares of Endeavor before the American Stock Exchange closes. Do it now! This stock is going to explode in price when word of their new bacteria gets out. Buy it now, don't wait until the price skyrockets and we can't make money!"

Peter's Public Relations staff distributed binders containing detailed information related to the development of the Model 276 Osiris Bacteria, and company financial reports, to each investor. After Peter answered their remaining questions, he and Roger led the men and women to limousines waiting in the company parking lot. The spectacular Miami skyline glistened in the late afternoon sunlight as people walked in the heat and oppressive humidity.

After Peter and Roger returned to the cafeteria, they spoke to company employees, and congratulated them for their efforts to make the test successful.

Thomas walked around the cafeteria, drinking the champagne remaining in glasses on the tables. "I'd say that whole affair was awesome. What'd you all think?"

"I'd say it became a bloody disaster the minute you started talking, you disrespectful fool!" Peter became furious. "What was that crap you told those investors? I didn't authorize you to use a presentation I didn't review!"

Thomas ran his hand over his shoulder length dark hair. It was unwashed, dirty, and shined as if greasy. "I put it together last night to impress those big wig money guys. No time to show you today, Kimosabe."

"Don't ever do anything that embarrasses me, or my company! Do you understand me?"

"You gotta chill out, my man." Thomas drank champagne from another glass. "I'm an innovator, a rebel!"

Peter grasped his own long ponytail. "This reassures my customers I'm progressive and open minded. They know I'm willing to take on new challenges. I don't pay you to take chances with my company!"

"Whatever!" Thomas unexpectedly laughed, before he drank more champagne.

"You don't do anything unless I approve it. Do you understand me?"

"No problem, Kimosabe! You're the boss. I'm only the vastly underpaid laborer." Thomas drank champagne from another glass, before walking from the cafeteria.

"He made all of us look ridiculous," Paul said.

"Relax, it's not a big deal." Roger opened a bottle of champagne. He handed a glass to each man, before filling it. "I propose a toast, to a superb company and an excellent product development team."

Peter savored the flavor of the champagne. He read a text message sent to his cell phone. "I need fifteen minutes of everyone's time. That includes you Harrison. Let's review the plans for the open air test."

Peter led the group into a large conference room filled with his senior managers. "Give us an update about the test preparations."

A woman stood, while holding a pad covered with hand written notes. "Arrangements at the Arizona landfill are moving forward as planned, according to our timeline."

"How much is this test going to cost me?"

"We've estimated the cost to be approximately four hundred fifty thousand dollars, to retool a building on the site. The improvements include the ability to store and spray Osiris, and collect the fuel byproduct."

Peter nodded. "I'll recover those costs in the first month after we begin selling Osiris. I'm not concerned about those minimal expenditures."

Another man stood. "We have a public relations concern."

"What does that mean? Say it in English!" Peter appeared frustrated.

"The landfill test site is located miles from the nearest town. We'll need to provide transportation for our invited dignitaries and their visitors, and the press."

"Is that beyond your capabilities? I can find someone else to do your job, if you can't figure out how to handle the work load."

"I can make the arrangements. I'm just saying we have a lot of logistical work to complete before the test."

Peter interrupted. "I want the guest list to read like it's a White House dinner party. I want the powerful people in Washington to be there to watch the test. Do you understand why?"

"You want them to invest in the company?"

"I don't want their money, you fool! The television cameras will follow them to the test. I want the publicity!"

"Ok, my office will make the arrangements."

"What's the date of the test?" Peter sat back on the chair, while feeling exhausted after the presentation to investors. "I can't make money until the world sees Osiris in action!"

"We're approximately eight weeks from the actual test date."

"Let's ensure nothing goes wrong in the lead up to the test." Peter looked at his watch. "It's been a long, but productive day. Let's go out and celebrate."

Chapter 2

The following morning Peter was surprised when he checked his company's stock on an investment site. The price doubled overnight after financiers around the world purchased millions of dollars of his company's stock, while hoping for a large return on their investment. He was elated the activity increased his personal net worth by approximately twenty-two million dollars. He became more excited while watching the news, after he saw a story about his company's efforts to develop the Model 276 Osiris bacteria. As he changed channels with the remote, he found every newscaster talking about his company.

Peter walked onto the lavish patio behind his large mansion. He smiled while inspecting his yacht docked in the nearby canal. He nodded to an attractive woman he met the previous night at dinner, and brought home. She lounged naked in a hot tub beside the pool. One of the housekeepers served breakfast to another beautiful woman wearing a skimpy black bikini. Peter ignored their need for attention. He walked to the towering decorative waterfall beside the large swimming pool.

The sounds of the falling and splashing water helped him to relax while he thought, '*I'm going to be famous! The world owes me this for helping everyone solve their environmental problems! I'll be the wealthiest man in the world, and I deserve it all! No one can dispute that! I deserve everything! I mentored my scientists as they created Osiris. I alone grew my idea into reality, and should get full credit for it! I secured the funding for my scientists without anyone's help! I led my project team to success while they developed Osiris. I showed my Marketing team how to publicize my bacteria. I'm the one who lost sleep worrying about the project every night. I'm the one who wants to save the world with Osiris. I'm the one who wants to make a difference! Every business executive will want to be like me! Everyone will want to be me. A young, dynamic, handsome, business genius!'*

Peter's fists clenched tightly as he felt victorious. '*I'm going to be worshiped like a god for saving this planet! I'm going to have money, wealth, and beautiful women begging to be with me. I'm going to have it all!*'

He turned to the two women. "Finish up and then get out of here. I can do much better than you two whores!" Then he walked into his house.

After a long and strenuous workout in his home gym, Peter drove to the office. When he turned his Jaguar sports car onto the street leading to his company headquarters, he abruptly braked. He was surprised to see approximately sixty news trucks parked around the building. Reporters and camera crews rushed into the street hoping to interview him.

"Hello everyone," Peter said after he climbed from his car.

"We'd like to meet with you to discuss the details of your Osiris breakthrough," a reporter said.

"We can talk on the lawn in front of my building." Peter led the reporters and camera crews out of the street, and onto the lawn, where he answered their questions.

As the news conference was concluding, Peter noticed an attractive reporter standing in the blazing sun. He studied her long dark hair, and the distinctive gray business suit she wore. His gaze settled on her long slender legs while he spoke. After answering all of the reporter's questions, he walked to her. "And you are?"

"I'm Bonnie Franklin, from the Independent News network." She smiled, while shaking Peter's hand.

"It's a pleasure to meet you, Ms. Franklin. Can I show you around my headquarters building?"

"Thank you. I would enjoy seeing your labs, to get a better understanding of how you created Osiris."

"Then we can discuss you having dinner with me tonight at a fabulous restaurant in Miami."

"I have a personal rule, where I don't date any of the men I interview as part of my job!"

"Why is that?" Peter became angry.

"So I can remain neutral when presenting the facts related to stories."

"If you can't find the time to have dinner with me, then I don't have the time to give you a personal tour of my building." Peter turned his back on Bonnie, and walked to his car. Then he sped past her, and into the parking garage.

"He's a charmer," Bonnie said, before laughing with her camera operator, and sound crew.

During the next seven days, Peter, Roger, and their staff gave interviews to reporters from around the world. Scientists, environmentalists, and world leaders hailed the Model 276 Osiris bacteria as one of man's greatest achievements. Scientists, politicians, and world leaders praised Peter's efforts to save the environment on news talk shows.

The following week, several prominent magazines described Endeavor as the most innovative company of the century. Peter perpetuated that image by allowing news camera crews to film the daily activities inside his building. He and his staff were quickly becoming celebrities.

When Peter attended a meeting to discuss the status of preparations for the test in Arizona, the cameras followed. His staff reported building preparations were continuing according to the timeline. Paul and Roger reported they were working with the Environmental Protection Agency to complete the documentation required to approve the test.

Thomas began describing the plans to grow large amounts of the Osiris bacteria at the test site, in twelve tanker trucks. He suddenly stopped talking, after the company cell phone on his belt began vibrating. He frowned while reading a text message. After realizing everyone was staring at him, he mumbled, "My mom needs some help. I'll call her later."

After the meeting, Thomas left the building to have lunch. He drove to a well-known and crowded strip club in Miami frequented by college students. Inside, he recognized an older man seated at a table, talking to a young woman. The man wore a dark suit, sunglasses, and a western style hat.

William Bascom motioned Thomas to sit down. He told the woman, "I'll meet you later, darling. We'll head out on my boat, and make some waves together."

"I'm getting hot and wet just thinking about it." She toyed with her hair, while walking away.

"Tom, find yourself a woman like her. She'll take your mind off science," Bascom said.

"I have no use for women." He wiped the perspiration from his forehead. "They don't find me interesting because I'm not a jock. They'll be all over me when I win the Nobel Prize for Science."

"Congratulations on your success with that garbage eating bug."

"Stop calling it a bug! Osiris will make me famous."

"I hope it does, my boy. It'll make me prouder to know you."

"I perfected Osiris without help from the interfering losers who claim to be my superiors. I'm more intelligent than all of them combined."

"You're a genius, my boy. I don't deny it." Bascom looked around cautiously. "When can I get the bacteria's complete genetic map?"

"I don't know." Thomas shook his head. "Selling the genetic blueprint of the bacteria so other companies can make their own versions just doesn't seem right to me."

Bascom changed his approach. He realized he had to become the man's friend and trusted advisor.

"My employer will make you a millionaire. Will Endeavor do that?"

"Peter will give me a bonus after he begins selling Osiris. He really cares about me."

"I told you, he's using you! I'm the only one who cares about you." Bascom clasped his hands together on the table. "I've guided you, helped you, and gave you genetic splicing information, since your first posting asking for help in the Internet scientific groups. Now I want to help you again, and make you wealthy and very happy."

"Stealing the formula doesn't seem ethical. It's not right."

"Endeavor got what they wanted from you. Don't count on getting that bonus."

Thomas looked into his eyes. "How do you know that?"

"All large companies are the same. They'll take your work, and forget about you, before they discard you. You'll get nothing in return. I won't do that to you. I'll never forget you, if you help me."

"You are a true friend, when I have none," Thomas said, confessing his inner most concerns.

Bascom knew he had the young man's attention. "I know other scientists like you. They give everything for one amazing discovery. Then the world forgets about them and they die alone with no money, while their employer makes billions of dollars with their ideas."

"You're right. Peter's not being fair to me. I can see it now. It's all clear after I talk to you."

"I'm only trying to help you. You're my friend, and I want to see you succeed."

"You're the only one looking out for me." Thomas felt comfortable. He felt as if he was speaking to his father. "What do you want from me?"

"I need a copy of the Osiris genetic map."

"That's all?"

"Then you need to get rid of Endeavor's version of the Osiris bacteria."

"Why do I have to do that?"

"Because my friend, you need to eliminate all of my employer's competition. Can you do that for me?"

"Sure, that's not a problem. It's easy to kill their bacteria."

"Do those things for me and I'll have your money waiting." Bascom knew a deal was close.

"Can I have a few days to think this over?" Thomas cradled his head in his hands, while confused.

"Of course you can. Relax." Bascom knew it would take one more meeting to convince Thomas to hand over the Osiris genetic map. This was the same tactic that worked for him in the past, when he purchased corporate secrets from other greedy individuals. "I don't want you to rush into anything."

"I understand you're concerned about me. Thank you."

"Call me if you want to talk. I always have time for you, my friend."

During several days of intense testing and television interviews, Thomas considered Bascom's lucrative offer. As Thomas walked to a meeting one day, a security guard stopped him and explained Peter's wanted to meet with him in office. There he found Roger, Paul, Ray, and several company attorneys, seated at a long mahogany table.

Peter slammed his office door closed. "I have something I need to get out in the open."

Thomas sat beside Paul. "Is there a problem with Osiris?"

"You are my only god damn problem." Peter pulled photographs from a large envelope, before he lay them out on the table.

Thomas began trembling after he saw them. His heart pounded. He could not think as he said, "Ah, ah."

Ray lifted a photograph. "The man in this picture with you is Bascom. He's an industrial spy working for Osanto Chemical. It's a Japanese biological engineering conglomerate."

"You had me followed?" Thomas felt the nervous perspiration running down his neck. "Why?"

"I've had investigators following you for months," Peter said. "What were you and Bascom talking about?"

"It was a chance meeting. It's nothing more than that."

"You're a lying bastard!" Peter started a recording stored on his cell phone. Everyone heard a conversation between Thomas and Bascom, arranging another meeting. "I know you've met him six times this month. I have the text messages from your company phone to prove it."

"You read my texts, and tapped my cell phone? That's illegal."

"And so is selling my company's secrets, you bastard!"

"Keep this professional," Roger said, warning Peter. "Don't let this get personal!"

"All right," Peter said. "How did Bascom know about Osiris in the first place?"

"I, I," Thomas felt his face becoming red from the growing embarrassment and humiliation.

"How did he know? I demand to know!"

"All right, I'll tell you! I posted messages to Internet scientific sites when I needed help. He read them, and called me, and then began helping me."

"You did what? That is the dumbest thing I've ever heard! Who else helped you?"

"Professor Valcoskovic in England, and Doctor McClellan right here in Miami."

"You took ideas from those people, and used them as your own?" Paul became angry after the admission. "The same ideas you said came from your superior intelligence?"

"Yes." Thomas' face turned red from the growing humiliation. "But they worked, and now we have Osiris." Peter took a deep breath. "For an MIT graduate, you're a terrible disappointment."

"Disappointment?" The insult angered Thomas. "You should thank me for taking the initiative, and reaching out for assistance. You wouldn't have lowered yourself to ask anyone for help."

"Anyone could have stolen the Osiris formula from the Internet! Did you think about that?"

"I wouldn't let that happened. I trusted the people who helped me."

"You trusted people like Bascom?" The veins in Peter's neck began bulging, as if about to burst. "You're a jackass."

"You're as dumb as your brother. You're too self-righteous to see my contributions saved your project. Roger and Paul couldn't have finished Osiris without my help!"

Peter pointed at Thomas. "You're not as vital to this project as you might think."

"What're you going to do, fire me? You need me to finish Osiris!"

"No, I don't need you any longer. But I'm going to keep you around to make your life a nightmare!"

Roger laughed. "I'll walk out of here today. Osiris will be a failure without my contributions."

"You're not taking any knowledge of Osiris to another company!"

"Watch me." Thomas stood. "I'll start my own company, and put you out of business!"

An attorney seated at the table interrupted. "Mr. Goldberg, you signed a five year contract with this company, and a binding non-disclosure agreement. In return Endeavor, paid all of your outstanding college tuition bills."

Thomas remembered the documents he signed. He collapsed back onto the chair, before sighing heavily. "Yeah, you got me for life on the Osiris project."

"That's where you're wrong," Peter said, "you're off the project."

"You can't do that!" Thomas was shocked. He looked to Paul and Roger for help. "Tell him you need me to complete Osiris. Tell him that!"

"You're reassigned to a do nothing project," Peter shouted, "where you sit around all day and look at your phone."

Thomas stood. "I know what you're doing!"

"I'm protecting my company from a thief."

"No, you want Roger to get the Nobel Prize for Osiris! I should get all of the credit for the creation of the bacteria!"

"This ridiculous conversation is ended, now!" Peter pushed a button on his office phone. Two security guards stepped into the office. "Help this man clean out his desk. Confiscate his company cell phone. Then move him to the laboratory in the sub-basement."

"This is so bogus!" Thomas stood, his chair toppling to the floor. He rushed from the office with the guards following. Peter slammed the door shut. "Do we have any information about those two individuals who helped Thomas look like a hero?"

An attorney opened a thick folder. "We have information about Doctor Steven McClellan."

"What do you have?"

"He's forty-five years old. He's been at Jackson Memorial Hospital in Miami for fourteen years. His specialty is nuclear medicine, with a background in genetics."

Peter wrote notes on a pad. "Do we know how much help he gave that fool Thomas?"

"Security reviewed the logs from Goldberg's cell and office phones. They talked many times. On many occasions they spoke for up to two hours at a time."

Ray added, "My guess is he knows everything about Osiris."

"Perfect. What else do we know about this guy?"

"He served three tours in Iraq with the Army Reserve. He was a surgeon."

"What else?"

"His great grandfather was a General during the Civil War."

"Is there anything else we should know about him?"

"We're hearing he has great personal integrity. He left the safety of a field hospital and went out into the war zone to triage wounded soldiers. He was wounded himself several times."

"This keeps getting better!" Peter angrily threw his pen across the room. "He's a war hero, who is waiting to take credit for developing my bacteria!"

"I think you're misreading Doctor McClellan's intentions," another attorney said. "He's highly regarded. None of our sources had anything bad to say about him."

"How much financial damage can those two men do to my company?"

"They can claim partial rights to Osiris in court, if they can prove they helped Goldberg."

Peter grasped his ponytail. "Ramp up our legal resources for a court fight. Get the background work going."

"We'll be ready if needed." The attorneys stood, before they walked from the office.

Peter took a deep breath, before exhaling loudly. "Roger, ensure the test plans remain on schedule, and ensure Osiris is ready for Arizona. We need to show the world what we've created."

"That's our plan. We're on top of it." Roger and Paul walked from the office.

Two maintenance workers carried a large red, blue, and yellow abstract oil painting into the office several minutes later. Peter looked at Ray. "Do you think that will look good hanging in here?"

"Abstract paintings are not my favorites. I like water colors on canvas."

Peter's temper flared. "I paid a million for that piece. You'd better learn to like it!"

That evening Thomas paced angrily in his small apartment. He repeatedly replayed Peter's derogatory comments in his mind, before he thought, *'I should get a gun and end my misery with a bullet to his damn head. I'd stand there and watch him bleed. I want him to see me laughing while the powerful businessman dies.'*

Thomas noticed the graduate school textbooks piled in a corner. He smiled after kneeling beside them. *'Why should I physically hurt Peter? I can make him suffer mentally. That's worse. It has to be something horrific. Something that embarrasses him before it puts him out of business. I know exactly what I'm going to do."* He smiled while opening a book.

During the following week, Thomas lined the walls of his bedroom with thick plastic sheeting. Sheets of plastic formed a door, preventing the flow of air in or out of the room. He purchased medical equipment and an incubator from a medical supplier website. After assembling his private laboratory, he purchased a dozen rats from a nearby pet store.

At the same time, Thomas quickly became the outsider within the company organization, after other employees learned of his demotion. They stopped speaking to him, and acknowledging him. His ruined reputation, and lack of personal hygiene, kept people away. He worked alone each day during the next six weeks in the isolated laboratory in the sub-basement of the building.

No one could imagine that late at night, after other employees were home with families, he was manipulating cells of the Model 276 Osiris bacteria he stole from an incubator. Then he continued his malicious activities into the early morning hours, in his apartment laboratory.

His growing hatred for Peter, and need to destroy the entire company and all employees, began creating unbearable stress. One night while working in his laboratory, Thomas looked up and saw Peter staring silently at him. He shuddered while Peter shouted humiliating obscenities. The humiliation became too much, forcing him to turn away. When he had the nerve to respond, he turned back to watch Peter's image evaporate into the air.

One week later, the growing stress slowly became debilitating. The smallest distraction or failure became mentally unbearable for Thomas. Tears streamed from his eyes when his repeated attempts to create a new bacterium failed. When he could not open a container of soup in his laboratory for lunch, he collapsed to the floor before he cried uncontrollably for hours.

Thomas unknowingly began talking to himself. He discussed his plans to humiliate and destroy Peter as if speaking with unseen assistants. Other times, he screamed instructions at unseen people. Strangers on sidewalks, in buses, began avoiding him.

Several weeks later, Thomas realized it was becoming difficult for him to sleep in the hours after he finished working in his apartment laboratory each morning. The lack of sleep, the growing exhaustion, and his need for revenge, caused him to make poor decisions. He purchased amphetamines from a dealer on the street. The drugs helped him remain awake, but forced him to take sleep-inducing medications so he could rest for a few hours each night. He was slowly becoming psychotic.

The stress and drugs began causing hallucinations, Thomas noticed Peter following him onto a bus. Another time, he saw Peter sitting in a fast food restaurant, silently watching him eat. He stood and began screaming and pointing at Peter, frightening nearby people, until the haunting image of the man he hated evaporated while he watched.

One morning as he worked in the laboratory in his apartment, Thomas imagined hearing a faint tapping sound. He convinced himself Peter placed an electronic surveillance device in the apartment. He searched for it, kicking holes in walls whenever he imagined hearing the sound. Several hours later, he finished destroying the walls in the living room, but could not find the device. He fell asleep on the floor crying, while curled up in a fetal position.

Then one rainy gray Saturday morning, while staring into the microscope in his apartment, Thomas became ecstatic. *'I did it! I alone created two different bacteria strains. I'm a genius! Now I'll use my intelligent bacteria strains to contaminate the Osiris samples they're taking to Arizona. When my two bacteria combine with Osiris, they'll alter the original genetic makeup. My bacteria strains will make Osiris do things Peter can't imagine. That demeaning bastard will be out of business a few days after a horrendous test!'*

One week before the test, Peter met with his senior managers in his large and ornate boardroom. Waiters served champagne as his staff gave updates. It was a cheap and meaningless gesture to thank them for their efforts. He also announced his personal net worth grew forty million dollars, due to the rapidly increasing value of company stock.

A secretary interrupted the meeting, and said, "Mr. Harrison from the Environmental Protection Agency is on the phone for you, Peter. He says it's very important."

Peter used a speakerphone so his managers could hear the conversation. "John, how are you?"

"I'm good, thank you. I have some great news, Peter."

"I need it today. What's going on?"

"As you know, the President is working to create new jobs with his stimulus package. He wants to leverage your bacteria, to create thousands of jobs recycling trash across the country."

"How does that help me?" Peter silently motioned to his staff, questioningly.

"The White House contacted me today. President Stillman will be in Arizona to watch the test, and promote your company and bacteria."

Peter became ecstatic. "He'll bring the press with him. Everyone around the world will know about Osiris the day after the test."

"That will be great advertising for your company. Congratulations."

"Thank you for your help." Peter ended the call. "Nice job everyone. Let's all work together to make this test a success."

After the meeting, Peter and Roger remained in the boardroom. Peter said, "What're you two going to do with the bonuses you're both going to receive after the Osiris test?"

Roger said, "I'll use it to help some of the charities in the city where I volunteer after work."

"Use your head! Don't give away your money. Life is short! Enjoy it."

"I will use the money to help people." Roger smiled while staring out a window. "We've come a long way since that little house in Boston where we grew up. I wish Mom and Dad were here to see us succeed today."

"If Dad wasn't a flipping alcoholic, they'd still be alive," Peter said.

"Mom tried to make him quit. She waited too long."

"She didn't use her head. She should never have let him drive that night. We're lucky we weren't with them, or we would be dead too."

"You can't say that." Roger became upset after his brother's remarks.

"He killed both of them when he drove into that tree! He was an alcoholic fool!"

"That's your opinion." Roger pictured his mother and father in his mind, smiling at him. He missed them. "They'd be proud of us today."

Chapter 3

Thomas carefully read the daily bulletins sent to all employees, describing the upcoming Osiris test. Late one afternoon he learned a critical event took place that day. The one event he impatiently waited to happen. Roger's team successfully isolated billions of Osiris cells into containers. They planned to transport the bacteria to Arizona the following day on a private jet, for the test.

That night Thomas hid in his laboratory until midnight. He began walking the halls aimlessly every hour, until he convinced himself the building was deserted. Then he carried two silver steel canisters into the Osiris development laboratory. Using his security badge, he opened the vault protecting all of the company's bacteria from a natural disaster or fire. He cautiously stepped inside.

'There you are my friends,' he thought. He lifted one of the containers holding the Osiris bacteria. He caressed it, while holding it to his chest. *'I've missed you very much during the past lonely weeks.'*

He quickly opened one of his steel canisters. He poured his bacteria solution into a dozen of the containers containing the Osiris samples prepared for shipment to the Arizona test site. Then he poured another very different bacterium in his second canister, into the Osiris containers. *'I want you to go out and show the world I'm a genius, so I can get another job with a good company'.*

As he was leaving the vault, Thomas stopped. He studied the Osiris bacteria growing in incubators.

'Why not ruin all of Peter's business?' He smiled while picturing Peter crying.

Thomas worked quickly to contaminate every sample of the Osiris bacteria with his own creations. Then he rushed back to his office, and eventually out of the building. *'I did it! Peter will have a heart attack when he sees what I did! I can't wait to see his face. I want to see him sweat and die'*

The bacteria Thomas created immediately began attacking the Osiris bacteria. His bacteria creations extended slender microscopic strands that attached to each Osiris cell. They transferred new genetic capabilities to Osiris. Seven hours later the transformation process was complete. Osiris was now a totally unknown recombinant bacterium, waiting to manifest itself.

The following afternoon a private jet carrying Peter and the others landed at Phoenix's Sky Harbor Airport. After checking into their hotel, they drove south to the landfill located at Casa Grande. Flat and seemingly endless sand dotted with cactus plants surrounded the two square mile landfill. The temperature was well above one-hundred degrees. The acrid odor of decomposing trash seemed to linger over the landfill.

News camera crews followed the group as they inspected the equipment installed in the vacant dilapidated building on the test site. The rusting sheet metal covering the building walls and roof made the interior feel like an oven.

Ralph Brady, an Endeavor site manager, greeted Peter and the others. "This building is larger than an airplane hangar. It originally housed fifteen furnaces that were used to burn trash. It has the space we needed to install our equipment."

Peter slid his hand over the black steel trough Brady's team installed in the building. "How long is this?"

"It's approximately three hundred feet. It's twenty feet wide with a conveyor in the center running the full length."

"What did I get for the money I spent in here?"

"Bulk loaders operating at the far end of the building will fill this trough with trash. The conveyor will move it forward. We'll spray Osiris onto the trash from those overhead rubber and plastic pipes and heads. By the time the plastic gets to the end of the trough, Osiris will have biodegraded it into fuel. It's going to be an impressive demonstration."

"How much trash do we have for the test?"

"We've pulled six tons of plastic and foam products from under the landfill by hand."

"Good job." Peter smiled. "That should be enough to make me a billionaire tomorrow."

Paul handed Brady a silver steel briefcase. "The Osiris bacteria for propagation are in the containers in this case."

"We've got the twelve huge tanks filled with the nutrient solution, and we're ready to incubate these samples. We'll get the process started now."

Peter motioned toward the reporters. "I want everyone out there giving interviews. Get the world ready for our test."

He noticed Bonnie Franklin talking to other reporters. She wore a short skirt, and tight white blouse. Her firm petite body and beauty intrigued him. He walked to her. "Miss Franklin, I'm happy to see you're here."

She smiled, while brushing back her long dark hair. "I wouldn't miss this amazing event Mr. Samulson."

"Please, call me Peter."

"Ok. How are plans for your test proceeding?"

"We're ready to shock the world."

"I can see that." She shaded her eyes from the sun to watch a variety of trucks speeding across the landfill in clouds of dust.

"I can show you around the landfill, and then we can discuss going to dinner tonight. My penthouse suite has a hot tub with a spectacular view of the city. Maybe we can enjoy drinks together in it."

"Peter, I learned a life lesson while covering the war in Iraq. Never mix anything with business. So I need to say no to your offer again."

Peter wondered if she could see the shocked expression on his face. Beautiful women never rejected him. "Well, I see we're back to that old maid philosophy crap. I hope you find something intriguing to report to your viewers." Peter noticed another attractive reporter in the group, and he stepped to her before introducing himself.

The following morning, Peter gave interviews to national talk shows, from the hotel lobby. He and others rode to the landfill in his stretch Hummer limousine. They were surprised to see a crowd estimated at five thousand people waiting to watch the test.

"Those people want to watch history being made today," Peter said.

"We're going to put on an amazing show for them, Peter. Everyone signed off on their tasks to indicate they're completed." Brady gave Peter a brief status of preparations.

"Perfect! It's sunny and hot. This is the perfect day to demonstrate our amazing Osiris product!"

"That's America at its finest!" Paul pointed at more than one-hundred fire trucks parked around the building. The breeze unfurled the large American flag attached to a pole on each truck. "Now we wait for the President!"

Doctor Steven McClellan walked into an employee lounge in a hospital in Miami. He found it crowded with doctors and nurses watching television. "What're you all doing here?"

Doctor Cindy Licitra said, "It's not every day we see your handiwork on the national news, Doctor."

"Believe me, it's nothing." Steve smiled while pulling several pieces of chocolate from his pocket. "I gave them some ideas, and encouragement. They did the rest."

"Don't be so modest," Doctor Daniel Citron said. "Everyone knows you solved a dozen genetics problems for that company."

"I gave them ideas to solve their problems." Steve laughed. The tall and handsome man adjusted his tie, jokingly. "I'm only keeping this day job until they award me the Nobel Prize for genetics."

"You should be In Arizona watching this test."

"I can't take time away from the hospital. I have work with my patients to finish here."

"I read that your very ill female patient is improving this morning," another doctor said. "Your gene therapy is showing remarkable results combating her liver cancer. Congratulations."

Steve smiled as others congratulated him. "Thank you, but we all collaborated to make that experimental cancer therapy a success!"

"My, my, Doctor," Nurse Jessica Shea said. She tossed back her long red hair. "You're helping to cure cancer. You're helping to solve the gas crisis. You're working to save the environment! You are quite the remarkable find. You're going to make some woman very happy!" She smiled with others as they laughed after her comment.

"No one's found me, and, I have no time for a social life. I'm not getting my hopes up."

A nurse said, "Why did you help that company develop the bacteria, Doctor? You received nothing in return for your efforts!"

"I helped them, to give back something to society." Steve paused while watching the television. "I see parents with kids in here every day. They can't pay the medical bills and feed their families at the same time. They shouldn't have to pay five dollars for a gallon of gas. I did it for them."

"That's a very good explanation," another doctor said. He shook Steve's hand.

At the landfill, a police officer told dignitaries waiting in the oppressive heat, "The President's motorcade is here." He pointed at six black utility vehicles, escorted by police vehicles, parking near the building.

President Stillman, a tall, young politician, stepped from a vehicle with his aides. Governor John Barrington of Arizona, Senator Judy Caliph, Representative Claire Hernandez, and Mayor Frank Mastrani, followed them out. State and local offices climbed from other vehicles.

John Harrison motioned Peter forward. "Mister President, I'd like to introduce you to Mister Peter Samulson."

The President extended his hand. "It's a pleasure to meet you. I'm looking forward to watching your test."

"Thank you Mister President. Let me explain what you're about to see." Peter turned to ensure he would appear in news videos beside the President. He noticed Bonnie Franklin, and waved to her. *'After this test, that bitch is going to be very impressed with my accomplishments. She'll beg me to get her into bed.'*

Thirty minutes later, several politicians gave short speeches at a podium on an observation platform built for guests, fifty yards from the building where the test was to take place. President Stillman then addressed the cheering crowd. "I'm excited by what Peter Samulson told me about Osiris. The development of his bacteria will be a blessing for our nation. It will reduce our dependency on foreign oil, while creating new jobs."

John Harrison stepped to the podium. "Mr. President, please push this big red button. We'll be the first to watch Endeavor's Osiris bacteria convert trash to fuel."

"It's my honor to initiate this process!" Stillman waved to the cheering crowd while depressing the button.

Two huge doors slowly slid apart, revealing the equipment and technicians inside the building. Large, loud, electric motors started. Equipment began pushing plastic trash onto the conveyor belt in the trough. The trash moved forward while pumps sprayed the Osiris solution onto it. The bacteria immediately began biodegrading the plastic. The synthetic fuel byproduct flowed along the sides of the trough to collection tanks. The spectators cheered as the biodegrading process performed flawlessly.

The President cordially extended his hand to Peter. "This is amazing. I'd like you to visit the White House next week. I want to discuss a federal program to license your bacteria, so we can utilize it in landfills across our nation. Osiris will solve one of our ecological disasters"

Peter smiled. "It will be a pleasure working with you Mister President."

Neither Peter nor his staff realized the Osiris cells were not dying as originally designed, after the biodegrading process was complete. Hundreds of billions of cells began dividing and multiplying in the nutrient solution in the storage tanks. In the tanks, and on the conveyor belt, the two strains of bacteria Thomas developed to genetically alter Osiris began combining. That radical bacterium, and the original Osiris bacteria, began evolving into a single new life form.

"We didn't see that phenomenon during testing." Paul pointed at the silver fog that began rising from the bacteria storage tanks, and the trough.

"Maybe it's a by-product created by the tons of dirty old plastic we're processing," Brady said, while reviewing notes on an electronic device. "No cause for alarm. I'll have my people check it out right now."

Dignitaries and technicians watched the swirling silver fog spreading through the immense building where the test was being conducted. Several minutes later, the fog became so dense technicians could not see through it. The fog filled the building as the Osiris solution continued flowing from the storage tanks used as incubators. Concerned technicians soon ran from the building. They congregated near the fire trucks. There they speculated about the source of the silver fog, which was now escaping through the building's doors and windows.

The primitive intelligence, which Thomas meticulously added to the Osiris bacteria, suddenly gained consciousness. It was the first moments of intelligent thought. It immediately understood hunger, and a need for nourishment.

Moments later, the fog began biodegrading tons of plastic trash stacked in the building for the test. The trash appeared to evaporate, as the bacteria converted it to a flammable liquid by-product on the cement floor. The swirling Osiris fog began biodegrading other plastic items in the building.

Telephones, cell phones, binders, office equipment, and even chairs, disappeared in the swirling living fog.

"We need to get everyone out of this building now," Brady said, before he began shouting other warnings to people. "Get out now!"

Osiris quickly learned the plastic coating on electrical wiring would serve as a food source. Exposed electrical wires created sparks on equipment, and inside the building's walls. All of the equipment used during the test unexpectedly shut down. That created an eerie silence in the middle of the desert. A deafening silence, which concerned everyone. No one saw the fires now burning throughout the building.

"I can't see what's going on inside the building," Harrison said, on the observation platform. "Where's that misty fog coming from? Why are those workers running from the building?"

"I can't explain that fog," Roger said. He was shocked after realizing the fog escaping from the building made a sound, somewhat like a mild summer breeze. "I never saw that strange mist during our testing."

Inside the building, Osiris suddenly realized it developed new biodegrading capabilities. Capabilities designed and manufactured by Thomas during his long hours of isolation and psychosis. As its hunger grew, the bacteria discovered it now had the ability to biodegrade rubber for nourishment.

Osiris began devouring the rubber hoses carrying the bacteria solution to the trough, from the incubation storage tanks. Thousands of gallons of bacteria solution flooded onto the floor. The mysterious fog began surging from the building. The fog unexplainably began to sound like the summer breeze, ahead of an imminent thunderstorm. The cloud rapidly and dramatically increased in size to envelop the entire building. It alarmed everyone after it swirled upward high into the blue cloudless sky, to resemble a tornado.

The cloud obscured the sun, raising the concern of the spectators. Many terrified people screamed as they ran to their cars, while others were already racing from the landfill.

Nurse Shea frowned at the television in the hospital lounge. "What's that misty fog Steve?"

"I'm not sure. Tom didn't talk about it during our lengthy discussions."

Osiris' growing intelligence understood it needed more nourishment to sustain the rapidly increasing fog of living bacteria. A large wispy area of the fog began advancing forward, over the landfill. Long fingers of fog inspected the breather pipes extending upward from the landfill's surface. The pipes vented dangerous gases from below the ground as the trash decomposed. The fog began surging into the pipes, spreading out under the surface of the landfill. The bacteria began actively searching for buried plastic and rubber trash for nourishment. That action shocked the spectators.

As the Osiris bacteria biodegraded plastic and rubber buried deep in the landfill, that created huge underground pockets of space. Large areas of heavy compacted trash above began collapsing into the pockets. The dirt covering the surface of the landfill began collapsing into the ground. Billowing clouds of orange dust rose into the sky, to accompany ominous groaning sounds deep beneath the landfill. Depressions in the dirt began appearing across the landfill, as Osiris discovered and devoured huge amounts of buried trash it needed to survive.

The primitive intelligence Osiris now possessed developed and learned faster than Thomas envisioned. It sensed a nearby source of nourishment. A large area of fog slowly rolled five hundred yards across the landfill to engulf several huge piles of discarded tires. Thousands of tires bubbled and slowly disappeared in the fog cloud while the bacteria biodegraded them. The fog cloud dramatically increased in size as the bacteria consumed other massive piles of tires. Hundreds of dislodged tires rolled through the fog, before they appeared to evaporate while consumed by Osiris.

The firefighters realized their vehicles were now in danger, after watching the bacteria cloud's movements. Drivers maneuvered them away from the building with sirens blaring and red and blue lights flashing.

Osiris sensed the movement and sound. Large areas of fog rolled forward to surround shocked firefighters, and vehicles. The bacteria did not harm the terrified firefighters, while devouring the plastic and rubber equipment on their gear.

The dense fog made seeing impossible, and when combined with driver's fears, made driving conditions treacherous. Many of the speeding firefighting vehicles crashed into one another, injuring and killing people. Some vehicles exploded upon impact, killing and critically injuring firefighters. Others rolled over to kill firefighters after Osiris destroyed their tires. Several of the firefighters that survived the accidents, were struck and killed by other speeding vehicles.

Paul was horrified while attempting to understand the situation, as he watched explosions, fires, and screaming spectators running from the test site. He began frantically pointing toward the cloud. "That, that fog is our Osiris!"

"It can't be!" Roger watched a fire truck explode, to create a huge fireball. "Our bacteria can't biodegrade rubber!"

"I'm telling you, somehow that's Osiris!"

On the observation platform, a frightened Secret Service agent said, "I radioed for your immediate emergency evacuation, Mister President." He pushed President Stillman backward protectively, after watching the bacteria fog engulf the presidential motorcade. The vehicles collapsed to the ground after Osiris devoured the tires. The bacteria destroyed everything in the vehicles made of plastic and rubber. Secret Service agents rushed the President across the hot desert sand, to a military helicopter that landed nearby. Minutes later, he was safely on his way to Phoenix.

In the hospital in Miami, a doctor said, "How does that fog fit into the biodegrading scenario?"

Steve squinted at the television. "Tom didn't say they engineered Osiris to destroy rubber."

"They'd be crazy to do that. How would they contain it?"

"The bacteria can't be contained if it has the capabilities to biodegrade both rubber and plastic. Something is terribly wrong." Steve attempted to call Thomas using his cell phone. He shook his head as he became frustrated and concerned. "He isn't answering his phone. He must be at the test site."

Osiris began biodegrading the plastic on electrical wires attached to telephone poles around the landfill. The exposed wires created showers of hot sparks that rained down and burned spectators. Many of the electrical transformers on poles began shorting. Smoke rose from the large steel cylinders on poles before they exploded. That showered the unsuspecting spectators with deadly metal fragments.

Senator Caliph rushed to the podium. She realized the public address system was no longer working. She screamed to horrified spectators and officials, "Evacuate the area! Get out of here! Get out of here now!"

Terrified spectators ran to their cars in the parking lot, and those parked along five access roads that led to the landfill test site. Drivers watching the expanding bacteria cloud sped thoughtlessly through the parking lots. They struck and killed other fleeing people. Speeding vehicles ran down and killed entire families. Many of the vehicles began crashing into one another in the parking lot. Violent accidents claimed hundreds of lives. In many instances, badly damaged vehicles exploded with people trapped inside. Intense flames made rescue attempts impossible. Black smoke began rising into the sky in dozens of locations, each signaling a terrible crash.

Moments later the fires inside the building used for the test, ignited the fumes created by the fuel by-product produced by Osiris. A powerful explosion blew all of the walls outward, off their metal frame. The concussion violently knocked fleeing spectators to the ground. It propelled fragments of metal outward like shrapnel. They injured and killed hundreds. The accompanying fireball incinerated the presidential motorcade, and most of the fire trucks, killing more firefighters. Suffocating black smoke settled over the survivors, as they stood to survey the dead around them. Body parts littered the ground.

"Oh my God," Doctor Licitra said while staring at the horrifying scene on the television. "What is going on there? Look at that carnage!"

Steve felt a sudden pain in his leg. A reminder from the war, when things went bad. "That looks like something I saw in Iraq."

"I see bodies everywhere on the ground," a nurse said.

He took a deep breath. "I helped create that disaster. I have to call Endeavor's headquarters and ask if I can help." He rushed from the room, while ignoring the concerns of his friends.

At the test site, Paul opened his eyes, and realized he was lying on the ground on his back. He heard screaming people all around him. He reached to his throbbing head. Then he saw the warm red blood on his fingers. "What, what happened?"

"I think a piece of the building hit you in the head when it exploded." Roger helped him to his feet. "We have to leave."

"I see our limo coming this way." Peter led the men to the parking lot, where he pulled open the vehicle's door. "Get in."

"Peter, help me!" Bonnie Franklin shouted. She ran across the parking lot in high heels, while avoiding speeding vehicles. "I can't find my crew. Please, I need a ride."

Peter saw the blood on her skirt. He climbed into the limousine. *I don't have time for you, bitch! You wouldn't have dinner with me, so why should I save you? I've got to save my company.*

"That reporter needs a ride out of here," Roger said. "Wait for her!"

Peter shouted at his driver, "Get us out of here, now! Don't stop for any of these losers!"

As the limousine sped from the landfill, Paul watched the mysterious fog. "I don't understand what went wrong."

"What happened to my test?" Peter screamed. "What's going on?"

"I don't know. None of this makes any sense."

"We need a plausible story to tell the press when we get to Phoenix."

"Why?" Roger looked at his brother.

"So my company doesn't look bad."

"What are you talking about?"

"I spent years building my company. You two almost destroyed it, in one hour."

58

Paul watched the towering silver fog through the rear window of the limousine. "How did everything go so wrong?"

At Endeavor's headquarters, horrified employees watched the disastrous test on television. Thomas hid his exhilaration as nearby women cried. *'I did it. Peter looks so stupid right now! The world is laughing at him, and now no one is laughing at me any more. He needed to be punished for talking to me the way he did. He treated me bad, and I destroyed his precious company. All of these people talk about me, and laugh at me behind my back, and now I'm going to make sure they all loose their precious jobs! I won't have to work here much longer. Endeavor will be out of business in a week! I'm a better man than Peter. I'm a survivor!'* Thomas walked back to his laboratory, passing hundreds of upset employees. There he enjoyed lunch for the first time in months.

Chapter 4

After his limousine arrived at the hotel, Peter heard the screaming sirens of a large number of emergency vehicles speeding toward the landfill. "They've got the situation under control. They don't need us."

He led the men to his suite. There he angrily threw his smoke damaged suit jacket onto the floor. He called his company headquarters. He demanded answers from his staff, threatening them with firing if they could not immediately respond to his questions.

Roger attempted to stop the blood flowing from Paul's head wound with towels. He began to panic after he realized he could not stop the bleeding. "I've got to call the hotel's front desk. I'll try to get a doctor up here to look at these gashes."

Ray rushed into the suite to join the group several minutes later. His light gray suit was scorched black by the fire. "How can Osiris suddenly be biodegrading rubber? We didn't design it with that capability!"

Peter stepped to the liquor bar. "We don't know that Osiris is biodegrading rubber. What we saw at that landfill could be a gasoline corporation plot to discredit my company." He opened a bottle of whiskey.

"What are you saying?" Ray was confused. "Explain that statement."

Peter poured himself a drink. "Osiris can cut oil company profits. Maybe they sabotaged our test."

"That's ridiculous. They don't have the background and ability to do this."

"They don't?" Peter raised an eyebrow questioningly.

"No, that will not explain what happened."

Peter silently gazed into a mirror behind the bar. "I know how to explain it."

"Don't fabricate a story," Ray said.

"Don't tell me what to do! You don't get ahead in business today, by telling the truth!" Peter laughed. "I'm going to say Osiris encountered hazardous waste buried in the landfill. The hazardous waste formed that cloud."

"You can't make up something like that!"

Loud pounding on the suite door interrupted the conversation. Harrison and four aides rushed in. The aides were on their phones, requesting a status from the landfill and the hospitals treating the injured. Dirt and blood streaked their clothes.

Harrison said, "Why did you leave the landfill? Everyone has questions only you can answer."

"We rushed back here to speak to my staff in Miami," Peter said. "They're insisting that landfill is your problem."

"My problem?" Harrison raised his hands questioningly. "How did they determine that?"

"They're saying someone buried toxic waste in the landfill. That waste formed that cloud."

"Your bacterium is out of control. Hundreds of people are dead. Now you're telling me toxic waste is the cause. Show me the research to back up that ridiculous statement."

"That's a preliminary conclusion." Peter drank the whisky, before filling the glass again. "I'll give you more information after I receive it."

"That's not a conclusion! That's a blatant lie!"

"Think whatever you want! That's what I know now."

"I need to know how to stop that cloud?"

"I don't know that cloud is my bacteria!"

"It can't be anything else but Osiris." Harrison paused to read a message on his phone.

"You're assuming it is, based on timing alone. You can't prove it!"

"Enough of this back and forth crap," Roger said unexpectedly. "This is getting us nowhere."

Harrison said, "I'm declaring an on-site emergency at the landfill."

Peter's hands clenched. "You're overreacting. You'll destroy my company if you do that!"

"Protecting people is my first priority. Your company means nothing to me." Harrison rushed out of the suite with his aides following, while they spoke into their phones.

Roger said, "We need to get our staff and documentation here as soon as possible. I want everyone here, including Thomas."

Ray nodded. "I'll make the call."

At six that evening Governor Barrington met with Peter. "That cloud is sitting on top of the landfill. Reporters are bombarding my office for information. So are federal officials. What can I tell them?"

"My scientists have concluded that cloud is not related to Osiris, or the test we ran today."

That response surprised Barrington. "Can you tell me how that cloud formed?"

"My people believe it formed after Osiris released toxic waste buried in the landfill?" Peter realized he needed to perpetuate the misinformation to save his company.

"Is the cloud going to evaporate in the heat? Will the wind blow it apart so it becomes harmless?"

"I can't tell you anything else, other than that cloud is not Osiris."

"That answer is not factual and is unacceptable. I need dependable information from you.__You manufactured and tested the bacteria. It now appears to be out of control, and a possible threat."

"I would tell the reporters the cloud, which no one can prove is my bacteria, will not harm anyone."

"You want me to say that, after people died today because of it!"

"That was an unfortunate series of events. They panicked and killed one another with their cars and trucks. We don't know what caused the explosion. Nevertheless, let me be clear. That cloud did not hurt anyone at the test site!"

"That cloud caused those tragedies!"

"You're not listening to me. Or, you're too stupid to understand what I'm saying." Peter poured himself another drink. "Leave your cell phone number. I'll call you when I have something to tell you."

"Talking to you is a waste of my time." Barrington abruptly walked from the suite

Harrison rushed in. "I have observers positioned around the landfill. They'll contact us if that cloud moves, or causes additional damage."

"Ok, thank you," Roger said.

"Representatives from the Center for Disease Control and the World Health Organization are on their way here to give us assistance."

"I'm sure they'll contribute a lot," Peter said sarcastically. "The only sicknesses afflicting everyone are panic and stupidity."

Roger shook his head after his brother's frustrating remarks. "I have a staff in Miami searching for a reason why that cloud formed. Another large group of my researchers is on the way here."

Harrison read a text message on his phone. "Scientists across the country are offering their assistance. I'm bringing them in to help you."

"We've got the situation under control," Peter said angrily. "I don't need outside interference!"

"Deal with it." Harrison read another message. "A Doctor McClellan and some other volunteers are joining us. He claims to know a lot about Osiris."

"I don't want him here," Peter said. "Tell the bastard to stay home!"

Roger motioned to his brother to relax. "We'll take all the help we can get."

"I'll have work areas prepared in the hotel's convention center." Harrison began speaking to his aides.

Peter watched a television newscast of the devastating test. *What did I do to deserve this? I should be having dinner with the President right now! Why is this happening to me?* He began walking toward the door.

"Where are you going?" Roger said.

"I need some air."

"You can't leave now."

"I can do whatever I want. I own this company! You work for me!"

Several hours later a news helicopter began circling the landfill. A camera operator filmed the silver fog glowing in the evening sun. It was one thousand feet wide, and extended several thousand feet into the air. The fog remained stationary, while the interior appeared to be in constant motion. Swirling areas of fog rose through the translucent main body. Other areas descended through the cloud formation until they were several feet above the ground. There they began rising again.

The noise and motion of the helicopter attracted Osiris. It became interested. A large area of fog rapidly extended outward to engulf the aircraft. The bacteria began biodegrading the plastic and rubber it found in the helicopter. Without critical aerodynamic components, the helicopter began spinning out of control. The motion caused the camera operator to fall out of the helicopter. His body crashed onto the desert below. The helicopter continued spinning, rapidly falling through the bacteria cloud, until it crashed. An explosion tore apart the wreckage seconds later.

Observers immediately reported the incident to Harrison. They retreated to new positions several hundred yards from the landfill. That night they used huge floodlights to illuminate the swirling fog. They did not realize Osiris was devouring the last of the plastic, foam, and rubber buried in the landfill. The floodlights shining upward did not reveal the entire dirt surface of the landfill already settled more than thirty feet into the ground.

No one could envision what was occurring inside the Osiris cloud. The bacteria slowly learned to create various types of cells each time they replicated. The primitive intelligence learned to utilize some specialized cells to search for nourishment. Other specialized cells biodegraded trash. Then those cells moved through the cloud to transfer nourishment to other cells. As the cells encountered one another, a primitive form of communication began evolving. The cells eventually matured into a huge organism, with a shared and growing intelligence. As the intelligence found it difficult to locate sustenance in the landfill, it suddenly sensed another source of nourishment.

Frantic pounding on the door woke Peter at five o'clock the following morning. Harrison led Roger into the suite. Both men wore pajamas. "My spotters reported Osiris just moved off the landfill!"

"I need some coffee before I can think." Peter lifted the telephone to call room service. "How can it be moving? Are you certain your spotters are correct?"

"It's been confirmed!"

Peter rubbed his eyes. "Where's it going?"

"It's headed for Phoenix!"

"What? Are you positive?"

"Yes!"

Peter met with his scientists who traveled from Miami overnight, and hundreds of government officials, in a hotel ballroom at seven that morning. He said, "Everyone is in a panic. The fog is moving toward Phoenix. Does anyone have any ideas to stop it?"

After speaking among themselves, a scientist said, "If that cloud is Osiris, it's comprised of bacterium just introduced into the environment. Spraying it with an antibiotic may kill it."

Peter thought, *'If my staff destroys that cloud, no one can prove its Osiris. I'll take credit for destroying the public menace. I'll make it sound like only my staff had the knowledge to stop the cloud. We'll rework Osiris and run another test. I can still get out of this looking good.'*

As the others discussed various ideas, Paul worked at a nearby table. The pain from the thirteen stitches needed to close his head wound became annoying. He carefully opened a vile of Osiris bacteria brought from Miami. He placed several drops onto a slide, before slipping it under a microscope. As he studied the bacteria, he frowned questioningly. "Something's wrong. This isn't our bacteria."

Roger read the label on the vile. "The code is correct. That's our Osiris."

"No, it's not. Take a look."

Roger stared into the microscope. "It's very similar to our bacteria, but something is different."

"Let me see." Ray looked into the microscope. "It appears something has been added to the cells. But, where could the mutation have come from?"

"What the hell is going on?" Peter appeared upset by the confusion. "How was the bacteria changed?

"I don't know how this happened," Roger said. "The samples were locked in the vault."

"Only one person has the knowledge to do this!" Paul said screaming, moments later. He startled everyone near him. "Where's Thomas? Where is he?"

Thomas immediately lowered his head. '*They weren't supposed to find out I changed the bacteria this soon.*' He attempted to remain inconspicuous. His heart pounded from apprehension and fear while he walked toward a door.

Paul pushed his way through the researchers. He grasped Thomas' arm. "You did this, didn't you? You changed the composition of Osiris!"

Peter rushed forward. "Did you alter the bacteria?"

Thomas slowly turned. "I may have done this, but you can't prove anything." He pulled a phone from his pocket.

Peter appeared stunned by the remarks. "What did you hope to gain by doing this?"

"I did it for you. You want to be famous. Now people will never forget your name!" He entered a code into the phone. He smiled, knowing a large bomb he meticulously constructed, detonated in his apartment to destroy the makeshift laboratory. He could not know the explosion leveled the building, killing dozens of innocent people in the ensuing inferno.

"What did you add to the bacteria?" Paul said, shouting.

"You can't imagine what I can do." Thomas laughed hysterically. "I altered it to be a helium producer. After the bacteria biodegrades plastic it produces a gas to manifest itself."

"That's why it formed into that cloud formation?" Paul said.

"I'm surprised your pathetically feeble mind grasps that concept." He sarcastically gestured a thumbs-up signal while laughing. "I also gave Osiris intelligence."

"You what?" Roger struggled to remain calm. "That's impossible."

"Nothing is impossible for me. You always underestimated my abilities." Thomas frowned, clowning, before he made an obscene gesture. "I used mice DNA to engineer a new intelligence."

Paul began to panic. "I don't believe what you're telling us! That's impossible!"

Thomas laughed hysterically. "Remember my thesis for creating intelligent bacteria to destroy cancer cells? I used that research as the foundation for creating stem cell intelligence in my laboratory!"

"You're flipping insane," Paul said, screaming. "What did you do to Osiris to make it biodegrade rubber?"

"I altered its capabilities to show the world my superior intelligence. The bacteria's need for rubber will lessen each hour, until it dies."

"The bacteria will die? When will that happen?"

Peter could no longer control his anger. He unexpectedly said, while screaming, "You did this just to get back at me?"

Thomas nodded. "The world is watching you Peter, and you're not looking too good. You're actually pale. But this is very satisfying for me."

"You've killed people with your ego trip!" Roger said. "You're responsible for their deaths!"

"Their blood is on Peter's hands. This is his fault. Let their deaths be his company's legacy."

"I want you to document everything you did to the bacteria. I want those details now!"

"You figure it out smart guy. You always said you were smarter than me."

Roger unexplainably felt compassion as he studied the overweight man's dirty clothes and hair. "I never said or implied that. I worked beside you every day as a colleague, and a friend."

"Don't be nice to me, now that you need me! You're using me just like your brother did."

"Someone call the police," Peter said. "I want this man arrested."

"Screw all of you!" Thomas ran through a door. He disappeared in the crowd of reporters in the hotel lobby.

Harrison and his aides rushed into the ballroom. "What happened in here? I heard shouting."

Peter rubbed his forehead. "One of my disgruntled employees just announced he altered Osiris to get back at me."

"Was that him running out of here?"

"Yes." Peter sat down. He buried his face in his hands.

Harrison motioned to his aides. "Contact the police and FBI. I want that man apprehended and brought back here."

Roger then told Harrison, "We have a way to stop Osiris."

"Give me the details. Tell me what equipment you need, and when we're going to do it."

"We want to spray pesticides onto that cloud. We're confident it will kill the bacteria."

70

"How do we do that? Can we use a fire truck's water cannon to spray the pesticide?"

"We'll deliver it from a helicopter hovering above the cloud."

"That's risky. It already destroyed the news helicopter."

"What do you recommend?" Paul said. "Spit pesticides at it?"

"I don't have another solution," Harrison said. "But I don't like the idea of putting anyone at risk."

"Get us a helicopter. I'll guide the pilot over the cloud to show I'm confident we'll be safe."

At four o'clock that afternoon Peter and his staff met Harrison and hundreds of state and federal officials, five miles north of the landfill. The heat was oppressive. Observers estimated the swirling mass was now one-quarter mile wide and several thousand feet high. Nearby, National Guard soldiers prepared a helicopter fitted with spraying equipment. A truck pumped an antibiotic solution into tanks mounted under the aircraft.

Roger was nervous. "We should have run some tests to ensure a pesticide solution will kill the bacteria."

"If we wait, that cloud will get larger and harder to stop. We have to do this now."

"Let him get to work," Peter said. "We all need to take chances to stop that cloud."

"I should be the one going up in that helicopter," Roger said. "You don't know how Osiris is going to react when it's attacked and dying."

"My friend, it's going to think it's a mouse, caught in a trap." Thomas shook Roger's hand. "It will be dead before it can escape."

Fifty minutes later the helicopter hovered three thousand feet above the cloud. The antibiotic solution began spraying from tubes under the aircraft. All of the observers reported the brown solution fell harmlessly through the bacteria before evaporating on the desert sand.

Everyone underestimated the bacteria's developing intelligence. Its primitive memory remembered the nourishment it found inside the news helicopter. A slender section of glistening silver fog began spiraling upward. Osiris was reaching out for nourishment. It surrounded the helicopter before the pilots could react to radio warnings from observers on the ground.

Osiris immediately began biodegrading the plastic and rubber in the helicopter. The aircraft began spinning out of control. The last thing people onboard saw were sparking electrical wires. Moments later an explosion tore the helicopter apart. A billowing red and black fireball formed in the sky, as burning debris rained down onto the desert.

"No one survived that crash," someone on the ground said.

"No, no, Paul can't be dead." Roger grasped his head with both hands. "We just talked."

Peter ignored his brother's mental anguish. "Why didn't the antibiotic kill Osiris?"

"Thomas that bastard must have made it antibiotic resistant when he changed the genetic structure."

Roger began wandering aimlessly in the sand. "I can't believe Paul is dead."

"Forget him. Concentrate on the problem of stopping the cloud."

Harrison watched panicking officials talking to one another. "What do we do now, Peter?"

"We're going back to the hotel to talk to our people. I need a drink."

Governor Barrington said, "I'm declaring a state of emergency. I'm asking for federal assistance."

As Peter walked to a limousine, Bonnie Saunders confronted him. "Thanks for leaving me at the landfill yesterday Peter. You're quite the hero."

"I'm not obligated to save your ass, bitch!"

"What you did, leaving me at the landfill, shows something about you."

"It shows I know my priorities. You're not one of them. Now stay away from me!"

"Can you tell me what you sprayed on the cloud? How are you attempting to destroy it?"

"I have no comment." Peter climbed into the limousine, after Roger and Ray.

Bonnie shook her head as the vehicle sped away. "I'd kill myself if I was married to him."

"I'd kill myself if I had to work for him," the camera operator said.

She lifted her long hair off her neck, which was wet with perspiration. "I'm thirty-three years old. I'm too old to be walking through this scorching hot sand."

"We did this for two years in Iraq, sweetheart. At least here, no one is shooting at us."

She shaded her eyes to look at the bacteria cloud. "I think this battle will be deadlier than the fighting we saw in Iraq and Afghanistan."

At five o'clock General Lawson of the Army National Guard read a statement to reporters. "My men are preparing to attack the cloud with flamethrowers. If heat evaporates it, which we're confident it will, I'll call in the Air Force to hit it with napalm."

After several hours of preparations, seven soldiers dressed in silver fire retardant protective clothing cautiously walked toward the Osiris cloud. They fired bursts of searing orange flames into the bacteria from flamethrowers strapped on their backs.

Osiris understood the danger after sensing the scalding heat. The bacteria cloud pulled back while forming tunnels that swirled around the streams of flames. An area of silver fog resembling a huge ocean wave suddenly crashed forward to engulf the soldiers. The bacteria began biodegrading the rubber hoses and plastic connectors on the flame-throwers. They exploded, creating huge orange fireballs that engulfed the soldiers and killed them almost instantly.

General Lawson turned to Governor Barrington. "My men never had a chance. Osiris overwhelmed them."

"Do you have anything else in your arsenal that will destroy that cloud?"

"We don't have anything to combat that cloud, Governor."

"Is the cloud still moving toward Phoenix?"

"Yes it is."

Chapter 5

Steve and volunteers from his hospital in Miami arrived in Phoenix later that night. A shuttle bus carried them to the hotel, where Harrison greeted them. "I want to thank you for volunteering your time and skills. We need your help to deal with this crisis. Please follow me, and I'll introduce you to the other scientists."

He led them to a ballroom. There he introduced each person to hundreds of scientists already at work. Steve was the last person Harrison introduced. "And this is Doctor Steven McClellan."

"Hello, everyone." Steve smiled. "I'm looking forward to collaborating with you."

Roger stepped forward to shake his hand. "I'm glad to meet you. Thank you for coming here to help us"

"I'll do whatever I can."

Peter stood with his arms crossed. He studied Steve's jeans and yellow tee shirt. "So you're the expert that bastard Goldberg used to get his ideas! Now you're going to be a hero, and solve all of our problems!"

Steve frowned, shocked by the verbal accusations. "Who are you?"

"I'm Peter Samulson. I own Endeavor. I know why you helped Goldberg. I know you want my money!"

Steve laughed, after the comments he considered absurd. "I don't want anything from you."

"Then why are you here?" Peter pointed at him accusingly. "I demand an answer!"

Steve realized everyone was watching silently. "I did help Thomas. He obviously made a mistake. I'm here to help him fix whatever he did wrong."

"That's a good response to harsh criticism, son." An older scientist shook Steve's hand.

Roger confronted his brother. "He's here to help us. You should be thanking him."

"All right everyone," Harrison said, "we're about to start another briefing session."

"I want to apologize for my brother's comments." Roger led Steve to another ballroom. On the way, he explained his understanding of how and why Thomas sabotaged Osiris.

Doctor Reglovic from the Environmental Protection Agency facilitated the briefing. He pointed to an area of a map projected on the wall. "Osiris continues moving toward Phoenix. It's currently located over this remote area of desert."

"What's keeping it alive?" A scientist said while studying the map. "It can't find nourishment in that desert."

"We performed a cursory analysis of the Endeavor bacteria design documents. It appears the bacterium may retain nutrients to keep it alive for extended periods."

"We have contradicting theories stating a lack of nourishment will soon cause the bacteria to die," Doctor Richard Meridian said. He represented the Sloane Kettering Cancer Research Center.

Reglovic removed his wire rim glasses. "Unfortunately, we do not have sufficient information, or time, to validate either hypothesis."

Governor Barrington rushed into the room with Mayor Frank Mastrani, and a large group of state officials. "Have you found a way to stop that bacteria cloud?"

"Not yet," Reglovic said. "We don't have enough information to develop a suitable countermeasure for stopping it."

"Will it reach Phoenix?" Governor Barrington waited for a response from the researchers. "If you feel it will make its way to this city, I need to order an immediate evacuation."

"We cannot speculate with any degree of accuracy." Reglovic stoked his long gray beard.

"What's your opinion Doctor Feltault?" Harrison asked his older, senior scientist.

"We don't understand the bacteria. We don't know what type of damage it will create." He paused while silently reviewing the facts. "I would evacuate the city as a precaution."

"I agree." Senator Califia said. "We can't place any additional lives in danger."

"The safety of residents is my primary concern," Barrington said. "I'm evacuating everyone."

A scientist stood and said, "Where will you put those people?"

"The military will set up tents in the desert to house the evacuees," Califia said. "They can go home after the cloud moves beyond the city."

"When do you expect Osiris to get here?" Steve said, while peeling foil from a piece of chocolate candy.

"The military estimates midday tomorrow, based on its current speed," Harrison said.

"We can't stay here," Reglovic said. "Where will we continue with our research?"

"I'll move all of the scientists to Flagstaff. It will be safe for you to work there."

"Let me in, now!" A reporter and camera operator pushed past the security guards at a door, startling everyone. She addressed the group. "I'm Bonnie Saunders, Independent News. I'd like to ask some questions about Osiris. What is it going to do? Should we be warning people to leave the city?"

Peter angrily pointed at the guards. "Throw that bitch out of here on her ass! We'll tell people what to do when we're ready!"

"You can't wait any longer! People are already panicking," Bonnie said. "They know that bacteria cloud is moving this way, but you're not saying anything. They don't know what to think, or do, to stay safe!"

"I have to agree with her," Steve said after he stood. "You have to tell the people what's happening."

"What the hell do you know?" Peter said, shouting. "Get your ass out of here and go home to Florida! We don't need your ideas!"

"What is your problem?" Steve stared at Peter. "You need people to stay calm during the evacuation. Keeping them informed will lessen their anxiety. This is the same approach I use when caring for terminally ill patients."

"You don't know what you're talking about! We're not in a hospital you god damn fool!"

"We have to warn people to evacuate. This reporter can reach millions of people with one television news report."

"The Doctor's ideas do have merit," Harrison said.

"No, I want that bitch out of here now!" Peter said, shouting. "She lies!"

Bonnie laughed. "Are you pissed because I wouldn't sleep with you Peter? Is that why you're acting like a child?"

"She's lying about me now! That's a lie she's trying to spread!

"I've heard enough," Governor Barrington said. "I've seen Ms. Saunders work. She's a professional."

Harrison said, "Ms. Saunders, you're now our liaison with the reporters. You'll collect information and distribute it to the news agency reporters every day."

"Thank you. I'll do everything I can, to help out during this crisis." She nodded to the group.

Several hours later Steve sat in the hotel lobby reading the details of the Osiris genetic composition. He noticed Bonnie conducting an interview with Harrison nearby during a live television broadcast.

After the interview, she walked across the lobby to where Steve sat. "Hi. I hoped I'd see you again. I want to thank you for supporting me today."

"My pleasure. It was the right thing to do."

She extended her hand. "I'm Bonnie Saunders."

"I'm Steven McClellan." He gently grasped her petite hand, while admiring her deep red nail polish.

Bonnie smiled. "I would like to interview you. They say you may know more about Osiris than any of these other scientists."

"I don't think so." He laughed. "I'm not good in front of a camera."

"That's too bad. Something tells me you're going to be a big story." Bonnie walked away with her crew.

Steve woke at five the following morning. He met other researchers in a ballroom for breakfast.

"How are you this morning?" Roger said, while pouring himself a cup of coffee.

"I'm good. How about you?"

"I'm very worried, about what's going to happen today." Roger clenched his trembling hands while attempting to relax.

"Is Osiris still moving this way?"

"The military reported Osiris is sixty miles south, and moving straight toward the city."

"I have to ask. Why did you name the bacteria after the Egyptian god of the dead?"

Roger shook his head. "It was Peter's idea. He read a magazine story about Egypt. He thought it's a unique name for a new product that everyone would remember."

"Makes sense from a marketing perspective." Steve sipped black coffee.

"Harrison asked me to join a group that's going to watch Osiris when it reaches the city. Would you like to join us?"

"Sure. Maybe we'll see something we can use to stop it."

Harrison walked into the room carrying a clipboard. "It's time to move you people and your equipment to Flagstaff."

One hour later Steve waved to volunteers on buses pulling away from the hotel. The heat was already oppressive. Even with shorts and a light shirt he wore, he was already sweating.

Bonnie walked out of the hotel wearing short white shorts and a red blouse. "Good morning, Doctor."

"You can drop that Doctor thing. It's Steve."

"I like saying that." She whispered, "You never know when I'll need you to examine me."

He laughed, while enjoying her dark sense of humor. "I see."

Several minutes later, twelve Army Hummers parked in front of the hotel. Harrison explained, "These vehicles will take us to an area where we can watch Osiris."

At noon, a group of anxious people stood on a highway overpass six miles outside the city. Governor Barrington, Mayor Frank Mastrani, General Lawson, and Representative Claire Hernandez joined them. Hundreds of state and federal officials nervously waited with them.

"Where's Osiris, General?" Roger asked Lawson.

"It's four miles south of the city."

"Has the cloud decreased in size?"

Lawson shook his head. "The Air Force estimates its now one mile wide, and a quarter mile high."

"Did they finish evacuating the city?" Steve said, while taking binoculars from a soldier.

"That activity is still underway," Mayor Frank Mastrani said. "It's taking longer than anticipated."

"Osiris is about to overrun a suburban area," a soldier said while listening to a radio.

General Lawson said, "This will give us an idea of what we're up against."

A wispy area of the swirling silver cloud extended outward to engulf an area of houses in its path. Osiris unexpectedly stopped moving. The primitive intelligence needed time to analyze the unfamiliar structures. After recognizing a new source of nourishment, the cloud settled over a five square block area.

Sparks rained down onto city streets after Osiris biodegraded the plastic around electrical wires attached to poles. Shorting electrical transformers began burning, and exploding, several minutes later.

"Something is happening to the vinyl siding on the houses," Steve said. "It appears to be bubbling."

"The bacteria is eating it!" Bonnie watched colored siding and plastic shutters disappear from the exterior of houses. "It took only seconds to biodegrade all of that plastic!"

Everyone watched garden hoses vanish silently in the swirling cloud. Water flooded from above ground swimming pools after the bacteria devoured plastic liners. Outdoor items such as plastic furniture, tables, chairs, flowerpots, trash containers, children's play sets and swimming pools, sheds, toys, rubber balls, and car tires disappeared in the fog, without a sound.

"Osiris is biodegrading everything," Governor Barrington said. "It's not leaving anything behind."

Representative Claire Hernandez said, "The bacteria is moving into houses through the open windows. What's it doing in there?"

No one could imagine the unseen destruction Osiris was causing. Wiring, plastic flooring, and plastic plumbing disappeared in the fog. In kitchens, bacteria devoured plastic plates, cups, utensils, food containers, and trash bags. The surfaces of microwave ovens disappeared, as did parts of other appliances, and tools. In living rooms, furniture, sculptures, models, compact discs, picture frames, and wall hangings disappeared. The bacteria consumed all electronic devices such as computers, televisions, surround sound systems, receivers, and speakers. In other areas of the house, the bacteria devoured vinyl records, picture frames, eyeglasses, and even credit cards. In garages, Osiris biodegraded storage cabinets, and the plastic and rubber components of cars, trucks, motorcycles, boats, and recreational vehicles. The bacteria eventually destroyed every object made of rubber, plastic, and foam inside the houses. The only remnant of those objects was the black fuel produced by the biodegrading process.

Harrison shaded his eyes from the sun with a hand. "The upper area of the cloud is expanding."

"The cells may reproduce faster when they have a source of nutrients," Steve said. "That reproduction causes the cloud to increase in size."

"The cloud is moving forward faster," Roger said. Perspiration streamed down his forehead.

Osiris moved over a business area of the city. It paused while studying the buildings. Then it engulfed a ten-block area. Nothing was immune from its devastating effects. It devoured components of construction equipment, delivery trucks, cars and trucks, and tools.

Inside a natural gas terminal building the bacteria devoured the seals of huge supply pipes. Sparking electrical wires ignited the released gas several minutes later. A loud and blinding explosion leveled the building, along with other buildings in a four-block area. The intense heat ignited fires in the flattened debris. Moments later the underground supply pipeline exploded with a deafening roar. The blast propelled tons of dirt high into the air. It briefly obscured the sun while falling back to the ground. A wide column of gas fed red-blue flames created a shrieking sound as it swirled violently almost a mile into the sky. Debris around the inferno immediately burst into flames.

Harrison surveyed the damage. "I never envisioned the destruction being this severe."

"The loss of personal property is terrible," Hernandez said. Tears flowed from her eyes.

"The cloud is moving toward the airport," Mayor Frank Mastrani said. "It's headed for the aviation storage tanks!"

Osiris destroyed rubber seals in the storage tanks, and pipelines supplying fuel to various areas of the airport. Released aviation fuel began flowing onto airport streets and into storm sewers. A fire truck speeding to the storage tanks skidded on the fuel. It crashed into a concrete road divider, before bursting into flames. The flames ignited the aviation fuel. An inferno of scalding blue flames began advancing outward in all directions on the streets. The flames engulfed nearby airplane maintenance hangers.

Aviation fuel in the storm sewers ignited moments later. Violent underground explosions began destroying the roadbeds. The flames quickly made their way back to the fuel storage tanks. Each tank began exploding with a deafening roar. Huge swirling clouds of flames and black smoke violently billowed into the sky from the ruins of each tank.

"I see airplanes taxiing on the runway," Senator Califia said. "What're they doing there?"

"Why is the airport still open?" Harrison said as he panicked. "Those people aren't safe!"

"We're trying to get the last flights out," Mayor Mastrani said, before he spoke into his cell phone.

Terrified passengers watched the advancing cloud surround their aircraft as they waited to take off. The bacteria began devouring everything made of plastic and rubber. Jet engines burst into flames after Osiris destroyed crucial components. Powerful explosions, created by ignited aviation fuel, destroyed ten aircraft waiting on the runway. Thousands of passengers and airline crewmembers died in the ensuing infernos.

"Thank God they made it out!" Mayor Mastrani pointed at two large passenger jets taking off.

Everyone was horrified moments later, after Osiris seemingly reached out to engulf the departing aircraft. As Osiris biodegraded and disabled their controls, each aircraft veered sharply before crashing into the city where they exploded. A third aircraft taking off exploded inside the bacteria cloud. Flaming debris and bodies fell to the ground through the swirling silver cloud.

The crew of a jumbo jet waiting to take off panicked while watching the approaching cloud, and the destruction it created. The pilot said, "Let's taxi back to the terminal and get the passengers offloaded!"

Ignoring safety procedures, the crew taxied forward with engines at full power. As the aircraft approached the terminal building, Osiris engulfed it. Terrified passenger screamed as the plane lurched after Osiris devoured the tires. The crew could not stop the aircraft and it crashed into the terminal. One engine exploded, creating a deadly fireball inside the building filled with people.

A fire quickly engulfed the airplane fuselage, before a powerful explosion destroyed it, and a large portion of the terminal. The explosion destroyed nearby aircraft, killing the screaming passengers rushing from them. A fast moving fire engulfed the entire terminal. The explosions and fires killed thousands of people attempting to flee the city, and the air traffic controllers trapped in the control tower.

Osiris advanced to surround buildings in the city's financial district. The cloud wrapped itself around the base of a high-rise building. It investigated the structure, before exploring the interior of the building. Then it slowly floated upward to surround the structure. Plate glass windows fell from the building after Osiris devoured rubber fasteners. After the bacteria filled the interior office areas, it consumed everything made of plastic and rubber. While biodegrading those materials, the bacteria produced large amounts of the fuel byproduct. After feeding inside the building, the cloud descended over a large area of the city.

Bonnie pointed with a trembling hand. "I see dark black smoke coming from the upper floors of that bank building." The group watched as intense blue flames spread rapidly through the structure. They did not know the fuel Osiris produced was feeding those fires.

The group was also not aware of the thousands of people who refused to evacuate the city. Windows falling from high-rise buildings crushed the now fleeing people on streets below. After Osiris destroyed electrical systems, thousands found themselves trapped in elevators. With safety systems destroyed by the bacteria, elevators eventually plummeted into the basement of buildings, killing screaming occupants.

In a high-rise apartment building, a young woman knelt in prayer surrounded by lighted candles. Osiris swirled harmlessly around her while biodegrading rubber and plastic. Twenty minutes later a powerful explosion ripped through the apartment, after the candles ignited released natural gas. The explosion ignited gas in other areas of the building. Boiling clouds of flames blew out windows and doors around the building to release dense black smoke. The structure became a crematorium for hundreds of terrified people.

The bacteria devoured the plastic and rubber components of cars and trucks abandoned on city streets. Gasoline released from tanker trucks refueling gas stations, flooded into the storm sewers. In several locations, it made its way into underground conduits housing high voltage electrical wires. Sparks from the bacteria stripped wires ignited the gasoline. Powerful and deafening underground explosions began destroying city streets. Released clouds of red boiling flames engulfed nearby buildings, causing them to burn.

Governor Barrington wiped away the tears in his eyes. "Can we send firefighters in there to put out those fires?"

"Not while Osiris is in the city," Mayor Mastrani said. "It's too dangerous."

"Send in military helicopters! Have them drop water from above!"

"I will not risk my crewmembers in futile attempts to save the city," General Lawson said. "That bacteria cloud will kill them."

Governor Barrington pointed at Peter. "This is your fault. You and your company destroyed our city and killed innocent people!"

"Oh my God, the cloud is moving toward the hospital," Senator Califia said. "It's going after the hospital!

Osiris surrounded the St. Joseph's Hospital and Medical Center, while firefighters continued evacuating patients. The bacteria biodegraded plastic pipes carrying oxygen and ether throughout the building. Several minutes later sparks ignited those released gasses. A powerful explosion shattered windows outward around the building. Black smoke and embers billowed into the sky, after the weakened roof collapsed into the structure. The walls collapsed inward soon after, killing hundreds of people trapped in the hospital.

Mayor Mastrani watched clouds of dense black smoke rising into the blue cloudless sky over his city. "That bacteria is destroying my city, and there's nothing we can do to stop it!"

Steve focused his binoculars on a group of homeless people on a city street. A man frantically waved his arm through the silver bacteria fog swirling around him. "That's a good sign. Osiris isn't harming people."

After watching the devastation for six hours, Steve scanned the city with the binoculars one final time. He saw the bright red flames of thousands of fires burning in the city and suburbs. Dark plumes of black smoke rose from those fires. A thick dense cloud of choking smoke hung over the city, darkening the sun.

He cringed every few seconds after hearing distant explosions. He attributed them to propane storage tanks, and entire gas stations, exploding in the city. Each violent explosion propelled flaming debris high into the sky. Those flaming materials ignited more fires when they fell onto nearby buildings. In other areas, the intense heat of fires caused cars and trucks to explode. Those explosions spread the fires to other structures.

Steve focused his binoculars on a high-rise apartment building in the distance. Raging orange flames shot through shattered windows as an inferno destroyed the interior of the structure. The intense heat soon weakened the structural integrity of the towering building. The screeching of twisting metal signaled a disaster was imminent in the moments before the burning high-rise luxury building collapsed onto nearby apartment buildings. A huge swirling cloud of dust, flames, and smoke, erupted into the sky after the building collapsed.

"Hey Doc, we have to go," Bonnie said, as she motioned toward people climbing into the Hummers. "There's nothing more you can do here."

"I need to make some notes."

"I can take notes on my I-pad for you.

"Thank you." He smiled while helping her into a Hummer. Then he discussed his thoughts with Bonnie, during the ride to a hotel in Flagstaff.

Julie Tarallo, a volunteer from Steve's hospital, greeted him with a can of soda in a large hotel banquet hall in Flagstaff. "Hi, I watched Osiris decimate the city on a television news channel."

"Osiris is out of control. It's destroying the city. We need a way to stop it."

"President Stillman is preparing to address the nation," Governor Barrington said. "He's attempting to avert a nationwide panic."

"Is he going to mention my company by name?" Peter asked. He began to panic.

"I don't know! I don't care if he does!"

"If he says my company created that cloud, I'll be out of business!"

"You should be more concerned about the destruction you just witnessed in Phoenix!"

Steve walked to Harrison from the Environmental Protection Agency. "John, does your agency have satellite pictures of the bacteria cloud moving across the city?"

"We can request them." John drank from a cold bottle of water. "What will they show us?"

"We may learn something about the bacteria if we watch how it advances."

"That's a very good idea Steve," Doctor Feltault said. "I'll call Washington, and ask for images."

"Roger, did anyone else outside your company assist your man Goldberg with the development of Osiris?" Doctor Reglovic said.

"A Doctor Valcoskovic in Moscow offered suggestions to Thomas. We're trying to locate that doctor."

"I have some bad news." Harrison pressed the water bottle to his forehead. "My staff informed me that doctor died in a traffic accident on the way to the airport this morning. He was coming here to help us."

"This keeps getting worse," Roger said.

Doctor Feltault said, "We'll need to rely on volunteers for solutions to stop Osiris. We've faxed the Osiris design documents to scientists across the country, and in other nations."

"You're giving away my patented research secrets?" Peter said, angrily.

"Maybe a scientist will find a flaw in the genetic mapping. Something we can use against the bacteria to destroy it."

"I'll sue the government for billions for giving away my trade secrets." Peter's anger flared.

A man shouting loudly in a corridor interrupted the altercation. The man ran into the room. "Where's Harrison? I've got to talk to Harrison."

"I'm over here." John became concerned after recognizing the man was one of his staff members. "Cole, what's going on?"

The man fell against a table while catching his breath. "Osiris started moving! It's moving!"

"Moving where?" John frowned questioningly. "Where's it going?"

"It's following the electrical transmission lines. It's moving this way! Toward Flagstaff!"

John looked at Doctor Reglovic. "Can you estimate when the cloud will reach this city?"

"My best guess, based on the current speed?" He slid a hand over his unshaven face while thinking. "Twenty-four to thirty-six hours!"

Chapter 6

"We have to evacuate this entire city!" John suddenly felt exhausted.

"Flagstaff is filled with transients from Phoenix." Mayor Alex Goodale said, as he pulled a cell phone from his pocket. "This will be a mammoth undertaking!"

"It has to be done!" John said, shouting uncharacteristically. "Get started, now!"

As state and federal officials began the evacuation, the researchers returned to work. They formed study groups based on scientific and medical backgrounds. Hundreds of other researchers from across the country joined them during the day.

John Harrison met with the group at eleven that night. He learned they were unable to develop a suitable technique for destroying Osiris. "We all need some sleep. Be back here at six tomorrow morning."

At four o'clock the following morning, frantic pounding on his hotel room door woke Steve. When he opened it, he saw researchers running in the hallway. "What's going on?

"Harrison wants everyone downstairs," a man said, while pounding on room doors.

"Why?"

"I don't know. Get downstairs now!"

Steve pulled on a robe. As he walked toward an elevator, Bonnie stepped from her room. She wore blue sweats. "Where's everyone going?"

"Harrison wants to see us." They stepped into an elevator together.

"Why is everyone panicking?"

"I don't know." Steve took a deep breath. "I hope he's going to tell us Osiris died."

"I see huge colored maps taped to the walls of this room," Bonnie said, after they walked into a ballroom that now served as a laboratory. "Where did all of those soldiers come from?"

Steve looked around. "I don't know. Why is the military here?" He was confused.

John Harrison stood on a chair. "Ok, quiet. Quiet! I'm sorry I had to wake you. This is important. Osiris started moving in a north-westerly direction about an hour ago."

Doctor Reglovic studied a map. "There's nothing in that area but desert. Why is the bacterium suddenly acting so erratically?"

'Why would it move away from Flagstaff?" Roger said. "It knows there's food in this city."

"Let me finish!" John said, shouting. "There is something out there, and Osiris must be aware of it."

"What does that mean?" Peter shouted, startling those beside him. "Tell us everything you know, damn it!"

"On its current course, Osiris is moving directly toward a military laboratory." The revelation shocked state and local officials.

"How far is the cloud from the lab?" Steve said.

"Osiris is approximately seventy miles from that location."

94

"How much time do we have before Osiris reaches it?" Doctor Meridian said.

"Military intelligence estimates the cloud will impact our facility in five hours." A tall military officer stepped forward. "I'm General Brenton of the Army's Central Command."

"What is the nature of the experiments the military is conducting in that laboratory?" Doctor Hoffstein from the Center for Disease Control said.

"That information is classified. I can tell you the complex consists of twelve surface buildings. They sit over a secure multilevel underground laboratory."

Steve studied General Brenton, a man in his early fifties, with graying hair. "Osiris will eat through every seal in that laboratory. You can't stop it. Does anything in that facility present a danger to the public?"

Brenton considered the warning. "The laboratory complex contains various chemical weapons. We're developing methods to safely and effectively neutralize them."

Governor Barrington became outraged. "You're conducting military weapons research near major cities?"

"We have systems to ensure biological agents will not escape. We're prepared for that cloud."

"No, no, you're not!" Roger pushed his way through the researchers. "Osiris will attack your buildings from the outside. It will get into your laboratories. You can't stop it!"

Brenton frowned. "You're implying the facility will not withstand a direct hit from the cloud?"

"Osiris will inundate all of your buildings, and underground laboratories."

"How many people are working in that facility?" Steve said.

"Approximately five-hundred scientists, and one-hundred support staff."

"Tell them to leave now," Roger said. "Get them out while you can!"

"They're required to secure the chemical weapons before leaving. That's protocol."

"General, our AWACS surveillance aircraft just reported the cloud's forward speed is rapidly increasing," a soldier said. She studied video on a laptop computer.

"When do they expect the cloud will overrun our facility?"

"Impact is imminent!"

"Tell your staff to get out of that laboratory now, General!" Steve shouted. "Don't wait!"

Brenton motioned to other soldiers. "Evacuate the facility, immediately. Notify Washington we're shutting down and evacuating the Long Hill Laboratory."

Several minutes later, loud alarms began sounding throughout the Long Hill Laboratory complex. Frightened staff soon ran toward the parking lots. Their vehicles eventually jammed the two access roads leading to the remote facility. Several minutes later, people were shocked when floodlights around the secret laboratory lighted the towering silver bacteria cloud as it moved toward them. They stopped to stare and point at the ominous approaching cloud.

Osiris surrounded the facility several minutes later. It began biodegrading the rubber and plastic components of cars and buildings. The bacteria began invading the underground laboratories. It traveled downward through the ventilation system, completely filling one floor of the complex after another. The bacteria destroyed electrical wiring, which plunged the underground facility into darkness while trapping people underground. It destroyed rubber seals around airtight doors to enter secure laboratories. As Osiris filled what the staff was told was the lowest underground level of the laboratory, the bacteria traveled down a secret elevator shaft to enter another large laboratory complex.

Osiris examined the blue nutrient solution it found in hundreds of glass flasks in incubators, and secured storage containers. Then the bacteria's intelligence made a startling discovery. It sensed something familiar. A primitive life form similar to its own genetic structure lived in the nutrient solution. Osiris ordered its worker cells to attack and dissolve the cell walls of the foreign bacteria. When that was completed, the worker cells quickly assimilated the foreign DNA to create a new lifeform.

The Osiris cloud began changing color as it acquired the genetic properties of the foreign bacteria. It began glowing with an ominous silver hue. The worker cells that normally carried nourishment throughout the cloud now carried the DNA from the foreign bacteria. The genetic transformation continued throughout all areas of the cloud, inside and outside the laboratory complex. At that very moment, as the bacteria sensed its new capabilities, it's now enhanced intelligence became aware of a new source of nourishment.

A young woman running through the bacteria cloud toward her car, unexpectedly felt a burning sensation on her fingers and face. She was horrified after she saw the skin of her fingers bubbling, as if dissolving. The flesh began disappearing, evaporating, exposing the bones of her fingers and hands. As she screamed hysterically from the agonizing pain, bright red blood spilled from her mouth. The blood appeared to dissolve in the cloud and disappear as it fell to the ground. The woman reached for her eyes while screaming from a sudden and unbearable pain. She did not realize Osiris was devouring her flesh for nourishment. The bacteria invaded her skull through her mouth, eyes, and ears, to consume her brain. Osiris stripped the flesh completely from all of her bones, before the woman's skeleton collapsed to the ground.

Several men ran to a stumbling screaming man after he fell. They watched in horror as the flesh of his head, and his hair, bubbled away to expose his skull.

"I feel strange," one man said, before he and a large group of fellow scientists screamed hysterically for several seconds while the Osiris bacteria devoured their flesh. Seconds later, their skeletons fell to the ground.

Hundreds of other fleeing people began screaming as Osiris agonizingly consumed their flesh by biodegrading it. Military guards futilely fired weapons into the cloud in the moments before the bacteria stripped the flesh from their bones.

The Osiris bacteria eventually destroyed all life above and below ground. The bacteria's growing intelligence learned human flesh could now provide it with more nutrients than plastic or rubber. It also learned not to overlook any nourishment. The bacteria methodically biodegraded all of the rubber and plastic it found throughout the Long Hill Laboratory complex. Raging flames soon began consuming the buildings, and underground laboratories.

After exhausting the food supply at the laboratory, Osiris began moving. It remembered Flagstaff. The bacteria's intelligence now sensed not only a distant source of plastic and rubber. Osiris sensed an abundance of human flesh in the distance.

Steve glanced at his watch. He said, quietly, "Come on someone, tell us what's going on out there at that lab."

"Hey, calm down." Bonnie smiled compassionately. "It'll be okay."

"I don't like seeing military people in danger."

"Isn't that their job?"

"I don't want to see any kids go home to their parents in body bags."

She appeared shocked by his response. "Were you in the military?"

"I was with the Army, in Iraq and Afghanistan."

She paused. "I want you to tell me about it when you have time."

"Why?"

"My dad died there. He was in the Army, and was killed when a roadside bomb detonated."

Steve did not know how to respond when he saw tears welling in her eyes. "I'm sorry." He gently grasped her hand.

She smiled. "It's okay. He's my hero, and my guardian angel now."

Forty minutes later a soldier said, shouting, "General, Alpha Zero Zero is one mile from the Long Hill Laboratory. They're radioing a status."

"Put it on the speaker. I want everyone to know what's going on out there."

The conversation began blaring from speakers, "Alpha Zero Zero, what is the situation? Over."

A distraught soldier said, "This is Zero Zero. The bacteria cloud destroyed the installation, and its burning. The fire is out of control. Everyone is dead."

"Alpha Zero Zero. Say again. You say, everyone is dead? How can everyone be dead? There are no survivors?"

"This is Zero Zero. I see skeletons everywhere."

"Alpha Zero Zero. Say again. Where do you see skeletons?"

"Around buildings, on roads, in parking lots! There's dead bodies everywhere!"

Brenton raised a hand to quiet the shocked researchers as they began talking to one another. "Zero Zero, this is General Brenton. Calm down, son. I heard you say skeletons. Explain the situation to me."

"That's, that's, what's left of the staff! Bones with clothes on them, lying on the ground!"

Brenton frowned. "Are there any signs of life?"

"Negative! Everyone is dead. Everyone is a skeleton!"

"The cloud killed everyone?"

"That's affirmative!" The researchers began expressing varying and ominous opinions.

John Harrison pulled out his cell phone. "I'm forcibly evacuating everyone in the cloud's path, until we understand this situation."

"I'll speak to the reporters and ask them to warn people to move away from the cloud until we know more." Bonnie ran from the room.

Steve stood. "General, can your men bring three skeletons to me?"

"Why do you want them?" Brenton appeared shocked after the macabre request.

"The remains might tell us what happened to those people. It will give us insight into how the bacteria functions."

Brenton contemplated the request. He nodded. "We can do that."

Roger swallowed hard. "How much time do we have until Osiris reaches this city?"

"Our best guess is thirty-five hours," General Lawson said.

"We need to get everyone out of this city." Roger noticed Steve deep in thought while drawing a diagram on a pad. "What are you designing?"

"I want to build something to get us a sample of the bacteria."

"That's going to be risky," Harrison said. "Is that attempt absolutely necessary?"

Steve nodded. "We need the sample to determine how Osiris mutated."

"That's an excellent approach for analyzing the bacteria, Doctor!" Doctor Reglovic smiled as he placed a hand on Steve's shoulder. "Good thinking, my boy."

Brenton said, "My engineers will help you construct your capture device, Doctor."

When Steve walked out of the ballroom, he saw Bonnie speaking with a large group of reporters. She began walking with him. "I told the reporters to tell people Osiris may now be a killer. They'll warn everyone they must evacuate the city."

"Nice job."

"Thanks." She smiled. "Where are you going now?"

"To shower and change before I begin working with Brenton's men."

"I need a shower so I can do a newscast. But my crew is using my room to edit video."

"Get your clothes. You can shower in my room."

She smiled. "I'll owe you big time for this."

"Yes you will." He smiled as they walked toward the hotel elevators.

As Osiris continued moving forward, it changed direction slightly after sensing a large nearby farm. Young children heard the faint cries of birds dying as they flew through the bacteria cloud.

"Where can we go to hide from that cloud?" A woman stared at the advancing cloud apprehensively, before calling her children into the house.

"We'll hide in the cellar until it goes by." Her husband led his family into the basement. The entire family died soon after Osiris filled the house. They screamed in agony in the darkened basement while the bacteria devoured their flesh.

In another area of the farm, Osiris engulfed and devoured seventy migrant workers hiding in a barn. The cloud cautiously surrounded and studied cows and goats, and other farm animals. The developing intelligence quickly discovered they would also provide ample nutrients to sustain its growing need for nourishment. Osiris devoured the flesh from every animal, leaving only skeletons on the ground. The cloud then spread out to engulf the entire farm. It biodegraded all of the plastic and rubber it found. Then it began moving forward, leaving the burning ruins of the farm behind.

At nine o'clock, Steve and Roger met with Army Engineers. Steve explained the details of his sketches, which depicted a device to capture bacteria. He said, "We only need a few cells to study."

"Can you put it together, gentlemen?" Brenton asked the soldiers.

Colonel Charles Straley studied the sketches. "Yes sir, we can build the Doctor's device."

John Harrison appeared pale and somber as he walked into the ballroom. "The bodies brought back from the military laboratory just arrived. The body bags are on the loading dock."

"I want to see them." Steve led the group to the loading dock where armed soldiers guarded three black plastic body bags. When he unzipped a bag,

103

the exposed white skull stripped of flesh shocked him. The jaw appeared frozen open, as if the person was screaming while dying. "This is much worse than I expected!"

Roger appeared visibly shaken. He sat on the concrete floor. "What have we done to these people?"

"Jesus Christ!" Brenton began pacing after he saw the skull.

Steve carefully opened the shirt to examine the grayish-white skeleton completely stripped of flesh. "Osiris destroys every type of body tissue. The hair, brain, heart, and liver. Everything is gone.

"There's no blood on the clothes, Steve," Reglovic said. "Their death was so fast, these people didn't have time to bleed."

"Did everyone at the laboratory die this same way?" Steve said.

"They all look like that," a soldier said. He appeared to be in shock. "They're skeletons!"

While he studied another skeleton, Steve noticed a small brass medallion hanging from a chain around the vertebral column, securing the skull to the spine. He read the letters stamped into it. He found a similar medallion on the other skeletons. "I need a walk, and some air."

Roger followed him onto a wide driveway. "That was a shock. Are you all right?"

"I'm good." Steve pulled a pen from his pocket. He began writing on his hand.

"What are you doing?" Roger frowned.

"Those medallions are name tags. Why would they be made of metal, and not plastic?"

Roger shook his head. "I don't know. Where are you going with this?"

"I'll ask Bonnie to locate information about these people."

Roger wiped the perspiration off his forehead. "How is that going to help us?"

"Maybe their backgrounds will tell us what they were doing in that military laboratory." Steve led Roger back to the ballroom where Straley talked with other soldiers. He reviewed his diagrams with them, as they began planning how to build the collection device.

Several hours later Bonnie returned from doing a live newscast, where she explained the destruction caused by Osiris in Phoenix. She walked into the ballroom and smiled while handing Steve a cold can of soda. "What are you mad scientists huddled around?"

Steve and the soldiers laughed. He said, "It's a device to capture cells from the bacteria cloud."

"What? Isn't that dangerous?"

"We have to do it, to get a view into the bacteria's cells."

She studied the device as the men and women worked. "How does it work?"

"The Osiris bacteria will fill this glass cylinder inside the cloud. After it biodegrades this piece of rubber, this spring will seal the end of the cylinder with a non-rubber gasket."

"Did you design this, Doctor?"

"I scribbled on a pad. These talented engineers built it."

"It's ingenious. You're using the bacteria to trap itself."

"It's only ingenious if it works." He smiled as the others laughed.

She looked into his eyes. "How are you getting your bacteria trap into the cloud?"

"We're going to use a weather balloon to float it through the cloud."

"I don't like that idea." She pictured the destruction in Phoenix in her mind.

"We don't have any other way to do it."

"If you capture a cell sample, how do you study it?" She felt an unusual nervous tightness in her chest. "Where will you keep it? It eats rubber."

"NASA is sending a laboratory trailer they built to study alien organisms. The seals are made of non-rubber based materials. They should contain the bacteria."

"Who gets to test that theory?" She began taking deep breaths.

"Me, I guess." He noticed her growing apprehension.

"I don't like this plan."

"Let's talk. I need your help." He led her out of the hotel. Cars and trucks filled with people evacuating the city jammed the streets.

"How can I help a brilliant doctor destroy Osiris?" She smiled, while taking a piece of chocolate he offered.

"I need you to research some names I found today." He pointed at the writing on his hand. "Find out everything you can about these people and their backgrounds."

106

She entered the names into her I-Pad. "Who are they?"

"They're dead scientists that were working at the military laboratory. I need to know their medical specialties."

"I understand." She closed her eyes before sighing heavily.

"Are you alright?" He gently touched her long dark hair. He admired her firm petite body, and her attractive face.

"I'm worried about you." She turned, before silently walking back into the hotel.

At six that evening, as Harrison planned, the military moved the researchers out of the city with their equipment. Steve watched the busses filled with researchers pull away from the hotel with a heavily armed military escort.

When he walked into the lobby, he was surprise to find Bonnie entering notes into her laptop computer. "What're you still doing here?"

"My crew and I are staying to film Osiris when it reaches the city tomorrow."

"I realize that's your job. Please be careful." He paused, before smiling. "If we're stuck here tonight together, can I buy you dinner?"

"I'd enjoy that." She laughed. "But all of the restaurants are closed."

"Let's raid the hotel kitchen." Steve took her hand, and led her through the almost deserted hotel.

She laughed. "This is so crazy!"

"Yes it is. But it's fun." He opened a door to the kitchen, and led her to the tall stainless steel refrigerators. A short time later, they were enjoying a variety of cold meats and rolls on the balcony of his room.

Bonnie finished eating a piece of sumptuous ham. "What do you do besides work?"

"I volunteer at a Boy's Club. I like to jog and work out in the gym when I have time."

"I like the gym too. I lift weights. And, I do a lot of aerobics."

"You look terrific." He studied the smooth skin of her legs, now exposed by her short jean shorts. It was a contrast to the black hair covering his legs and arms.

"What kinds of music do you like?"

"Jazz." He opened a bottle of wine, before pouring two glasses. "I listen to the music on my phone and watch the waves when I go to the beach."

"That won't work if we go to the beach together, Doc." She sipped the wine.

He laughed. "What works for you? Do you want me to rub oil on your body?"

"That sounds interesting." She pulled down the waistband of her shorts to expose a narrow tan line. "I want you looking at me! This is from my bikini. Do I have to say more?"

"I don't think so." Steve felt himself becoming more relaxed with the woman.

"What kinds of food do you like?" She lifted a piece of decorated dessert pastry.

"I enjoy everything from pizza and hot dogs, to candle light dinners in nice restaurants."

"Those are some of my favorites too. We have a lot in common, Doctor."

They talked and laughed for several hours. They discussed families, work, and interests.

At midnight, Bonnie stood before she stepped to the balcony railing to look at the city. She smiled when Steve stepped behind her. She enjoyed the feeling when his body pressed against her from behind. "This city will be gone tomorrow."

He slid his fingers through her soft warm dark hair. "Some things last longer than cities."

She turned to face him. Her breasts pressed tightly against his chest. "And what is that, Doctor?"

"Two people who somehow may have found each other in the chaos."

"I was thinking the same thing." She smiled. "We're all alone in this big hotel. We can be as loud as we want."

He smiled, after kissing her cheek. "And if you have a sudden shortness of breath, I can give you mouth to mouth!"

"And I can do the same, all over your body."

"I think you need that examination." He kissed her passionately.

"I want to see your bedside manner, Doc. I need a very thorough examination."

"I'll undress my patient." He led her into the air-conditioned coolness of the hotel room. Then he lifted her in his arms, before gently placing her on the bed.

At noon the following day, Roger, Steve, and Straley waited anxiously in a Hummer on a street overlooking the city. Soldiers and equipment filled a dozen nearby vehicles. Bonnie and her crew waited in another. Everyone apprehensively watched Osiris approaching in the distance, while listening to military damage assessments on radios.

The bacteria cloud now extended approximately two miles above the ground. It resembled a cresting ocean wave, two miles wide. Enormous sections of the silver cloud fell forward to engulf sprawling residential areas in its path.

When Osiris was several miles from them, the soldiers inflated a towering brightly colored orange weather balloon. Steve attached the collection device to it. When they released the balloon, it floated upward silently into the cloudless sky. The winds blowing toward the raging firestorms behind Osiris began carrying it toward the bacteria. Thirty minutes later, everyone cheered after the balloon floated into the silver bacteria cloud.

"Hopefully, we have the Doctor's sample of the bacteria. Bring down that balloon," Straley said. He watched one of his men shoot at the balloon with a loud high-powered rifle. Then he and Steve tracked the punctured and deflating weather balloon's descent electronically, before marking the location on a map.

"Congratulations, Doctor." Bonnie slid her hand on his arm while smiling. "All of your ideas are amazing!"

"I see something happening to the right side of the cloud," a soldier said. He pointed at a misty tentacle of the silver cloud rapidly extending outward, toward them.

"Osiris somehow senses we're here!" Steve frowned at the approaching cloud formation.

"It's moving directly toward us, and picking up speed!" Straley shouted. "Get into the vehicles! We have to move out, now!"

"Let's go!" Steve led Bonnie and Roger to a Hummer. He climbed behind the wheel. He began speeding on the city streets, while driving ahead of the other vehicles.

"The cloud is chasing us!" Roger stuck his head out the window to watch the silver cloud rapidly moving forward.

"We'll take the highway!" Steve turned the Hummer sharply to the right and drove onto an entrance ramp. The other vehicles followed. "Maybe we can outrun it."

Bonnie pulled windblown hair out of her face while watching out a window. "Oh my God! Two of the trucks just rolled over!"

Roger watched soldiers crawl from the overturned vehicles, as the silver cloud surrounded the men. "Osiris got them! They're dying! The bacteria are killing them!"

"It's going to get us too!" Bonnie trembled uncontrollably from fear. She watched a Hummer crash into a guardrail after Osiris devoured the tires. The vehicle rolled over several times before exploding. "Oh my God! Those men just crashed too!"

Steve tightened his grip on the steering wheel. He felt his heart pounding in his chest. This realized this was another war, and he might be a fatality. "Where is that damn cloud now?"

"It's still gaining on us," Roger said, shouting while looking out the window. "It's half a mile behind us!"

"No! No!" Bonnie said, screaming hysterically. "It just surrounded three more trucks!"

"This can't be happening," Roger said, shouting. He watched three other vehicles skid across the road before crashing. Two of them burst into flames. The fires burned the uniforms from the skeletons.

"It's stopping! The cloud stopped!" Bonnie struggled to control her breathing. She watched the silver tentacle retreat back to the main cloud.

Steve stopped and parked on the highway. He watched the undamaged Hummers and trucks park beside him. As soldiers climbed from the vehicles, he checked to ensure everyone was unharmed.

Bonnie frantically looked for her camera crew, but they were not among the survivors. "Oh my God! My crew was in those other trucks." She began running toward the vehicles burning in the distance.

Steve chased her, to stop her. He grasped her arm. "I'm sorry, but they're dead. You can't help them."

"They can't be dead! How did this happen?" She watched the smoke rising from the burning vehicles.

"Are you all right?" Roger asked Straley, when he saw him lying on the highway on his back.

"No, I'm not." He sat up slowly. "I just lost a lot of good men."

"I don't know what to say." Roger sat down beside him. "Saying I'm sorry isn't enough."

"That bacterium is the perfect killing machine! It grows as it feeds on its victims."

"I'm sorry about your men." Steve said. "It's not easy to lose your team members."

"I never expected that cloud to attack us. This is my fault. I didn't keep my men safe!" Straley made a fist as his anger increased.

"There's no blame here, Colonel. We're dealing with a new enemy. An enemy that's learning quickly. Much more quickly than anyone expected."

Bonnie grasped Steve's muscular upper arm with her hands to support herself. "Now what do we do?"

"We have to find the collection device," Steve said. "We need the bacteria to study."

"What?" Her body began trembling. "You can't do that! Not after what just happened!"

"The Doctor's right." Straley stood. "If we don't retrieve the device, my men died for nothing."

"I know we have to do it." Bonnie took a deep breath. "I'm terrified now!"

"Come on, let's go." Steve put an arm around her waist, before leading her to the Hummer.

The Hummers and trucks began cautiously driving around the cloud. The route took them through areas of the city completely devastated by Osiris. Dense black smoke blown by hurricane force winds from intensifying firestorms obscured the landscape. The smoke obliterated the sun, turning day into night, while making breathing and seeing almost impossible. Explosions and fires destroyed houses and commercial buildings on both sides of every street. Flaming debris crashed down on the vehicles and roads, adding to the danger and fear.

Automobiles and gasoline powered equipment exploded in burning buildings, destroying the structures and igniting more fires.

After hours of searching, the group eventually found the weather balloon lying in a residential area, behind houses engulfed in raging red flames. The howling winds blew huge clouds of hot red embers across the streets and lawns, along with dense acrid smoke.

"Stay here. You'll be safe," Steve told Bonnie.

"I'll be waiting for you." She began to panic after the men disappeared in the black smoke. The hurricane force winds violently shook the Hummer.

"I don't like this!" Roger shuddered after violent and deafening explosions completely destroyed several nearby houses. Dense black smoke suddenly made seeing almost impossible.

"I can't breathe!" A soldier gasping for air collapsed to the ground. Several of his companions helped him to his feet.

"I see our collection device!" Steve squinted while pointing ahead. He ran into the smoke and soon returned with the device. He cautiously carried it to the Hummer.

"What took you so long, Steve?" Bonnie said. "I got scared."

"You're safe now." He wrapped the glass canister in a blanket.

"The fires are creating their own weather and we couldn't see anything," Straley said, as bright red burning embers and dense smoke filled the sky.

After several more nearby houses exploded, Steve said, "We have to leave now!"

"It'll take a century to rebuild this city," Bonnie said after the group drove to a safe location well away from burning buildings. There she watched the raging firestorms consuming the city. Tears began streaming down her cheeks.

Steve listened to a radio transmission, as Straley explained the situation to Brenton. "Osiris killed twenty-four of my men. Ms. Saunder's crew is also dead."

"That's not the scenario I expected." There was a long silence. "Did you get a sample of the bacteria?"

"Yes sir."

"Bring it in. Our command center is located on the Hualapai Indian Reservation, north of Flagstaff."

At nine that night, the Hummers drove onto the Indian reservation. The command center consisted of forty large trailers airlifted to the site, and a large group of tents. Portable generators provided electricity to the site. Loud helicopters landed to unload supplies and people.

Brenton met the group. "I'm glad to see you Colonel. How is everyone?"

"Shaken, and lucky to be alive, Sir."

"Are the people you evacuated from the city safe?" Steve said.

"Yes they are. They're staged in the desert sixty miles west of here. Most are sleeping in their vehicles. Some brought tents and trailers. We're trying to get food to them, but it's a logistical challenge."

Peter Samulson rushed to the group, before he shook Straley's hand. "I heard what happened to you, Colonel. Losing your men is a tragedy."

John Harrison joined the group. "Ms. Saunders, I need you to tell the other reporters what took place today. Emphasize how deadly Osiris has become."

"Come with me gentlemen, we need to talk." Brenton led Roger and Steve into a long camouflaged windowless trailer. Overhead lights illuminated a narrow central corridor lined with doors. He opened two of them. "This is a mobile barracks. These are your quarters. It's tight, but you have a bed, desk, television, Internet connectivity, and cell phone service. It's also air conditioned."

"Where can we take a shower?" Steve said, after they stepped outside. "I smell like smoke."

"We have four outdoor shower units." Brenton led them into a long tent. "We have a full kitchen in here. Get yourselves something to eat."

"Two cheeseburgers, please," Steve said, after soldiers asked to help him.

Brenton filled a cup with soda. "Do you have any ideas related to what happened to Osiris after it encountered our laboratory?"

Steve shook his head. "Something must have altered the bacteria. We have to figure out what that is." He sat at a table with a tray of food and waited for Roger to sit beside him.

"The Pentagon confirmed there were no chemical weapons being developed in that facility, Doctor."

One of Brenton's aides rushed into the tent. "General, the FBI found Thomas Goldberg."

116

"Get him here as soon as you can," Roger said. "We need to know what he did to Osiris!"

"It's not that easy." The aide read the report he carried.

"Explain," Brenton said.

"They think they found what's left of Thomas Goldberg."

"What does that mean?" Steve frowned.

"Initial reports indicate he was on an airplane Osiris destroyed in Phoenix."

"Osiris killed him?" Roger was shocked. "Now we'll never know how he altered Osiris!"

"You're sure he's dead?" Steve asked skeptically. "This isn't another one of his tricks?"

The aide nodded. "The airline computer indicates he had reservations on a flight to England."

"He was running to another continent," Steve said. "He may have thought he would be safe on an island!"

"I want to confirm that man is dead," Brenton said.

"I'll go with you." Roger followed the men out of the tent.

Bonnie walked into the tent and ordered food. She smiled as she sat beside Steve. "Hey, thanks for dragging me into that truck today. I was too scared to move."

He smiled. "I just started running before you did."

"You saved my life." She gently kissed his cheek. "I'm grateful for that."

Moments later a loud gunshot startled them. They heard a woman's hysterical screams soon afterwards.

Steve took Bonnie's hand after they stood. "Let's find out what's going on."

They ran behind a trailer where researchers were gathering. Steve saw Peter's body lying on the ground. The bullet from a self-inflicted gunshot ripped away a large portion of his skull. Bright red blood pooled under the lifeless body.

"Oh my God!" Bonnie covered her face with her hands while pressing her body against Steve.

Steve saw the shocked expression on Roger's face after he pushed his way through the crowd. "I'm sorry."

Roger took a deep breath while staring at his brother's body. "Peter always took the easy way out. Now he doesn't have to deal with Osiris."

After military police and medical personnel asked everyone to leave the area, Steve grasped Bonnie's hand. "You're staying with me."

"When are people going to stop dying?" She asked. "When is it going to end?"

Chapter 7

Early the next morning Steve, Brenton, Mayor Goodale of Flagstaff, and John Harrison, met in an Army communications trailer. Fifteen meteorologists from the National Weather Service, and the National Hurricane Center joined them. They discussed the changing characteristics of the deadly bacteria cloud. It was forming into a cloud formation that resembled a hurricane. The circular cloud four miles across rotated in a counter clockwise pattern, but did not produce wind. The well-defined eye at the center of the spiral cloud puzzled everyone.

Steve studied the faces of the young military men and women. A soldier reminded him of a friend killed by a roadside bomb in Iraq. He thought, *'Why do we always put our kids, our most precious resources, into dangerous and deadly situations? When are we going to learn to stop doing this?'*

Images from a reconnaissance satellite approaching Flagstaff appeared on several monitors. An officer said, "You're seeing video of the city from our most sophisticated surveillance platform." Everyone studied the huge firestorms consuming hundreds of buildings.

Steve said, "Can you show us where Osiris is located now?" An image of the entire city appeared on the monitors. He was shocked when he saw the cloud dramatically increased in size overnight.

"It appears Osiris has stopped moving," Harrison said. "Why is it stationary?"

119

"Show us the streets Osiris passed over," Steve said. The monitors soon displayed a startling image.

"I don't know what to say!" Alexander Drouin said. The renowned pathologist from France, was accustomed to working with cadavers. He was not prepared for what he saw on the monitors. "This scene is quite unbelievable!"

"The city streets are covered with thousands of clothed skeletons!" John pounded his fist on a table. "Osiris killed those people as they were fleeing."

Brenton said, "That may not be the circumstances. Military Intelligence reported thousands remained in the city despite the mandatory evacuation. They stayed to loot stores and malls. That decision cost them their lives."

"That explains why the cloud isn't moving," Steve said, coldly.

Brenton frowned. "I don't understand."

"The bacteria are hunting the people hiding in those buildings in the city."

A soldier reported, "You're now seeing a departing view of the city." Everyone silently watched the smoke rising from raging firestorms.

"This situation is rapidly deteriorating," Brenton said, somberly.

"And it's going to get worse if we can't stop that bacteria," Steve said. When he stepped from the trailer thirty minutes later, he saw Roger reading a report. "What's going on?"

"This is a press release about Peter's suicide. They're blaming him for Osiris!"

"There's no reason to do that." Steve realized Roger's uncharacteristic anger indicated his mental stress was becoming unbearable. "Why don't you take a few days off and get some rest? You need a break."

"No, thanks." He nodded to several people expressing their condolences. "I don't want time to think."

Steve paused. "I understand."

Roger crushed the news release in his hands. "Let's check out our laboratory trailer." The NASA trailer located in the center of the command center measured seventy feet long, twelve feet wide. The windowless silver metal exterior reflected the sun. Thick black cables carried electricity, Internet, and telephone access to it.

"How is everyone?" Steve said, after he stepped inside and found researchers already at work. He studied the equipment lighted by fluorescent lights.

"We're good," Ray Jacobs said. "We're about to confirm you captured a sample of bacteria for testing."

"How are you doing that?" Steve suddenly felt uneasy. He nervously slid a hand over his short dark hair.

"We put pieces of a rubber tire into this isolation chamber," Barry Hazlett said. The oncology doctor took a deep breath. "After we open your collection canister, any bacteria you captured should digest it."

"It's a primitive test," Ray said, "but it'll tell us what we need to know."

"I agree." Steve crossed his arms defensively. Being near the bacteria again made him uncomfortable.

Several researchers stepped to the window of the isolation chamber. Constance Gendrone, a NASA Engineer, grasped the mechanical hands dangling from the ceiling of the trailer. They controlled two mechanical hands inside the chamber. She locked one hand around the collection device, before opening it with the other hand. The researchers watched as the pieces of rubber in the isolation chamber began bubbling. The rubber seemed to evaporate as Osiris biodegraded the material.

"We've got live cells for testing." Ray shook Steve's hand. He smiled as several scientists expressed their appreciation to Steve.

Doctor Licitra said, "We have a dozen isolation chambers in this trailer. Twelve teams working independently can search for ways to destroy the bacteria."

During the next five hours, teams of researchers isolated bacteria cells. After successfully placing one cell into an electron microscope, they huddled around large monitors to view it.

A fascinated scientist staring intently at a monitor said, "So that's our bugger flesh eater."

Doctor Licitra said, "The cell isn't symmetrical as I expected. Strange, it's shaped irregularly."

"It looks like a very radical form of cancer," Doctor Navickis of the Dana Farber Cancer Institute said. "I've never seen anything like it."

Doctor Judith Bechthold from the German Academy of Sciences removed her glasses. "Those hair like filaments extending outward from the cell puzzles me. They might hold the cells together in the cloud formation."

"I don't recognize the dark half circle areas around the exterior of the cell," Roger said.

Doctor Sarah Berrutti said, "Those areas of the cell might expel helium. That allows the cells to form into the cloud."

Doctor Meridian suddenly felt helpless and confused. "It might take years to understand this organism."

"The human species doesn't have years," Steve said. "We need to kill this monster!"

Doctor Reglovic looked at the clock. "I suggest we work around the clock in shifts to maximize our efforts." Everyone agreed. They began developing a research schedule.

At seven o'clock that evening Bonnie stepped into the trailer crowded with researchers. She watched Steve staring into a microscope while others explained their theories. She studied his body movements. She noticed how the handsome and intelligent man dressed in shorts and a tee shirt, intently listened to varying ideas. She felt herself unexplainably becoming excited.

When he looked up, he saw her. He immediately smiled. "How are you?"

"I'm good. Are you hungry?"

"I'm starving. Let's get something to eat."

As they walked to the kitchen tent on a road crowded with researchers and soldiers, they talked and shared their thoughts.

Bonnie took his hand, before she squeezed it tightly. It made her feel safe. "I missed you today, Doc."

"Me too. What did you do today?"

"I filmed a new story warning people Osiris will kill them, even if they try to hide from the bacteria. They need to evacuate to stay safe. I'm attempting to calm the people with the facts, instead of sensationalizing the situation."

"I haven't seen the news for days. How's the country dealing with Osiris?"

"Everyone is panicking. They're booking flights to get overseas. The roads to Canada and Mexico are jammed with cars, but the borders are closed."

"The situation will get worse if we can't find a way to stop Osiris."

"I wish we were somewhere else right now. At a different time." She took a deep breath.

"I do too."

"Why couldn't I have met you when I was on vacation in the Bahamas?"

"The Bahamas?" Steve laughed. "I can take you diving."

"Diving?"

"I've been doing it for years. I'd love to see you underwater in a bikini."

She laughed. "What's up with you today?"

He sighed. "The stress. I can't handle it if I'm serious all day. I'm sorry."

"Don't ever be sorry for being you." She led him into the kitchen tent.

Later that night, Steve stepped into his sleeping quarters. He found Bonnie lying on the bed watching the news. "I hope you don't mind I'm in here. I couldn't get to sleep in the heat."

"I enjoy having you with me." They kissed passionately, before helping each other to relax.

At five the following morning a hand grasped Steve's shoulder. It startled him to consciousness. He opened his eyes and saw Roger kneeling beside the bed. "What's going on?"

Roger's head fell forward in the dim light. "Osiris is moving."

"What? Where's it going?"

"It's headed for Las Vegas."

Steve's eyes widened from shock. "Give me ten minutes." When he stepped out of the trailer, he momentarily enjoyed a spectacular red sunrise. Then he and Roger ran to a military trailer to view images from a reconnaissance satellite.

General Brenton appeared exhausted while pointing at a large monitor. "This is an infrared image taken of Flagstaff thirty minutes ago. The black areas are intense fires. This cooler blue mass is Osiris moving away from the city."

"Why did it start moving now?" Steve stared at the monitor. "It couldn't have biodegraded all of the rubber and plastic in the city."

"Maybe the fires are too hot for the bacteria to survive," Brenton said. "Those fires are melting steel in some buildings."

"I don't think that's it," Roger said. "The bacteria appeared impervious to flames and heat in Phoenix."

A view of the city appeared on another monitor. A soldier explained, "We animated the movement of Osiris across the city." Everyone watched the seemingly random forward progression of the hurricane shaped cloud.

"Why does the cloud make turns as it moves?" Roger said.

"I don't like what I'm seeing." Steve rubbed his forehead.

"What do you think is happening, Doctor?" Brenton noticed Steve looked unexplainably traumatized.

"I shouldn't speculate without more information." He stared at the monitor as if transfixed.

"We don't have time to assimilate more information Doctor! Speculate for us."

"I think the cloud zigzagged across the city because it's hunting humans as a food source."

"How can that be happening?" Brenton was shocked, and looked at his aides.

Steve took a deep breath. "Osiris is moving away from Flagstaff because it destroyed every living creature in the city. It's looking for more human flesh!"

"Oh God, don't tell me that." Roger collapsed onto a chair. His head fell back as if defeated.

Steve said, "It may know flesh provides it with more nutrients than rubber or plastic."

"How does it know Las Vegas is another food source?"

"Maybe, as the cloud increases in size General, maybe its ability to find food is developing."

"When will it reach Las Vegas?" Roger said.

"Thirty hours." Brenton looked at a map. "Then what happens? Anyone?"

Steve pictured the city in his mind. He remembered being there only three months ago, attending a symposium. "After Osiris destroys Vegas, it'll probably move west into the heavily populated areas. It'll kill millions of fleeing people."

"Then what will the bacteria do?" Brenton studied a map on a table. "I need your thoughts for planning purposes."

"It'll work its way up the west coast. After destroying Seattle, it'll invade Canada. After destroying North and South America, the cloud will be large enough to move across the Bering Strait to Russia. It'll destroy Europe."

"How can this be happening?" Tears filled Roger's eyes. "Where does this end?"

Steve stared at a map of the world on a monitor. "I wouldn't publicize this yet, but I believe Osiris has the potential to destroy all forms of life on our planet."

"That's a very grim assessment, Doctor," Brenton said.

"Let's wake everyone and tell them what's going on," Roger said. "We need their ideas!"

One hour later the researchers met in the kitchen tent. Many still wore pajamas and robes. They listened intently to the cloud's movement update from Brenton's staff.

Reglovic wore a bright green and blue striped bathrobe. He read his notes. "We've completed three hundred tests using fire, heat, cold, steam, pesticides, and a variety of chemicals. Nothing we've tested kills the bacteria."

Steve's determination increased after the disheartening report. He began pacing nervously. "It's time to get radical and unconventional."

"Explain your thinking son," Reglovic said.

"It's time to consider bizarre and unorthodox ways to kill the damn bacteria."

"Your approach is sound. It can't be impervious to everything."

"Exactly, my thinking. Something has to stop it. It's something we haven't tried yet!"

General Lawson interrupted, to introduce a large group of researchers who recently arrived. They were from Russia, Sweden, France, China, and England. World governments now perceived Osiris as a threat to all people and nations.

Late that afternoon Steve, and Kirstin Rusnak an Oncology nurse who worked with him in hospital, took a break. They stepped out of the laboratory trailer and into one hundred degree heat. While walking toward the kitchen tent for water, Steve watched hundreds of researchers working in huge military tents. Most wore shorts and tank tops. A few women wore short skirts. Many wiped away the perspiration on their hands and faces with towels.

Steve said, "I don't see how they can work and think in this heat."

"You make them determined to be successful."

"What does that mean?"

"They're watching you drive yourself. They're trying to work as hard as you do."

"You're saying I'm their role model?" He frowned skeptically. "I don't think so."

"You're giving us the incentive and inspiration to work harder."

"I'm helping everyone to succeed and be successful. It's what I do best."

"We all see that in you. You're setting the example. You're the leader we're following."

Brenton stopped them. "Doctor, do you want any of your people to accompany the intelligence gathering teams I'm sending to Las Vegas?"

Steve's heart began racing. "Why are you putting soldiers in the path of that cloud?"

"The Pentagon wants a video feed from the city. They want to see Osiris in action."

"I don't want to put any of our people in danger. I'd rather keep them working here."

"I agree completely."

"Can we watch the video here? We may see something we can use to destroy the bacteria."

"We can do that." Brenton watched low flying helicopters carrying supplies to the command center. "Ms. Saunders asked if she can accompany my teams. You may want to warn her to watch her step in Vegas."

"I'll do that." Steve saw Bonnie walk out of a press tent with reporters. He smiled as she motioned him toward the group.

"Talk to her and take care of what's important to you Steve," Kirsten said.

"Yeah, I should do that now." He remembered the deadly encounter, when the cloud chased the Hummer he drove. He walked to the press tent.

Bonnie smiled as she spoke to the reporters. "This is Doctor McClellan. I put his background information in the news packets I distributed to all of you today."

Steve shook the reporter's hands, as he answered questions. When he and Bonnie were alone, he said, "Brenton told me you're going to Vegas. Is that necessary?"

"My network wants me to do a live report from the city when Osiris gets there." She read the text messages on her phone.

"I don't like the idea of you being near that damn cloud."

"I'll be fine." She smiled. "I'll do the story and then come back here."

"I need you to be safe." He leaned forward to kiss her lips.

Bonnie smiled as researchers walking past them smiled. "I'll be safe with you watching over me, Doctor."

He smiled. "Let's meet for dinner later."

At four o'clock the following morning, bright floodlights illuminated soldiers loading helicopters with equipment. Steve and Roger helped Bonnie's crew move their equipment onto a helicopter.

"Thanks for your help Roger," Bonnie said, shouting over the sounds of arriving helicopters.

"Please be careful." He hugged her.

"I will. You keep this one calm while I'm gone." She grasped Steve's shirt tightly while smiling at him.

"I won't be there to watch your ass, so keep an eye on Osiris." He caressed her long hair.

"I didn't know you watch my ass!" She joked, attempting to coax a smile from him. "I'll be back before you know it. Give me a kiss for luck."

Steve watched her run to a helicopter. He saluted Brenton and Straley before they climbed aboard another. Ten minutes later, twenty-four helicopters departed from the command center. They soon disappeared in the darkness, as the sound faded away.

Military technicians began broadcasting from Las Vegas at noon. In the laboratory trailer, researchers watched the swirling silver cloud as it silently began engulfing entire blocks of city buildings.

Doctor Reglovic frowned while watching a monitor. "It appears Osiris is moving much faster than it did, while it consumed the cities of Phoenix and Flagstaff."

"I'm picturing millions of terrified people running from the cloud on city streets right now," Doctor Carol Louth from the University Of Connecticut School Of Medicine said. She shuddered. "God help and protect those people who remained in the city."

Roger heard a faint rumbling sound in the distance. The sound became louder with each passing second. "What's that noise?"

"Earthquake!" Doctor Reglovic shouted. "Everyone get outside before the isolation chamber shatters and releases Osiris!" He guided researchers rushing toward the trailer door, to join hundreds of frightened people standing outside.

"The sound is coming from over there." A woman pointed to the east. "Over those mountains."

Steve shaded his eyes. "I see black specs above the horizon. They're moving this way."

"They're too loud to be helicopters," a soldier said.

Several minutes later, everyone saw approaching aircraft high in the sky. Another soldier said, "They're Air Force transports."

"I count thirty aircraft," Roger shouted, over the growing rumble of engine noise.

"They're flying west," Doctor Satriano from the Harvard School of Medicine said while pointing at the aircraft, "toward Las Vegas!"

Steve rushed into the trailer and lifted a telephone. He watched Osiris surrounding buildings on a monitor. He squinted at the monitor after he heard someone say, "Rolling in Strike Package B."

When a military operator answered, Steve shouted, "This is Doctor McClellan. I have to talk to Brenton!"

"The General is away from the helicopters and doesn't have a portable radio."

"Get me Straley!" Steve watched the researchers rushing back into the trailer. "Get me anyone! I need to talk to someone to stop this insanity!"

Doctor Meridian said, "I'm becoming very concerned."

Steve was shocked after he unexpectedly heard Bonnie's voice on the phone. "Steve, I see planes flying toward Osiris!"

"Tell Brenton to divert them! Do it now, before it's too late!"

132

She frantically looked around. "I don't know where he is!" She shaded her eyes from the sun to watch the approaching aircraft.

"Those planes are too close to Osiris!" Roger cried. "Didn't Brenton warn them about the bacteria?"

Bonnie said, "The planes are about a mile from Osiris. Oh my God! What are they doing?"

"What? What's happening?"

"They're flying over the cloud! They just started spraying a bluish liquid onto it!"

"They're doing what?" Steve looked at the others when she did not respond. "What's going on?"

"Now all of the planes started spraying that blue liquid!"

"Tell someone they need to stop! Get the planes out of there!"

"Oh my God!"

Steve felt his heart pounding after she suddenly stopped speaking. He panicked, wondering if Osiris attacked her. "What is it?"

"Part of the cloud started spiraling upward in a counter clockwise direction."

"How can it do that?" Steve motioned to the others to stop screaming questions at him.

"The cloud is climbing into the sky like a tornado." She paused for several seconds. "The top of the funnel cloud is almost a mile wide!"

"How can that be happening?" Steve looked at the others. He waited, but no one could give him an answer.

"The top of the cloud is almost two miles wide now. It just surrounded the first group of airplanes! Oh my God, what's happening up there?"

Osiris began biodegrading the plastic windshields, before flooding into the interior of each aircraft. Plastic controls began disintegrating in pilot's gloved hands as the bacteria devoured them. Entire plastic instrument panels and instruments disappeared. Metal gauges and switches fell from the ceiling after Osiris destroyed plastic panels.

Screaming crewmembers clawed savagely at their flight suits while Osiris biodegraded their flesh. A pilot in agony reached for the ejection seat handle. He screamed when he saw his fingers and hands stripped of flesh.

"What's happening now?" Steve shouted. He began pacing nervously.

Tears began flowing down Bonnie's cheeks. "Osiris must have killed the crews. The planes are in steep dives. They're all trailing black smoke."

"Where is Brenton? Tell him to get the other planes out of there!"

"Two planes just crashed into the desert. They exploded! The others crashed into the city and exploded."

"What about the other airplanes? Are they safe?"

"The cloud is still spiraling like a tornado. It surrounded the other airplanes while the pilots tried to veer away." She paused and helplessly watched the bacteria cloud. "Osiris must have killed those crews. Some of the planes are crashing into the city. Oh my God, they're exploding!"

134

Steve heard an unusual sound on the phone. "What was that?"

"Three of the airplanes just exploded in the air after Osiris surrounded them."

"What's going on now?" He gasped for breath, while panicking.

"Two of the airplanes are descending toward the city trailing flames and black smoke. My God, one crashed into the Luxor Hotel!" She watched flames explode outward through every window and door of the building moments later.

Bonnie wiped away tears while staring through binoculars. "Another just crashed into the side of the Bellagio Hotel." She watched a series of violent explosions quickly engulfed the building in a raging inferno. "Can we do anything?"

"It's too late to help those flight crews."

"Another plane just crashed into the base of the Excalibur Hotel before it exploded." She watched a swirling fireball rise above the hotel, before powerful explosions ripped through the building. The structure rocked. Then it toppled to the side and crashed onto the casino complex with a deafening rumble. Clouds of dust and black smoke swirled violently into the sky. "Oh my God! The entire building just collapsed! It collapsed!"

"Did any planes make it out safely?"

Bonnie scanned the sky with the binoculars. "Osiris destroyed all of them! None of them escaped!"

"What's Osiris doing?"

"The cloud is still moving forward. The blue liquid didn't affect it."

The researchers in the trailer silently watched the monitors. Reglovic said, "That was our government's pathetic attempt to destroy Osiris. They must feel they have a better grasp of the situation than we do."

"What a waste of human life." Steve rested his head on his hands. He thought about the dead crew members, and how they suffered before they died.

Late that afternoon, the helicopters returned to the command center. Steve, Reglovic, and Roger met them.

Steve ran to a helicopter after Bonnie climbed from it. He said, "I was so worried about you. Are you all right?"

She hugged him tightly. "I felt so helpless. I knew Osiris was killing the pilots, but I couldn't do anything to help them." Then she began crying.

As Brenton walked toward a Hummer, Reglovic shouted, "Where did those airplanes come from, General?"

"That was a Central Intelligence Agency operation. The President authorized it, after a recommendation from his advisors."

"How many men just died needlessly?" Steve said, angrily. "That didn't accomplish anything."

"I'll relay your objections to Washington."

"Why is Central Intelligence running an independent operation? Why aren't they working with us, and collaborating to find ways to stop Osiris?"

"I assume they're trying to help us destroy Osiris."

Reglovic became angry. "Get us the formula of whatever they sprayed on the damn cloud. We know it won't stop the bacteria."

"I'll request that information."

During the next three hours, researchers reviewed the video of Osiris destroying Las Vegas. It provided them with a better perspective of the bacteria's capabilities. It did not provide any new theories for destroying it.

At seven o'clock Brenton, John Harrison from the EPA, and three civilians stepped into the NASA trailer. Four high-ranking military officers followed them. Brenton said, "Can I have your attention please. This is Mister Jeffery Thompson of the Central Intelligence Agency."

Roger immediately pointed at Thompson. "You're the fool who sent those planes to Las Vegas? You sent those pilots to their deaths!"

"Take it easy Roger," Brenton said. "These military officers directed the activities in the military laboratory Osiris destroyed. They have an inventory of the biological agents stored in that facility."

"Please review this list." Major Johnson said, after he placed a document on a table. "Ask us any questions you feel are important."

Doctor Feltault carefully scanned the document with others. "Nothing here caused Osiris to turn deadly."

Major Johnson motioned to Thompson. "Did you bring your inventory list?"

He ignored the question. "It's not important. Forget about what my agency was doing in that laboratory."

"What are we discussing?" Brenton asked the officer.

"There were rumors Central Intelligence stored chemical agents in a restricted area of the lab."

"That's enough Major," Thompson said. "My organization will not tolerate military interference!"

Steve watched Thompson intimidate Major Johnson by shouting warnings of government retribution. He guessed the man to be in his late forties. He noticed Thompson wore two gold rings on the fingers of each hand, and a terribly fitted brown wig. A nervous twitch in the man's left arm caught his attention.

Johnson angrily said, "You're withholding information during a national crisis."

Thompson ignored the remark with a gesture of his hand. "General, order that man to restrain himself."

Brenton look directly at Johnson, before he said, "Colonel, I'm ordering you to tell these researchers what they need to know!"

"You'll find yourself court-martialed if you continue," Thompson said, threatening the officer.

"Central Intelligence was developing something in the lab. It may have impacted the Osiris' genetic structure."

"You're through in the Army!" Thompson pointed at Johnson. "I'll contact your commanding officer and explain your refusal to obey my orders."

Steve's anger flared, before he pointed at Thompson. "Shut your god damn mouth, you flipping idiot! I've had enough of your crap!" The crude remark shocked and silenced everyone.

Thompson appeared surprised. His mouth briefly fell open. "And who might you be?"

"I'm Doctor Steven McClellan."

"Something in that lab caused Osiris to mutate," Doctor Meridian said. "This man knows what it is."

"That's absurd!" Perspiration began forming on Thompson's forehead in the air-conditioned trailer. "Our project involved biodegrading oil spills before they can pollute the environment. The experiments were nothing more than that."

"I want the formula of whatever you're developing." Meridian crossed his arms, defiantly.

"That information is classified. It's not for your eyes!"

Steve laughed. "An oil biodegrading formula is classified? Do you expect us to believe that, you fool?"

Meridian was determined. "Get on the phone, and get us that formula!"

Thompson shuddered theatrically. "I make minor annoyances like you disappear in the night."

"Threats don't work with me," Meridian said. "I want the truth."

"My agency is dealing with this situation. We'll have a solution for stopping Osiris within several weeks."

"We'll have no nation left in a week, if we don't stop the bacteria now. You have two minutes to get the formula!"

"Or what? You'll pack your bags and run home?"

"Should I get the President on the phone and explain the situation where you're being uncooperative?" Brenton said, threatening Thompson.

"The President? He can't decide what to have for lunch. You expect him to deal with this situation?"

"We don't need the President." Steve smiled. "If we don't get the formula I'll tell the reporters an experimental bacteria your agency developed caused Osiris to turn deadly."

Thompson appeared shocked by the threat. "You can't substantiate that! No one can!"

"You're right. However, the press will run with that story and implicate you. They'll tell the world your agency created the killer cloud!"

"If anyone discloses that information I'll have you arrested."

Feltault said, "There are forty people in here. Are you going to arrest everyone?"

Doctor Carol Louth angrily said, "I'll ensure those reporters drag your agency down. Congress will shut you down."

Thompson silently contemplated his options. He nodded to one of his staff. "Give these fools what they want."

The man pulled several pages from his computer bag. "This is the breakdown of the chemical agents we're developing."

"You'll see it did not affect Osiris," Thompson said.

"We'll determine that," Meridian said. "You can leave."

"You're dismissing me?" Thompson pushed his way through the researchers. Outside the trailer, he asked the aide, "What did you give them?"

"The Omega Eleven formula. It was a failure we worked on ten years ago."

"Good work. Keep an eye on them. I want to know if anyone figures out what's really going on."

Chapter 8

The scientists analyzed Thompson's formula until exhaustion impeded their thinking at midnight. Colonel Caraster from Walter Reed Army Hospital studied notes covering six whiteboards. "I'm not convinced this bacterium altered Osiris. It has no basis for turning Osiris into a deadly organism."

"Your statement makes me suspicious." Steve intently stared into a microscope.

"Suspicious of what?" Doctor Meridian said, unsure of his colleague's concern.

Steve looked up. "Our government and their information sources."

"It would be disconcerting to learn our government is providing us with misinformation."

"I know how they work from my time in the military."

"That's why I'm troubled by your remarks." Meridian nodded, while stretching his arms.

"I've got to get some sleep." While walking to his quarters, Steve stepped into an Army Intelligence trailer. The only light came from dozens of radar screens. He asked the soldiers studying them, "What's Osiris doing?"

"The cloud is covering one sixth of Las Vegas, Sir," a high-ranking officer said.

"Are you sure?" He appeared visibly shaken by the unexpected response.

"This is an infrared image of the cloud."

Steve studied the red and black image on a monitor. "How are we ever going to stop that monster?" His remark shocked the soldiers. They looked at one another questioningly after he walked out.

He found Bonnie asleep in his dimly lighted and small quarters. He studied her face, and hair on the pillow. He thought, *'I'm falling in love with her and she doesn't know it. I'm fourteen, maybe fifteen, years older than her. That's a problem.'*

She woke as he undressed. "Hey, how are you? I'm sorry I fell asleep waiting for you."

"Don't be sorry." He sat beside her. "You need some sleep."

"Did you figure out how that government bacteria altered Osiris?"

He shook his head. "The documentation Powell gave us doesn't make any sense."

She rolled onto her side. The white sheet slid from her shoulder to expose her naked body. "Are we all going to die?"

"We'll find a way to kill Osiris." He looked into her eyes. "I won't let anything hurt you."

"I want the truth." She sat up. "If I'm going to die I need to do some things."

"Like what?"

"I want to get home and see my family. I've been away from them much too long."

"We all spend too much time away from the ones we love."

"That was a mistake I regret." She toyed nervously with her long dark hair while it rested on her breasts.

"Death has a way of putting everything in prospective. We realize we put off the important things until it's too late."

"If you can't kill Osiris, what will it do?"

"Computer projections show the cloud increasing in size as it moves around the planet."

"Will it eventually die from a lack of food?"

"It'll take fifty years for the bacteria to devour all of the rubber, plastic, and people."

Tears began filling her eyes. "I want you to make me a promise."

"What am I promising?" He was surprised by her comment, and attempted to comfort her while gently rubbing her shoulder. The skin felt smooth and warm.

"If Osiris is going to attack us, I want you to kill me before it does."

"Kill you?" He appeared shocked by the request. "I don't understand."

"The thought of dying in agony while the bacteria eats my skin, terrifies me."

"I have the same thoughts and concerns."

"I think about the bacteria killing me every minute I'm awake! I have nightmares about it whenever I'm asleep!"

He gently brushed her hair back, and off her shoulder. "I'm not sure I can do what you're asking."

"Promise me. I don't want to die that way. I don't want to suffer."

He paused, before nodding while staring into her eyes. "I won't let Osiris hurt you."

She understood his commitment to her. "Thank you."

He stretched out on the bed beside her. "Why don't you go home? Stay with your family until this is over."

"I can't leave you here." She slid her fingers through the black hair covering his chest.

"I'll be safe."

"But I'll be away from you, and that would be very difficult for me."

Steve looked into her eyes. "What's going on here? I feel the same way about you, when we're not together."

She smiled. "This disaster brought us together. I know you care about me, and take care of me, and watch over me. I'm beginning to fall in love with you, Doctor."

He pulled her tightly to his chest. "I'm falling in love with you too."

She smiled. "How did that happen, Doc?"

"I have no idea. But it's a very good feeling."

"What do we do?"

He kissed her. "We continue on this journey together."

"I like that, Doctor. Me, and you."

They held each other and talked about their relationship until they eventually fell asleep.

The following morning Steve ate breakfast with Doctor Elaine Murphy from Saint Catherine's Hospital of London, and Doctor Lancome. It was hot and humid. His yellow shirt and brown shorts were already wet with perspiration.

Doctor Murphy said, "I'm thinking we might vacuum the blooming cloud into a flask. We might evaporate it from there."

Doctor Lancome wiped the perspiration from her forehead with a white towel. She started every day with a twelve-mile run. "We'd need the heat of a nuclear reactor to evaporate a cloud that size."

Murphy paused. The women looked at one another. "That's a blooming thought we didn't pursue."

"What's that?" Steve was confused.

"We decided against using radiation several days ago," Lancome said. "We didn't conduct any tests."

"There's no feasible way to expose the entire cloud to radiation," Murphy said. She began speaking to excited researchers sitting nearby, as they expressed ideas for utilizing radiation to attack the bacteria, after hearing her thoughts.

Steve notice Brenton walking into the tent with his aides. He motioned him to the table. "Can you get us a radioactive isotope, General?"

"You'll have it in a few hours." Brenton nodded to an aide.

John Harrison walked into the tent carrying a status report. "Good morning everyone. FEMA is planning to allow displaced residents to return to Phoenix tomorrow."

Louth became upset. "There's no water or electricity available for those people. There's no food. How will they survive?"

"Those people whose homes Osiris destroyed will stay in shelters. The military is setting up kitchens in public buildings to serve food. They're also locating a mobile military hospital in the city to care for the sick."

Feltault removed his glasses. "Are you providing toilets, and shower facilities?"

"People will be using portable units."

"Millions of people? That presents a risk for an outbreak of dysentery."

"The government doesn't have a choice, Doctor. They're seeking refuge for those people!"

"Refuge from what?"

"They'll find safety in a city the bacteria cloud already destroyed."

"When can you get fresh water flowing into the city?" A researcher said.

"That will take years. Osiris destroyed the water purification plants. It even devoured the plastic plumbing in buildings. There's no water going into the city, and no way to get wastewater to the treatment plants. Osiris destroyed those plants too."

"What's the timeline for restoring electricity?" Steve said.

"There's no estimate. The bacteria destroyed the power transmission lines. The electrical infrastructure is gone."

"The cloud devastated both cities," Brenton said. "It'll take twenty years to rebuild them."

"The loss of human life is unimaginable," Harrison said. "Osiris killed hundreds of thousands."

"Possibly millions," an aide said solemnly.

"This is all because my brother wanted to be famous?" Roger stood in the door of the tent. "I'm so sorry everyone."

"The past isn't your fault," Steve said. "You're working to correct his mistakes now. We can't ask for more than that."

Early that afternoon the radioactive isotope arrived. Several hours later, in the NASA trailer, Doctor Lancome looked at researcher and said, "We moved a dozen Osiris cells into this isolation chamber. We're about to expose them to radiation."

"Releasing radiation in three, two, and one." Doctor Judith Bechthold pushed two red buttons. Warning alarms sounded, signaling the release of deadly radiation.

Researchers studied the bacteria's silver cells on monitors around the trailer. They waited and hoped, but became disappointed when they did not see the positive reaction they expected. Instead of destroying the cells, the radiation appeared to excite them. They began multiplying faster.

"I don't think there's any feasible method to stop Osiris," a dejected Doctor Satriano said. She thought about her young children playing in the warm sun, on a beach in Florida.

Roger unexpectedly let out a high pitched, primal scream. It startled everyone. He struck his chest with a fist. "That was our last hope! Nothing can stop Osiris! Nothing! Nothing in this world!"

"What are you saying?" Doctor Meridian said.

"We can give up trying to stop Osiris!" Roger's arms flailed wildly. "It may not be today, or next week, but Osiris will kill all of us!"

"He's falling apart mentally," Steve said, whispering to Straley. "Get a doctor in here. We may need a sedative."

"What's going on Roger?" Louth laughed nervously, unsure of his intentions. "Don't let one bad test defeat you."

He began pacing in the trailer. "All of you should go home! Spend the time you have left with your families and loved ones! We're all going to die! Osiris is going to kill all of us!"

"We're all going to die, but not today." Steve attempted to remain calm. "We need to sit down and talk this over, Roger."

"It's too late for talking!" He stared into the isolation chamber. He unpredictably smiled. "I finally understand what Osiris wants!"

"What are you telling us?" Steve felt the hairs on his arms stand on end, as they did many times in Iraq when situations were going bad. He realized Roger's voice sounded ominous. "Explain it to us."

"Osiris killed Goldberg and Jackson! It wants to kill me too! Then it will let everyone else live."

"The bacteria doesn't want you, Roger." Steve saw Straley lead a military doctor into the trailer. "You're tired and you need some rest."

"I know what I have to do." Roger rushed to a control panel. He violently pushed four technicians aside. Then he depressed two red buttons.

"Stop him," someone screamed hysterically. "He's releasing the Osiris bacteria into the trailer!"

The researchers were horrified, after the exterior glass wall of the isolation chamber containing the Osiris bacteria, slowly began sliding open. Alarms began shrieking inside and outside the trailer. They signaled the accidental release of the deadly bacteria.

"Kill me! Then let everyone else live!" Roger smiled as he leaned into the isolation chamber.

"Get out of there, damn it!" Steve tackled him around the waist. Both men fell to the floor.

A terrified researcher screamed, "We have to get out of this trailer before Osiris kills us!"

That hysterical statement caused many others to panic. They began rushing toward the trailer doors.

"Let me go!" Roger struggled wildly with Steve on top of him. "I want Osiris to kill me!"

"This is not how I want to die!" Steve groaned after Roger punched his face.

"Get off me!" Roger punched Steve's chest repeatedly. The two men continued struggling on the floor. They rolled into a table, causing instruments and a variety of containers to crash onto the floor. Red and yellow chemicals mixed to create a foul odor.

"Someone help me," Steve said. He thought, '*Don't hurt Roger! He doesn't know what he's doing.*'

Roger's legs thrashed wildly before Straley sat on them. He pointed at the doctor and said, "Sedate this man, so he calms down!"

"Hold his arm!" The doctor pushed the needle of a syringe into Roger's shoulder. The sedative quickly numbed his mind.

Steve slowly stood, while studying Roger's unconscious body. "I feel like I was in a bar room fight."

"The doors are sealed!" Constance Gendrone said hysterically. "We're trapped in here with the Osiris bacteria!"

150

"Can we force the doors open?"

"They can't be opened." Reglovic sat at a computer. "The computers sealed them to prevent a biological release."

Steve flinched as the shrieking alarms hurt his ears. "Someone shut off those damn alarms."

Straley nervously pointed at the open isolation chamber. "Was there enough bacteria in there to hurt us?"

"More than enough to kill all of the people in this entire camp," Doctor Navickis said, almost hysterically.

"It can't get any better than this." Steve pushed two buttons, and took a deep breath while watching the isolation chamber close.

Doctor Judith Bechthold said, "I don't understand why we're not all dead already, Steve."

"None of this makes sense." He looked around ominously, waiting for the Osiris bacteria to attack. "Is everyone okay?"

"We're all right," Reglovic said, after watching frightened researchers nodding to him.

"For now," someone else said.

After cell phones in the trailer began sounding, Feltault said, "Everyone answer those phones. Tell people we have a crisis in progress in here."

"What do you think is happening?" Steve said, after he walked to Doctor Meridian. "Why hasn't Osiris attacked us? What's your best guess?"

"Maybe it's stalking us. Much like the animal that Goldberg used to give the bacteria intelligence."

151

"The bacteria are moving around inside this trailer?" Straley looked around ominously. "It's waiting to attack us?"

"That's not an encouraging thought, is it?" Steve said.

Reglovic motioned to his assistants. "Scan the isolation chamber. Tell us if the Osiris cells are still inside." Using a powerful microscope, they thoroughly examined the interior chamber.

Twenty minutes later one of the assistants said, "The chamber is empty, except for debris we can't identify."

Steve frowned questioningly at Meridian before he said, "Where are those damn bacteria cells?"

"Did the radiation destroy the bacteria?" Lancome said. She felt her body trembling with debilitating fear.

"It's possible radiation may have destroyed the cells while Roger distracted us," Reglovic said.

"We need to definitively confirm that scenario took place," Feltault said.

"Lets run another test to understand exactly what happened," Steve said. "We can't open the trailer doors until we're sure Osiris isn't alive and hiding in here."

"And if it is? What're we going to do?" A technician said.

Steve shook his head. "I don't know. Tell people outside the trailer about our plan to run another radiation test."

Three tense and emotion filled hours later, the researchers were prepared to bombard ten cells with radiation. Louth stepped to the control panel.

"Three, two, one." She pushed the buttons. The alarms sounded again, signaling the release of the deadly radiation.

Everyone remained silent while staring at the pulsating cells displayed on monitors. Someone said, "Nothing is happening to them. I knew radiation wouldn't affect it! Nothing will kill Osiris."

"The bacterium is waiting to kill us in here!" A man screamed. He looked at the ceiling ominously, searching for an invisible but deadly enemy.

"We don't know that! Calm down!" Steve sensed a growing hysteria among the researchers.

"I saw a fire axe in that cabinet," a man said shouting. He watched the others panic. "Let's break down the doors and get out of here."

"Stay where you are." Straley stepped forward. "Steve will decide what we do next."

"You can stay in here and die with him!" The researcher rushed toward the cabinet. "I'm getting out of this coffin!"

"I don't think so." Straley knocked him to the floor with a solid punch to the jaw.

"I don't want to die!" A hysterical woman screamed. Her frightening words caused other people to become overexcited. They became an uncontrollable, unthinking, and terrified mob.

"Oh my God! My God!" Doctor Lancome said shrieking, while she pointed at a monitor.

Meridian appeared shocked by what he saw. "That cell's outer membrane is disintegrating. It exploded!"

Reglovic said, shouting, "White bubbles are forming on the exterior of the other cells. Are they falling apart?"

Kirstin Rusnak said, "It appears the cells are dissolving!"

"What are those flashes of light inside each cell?" Straley squinted while staring at a monitor.

"I couldn't venture a guess Colonel," Meridian said. "I can't explain what I'm seeing."

"The radiation is somehow shredding the cell's exterior membrane." Steve took a deep breath.

"All of the cells are rupturing," Reglovic said. "The radiation is destroying them."

"The nucleus of each cell appears to burst last," someone said. "That creates the blinding flash of light."

"The radiation did it," Colonel Caraster said joyously. "Radiation kills Osiris!"

Doctor Rocco of the Italian government said, "I'm thinking the radiation destroyed the cells in the isolation chamber before Roger opened it. That's why we weren't hurt by the bacteria."

Reglovic smiled, but cautiously said, "Let's not make any quick assumptions. Let's ensure the cell fragments do not regenerate into a new organism." He and the others nervously watched the remnants of the destroyed cells for signs of continued life.

Two hours later Feltault took a deep breath before he smiled. "Now we can begin celebrating. We've shown radiation will stop Osiris!" He watched researchers clapping as they began to relax.

"Open the trailer doors," Steve said. He watched as relieved researchers began rushing outside. He stepped out last, behind the soldiers carrying Roger's body on a stretcher.

Bonnie rushed to him. Tears filled her eyes as they hugged in the blazing sunlight. "I was so afraid I lost you. I love you."

"I love you too." He kissed her. "I didn't think I was going to see you again."

"What happened in there?"

"We just found a way to stop Osiris."

"Tell me what happened!" She felt overwhelmed with relief.

During a lengthy debriefing with all of the researchers in a kitchen tent, Reglovic described the deadly effects of radiation on Osiris. He paused. "Where's Steve? If he didn't remain calm during the tense situation in that trailer, we might have overlooked our only method for destroying Osiris."

"I'm very proud of you sweetheart." Bonnie grasped his hand as she sat beside him.

He smiled while all of the researchers clapped. "I don't deserve this."

"Yes you do. You helped these people through a crisis. They're grateful." She smiled after nearby researchers began shaking Steve's hand.

The following morning as Steve ate breakfast, Straley said, "Roger is awake in the hospital tent. He's asking to see you."

"I'll check on him now." Steve walked to the large tent filled with sick and injured researchers. He asked a doctor for a status.

"Roger seems much better and relaxed this morning." She pulled the stethoscope from around her neck. Then she pushed back her long red hair.

"You're the only one who knows him well enough to say he's no longer a danger to anyone."

"Now I'm a psychiatrist?" He laughed.

"I hear you're playing all roles very well, Doctor." She smiled.

"Good morning." Steve quietly moved a chair beside Roger's cot. "How are you this morning?"

"Not good." He appeared embarrassed, and covered his eyes with an arm resting on his head. "I made a fool of myself."

"I do that at least two dozen times every day." Steve laughed.

"I almost got everyone killed." Roger rolled onto his side, looking away from Steve.

"You worked non-stop for seventy hours. The stress and exhaustion got to you, my friend."

He looked at Steve. "Do the others want me to leave? Do they think I'm crazy and dangerous?"

"Of course not. When you're rested, you can rejoin the group. We need you back in the lab."

"Someone said radiation will kill the bacteria."

"Yes it will. Knowing that should make you feel better."

"It does." Roger smiled. He sat up on the cot.

"I have to get back to work." Steve stood.

"Thanks for all of your help." Roger extended his hand. "I really appreciate what you're doing."

"My pleasure." On his way out Steve told the doctor, "He's ready to get back to work."

A soldier stopped Steve outside the tent. "The General wants you in the command center immediately."

Inside a large tent filled with frantic soldiers, he saw Brenton directing activities. "What's going on?"

"Intelligence just reported Osiris is moving."

"Moving?" He frowned. "Which way is it moving?"

"South west." Brenton paused. "The damn cloud is headed for San Diego."

"That's not good!" He took a bottle of water from a soldier. "When will it reach the city?"

"In approximately seventy-two hours."

Steve frowned again. "How can it get to San Diego that fast?"

"The cloud has doubled in size. It's forward speed tripled."

"This situation continues to deteriorate!" He studied a map. "Can we evacuate the city in three days?"

"We're going to attempt it." Brenton read a message handed to him. "Washington is requesting a report detailing the effects of radiation on Osiris. Can your team pull it together?"

"You'll have it this afternoon."

At three-thirty that afternoon, Steve and other researchers sat and composed the report in the kitchen tent. Benton led men and women wearing suits into the tent. "Forget writing that report. This is Mister Powell. He's the President's personal advisor. He's here to understand how radiation destroys Osiris. He will relay the information directly to the President."

"Excellent," Reglovic said. "Now we have a direct line to the White House."

Powell removed a dark blue jacket. "This heat is ghastly. I need some ice water! Get it for me immediately!" He watched an aide rush to a counter for a glass.

Steve studied the middle-aged man with short red hair. "What's your background, Powell?"

The tall man peered at him over the top of black glasses. "People normally call me Mister Powell. I expect nothing less from any of you, even during this difficult situation."

Steve smiled. "Have it your way. What's your background? I've never heard of you."

"I am a forward thinker. A visionary in times of despair. I fix situations for the government"

"Is that right?" Steve smiled at Reglovic.

"My specialty is analyzing critical situations. I formulate comprehensive and efficient solutions for the President."

"Which crisis have you resolved lately?" Reglovic said. "Iraq? Afghanistan? Global warming?"

"I'm not here to answer your questions! You're here to educate me! Now get started!"

"That says it all!" Steve smiled at the others. "Let's tell him what we know."

The group explained the process where radiation destroyed the Osiris cells. Several of Powell's aides asked questions while they took detailed notes.

"Hum, I see," Powell occasionally said. At other times, he appeared bored and uninterested, while looking around the tent at people eating.

At nine that night Powell stood, interrupting a researcher as she spoke. He stretched his arms.

"This meeting is over. I have a good understanding of the situation. I'll put together a list of my recommendations for the President."

Meridian closed a leather notebook. "Can we assist you? We can provide scenarios for stopping Osiris."

Powell laughed after the question. "That won't be necessary. I'll deal with this situation." He led his staff from the tent.

The following morning, Bonnie filmed a story inside the NASA trailer with the researchers working behind her. She planned to show the researchers discussing how to attack the bacteria with radiation. She hoped it would dispel the growing hysteria spreading across the nation, when people learned a method for destroying Osiris existed.

The researchers stopped talking after Roger stepped into the trailer. "Hello everyone," he said, hesitantly.

"Where have you been? We have a lot of research work we need you to finish." Steve said jokingly. He laughed, and then shook Roger's hand. "How are you?"

"I'm feeling much better, thank you." He began to relax when all of the researchers began speaking to him cordially. He appeared relieved. "I'm sorry I lost my head in here."

"You did?" Doctor Reglovic said, as he frowned. "I didn't notice anything unusual. You must be mistaken."

Steve laughed. "Neither did I." He began explaining the researcher's progress to Roger.

159

Several hours later Brenton led Powell and Thompson into the trailer. "I'd like your attention. I want everyone to be ready to leave in twelve hours. Your job here is done."

"What are you talking about? How can we be done?" Doctor Satriano frowned at his associates. "We're just beginning to develop scenarios which utilize radiation to stop Osiris."

"Mister Powell has determined how to deal with Osiris. The President accepted his recommendations. He's now in charge of all efforts to destroy the bacteria cloud."

"I'm confused." Reglovic became angry while sliding off a stool. "Are his recommendations based upon scientific fact?"

Powell laughed. "That's a naive question, I would have expected from you microscope nerds! You reported radiation will stop Osiris. I recommended the use of a nuclear weapon to destroy the bacteria cloud. The President agrees with my reasoning and justification."

"Are you out of your god damn mind?" Steve said. He appeared incensed. He paused when others began expressing outrage while shouting in the trailer.

Powell raised his hands to calm the growing anger. "The military will detonate a device while the bacteria are destroying San Diego. The radiation will obliterate the cloud. That action will end this untidy situation which science, and scientists like yourselves, created."

160

"Are you getting this on tape?" Bonnie whispered to her camera operator. She watched him slowly nod while adjusting the camera.

"You can't destroy the entire city," Reglovic said. "That's absurd!"

"That destruction is acceptable if we can stop Osiris," Powell removed his jacket, before handing it to an aide. "It's stifling in this trailer. How can you breathe?"

Steve looked at Brenton. "You've got to tell your superiors this plan is ridiculous!"

Powell laughed after the statement. "The General has no say in this. I answer directly to the President."

"I'll find a way to stop you, you pompous bastard!" Steve's face became red with anger.

Powell said, "General Brenton, get everyone out of this trailer except Reglovic, Meridian, Harrison, and McClellan. Shoot anyone that does not leave. I want to speak to these men alone."

When the researchers began protesting, Steve raised his hands. "You don't have a choice. Please leave so you don't get hurt."

"Don't take any crap from that government fool!" Bonnie led her crew from the trailer.

After the last researcher stepped from the trailer, Brenton's aide closed and locked the door. "The area is secure, General."

Powell said, "Let me explain the wonderful opportunity being presented to us."

"Enlighten us," Harrison said. "What's really going on here?"

"We must attempt to stop Osiris, before it destroys more of our nation." Powell smiled as he lifted a beaker of blue liquid to study it. "All losses, both personnel and property, are acceptable in the process."

"That explanation is not logical," Reglovic said. "This course of action, where you completely decimate an entire American city, and contaminate the ground with radiation for hundreds of years, makes no sense!"

"What if we do nothing, Doctor? Imagine the scenario if Osiris moves into Canada or Mexico."

"The bacteria will kill millions of people in those nations," Meridian said, "as its doing in our own nation."

"Exactly. World opinion will condemn the United States for its inactions."

"Why does world opinion need to be on our side?" Steve said skeptically. "How does that help us?"

Meridian frowned, and raised a finger while thinking about the situation. "This has nothing to do with stopping Osiris!"

"That's a very perceptive observation, Doctor." Powell smiled at his staff. "The President will inform the world before he detonates a bomb. World leaders will watch San Diego disappear in a fireball."

"Osiris isn't the real target in the scenario," Reglovic said, disgustedly.

Powell snickered. "Of course it isn't. We're doing this to position ourselves politically as a nation."

"For what reason?"

"For and when Osiris invades another country. Other nations won't be able to criticize our government when that happens."

"What will prevent them from being critical?"

Powell became frustrated by the questions. "The world will understand we decimated an entire American city in an attempt to destroy the bacteria. Sympathy is our key to maintaining our position as world leader, after this situation is resolved."

"What's your freaking plan for dealing with the radioactive ruins you create?" Steve said.

"Other nations will view the destruction with a sympathetic eye. They'll help our government rebuild with monetary contributions, and advanced technology, after we destroy Osiris."

"You're suggesting destroying an entire city and the land mass around it, and the people who remain there and refuse to evacuate," Harrison said. "This is a ridiculous plan, and I have the feeling there's more to your insane recommendation. Stop lying to us with some bullshit explanation you fabricated, and tell us what's really going on!"

Powell smiled, before he said, "Think of this situation as a marvelous learning exercise for our military analysts, and civilian weapons designers."

"What can they possibly learn while destroying Osiris?"

"A leading edge nuclear device has never been detonated over a modern city. Our military will acquire infinite volumes of performance information, when they monitor the destruction a nuclear weapon detonation creates in San Diego."

"Are you insane?" Meridian said. "Destroy a city to observe how a bomb works? It destroys everything. What do you think happens, you bureaucratic fool?"

Powell frowned after the derogatory remark. "Monitoring the destruction will help us develop far more efficient nuclear weapons for the future."

"I'm sorry Osiris didn't get loose in Washington first," Steve shook his head while pacing. "If it killed all of the politicians like you, no one would have noticed for months."

"You're being naïve, Doctor. Leave the future of our nation to the forward thinkers and experts in Washington. We know what's best for the country."

"I can't take any more of this absurdity." Meridian angrily pushed open the door, before walking from the trailer.

Powell and his aides followed. "I'm glad you concur with my recommendations!" He began laughing while leading his team to the command center tent.

Bonnie rushed inside with her crew. "What just happened in here, Steve? You all look upset!"

"The government is planning to use an atomic bomb to protect its reputation!" He explained the details of the confrontation with Powell.

"This is so bizarre. Do you have anything he put in writing, which I can use in a story?"

"Powell isn't going to give us any documentation," Reglovic said. "He's sending information directly to the President."

Bonnie silently thought about the options. She pointed at a news camera mounted on a tripod in the trailer. "We may have what you need to stop Powell right there."

"How's that?" Meridian said. He appeared confused.

"My crew left that camera running when Powell forced everyone to leave the trailer so he could talk to you."

"You recorded us?" Steve became excited. "You have our conversation on tape?"

"I don't know." She nodded to her crew and watched as they began dismantling the camera. "We need to review what we captured."

"When can we do that?"

"We can do it now." Bonnie led the group to her broadcast truck, where her film crew began working.

One hour later, Steve appeared overjoyed. He said, "You have Powell's entire conversation on video."

"How can we leverage this information you captured to prevent the destruction of San Diego?" Meridian said.

Bonnie entered notes into her phone. "I can ask my producers to distribute the video to television networks. Those national television networks will include it in their news programs."

"Can you give copies to other news organizations, Ms. Saunders?" Reglovic said. "We need to get this information out so everyone can see it."

"I'll publish a story with the video to Internet news portals. News organizations around the world will pick it up and use it."

"You are so evil." Steve kissed her cheek. "You're beautiful."

She smiled after the compliments. "Thank you, Doctor!"

That afternoon, Steve discussed scenarios for utilizing radiation to destroy Osiris with researchers in the kitchen tent. They drew sketches on several pads, but could not determine how to effectively attack the huge bacteria cloud with radiation.

Powell rushed into the tent, leading a large group of federal agents. He pointed at the researchers. "Arrest McClellan, Reglovic, and Meridian. I want them in handcuffs. We'll find Harrison later. Arrest all of them now!"

"What's the charge?" Meridian's voice wavered under the stress of the unique and tense situation.

"We'll start with treason. You knowingly disclosed government secrets to the public."

"We told the world what everyone in Washington already knows about you, ass hole," Steve said sarcastically. "You're fucking insane!"

Powell's face became red with anger. "Even now, you continue to disrespect me, Doctor. You'll have time to think about your stupidity, while you're sitting in jail!"

"The President must be pissed." Steve stood.

"How did you record our conversation?" Powell grasped his shirt. "You'll pay dearly for making me look foolish!"

"Take your hands off me, you freaking idiot!" Steve grasped the man's wrist, before he pinched a nerve.

"You're hurting me!" The sudden stinging and burning pain radiating along his arm, immediately caused Powell to scream. "Acts of violence are uncalled for, Doctor."

Brenton rushed into the tent, after pushing aside shocked people in a huge group now surrounding it, to watch the action. Six soldiers, members of a Special Forces team, followed closely behind. "What the hell is going on in here?"

"I'm arresting these men," Powell said while rubbing his arm, "utilizing the conditions set forward under the Patriot Act."

"No, you're not arresting anyone in my base camp! These people are working diligently to stop Osiris, while you're creating chaos!"

"I answer directly to the President! That exceeds your insignificant authority!"

Brenton stopped to take a deep breath to calm himself. "I've had enough of you, Powell!"

"I'm in charge here, General! The President said I am!"

"You're nothing more than the President's errand boy!" Brenton pushed the man backward. "Do you understand me?"

Powell appeared shocked by the sudden physical confrontation. He looked to the federal agents for assistance. "Don't just stand there! Do something to protect me. This man just assaulted me!"

"Everyone stay where you are," the agent in charge shouted. He motioned to three other men who immediately pulled handguns from their jackets.

"They've got weapons!" One of the soldiers accompanying Brenton said, screaming a warning. He stepped in front of the general to protect him. Frightened groups of screaming researchers began running from the tent, adding to the escalating confusion and fear.

"At ease," Brenton said, shouting at the soldiers. "Stand down!"

"Drop those weapons," another soldier said, while pointing a handgun at the federal agents.

"This is not a military problem," the agent in charge said. His body trembled while reaching into his jacket to retrieve a cell phone.

"He's going for a gun!" A nervous soldier said, screaming. He began pulling the trigger of a handgun to shoot at the agents he perceived as a deadly threat.

"Stop shooting!" Brenton stepped forward with arms flailing. "Secure those weapons immediately!"

"You don't need to shoot!" Steve grasped the barrels of weapons several soldiers held at the ready, and lowered them toward the ground.

"I need medics in mess tent seven, now," Brenton's executive officer said, speaking into a portable radio.

Powell stared at the four men lying on the floor in a growing pool of red blood. "The President won't be pleased with your actions, General."

Brenton stepped aside as a medical team rushed into the tent with their equipment. One soon reported, "These men are dead, General. There's nothing we can do to help them."

"You just murdered government agents!" Powell said. "I'll personally see that you are charged with the murders of these fine men!"

A soldier rushed into the tent, and appeared shocked when he saw the bodies on the floor. "I have a priority message from Washington for you, General."

Brenton read it. He took a deep breath. "If this came a few minutes earlier, these men would still be alive."

"Am I now in charge of this entire area of the country?" Powell said, before smirking.

"You're nothing more than a piece of shit!" Brenton stared at him. "Drag your ass out of my command center, now!"

"Is that a threat, General? I'll have you fired this afternoon if you attempt to intimidate me!"

"The President is not pleased with your actions, and he's recalled you to Washington. He wants to talk to me."

"I want to speak to him. I want him to know you've hindered my progress."

"Get this man out of my sight!" Soldiers dragged the struggling man from the tent. His staff followed. "If he does not leave within the hour, arrest him and his people."

"You'll pay for this harassment, General!"

"I'm paying for it already, being forced to deal with you!"

"That got a little too tense for me, General." Steve sighed while helping the medics place the dead agents into body bags.

Brenton said, "The President wants to speak with the scientist coordinating activities at this camp, doctors. Who is that spokesperson going to be?"

"That would be Steve," Reglovic said, before anyone else spoke. He nodded as others agreed with his statement. "He's coordinating all of the activities. Everyone looks to him as our leader."

"That's completely wrong." Steve still trembled from fear after the deadly confrontation. "I'm not doing anything special."

"You're leading all of us with ideas, and insight, and attitude, my boy!"

Straley said, "He's right. It's you Steve." He smiled and nodded.

"I'm not the guy to do this. I'm scared and confused."

"That's why you're the correct person to be leading this effort," Brenton said. "You're determined to destroy Osiris, and you're inspiring others to look for solutions."

"Thank you all for your support. I could not imagine doing this work without all of your expertise, ideas, and skills. Thank you for being part of this undertaking." Steve looked around the trailer, at the researchers he already considered colleagues and good friends. He felt overwhelmed with emotion as he smiled, while thinking about the unique situation where he was the leader. He took a deep breath. "Let's not keep the president waiting, General. We have a lot to talk about!"

The researchers began clapping and cheering. Many shook Steve's hand after his profound statements, as he walked toward the trailer door.

"Tell the President using radiation is the only way to destroy Osiris," Reglovic said. "But, you must convince him not to drop a bomb onto the cloud."

"I'll attempt to convince him there are alternate ways to deliver the radiation. He may not listen to me." Steve suddenly felt unsure of himself.

"You're leading the activities here," Meridian said. "You're keeping everyone focused on the problem. Present a case to the President. You can do it."

"I agree. You can convince the President he has alternatives," Doctor Carol Louth said, while shaking his hand. Then she gently kissed his cheek. "You speak for all of us."

"I'll tell the President everything we know about Osiris, and how to destroy it." Steve stepped out of the trailer.

Brenton led him into a windowless trailer at the other end of the compound, guarded by armed Marines. "This facility is used for secure video conferencing with Washington."

Steve sat at a long table to study the monitors attached to the walls around the interior of the trailer. He took a deep breath before he slid a hand over his short dark hair. "I wasn't expecting to be the spokesperson, General. There are much more qualified people in this compound that should be filling this role."

"You're doing one hell of a job, Doctor. Stay calm, and tell the President the facts he needs to know, to make sound decisions for the nation."

Monitors in the trailer began to brighten. Steve saw a huge room with a large group of men and women he assumed to be presidential advisors, seated around a wide circular table. President Stillman sat at it with civilian advisors, and commanders of all the military branches. He wrote notes on a pad during a seemingly heated discussion. The middle-aged man with blonde hair appeared exhausted, with his blue tie pulled down and his white shirt collar unbuttoned. Gray smoke from a cigarette clenched between his fingers drifted toward the overhead lights

Chapter 9

President Stillman looked up, after writing several additional notes. "General, I want to thank you for joining this hastily convened meeting."

"It's not a problem Mister President." Brenton took a report from his executive officer, who sat behind him.

"Being on the front lines of this battle must be more difficult than the years you served commanding forces in Iraq and Afghanistan."

"This is a very frustrating situation, Mister President. It's the first time we're fighting a deadly war on our own soil. We're losing, and our people are dying."

"I can sympathize with that statement. Please, give us your current assessment of the situation."

"Unfortunately, it's worsened during the past few hours."

The President frowned, before looking at several advisors. "Explain what changed, General."

"Osiris began forward movement toward the City of San Diego."

"I'm aware of the change in the cloud's forward direction." Stillman frowned at his advisors.

"The Joint Chiefs informed me you've ordered the evacuation of the city."

"That's correct." Brenton paused, as if searching for the correct words. "I have a concern."

"What's troubling you?"

"We may not be able to successfully evacuate everyone out of the city before Osiris strikes it."

"I've ordered FEMA and Homeland Security to assist with the evacuation." The President nodded to the federal officials responsible for those agencies in the room.

"I'm utilizing resources from those government agencies to coordinate the evacuation activities across the city. Military personnel from all bases on the west coast, and the National Guard, are also engaged in the evacuation."

"Let's make this process work as efficiently as possible. Get those people to a safe location, away from the bacteria cloud."

"Yes sir. That's our plan."

The President nodded. "Who is that with you?"

"This is Doctor McClellan. He's organizing the work of the researchers searching for ways to destroy Osiris."

The President stared at the monitor, studying Steve. "It's a pleasure to meet you Doctor."

"I'm honored to meet you Mister President." Steve felt out of place. He took a deep breath.

"Has your team made any progress finding a way to destroy Osiris?"

"We've determined radiation will kill the bacteria."

"I'm encouraged to hear that. Have your researchers formulated a plan for using radiation to attack the cloud?"

Steve sat forward. He realized his hands were wet with nervous perspiration. "We're still putting that together Mr. President. We need more time!"

"I see."

"Powell explained a ridiculous plan to attack the cloud with a nuclear weapon. All of the medical experts here disagree with that approach for eradicating the bacteria."

"Mr. Powell was mistaken," President Stillman said, interrupting. "I'm not planning to attack the cloud with a nuclear device."

Steve sat back, relieved. "We're developing a plan to attack the cloud without destroying the city."

"I need to see that plan soon. Osiris is about to attack one of the most densely populated regions of our nation, and I need to stop it."

"The researchers are making progress," Brenton said.

"You've got to give me a solution you believe will work. Millions of lives are in jeopardy, and you're their only hope."

"Yes sir," Steve said. "We're all aware of the urgency of this deadly situation."

The President silently read a message an aide handed to him. "I must attend an urgent United Nations meeting immediately. General, I need a status report from you every six hours. Good luck gentlemen." The monitors darkened, signaling the meeting concluded.

The President took a deep breath. He looked around the room at advisors, military leaders, and the heads of federal agencies. He felt angry and upset. "I don't enjoy misleading the people risking their lives to save our nation!"

"History will not judge you harshly," General Frederick Flarrity from the United States Marines said, attempting to assure the President. "Not during this time of crisis."

"You're taking this much too personally, Mister President," said Helen Simmons, the Secretary of the Interior. "We'll all work together to support you as you rebuild the nation. This is nothing more than a job."

The President angrily crushed out his cigarette. "This is more than a job for me. My administration is responsible for the deaths of millions of our own citizens! Osiris is killing the people who voted me into office. The people who trusted me to keep their families safe are dying out there. I let all of them down."

"The press, and public, and world opinion, are behind you Mister President," Robert Thorton said, after sipping coffee from a cup. The Senior National Security Advisor nodded. "They say you're doing an outstanding job battling Osiris."

"If the press finds out what really caused Osiris to mutate, they'll call for my impeachment, and public execution."

"My organization, and our CIA partners, will ensure the press doesn't learn the true nature of what's taking place, or what took place previously," John Leckowicz said, the Director of the Defense Intelligence Agency. He crushed a cigarette in an ashtray. Then lit another. The older man's skin was aged beyond his years from his time in the military, and appeared rough and creased. His graying blond hair appeared dirty as it rested on the collar of his white shirt.

"People talk, rumors start, the press reports them, and Congress investigates." The President leaned back on the chair. "My administration will be condemned because of your agency's questionable activities!"

"My agency? How do you see that we did anything incorrect, or improper?"

President Stillman slid a hand across his cheek nervously. "You proceeded with Project Frostfire after I specifically instructed you to curtail that activity! Your blatant disregard of my executive order led directly to this catastrophe!"

Leckowicz frowned. "My organization was forced to secretly proceed with Frostfire, because of your inability to ensure this nation's national security."

"Pardon me?" President Stillman leaned forward, while staring coldly at the man seated across the table. "Explain that statement."

"You suggested releasing bacteria into the water system in Tehran Iran, and Kabul Afghanistan. Your agency planned to kill millions of innocent people, civilians, with a flesh eating bacteria."

"I only mentioned the idea during a brainstorming National Security session. It was nothing more than that."

"You took that flesh eating bacteria into the research phase, without my damn approval!"

Leckowicz smirked. "You wanted to topple the Iranian government, and the Taliban government ruling Afghanistan, with a violent public uprising. You want the world to think those backwater governments have weapons of mass destruction that got loose, and killed their own people!"

The President suddenly appeared tense. "That was a poor choice of words on my part. Nothing more. I did not give you approval to move Frostfire forward!"

Leckowicz crushed out his cigarette. He fumbled with a pack for another. "All of my highest level security analysts felt the killer bacteria scenario had great potential to topple foreign governments. That's why we began development of the prototype strain."

"You stole the basic concept for your Frostfire bacteria from that scientist Goldberg, at Endeavor Engineering," said Robin Furloong, one of President Stillman's National Security advisors, while reading notes in a folder. She brushed back her long bleached blonde hair, as if annoyed with the conversation. "You didn't develop the bacteria!"

"It's simply a matter of interpretation," Leckowicz said angrily, while pointing at the woman. "You're incorrect, and don't know what you're talking about!"

"Everyone calm down." The President frowned at Furloong. "No one has provided me with the complete scenario. What really happened to create this disaster?"

She reviewed the information in the folder marked Beyond Top Secret with bold red lettering. "The flesh dissolving bacterium Defense Intelligence scientists developed, is based completely on the original Osiris genetic structure created by Endeavor Engineering researchers."

"Government scientists and Endeavor people knowingly collaborated to develop the bacteria?" President Stillman appeared confused after the revelation. "Is this a coincidence?"

"No, this was made to happen, Mister President."

"How was this series of events orchestrated? I want the specifics that led up to this national catastrophe!"

Furloong stared at Leckowicz as she said, "Defense Intelligence had their highest ranking senior scientists misrepresent themselves. They posed as college students to get Goldberg's ideas, information, and thoughts, related to his bacteria."

"Your people did what?" President Stillman turned to Leckowicz.

"Hey, the dumb college kid hotshot was posting messages on science bulletin boards on the Internet. He was looking for help. We gave him the assistance he needed. This is our standard operating procedure for developing new weapons. We do this all the time! We take radical ideas from the public sector, and attempt to develop those ideas into weapons!"

"No you didn't provide him with information," Furloong said. "You reached out to him so you could steal his bacteria formula! Goldberg's email exchanges with your people are in this folder. Your people lied and misrepresented themselves to steal his ideas when he felt betrayed by Peter Samulson, and wanted revenge!"

"Did you send agents to Endeavor?" President Stillman appeared shocked again. "Did they enter that facility illegally to steal the bacteria under false pretenses?"

"My agents did not do that. That's illegal." Leckowicz appeared shocked when several people laughed after his comment.

"How did you get the bacteria from Endeavor?"

"The fool kid shipped a sample to my people to study, when we mentioned we could help."

"He did that because he believed your scientists were college students!" President Stillman felt his face becoming red from anger.

"I guess." Leckowicz raised his hands questioningly. "I don't know what was going through the fool kid's head."

"What did you do with the bacteria he sent to your staff?"

"It's a complicated process."

"I'm the President of the United States! I'm fairly intelligent! Tell me what your people did with the bacteria."

Leckowicz laughed after the question he considered naïve. "My researchers genetically enhanced the original strains of Goldberg's bacteria, with our altered and very aggressive and deadly versions of e-coli and Mersa bacteria."

"You made two deadly strains of bacteria more efficient? More deadly? How do they fit into the Osiris mutation scenario?" The President felt extremely agitated as he sat on the edge of his chair.

"We genetically combined them with Osiris. We made the plastic eating bacteria crave human flesh. End of story!"

"I don't believe what I'm being told!" President Stillman rested his head on a hand. "What's the correlation between your activities, and the cloud that formed over that landfill Arizona?"

"Our leading scientists agree it was not the Defense Intelligence bacteria that caused Osiris to mutate, and form into the cloud over the landfill," Robert Thorton said. "That was caused by Goldberg's tampering with the original strain of bacteria, during a quest for revenge while attempting to punish Peter Samulson."

President Stillman became frustrated. "Someone tell me the events that led to Osiris being transformed into a flesh eating monster! How could that have possibly happened?"

Robin Furloong stood and walked to a map attached to a wall. She pointed at key details on the map as she said, "The rubber devouring Osiris bacteria attacked and destroyed this military laboratory. This is the site where the Defense Intelligence scientists created their flesh eating bacteria. That one random incident gave the two similar strains of bacteria the opportunity to combine."

"They combined? And then what happened? I still don't understand the series of events."

"The most agreed upon scenario is the Defense Intelligence flesh eating bacteria variant was the dominant strain. It mutated the bacteria in the entire cloud into the killer version which is now crossing our country, and killing our citizens."

"The entire massive bacteria cloud took on the properties of the killer bacteria being developed in

181

the military laboratory, Mister President," Robert Thorton said. "As the bacteria multiplies, it retains the flesh eating characteristics."

"What does that mean? Does that improve, or exacerbate the situation we're facing?"

"As the bacteria multiplies, it replicates more of the killer cells. That causes the bacteria cloud to expand. As it does, the bacterium seeks out more people and plastic to eat to sustain itself."

The President took a deep breath while slowly shaking his head. "This is a nightmare. A living nightmare." He wrote notes on a pad.

"This isn't as bad as it may appear," Leckowicz said. He smiled.

"How do you see it that way?" President Stillman said. "Your actions in this situation are irresponsible!"

"Well slap my wrist! Who knew Endeavor's bacteria would get loose half way across the country? Who could have guessed it would find our lab? Who knew the two bacteria would combine? No one did! So don't put all of the blame on me and my dedicated people!

"Your entire agency acted irresponsibly! There's no excuse for your behavior!"

"You'll thank me when you order us to execute your attack plan against Iran and Afghanistan with our bacteria strain next year!"

"What was that reference to Iran and Afghanistan?" Robert Thorton sat forward while frowning. "This is the first I'm hearing of an attack on two foreign nations!"

"That was idle chatter," the President said. His voice seemed to crack from nervousness. He pointed at Leckowicz. "You just overstepped your authority."

"You're an outsider looking into our world of national security. There hasn't been a president who understood us, or our ways of protecting this nation."

"I'm going to expose and change your secretive ways. I'm not like my predecessors. My eyes are open."

"Maybe you are seeing too much for this nation's good." Leckowicz shook his head. He looked around the table at the others.

"Can anyone link your agency to Frostfire?"

"Of course not. We destroyed all of our documentation. Osiris killed our research staff at the lab. There are no witnesses."

"Are you sure there is no one alive that can connect my administration to Frostfire?"

"Major Troxell is the only person we extracted from the laboratory before Osiris destroyed it." Leckowicz nodded to a man in uniform seated in the rear of the room.

"I'm Major Troxell, Mister President." The tall man with the shaved head and stern stare, slowly stood.

The President appeared shocked. He looked at Leckowicz. "You left everyone else in your organization in that laboratory to die?"

"We didn't know Osiris would eat the flesh off their bones. Those resources were nonessential and expendable. The Major's expertise is vital to our nation's security."

Marine General Frederick Flarrity said, "Did we salvage samples of Frostfire for evaluation and replication?"

"The Major risked his life while unsuccessfully attempting to retrieve bacteria samples, before Osiris destroyed the laboratory."

The President said, "Why do you want samples of that deadly bacteria?"

"It could become our nation's ultimate weapon. We could release it inside an aggressor nation's borders to decimate their infrastructure and people."

"But you can't control the bacteria!"

"We'll find a way to manipulate the bacteria, so it becomes our perfect killing machine."

President Stillman studied the young Marine officer standing against a wall. "What do you think of the situation, Colonel?"

Troxell immediately stood upright, as if at attention before responding. "Civilians always inadvertently die in friendly fire when we're fighting to protect our nation. We're seeing acceptable losses."

"How can you say that?" The President frowned while studying the numerous ribbons and awards on the officer's uniform.

"We can release Frostfire in any aggressor nation to create panic and turmoil. It's been successfully tested on live subjects."

The President sighed. "Unfortunately, we tested the bacteria using our own people!"

184

"Let's end this conversation so we can get back to work protecting our nation," Leckowicz said.

"We need a better assessment of what those scientists are doing to destroy Osiris," said Craig McCarthy, Director of the Central Intelligence Agency. "I'll put some scientists into Brenton's camp today."

"Do that as soon as possible," the President said. "We need to understand what they've learn about the bacteria."

Robin Furloong took a message from an aide. "We need to schedule a press conference to address the Powell video."

"Handle it for me. I sent Powell there to diffuse the situation. Instead, he's focused world attention on my White House." The President stood before pulling on a suit jacket. Then he led his advisors from the room.

Carl Rutherford, The Director of the National Reconnaissance Office, said, "I'm thinking the President may become a problem for us during the next few days, if this situation continues to escalate."

Leckowicz said, "He's coming apart mentally! He's not fit to be the President. He can't handle high stress situations."

"If our President decides to goes public with a Frostfire Osiris correlation story, we're all screwed," General Frederick Flarrity said.

"We cannot let that happen under any circumstances." Craig McCarthy looked at several men seated across the table from him. "Presidents have a habit of dying in their sleep."

Ruth Karrington, a senior Central Intelligence Agency senior analyst said, "Are you suggesting another operation to silence the White House, as they did when our predecessors orchestrated the John Kennedy assassination?" She closed a red leather notebook, before clasping her hands together on it.

"No, I'm not suggesting we plan to eliminate the President at this time. Nevertheless, it's an option we should be considering if he's going to say too much, and implicate us in a national scandal. We need to retain our crucial positions in our government to protect our nation, and our citizens."

"If Brenton's scientists determine a government bacteria is the contributing factor in this national disaster, we will all have insurmountable legal issues," John Kump, the Secretary of Defense said. "We might possibly be facing prison time, for reckless endangerment and homicide."

"That travesty of justice cannot be allowed to happen." Leckowicz crossed his arms defiantly. "The nation needs everyone in this room at their jobs, to maintain its national security. You are all critical components of our government, and we must ensure none of us are prosecuted and imprisoned by an uneducated press and public!"

"How do we ensure those scientists don't inadvertently link the work your team was conducting in that military laboratory, to Osiris?"

Leckowicz smiled. "Major Troxell will join the people working at Brenton's camp, impersonating a civilian doctor. If any of the medical or computer geeks knows too much, he'll identify them as an imminent threat, and eliminate them."

Troxell nodded. "I can deal with any situations. I'll protect our government, and all of you."

"Do not allow them to destroy the Osiris cloud, until scientists from the Central Intelligence Agency and the Defense Intelligence Agency, come up with a way to secure samples of the bacteria. You are to defend the bacteria and keep it alive at all cost, regardless of who you need to kill and how."

"I understand, Sir." Troxell nodded, indicating he understood the order.

"Eliminate that Doctor McClellan as soon as possible," said General Flarrity. "His death will disrupt the progress of those inquisitive researchers he appears to be leading."

"Consider him already a dead man." Troxell smiled before he walked from the room.

"Can we trust that man?" Army General Fenoglio said, after military guards closed the doors.

"Implicitly," Marine General Miscel said. "He's one of my best officers. Dedicated, disciplined, and loyal."

"What about the Powell situation?" Kump said. "He is aware of some very minor details about Frostfire. He may talk to the press if he's trying to salvage his reputation, after his disastrous performance at Brenton's camp."

"My agents will effectively deal with him," Craig McCarthy said. "Central Intelligence will ensure he does not speak to anyone!"

"Excellent." John Leckowicz finally felt relieved, and in charge of the situation. He smiled at the others. "I'm glad we're in agreement. We'll meet tonight at midnight as scheduled, to review our progress."

Late that afternoon, Brenton interrupted the researchers during their work. "Satellite reconnaissance videos and images, and our ground based observers, confirm Osiris is moving over the Providence Mountains, in the Mojave National Preserve."

"Where is that?" Steve said.

It's one quarter of the way to San Diego."

"Thank you for the update General. We're searching for alternative methods to destroy Osiris, but we have not been successful."

"Keep working ladies and gentlemen. Your heroic efforts and ideas may be the only way to save mankind."

At eleven that night, Steve led Bonnie to the outdoor stall showers. He was disappointed, after viewing a frustrating series of failed radiation tests. He stood under the steaming water, staring at the bright moon overhead in the dark sky. "Did I ever tell you I wanted to command the first base on the moon?"

"You may get your wish." Bonnie washed her hair in the shower across from him. "We'll be living there sooner than you think."

"We may not see that happen for quite some time."

"What'd you mean?" She rinsed her hair.

188

"Osiris may set the world back a thousand years." Steve watched loud and huge out bound helicopters fly over the camp.

"How?" She was confused. She sensed something was troubling him.

"Osiris is destroying the plastic components of our current technology. It's destroying everything from toasters, to computers, to medical equipment. Even our conveniences like electricity and fresh water are in jeopardy."

"This nation started with nothing except land. We'll rebuild it."

"I'm concerned they'll be no schools or colleges left to teach the survivors how to rebuild to today's levels of technology and sophistication."

"You're worried Osiris will kill the teachers?" She frowned while remembering her days in college classrooms.

He nodded. "We'll be thrown back into the stone age. It may take ten to twenty generations to get back to today's technology level."

"Do you think it'll get that bad?"

"It could get much worse."

"What are you saying?" She swallowed hard while stepping from the shower wrapped in a towel. "How could it be worse?"

"If the Osiris cloud continues expanding as it kills people and destroys cities, foreign nations may meet to take unilateral action to protect themselves."

Her eyes narrowed, questioningly. "What type of action?"

"European and Asian nations may agree to hit us with nuclear weapons. They know radiation destroys the bacteria. A nuclear attack would be their attempt to stop the cloud."

"They wouldn't do that. They'd kill hundreds of millions of innocent Americans."

"They'd justify an attack by saying they need to destroy Osiris." Steve stepped from the shower with a towel around his waist.

"Don't you think those leaders value human life?"

"Yes they do; the lives of the people of their own nations. I would be concerned about the leaders of foreign governments taking matters into their own hands, during this time of global crisis."

"You're scaring me." She took his hand. "Let's get some sleep. I'm exhausted."

The next morning Brenton introduced volunteers who arrived overnight, to the researchers. Troxell stood in the group, smiling while shaking hands. He wore a gray suit. He thought, *'What a bunch of flipping medical nerds! My job here will be much easier than I thought!'*

"We're going to bring everyone together to discuss plans for using the radiation from a nuclear reactor to stop Osiris," Roger said, after he introduced himself to the group of researchers. "We'd like all of you to join the meeting after General Brenton's staff assigns you a place to sleep."

Moments later, Brenton's executive officer rushed into the tent. "General, we just received a message stating Powell's plane crashed while landing in Washington!"

"How could that have happened? Was anyone injured?"

"The aircraft crashed in flames. There are no survivors."

Troxell smirked silently while looking at the floor. *'Stinger missiles fired from the shoulder of a government assassin always brings down planes, when you want to ensure there will be no survivors. No one ever knows what hit them. That's how that big mouth Powell died!'*

"We can't get hung up on Powell again, and we have to move on," Roger said, "General, are there any nuclear power plants north of San Diego?"

"Do we have that information available," Brenton asked an aide.

"I know there's a plant at Mission Viejo."

"I found the location on this map." John Harrison pointed at a spot near the Pacific Ocean on a large map resting on an easel. "You want to lure Osiris to a power plant after it destroys San Diego?"

"How can that be accomplished?" Brenton said.

"It's conceivable we could stack rubber tires around the plant," Doctor Lancome said. "We can also pile corpses around the plant if necessary."

"That'll get the bacteria's attention." Steve swallowed hard while imagining bodies stacked around the familiar rounded reactor building.

"How do we release radiation from a nuclear power generation plant?" Doctor Navickis said. "They're built to prevent the release of radiation."

"The containment building will require modifications." Roger paused. "And, we're thinking someone, a volunteer, will need to stay at that plant to ensure the release of radiation."

"That person won't be safe," General Lawson said. "They'll be no place to hide from Osiris."

"Can we release radiation remotely?" Doctor Hatacher of the University of Tokyo said. "That will eliminate the need to put anyone in danger."

"That's not feasible," Harrison said. "If Osiris destroys the wiring, instruments, and computers in the plant's control room, the radiation will need to be released manually."

After several hours of discussion, the group drafted a preliminary plan for attacking the bacteria cloud with a reactor. As they walked toward the NASA trailer in the hot sun, Roger told Steve, "I have to be the one who stays at the plant."

"You don't know how to operate a reactor." Steve laughed.

"We'll find someone who does. I'll stay there with him and protect him from Osiris if we need to run."

"You're not thinking your death will appease Osiris again, are you?" Steve appeared concerned.

"No, not this time." Roger felt embarrassed after remembering the incident in the research trailer.

"Why are you suggesting you be the one to stay at that plant?"

"I can't ask someone else to risk their life, trying to destroy a deadly monster I created."

Steve smiled. "I would feel the same way."

"I'm glad you agree. Then I'm not losing my mind." He laughed.

"I'm not a good psychologist." Steve stared at the picturesque mountains in the distance. He suddenly felt relaxed. "I'll be there at the plant with you."

"What are you thinking?" Roger shook his head. "It's too dangerous. If radiation doesn't kill the bacteria, you'll need to find another way to stop Osiris."

"If radiation doesn't stop it, nothing will. My work will be done."

Brenton called to the two men as he ran toward them with his staff following. "We have confirmed intelligence reports stating Osiris is two thirds of the way to San Diego."

"How did the cloud's forward speed increase so dramatically?" Roger appeared shocked by the news.

"I can't explain it. I arranged a meeting with Governor Wagner of California. I'd like both of you to be there at that meeting."

Several hours later, Governor Wagner along with a large contingent of state officials, intently listened to the researcher's plan to destroy Osiris with radiation. He was obviously concerned. "This is a very risky venture. It has no guarantees of success."

"I agree it's risky," Brenton said. "The alternative is the President drops a bomb onto the cloud while it's over San Diego."

"Where are you planning to attack Osiris?" Wagner studied a detailed map of California on a table.

"At a power plant directly ahead of the advancing cloud," Roger said.

The conversations abruptly stopped and everyone became alarmed after they heard shouting and screams across the camp. Large groups of researchers and military personnel began running past the tent, increasing the growing apprehension and concern inside.

Brenton led the researchers and state officials from the tent. "What is going on out here?"

His executive officer ran from the command center. "General, Osiris just moved into the outskirts of San Diego!"

Brenton appeared shocked as he turned to Steve. "We estimated the bacteria cloud would not reach the city for another twenty hours."

"We've got six hundred thousand people in staging areas inside the city, waiting to be evacuated!" Governor Wagner pointed at his aides. "Contact the evacuation command center. Tell everyone to get out of the city any way they can!"

"Tell them to run on foot if necessary," Brenton said. "They need to flee the city now!"

"What have I done?" Roger moaned. He leaned forward, resting his head on his hands.

"What's going on?" Steve said.

"Ray Jacobs and a group of my company executives flew to San Diego. They're helping out in the evacuation center."

Steve began to panic. He handed a map to Governor Wagner. "Where's that command center located in the city?"

"It's in this area, approximately." He pressed a finger to the map.

Steve showed the map to Brenton. "Can we check the radar and see where Osiris is located?"

"Let's do it." Brenton led the group across the camp in the blazing sun.

Governor Wagner was surprised to find one of his senior aides sitting on the ground outside a military communications trailer. He was crying hysterically. The Governor knelt on one knee beside the man. "John, did you tell our people the cloud is already in the city? Did you tell them to warn everyone to evacuate any way they can?"

The man shook his head while wiping tears from his eyes. "I can't get anyone on the phone." He continued crying.

"Why not?" Wagner looked at his other aides questioningly. He was confused. "What's going on, John? What happened?"

"It doesn't matter anymore. Nothing matters."

"Tell me what happened?"

"My wife and kids were waiting for me in the evacuation center! They're all dead! Osiris killed everyone!"

"Maybe they were already evacuated from that building and location." Wagner looked at his other aides, who now appeared horrified.

"Oh my God, I've got to call my family in the city." A hysterical female aide ran from the group.

The senior aide sitting on the ground said, "No one will answer the call, Marci! Everyone is already dead! The cloud killed our staff, and everyone else! The bacteria attacked the evacuation center!"

Wagner wrapped his arm around the man's shoulders. "John, I'm so sorry. I don't know what to say!"

"Let's get an up to date briefing." Brenton led the others into a trailer where he requested a status. A radar operator said, "Osiris is already covering a hundred block area of San Diego."

"Why, how, did the bacteria cloud move forward so quickly?" John Harrison stared at the radar image on a monitor in shock, and disbelief. "That cloud is out of control and unpredictable!"

Doctor Reglovic frowned at the results, after entering information into his handheld computer. "We may be seeing the bacteria's primal instinct to survive, under harsh conditions and circumstances."

"Meaning what?" Brenton said. "Please explain that statement."

"The bacteria's intelligence must have sensed some of the cells died while crossing the Mojave Desert, due to a lack of nourishment in that desolate area, and the intense heat."

"Tell me how those conditions influence the cloud's forward movement?"

"The bacteria's primal instinct to survive may have caused it to increase its forward speed, to find nourishment to sustain itself, and to survive."

"It knew enough to speed up to find food?" Brenton was shocked, and intrigued.

"Its intelligence knew it had to find nourishment in San Diego, or die."

"Christ, you're saying the damn bacteria are getting smarter?" Harrison was shocked. "It's learning from new experiences?"

"Yes, the intelligence appears to be developing. Somewhat as a child learns as they develop, grow, and mature. We must think of the bacteria as a maturing entity, learning with each new involvement and engagement with the world around it."

"Damn it!" Steve pounded his fist down on a cabinet. "I should've seen this coming."

"You're the expert," Governor Wagner said, shouting. "Because of your negligence, and that of all of these other genius researchers, Osiris is killing hundreds of thousands of innocent and terrified people in San Diego, while we stand here confused."

"That's enough," Brenton said. "No one could foresee or anticipate these events occurring."

"This man is the expert!" Wagner pulled his tie down while staring at Steve. His actions reflected his anger. "He should have warned us of the possibilities, so we could have taken further precautions!"

"This situation is a best guess, given what we know," Brenton said. "Decisions are wrong only in retrospect. Only after you have more information about the situation."

Troxell saw a chance to strike out at the demoralized group mentally. He realized he did not need a weapon. "Doctor McClellan's inept evaluations of the situation delayed the evacuation of the city. His actions, or lack of them, to warn everyone, cost people their lives."

"You just got here," Roger said, angrily. "It's a little early for you to be criticizing anyone."

"Are you disputing the facts? McClellan failed to evaluate the situation correctly."

"None of us realized what Osiris might do. We didn't see this coming."

Troxell frowned. "You're losing your credibility with your poor judgment and decisions!"

"Perhaps we were mistaken, but we are not defeated!" Reglovic nodded to Steve. "And we fully support all of your decisions!"

"Using the power plant at Mission Viejo to destroy Osiris is no longer feasible, after the cloud moved beyond it." Harrison said.

"There's another nuclear power plant facility one hundred miles east of Los Angeles." An Army intelligence officer pointed to an area of a map. "It's located in this vicinity."

Harrison shook his head. "Why would the bacteria travel over desert again to get to that plant, when it can easily move over Los Angeles?"

"A very good observation," Reglovic said. "The bacteria will simply move north, into Los Angeles. It knows there's food there to sustain itself while expanding."

"Is there another nuclear plant in the area?" Brenton said, while looking to his staff for answers.

"There is," an officer said, while studying the information displayed on a computer monitor. "That facility is approximately one hundred fifty miles north of Los Angeles."

"We'll have to lure Osiris to that plant," Brenton said, "and kill it there."

"You can't allow the bacteria to destroy the damn City of Los Angeles, and the people in it!"

Governor Wagner frowned angrily. He crossed his arms defensively. "It'll take hundreds of billions of dollars to rebuild the city!"

"Your concerns are noted," General Brenton said. "They're unfounded."

"How can you say that, General?"

"Our emphasis has to be on destroying Osiris. The city is our secondary concern."

"This approach is wrong! Very wrong!" Wagner stormed out of the trailer. His staff, and Troxell, followed closely behind.

"That didn't go well at all." Steve said, as he and Roger stepped from the trailer.

"What's he doing now?" Roger said, after he noticed Troxell speaking to Wagner.

"Thank you very much for your insight Doctor." Wagner shook Troxell's hand, before leading his staff away.

"What was that all about?" Roger said, while staring at Troxell.

"I told him there may be other options available for stopping Osiris. Something you may have missed." Troxell realized he could create confusion, indecision, and in fighting within the group. Chaos would lead to the researcher's eventual failure.

"That's a very dangerous statement coming from you, who has very little knowledge of how all of our attempts to destroy Osiris failed!" Steve studied the perspiration streaming down the man's shaved head. "Radiation is the only viable option. There's no other way to stop Osiris."

"Hey, yah gotta give'm hope." Troxell laughed.

"This is not a romance novel. We're not going to find the miracle cure in the seconds before the patient dies!"

"Don't say anything until you know our position!" Roger became frustrated by the man's attitude.

When he led Roger and Troxell into Brenton's command center trailer to speak to the General, Steve appeared shocked by the frantic activity inside. He said, "What's going on now?"

"The Army and Marines have moved in to Las Vegas to secure the city, and stop the looting," an officer said. "They're taking hostile fire from buildings and vehicles, and have already sustained a large number of casualties!"

"Armed looters are in the city?" Steve shook his head. "What's left to steal after the bacteria destroyed everything?"

"Armed gangs are robbing the dead bodies, and the banks."

Steve slid a hand over his short dark hair. He quickly became frustrated. "This situation continues to get worse, and more confusing."

"What about the fires in the city?" Roger said. "Did they burn themselves out?"

"Those fires are more numerous, and they're still raging across the city."

"Can we get in there, and take a look around?" Steve said.

"That's going to be very risky while the military is engaged in firefights with looters on city streets," Brenton said. "I don't like that idea."

200

"That's a risk we need to take," Roger said. "We need a close up view of how Osiris works."

Brenton realized the men's determination. He nodded. "I'll arrange transportation. Colonel Straley and a security team will escort you."

"I want to tag along too." Troxell stared at the group who appeared shocked after his request. "Unless there's something you don't want outsiders to see."

"What is your problem?" Roger asked.

"No problem. I'm just here to give you guy's assistance."

Steve turned when a Hummer parked near them several minutes later. He smiled while helping Bonnie climb from the vehicle. "Hey, how are you?"

"I'm good, now that I'm with you." Her short blue skirt became tangled with the seat belt. That caused her skirt to slide up her legs. She noticed Troxell staring at her slender thighs. That immediately made her self-conscious. "Who is that guy?"

"A researcher who arrived last night." He kissed her. "Why?"

As she frowned at Troxell, she watched him smile before he walked away. "He creeps me out."

Steve slipped his arm around her waist, as they walked in the hot sun toward the mess tent for something to drink. "Where have you been?"

"I did a live television news report about Osiris moving over San Diego. It doesn't look good."

"Yeah, I know that." He looked down at the ground as they walked.

"Are you okay? Did something happen while I was away?"

He stopped, and then took her hand before he looked into her eyes. "What'd you say we take off and head to Greenland? Or someplace else that's safe?"

She squinted at him while appearing confused. "Are you serious? You're thinking about leaving here?"

He paused before he shook his head. "I can't leave, and I know it. I get depressed when I think about Osiris killing innocent people."

"I'm getting worried about you, sweetheart." She gently slid her fingers down his cheek. "I know the pressure on you must be unbearable. But you can't walk away. Osiris will find you somewhere, and you'll need to fight it again."

"This is like watching cancer kill my patients. There isn't a thing I can do to stop it."

"Are you going to let a flipping amoeba, or whatever the hell it is, beat you?"

"An amoeba?" He frowned.

"I sucked in biology! Can you tell?" She laughed.

"You're so great for my mind." He laughed with her, before kissing Bonnie.

"I'm glad you keep me around for something." She led him into the mess tent where they pulled bottles of cold water from a steel tub.

"Roger and I are flying to Las Vegas. We want to see how Osiris destroyed the city."

"What can I do to help?"

"Start doing more live stories, warning people north of San Diego to evacuate."

"How far north?"

"I'm guessing three hundred miles."

She was surprised. "What do you think is going to happen?"

"Osiris is going on a feeding frenzy."

"What do you think is happening in San Diego right now?"

"It's the closest to hell we can ever imagine, where people are running for their lives and dying horrible deaths."

Across the City of San Diego, terrified fleeing people filled the streets. They screamed hysterically as the towering silver cloud silently advanced toward them, rolling forward like an approaching ocean wave. The leading edge of the cloud cascaded forward to cover entire city blocks. Agonized screams echoed through the city, after the bacteria surrounded huge groups of people, to devour their flesh. Thousands died in the darkness of the subway system after Osiris filled the tunnels. Tens of thousands died agonizing deaths while waiting to board busses at the evacuation sites. Thousands of others died at the airport while waiting to board military transport aircraft scheduled to fly them to safety.

Explosions and fires began erupting across the city. Thick clouds of smoke and flames rose into the sky from the San Diego Naval Base, after Osiris destroyed the fuel storage area for ships. The bacteria also released millions of gallons of aviation fuel onto the base. The highly flammable liquid quickly became a raging inferno, which consumed buildings and structures on the base. The dense black acrid smoke of hundreds of raging fires across the city soon obliterated the bright sun.

Early that afternoon, six Blackhawk helicopters carried researchers and armed soldiers toward Las Vegas. Cobra helicopter gunships, and Apache attack helicopters, escorted the Blackhawks.

"What am I seeing up ahead?" Steve squinted at green patches dotting the desert ahead. Black smoke rose from all of them. He tapped the helicopter Crew Chief on the shoulder. "What are those burning areas?"

"Those are vacation resorts in the desert. They're spread out across this part of the country."

Roger stared through the helicopter's open door as they flew over a resort. "I see a lot of skeletons down there."

"Osiris was on top of these people before they had time to run." Steve shook his head while staring at the clothed skeletons below.

The Las Vegas skyline soon came into view. The helicopters began flying through dense black smoke rising from the fires still consuming buildings in the devastated city.

Everyone saw the large number of Apache helicopters flying over the city. Some fired machine guns toward the ground. Others fired missiles. The researchers realized those helicopter crews were battling heavily armed looters.

"Where do you want to land, Doctor McClellan?" A pilot said, as they flew through clouds of smoke.

"What's that large building to the left, up ahead?"

"It looks like a shopping mall."

"Can you put us down in the parking lot?"

"Roger that." The pilot radioed instructions to the pilots of other helicopters. "We have plenty of space to land safely."

"I see a large number of vehicles parked around the mall," Meridian said, as the helicopters circled the sprawling building. "I see hundreds of skeletons on the ground."

Straley frowned, while grasping his automatic weapon tightly, as if nervously preparing for a battle with the bacteria cloud. "Why were those people shopping while a killer cloud was moving this way?"

"They weren't shopping," the helicopter Crew Chief said while looking through binoculars. "They were looting the stores in the mall. I see boxes of televisions and home goods products, and clothes, scattered on the ground around those skeletons."

The helicopters cautiously landed several minutes later, before the researchers warily climbed from them. They were shocked by the devastation they saw around them. They noticed flames destroyed many nearby buildings. Other structures collapsed after the intense heat of fires weakened the metal support structures. Acrid choking smoke caused some of the researchers to cough uncontrollably.

"Listen to that, Steve!" Julie Tarallo, said while frowning at him.

"What do you hear? I don't hear anything."

She nodded, while suddenly appearing to be in shock. "There isn't a bird, bug, or animal making a sound. There's no cars, or people. Osiris destroyed every living organism."

"This place gives me the creeps," Doctor Lancome said, as if confessing. She looked around nervously.

Steve turned to the helicopter Crew Chief and said, "Wrap up three skeletons in body bags. We'll take them back with us for analysis."

"I suggest we split into smaller groups and look around," Meridian said. "It'll save us some time, and we can cover more areas of the city."

Straley and four soldiers led Steve, Roger, and a group of researchers toward the mall. A hazy black soot from the fires covered everything. They studied the clothed skeletons littering the parking lot, sidewalks, and grass. Inside the darkened mall, there was an eerie silence. There were no shoppers talking, children running, or infants crying. Instead, clothed skeletons covered the various floors throughout the building.

"I'm surprised to see no blood, anywhere," Doctor Sarah Berrutti said. "No splattered blood. No pools of blood. Nothing to indicate these people died agonizing deaths.

"The bacterium devours the victim's tissue and blood before it can fall from the body," Roger said, before he took a deep breath while feeling personally responsible for people's deaths.

The group cautiously walked through the mall looking for survivors. They were disappointed when they did not find anyone alive. Outside, at the other end of the mall, they found streets littered with skeletons. Dense smoke drifted from nearby fires to darken the sky. The powerful concussion of an exploding gas station several blocks away startled everyone. They were shocked while watching a violently swirling red and black fireball billowing upward into the sky.

Everyone became alarmed and frightened after hearing the sounds of automatic weapons in the distance. Warning messages blared from portable radios. The soldiers immediately formed a defensive perimeter around the researchers as they walked on the wide city street.

Straley said, "The looters are making this city a war zone."

Roger unexpectedly knelt on one knee on the street. "This is the skeleton of a young woman. She had a dog on a leash."

A doctor studied the bones of the dog's skeleton. "This confirms Osiris doesn't differentiate between humans and animals. It kills all living organism for nourishment."

Meridian looked at the nearby historic brick buildings housing retail stores. "Let's check out all of those stores and see what we can find inside."

Troxell accompanied Japanese Doctors Haru Katana and Akari Higuchi into a clothing store. He watched the man and woman kneel beside several skeletons. He frowned when they began talking excitedly in their native language, as if they suddenly discovered something important. He immediately became concerned. *They know something! They see something the others missed! I can't let them tell anyone what they know.'*

Akari began franticly writing notes on her pad, while Haru examined a skeleton with his fingers and explained his discovery.

"Look at me, ass holes!" Both the man and woman appeared shocked after Troxell unexpectedly stepped in front of them. He saw the confused expressions on their faces, while he pressed a white cloth over his mouth and nose, as he raised a small silver canister in his other hand.

Doctor Haru Katana said, "What do you think you're doing?" He frowned as he began to stand.

"I'm killing you two fools before you can talk to the other nerds." A cloud of deadly Saran nerve gas shot from the canister to surround the two researcher's heads.

The terrified man and woman grasped their throats as the nerve gas attacked their central nervous system, before they fell to the floor. Their bodies began convulsing wildly while dying. Blood flowed from Haru's mouth after he bit off his tongue, before he died. White foam and red blood filled Akari's mouth, as her eyes remained open and staring at the ceiling after her agonizing death.

'You two ass holes are the first of many to die for what you know about Osiris!' Troxell pulled the notebook from Akari's hand while kicking her chest, before stuffing it into his pocket. He cautiously ran from the store after ensuring none of the researchers or soldiers were in the area.

Roger warily walked into a large and dark pet store. He used a flashlight while looking around. He shook his head while studying the skeletons of dead animals in cages. Then he made a horrifying discovery. He ran outside to find Steve. "Osiris killed all of the animals in the pet store. None of them survived."

"I would have expected that." Steve stared through the window of an appliance store shattered by looters.

Roger shook his head frantically. "No, no, you don't understand. The bacteria killed the fish in water in the aquariums!"

Steve stopped walking, shocked by what he heard. "Are you sure it was Osiris?"

"I just saw thousands of fish skeletons floating in the aquariums in that pet store! Osiris somehow got into or under the water, and killed them!"

"How can the bacteria survive underwater?"

"Maybe it got sucked in through the air pumps before the electricity went out."

Steve frowned. "Or, the bacteria learned to travel down into the water through the air bubbles to get at the fish."

"If Osiris gets into the oceans, or a lake, it can destroy all marine creatures. The bacteria can destroy all life on this planet!"

"Damn!" Steve saw the others walking from stores. He soon realized two researchers were missing.

"I think they went into that clothing store." Troxell pointed across the street. "I'm not sure. We got separated."

"Everyone stay here. Do not move from this location." Straley assigned two soldiers to guard the researchers. Then he led several other soldiers forward with weapons raised and readied. They cautiously entered the store. Several minutes later, they carried out the bodies of the Japanese researchers.

"What could have happened to these people?" Roger said, as he appeared horrified. He grimaced after seeing the blood on the faces of the dead man and woman.

"Something killed them very quickly," Straley said, "But I don't think it was Osiris."

Steve studied the horrified expressions on the faces of the two bodies. "Doctor Katana is an expert in communicable diseases. He was not expecting whatever killed them."

"I cannot explain it," Straley said. "There's nothing in the store to give any clues as to what happened to these people."

"I want to check out that store," Steve said.

Roger reached out to grasp his arm. "It's too dangerous. It may not be safe in there."

"Did you see what happened to them?" Steve said, after turning to Troxell.

"Can't venture a guess. Maybe your Osiris is mutating to kill in a variety of ways."

"These people died horrible deaths, but their flesh is intact," Meridian said. "This is inconsistent with what we know about Osiris."

Roger looked around. "Let's get out of here now, before someone else gets hurt."

210

Chapter 10

General Brenton waited impatiently in the scorching sun as the helicopters circled the camp before landing. Ignoring warnings from his staff, he ran between landing aircraft when he saw Steve and Straley. "What happened out there? The pilots radioed you encountered an incident."

"We split up to check out the Osiris damage in the city." Steve watched soldiers removing the two bodies from a helicopter. Blood drained onto the ground from their mouths. "We found two of our people dead, and we can't explain what happened."

Brenton watched Army medics sliding the bodies into black plastic body bags. "Did Osiris kill them?"

"I don't know." Steve slid a hand over his short dark hair. He appeared confused. "Maybe Osiris is mutating again and we're not aware of that change to its composition. I don't understand what happened out there! I don't understand any of this!"

"This situation where people died is too confusing to interpret, based on what we currently know, Doctor."

"I wish I could tell you more General. But I don't have any answers."

"I don't know which enemy we're battling." Brenton watched medics carrying away the body bags. "How do we determine a cause of death?"

"Can you send those bodies somewhere with facilities to conduct an autopsy?"

"That may not be possible for some time. That's a low priority request, based on the crisis we're facing." Brenton assigned the task to one of his staff officers. "I'll notify Washington the situation may be changing."

That night Steve and Bonnie watched a newscast in his sleeping quarters. The reporter looked exhausted, as if she had not slept for days. She said, "Sources confirm Osiris killed tens of thousands in San Diego. Gigantic fires are destroying the city's business and financial districts. Reports indicate the San Diego Naval Shipyard is completely engulfed in flames, as are large suburban areas." The live video-feed from a helicopter showed black smoke billowing from large orange fires raging across the city.

"This is terrible!" Bonnie's personal fear of Osiris caused her to tremble. "I feel so sorry for those people."

The reporter paused while listening to information relayed to her in a radio earpiece. "We're now switching to Los Angeles for a live report from Steve Reiner."

The scene changed to show a middle-aged man, Steve Reiner, standing on a highway overpass. He said, "The scene here is utter chaos, as millions flee from this city while Osiris moves north. The highways and secondary roads are jammed with traffic, and are at a virtual standstill. Officials are warning people to avoid the airports unless they have pre-purchased tickets. Amtrak reports they cannot accommodate the masses of fleeing people, even after adding trains to their schedules. To make the situation worse, service stations are reporting they no longer have gasoline. This scene is being repeated in every city as far north as Seattle. In a related event, Canadian officials mobilized their military forces to close the entire border with the United States. That government insists it cannot accept any more fleeing people from our nation."

"I've got to stop that damn Osiris." Steve turned off the television. "The dying has to stop."

Bonnie hugged him tightly. "Hold me for a minute. While we still have time."

'I need some god damn sleep,' Troxell thought while sitting at a table in a laboratory tent, as he appeared to read a medical report, at midnight. A large group of young researchers frantically worked around him. He heard rumors they might be on the verge of a breakthrough. He dozed off several times while listening to their discussions. The technical phrases were beyond his understanding. They bored him. A woman's elated screams suddenly concerned him.

"We collaborated and just accomplished the impossible! Antibiotic solution seven-two-four killed the Osiris bacteria!" Doctor Sarah Edwards screamed joyfully, while studying dead bacteria cells under a microscope. The woman in the short red skirt began clapping, congratulating her associates. She was ecstatic. "Our antibiotic will kill the bacteria immediately after exposure!"

"It's so simple," another researcher said. "The antibiotic creates fissures in the Osiris cell's outer membrane. The fissures allow oxygen to invade each cell. They die from an overabundance of oxygen."

213

"Now we can stop the killer cloud in a matter of hours," another researcher shouted, as he took Edwards' hand. He began dancing with her.

"The military simply needs to spray our antibiotic onto the cloud," Doctor William Chancelar said excitedly. "The bacteria will die immediately upon contact. Osiris can be destroyed tomorrow, and the death and destruction will end!"

"Simple over exposure to oxygen destroys the worst killer in the history of the world," a young scientist said while shaking the hands of others.

"Thank God we found a way to save our nation, and the world," an elated researcher said. He pulled off a green tee shirt. He began waving the garment triumphantly above his head. "We can stop Osiris before it reaches Los Angeles."

"We'll save millions of lives!" Another said, joyously. She hugged the others one by one. "Together, we accomplished the impossible."

"I'll ask the soldiers to wake Steve and Roger," Sarah Edwards said. She entered text into her cell phone. "They'll want to hear our news."

'I need to ensure no one knows there's a way to kill Osiris.' Troxell followed Sarah Edwards out of the tent. As he walked behind her in a secluded area he said, "You must be proud of yourself."

Sarah turned, and smiled. "This was a group effort. I'm happy we can help save the world." She self-consciously toyed with her short black hair after the unexpected compliment.

"You should be happy while you die, bitch." Troxell pulled back his arm. Moments later, he struck the woman's jaw with a fist. The violent

214

impact jerked her head backward. He smiled after she fell to the ground, unconscious.

"I have all the time in the world to use you, whore." Troxell admired the woman's slender body. He knelt and reached under her skirt to pull down her panties. Then he pulled down his jeans before he moved between her legs.

"What's taking Sarah so long out here?" A concerned researcher said, as he led others between the tents. "She's been gone too long."

"Let's look around for her, to ensure she's okay," another person said.

Troxell heard the concerned researchers talking about Sarah as they approached. He stood, before frantically rearranging his clothing. Then he lifted the woman's body off the ground before he carried her toward the people. He told them, "I just found her lying on the ground, pass out."

"Bring her back to our research tent," a man said. "Be gentle with her."

The horrified researchers guided Troxell into the tent as he carried the unconscious woman. A man pushed aside manuals on a table. "Put her on this table so we can examine her."

He placed Sarah's limp body on the table. He quickly looked around, ensuring the green canvas tent flaps were rolled down to conceal his activities.

"Get out of my way," Doctor William Chancelar said. He stepped forward carrying a medical kit.

"Don't ever talk to me that way, you god damn nerd!" Troxell violently thrust his arm backward to shatter the man's nose with his elbow. Troxell realized the impact drove cartilage into Chancelar's

215

brain, killing him instantly. He smiled as the man's body collapsed to the floor, horrifying everyone watching.

"Who wants to die next?" Troxell grasped a nearby researcher's head. He twisted it violently, breaking the young man's neck. He laughed as his victim made a gurgling sound, while he fell to the ground before dying.

Without hesitation, Troxell struck another researcher's throat violently with a fist. The impact crushed her larynx. She fell to her knees, gasping for air while dying, before she slumped onto the ground.

"He's, he's crazy," a terrified woman said, while pointing at Troxell as he laughed. She and a large group of horrified researchers warily backed into a corner of the tent. "Stay away from us! Stay away!"

"You're making this too easy." Troxell grasped and lifted a heavy microscope. He struck a man's head with it, shattering his skull. Red blood spattered onto the terrified onlooker's skin and clothing. He attacked fifteen others with the microscope, killing them with blows to the body and head.

"What have you done?" A blood spattered researcher screamed behind him. She felt paralyzed from overwhelming fear as Troxell turned toward her. Her body trembled while staring at the blood-covered, mutilated, bodies.

"I left the pretty one until last, so I can make you die slowly!"

"Please don't hurt me!" The woman began running toward the door.

Troxell wrapped an arm around her waist, grasping her from behind. "You ain't going nowhere, bitch!"

"Let me go!" The woman said, screaming hysterically. She kicked at him frantically. "Let me go!"

"I like it when hotties struggle as they're dying!" Troxell frantically grasped a long slender medical probe off a table as he struggled with the woman. He pushed the tip into the woman's ear.

"No, no, let me go! Don't do this to me!"

"You deserve to die for fighting so much!" Troxell forced the medical probe deep into her ear, savagely ripping apart the tender skin. He enjoyed her hysterical screams in the moments before he forced the medical probe deep into her brain while twisting it in his hand. He enjoyed the pleasure of her final scream before her body began convulsing wildly in his arms. Then she went limp after she died silently.

"Your discovery dies with all of you flipping losers." Troxell dropped the woman's body on the ground beside the others. He found large bottles of alcohol. He poured the liquid onto the bodies, notes, computers, and antibiotic samples. When Edwards began regaining consciousness, he splashed alcohol onto her face, hair, and clothing.

"Do you want to know what hell looks like?" Troxell laughed before he tossed a lighted match onto the bodies. Searing blue flames erupted immediately to engulf them. The flames spread to swallow up notebooks and laboratory equipment. The intense heat caused bottles of the antibiotic solution to shatter. The interior of the tent quickly became an inferno. Troxell smiled at his handiwork before running into the shadows behind nearby tents.

"Help me! Someone help me!" Edwards said, before she shrieked hysterically, after the flames spread to her clothing, skin, and hair. She rolled off the table, and staggered toward the door of the tent already engulfed in flames. She collapsed moments later, her skin burned beyond recognition by the intense flames.

Wailing alarms woke Steve several minutes later. He ran to the tent with hundreds of researchers and military personnel. There, he helped soldiers battling the flames with fire extinguishers. After the tent walls collapsed, he saw the charred bodies inside. "What happened here? Did anyone get out alive?"

"It doesn't look that way!" A soldier handed him another fire extinguisher.

Steve frantically pointed at the bodies when he saw Brenton approaching. "This is a tragedy. I don't understand what happened in this tent to create this intense fire and heat! Everything is destroyed. It was incinerated by the heat!"

"Those people must have made a very bad mistake. What else can it be?"

"This is terrible! Terrible." Steve paced while staring at the bodies blackened by the flames. He looked away after seeing the flesh burned from several human skulls.

Brenton grasped his arm. "What's going on here Doctor?"

Steve pointed at the bodies. "These people sent me a text message a few minutes ago. But I was sleeping and I didn't come to this tent after they asked me to rush over here."

"What did that message say?"

"They discovered a way to stop Osiris."

Brenton appeared shocked by the revelation. "Did they tell you how to stop the bacteria?"

"No, they wanted to tell me personally." Steve rubbed his neck while shaking his head. "The fire destroyed their documentation. We don't know what they were doing!"

"Well, we don't have any new options. These people gave their lives trying to save others. Now we move on and continue planning."

At nine o'clock the following morning General Brenton met with Steve, Roger, Governor Wagner and his staff, and members of several federal agencies. As they watched a monitor Brenton said, "The military shot this video in Las Vegas yesterday using our latest surveillance drones. They found thousands of human skeletons in the areas Osiris passed over."

"We've got to ensure we evacuate all of the people from Los Angeles," Steve said.

"There are approximately four million people living in the city and suburbs!" Wagner became angry. "Believing you can evacuate everyone is not feasible, and unrealistic!"

"We can't leave any stragglers in the city to die."

Lieutenant Governor Samuel Casey said, "Where are you planning an attempt to stop the advancing Osiris cloud?"

"At the San Luis Obispo power plant north of Los Angeles," Steve said.

"That's two hundred miles north of the city. Why will the bacteria cloud go there?"

"We're going to entice it to that location with a huge stockpile of rubber tires."

"Why will it go there to eat tires," Wagner said, "when it has all of California north of Los Angeles to feed on?"

"We're going to deprive it of that food source, so it has to go to the nuclear plant to feed."

"How do you deprive a run-away cloud of food? I don't understand any of this!"

"We destroy its food source." Steve pointed at a map taped to the wall of Brenton's command center trailer. "That red shaded area represents a forty mile wide corridor. It extends ninety miles south of the plant."

Wagner squinted, studying the map. "What are you going to do there?"

"We have to reduce that area to ashes."

"What are you talking about? Are you insane?" Wagner appeared shocked. He looked at his aides. He saw they were confused and shocked by Steve's response. "This is the best plan you geniuses could come up with?"

"This is our only option. Every building has to be burned to the ground. Osiris can't be allowed to find any nourishment in that area. That will force the cloud to move north, to the power plant!"

"Do you know what you're saying?" Wagner's arms flailed wildly. "Do you understand your talking about destroying people's life work with your asinine plan?"

"Yes, unfortunately I do." Steve took a deep breath. "This wasn't an easy decision."

"The people living in that area won't let you destroy their homes and businesses!"

"I'm afraid they won't have a choice." Brenton studied the map.

"They'll stop you." Wagner appeared defiant. "I'll be there to help them stop you."

"Then you'll die with them!"

"Don't threaten me, you pompous fool!" Wagner stepped toward Brenton.

"Stop this now! It's getting us nowhere!" Steve stepped between the men. "We don't have time to argue."

Lieutenant Governor Casey said, "You're going to attack the cloud with radiation at the nuclear plant?"

"That's correct."

"Who's going to do that?" Wagner said.

"Roger and I will stay at the plant and wait for the cloud," Steve said.

"What do you two know about running nuclear reactors?" Wagner sounded sarcastic and demeaning with the question.

"We'll find a company engineer to help us." Roger said, angrily.

"What'll happen if Osiris destroys the plant before the radiation kills it?"

Steve took a deep breath. "That's the big unanswered question."

"This plan is ridiculous!" Wagner paced in the command center. "Listening to you babbling is a waste of my time!"

"This is the only way we know to stop Osiris."

"We're moving forward with this plan immediately, gentlemen," Brenton said as he looked at Wagner and Casey.

"No, you're not!" Wagner motioned to his staff. "We're leaving. We'll find our own experts to destroy Osiris."

Brenton lifted a telephone. "Get me a secure line to the White House. I want to speak to the President immediately."

"What're you doing?" Wagner stared at him coldly.

"I'm declaring martial law in California."

"You can't do that." Wagner turned to his staff.

Lieutenant Governor Casey said, "The General will have control of the entire state after he declares martial law!"

Brenton said, "I'll run this state with my military commanders, after you're out of the way."

Wagner appeared shocked by the quickly escalating confrontation. "You, you're bluffing, General."

"I'll coordinate the attack of Osiris with my military commanders. The press will know you're being uncooperative. They'll know you're risking the lives of your state residents with your confrontational attitude."

Wagner suddenly appeared exhausted and overwhelmed. He rubbed his forehead. "You leave me with no options. We'll try it your way."

Brenton nodded to Roger and Steve. "It's your show gentlemen. Let's get started."

At one o'clock that afternoon Brenton, Straley, Roger, Steve, and Bonnie boarded a military jet at Pulliam Airport in Flagstaff. The ruins of fire-ravaged buildings smoldered around the runways. Military air traffic controllers managed the steady arrival of huge transport planes loaded with food and supplies for returning residents.

Several hours later, the jet landed at Los Angeles International Airport. The group saw seventy military and commercial airplanes filled with fleeing people, waiting to depart on the runway. Military police escorted the group to Blackhawk helicopters parked on the tarmac. The heat was oppressive. The deafening sounds of departing aircraft on nearby runways made hearing almost impossible.

General Alfred Grocey smiled while raising his hand to Brenton when they met in a large hanger filled with soldiers sitting at tables, coordinating the evacuation. "How are you John?" All of the National Guard units in California reported to Grocey.

"It's good to see you Al. Are you getting the people out of the city?"

"I have Military Police directing traffic to ease the congestion at city intersections, and on highways."

"Is that helping?" Brenton watched a large and loud departing Air Force jet speeding down the runway.

"It's a futile effort. The roads weren't designed to handle millions of fleeing people."

"What are you doing with the people who have no transportation?"

"We're using military trucks and civilian buses to evacuate them."

"Good thinking." Brenton read a status report handed to him. "I need to focus on preparations at the nuclear power plant, so we can be ready to stop that damn Osiris there."

"My most experienced pilots will transport your team to the plant. Their aircraft are fueled and they're ready to go."

"Thank you." Brenton shook Grocey's hand again. "Take care of yourself, and your men and women. I want to see your ugly face again after this situation is resolved."

Grocey smiled, before he saluted Brenton. "Yes, Sir!"

Fifteen minutes later a dozen Blackhawk helicopters carrying Brenton and the others flew over the city. They passed over highways where slow moving and stopped traffic stretched endlessly into the distance.

"I don't understand what's going on down there! People are abandoning their cars! They're running on foot," Straley said, as the helicopters flew low over a highway. He was shocked. "Don't they realize they can't outrun Osiris?"

"They're terrified, and they don't know what else to do, with traffic stopped on the highway." Steve frowned while watching the people running on foot in the oppressive heat and humidity. He saw some carrying children, while others carried pets. "I feel sorry for all of them!"

"That's the nuclear power plant directly ahead," the pilot said a few minutes later. He pointed at large groups of helicopters landing at, and departing from, an area in the distance. He began to circle the plant so Brenton and the others could view the entire facility.

One of Brenton's aides said, "The power plant occupies approximately two hundred acres, set in this remote location far from residential areas. Four tall barbed wire fences around the facility protect the entire plant from intruders. Two long access roads lead to the plant gates from a nearby highway."

"What are those?" Roger said, pointing out of the helicopter.

"Those three enormous cooling towers rise seven hundred feet into the sky. That's steam clouds you see billowing from them. The cooling towers are painted red so they can be seen, and identified, by the pilots of aircraft. The bright flashing lights at the top of each cooling tower warn approaching aircraft of potential danger."

"That's our men and equipment arriving at the plant," Straley told the group. He pointed at the military vehicles lining both sides of the access roads. Everyone saw the equipment on the trucks, and the soldiers standing around them, waiting for instructions.

Brenton's aide continued with his explanation of features at the plant. "Five large transfer stations containing electrical transformers are strategically located around the plant. You can see tall steel towers holding up power transmission cables that snake to the transfer stations, and then away from the plant to residential and commercial areas in all directions."

"Where is the reactor?" Straley said.

The aide pointed out of the helicopter. "A dozen administrative and maintenance buildings are located around the plant. The most prominent structures are the three towering nuclear reactor containment buildings. They house the reactors. Each building is constructed of stark gray reinforced concrete. Each building stands approximately three hundred feet high, and is approximately two hundred feet in diameter. The buildings resemble bullets standing on end, with a rounded dome at the top of each structure."

"That's where we have to stop Osiris." Steve sounded determined. "The madness and death has to end here!"

Colonel John Powers commanded the advance team Brenton sent to the nuclear plant days earlier to begin preparations. He stood beside the large grassy field in oppressive heat, which was being utilized as a helicopter landing zone. He greeted Brenton and the others as helicopters carrying supplies swooped in low overhead to land, before they were frantically unloaded by hundreds of soldiers. "We've got preparations well underway, General."

"You did an excellent job here, John. Thank you." Brenton watched military trucks loaded with equipment speeding past the group from the landing zone. Soldiers and sailors ran past them, headed for the containment buildings while carrying supplies. "Give me the layout, and the situation."

Powers pointed to the right. "Those tents house your command center, and medical and intelligence units. We've set up another sixty tents around the plant."

"What are we doing in them?"

"We'll use them for sleeping and mess facilities. We've got to provide our people with food, and a place to rest, if we expect them to have the plant ready."

"Good thinking." Brenton smiled while patting him on the shoulder.

Powers pointed at fifteen towering antennas, and several satellite dishes, positioned beside camouflaged tents. "That's our communications center."

"Excellent."

"If you look behind us General, you'll see large camouflaged trucks parked in a field beside rotating radar antennas. Radar technicians are monitoring the Osiris cloud movement in those trucks. They also have access to radar data from a dozen Aerial Warning and Command aircraft flying around Osiris. They'll give us a heads up if the cloud begins to do something erratic or unexpected."

"Is NASA rolling in their assets to assist us?"

"They're monitoring the cloud's size and movement each time the International Space Station passes over the area. The crew will relay information and images of Osiris from space."

Brenton led the group forward while watching the activities of soldiers. "How many troops do we have here to assist with preparation?"

"We have one thousand on the ground at this time. Another contingent of five thousand troops are currently being transported here."

"Very good." Brenton watched loud Chinook helicopters flying low over the power plant. "What do we do first to move our preparations forward?"

"I've scheduled an introduction meeting with all of you, and plant officials." Powers led Brenton and the others into an administration building.

"Where are the planning teams working?"

"In this area, Sir." Powers led Brenton into a large conference room.

"We need sound ideas from these talented individuals." Brenton studied hundreds of civilian men and women sitting beside, and working with military personnel, planning how best to attack Osiris. Empty pizza boxes and food containers filled trashcans, indicating the people were collaborating for several days.

"General Brenton, I'd like to introduce you to General Hank Phillips," Powers said. "The General commands the Marines stationed in California."

"It's a pleasure to meet you." Brenton shook Phillip's hand. "We need your men to save our nation."

"We'll do everything we can to get the job done." Phillips introduced his staff members.

Brenton smiled when he noticed an Army officer who served under him during operations in Iraq and Afghanistan. "Mark Hudson. Colonel Mark

Hudson? I'm impressed with your promotion, Son. It's well deserved."

"Thank you, General." The young officer smiled while shaking Brenton's hand. "It's good to see you again."

"We'll see if you learned anything during the time you served in my command." Brenton laughed with Hudson.

"General, I'm Admiral Garity," another officer said. "The Navy Seal and Seabee teams on the west coast are under my command."

"It's a pleasure to meet you, Admiral." Brenton shook his hand.

"What are Seals?" Bonnie said, while frowning at Steve.

"The Seals are the Navy's Special Forces teams. The Seabees are the Navy construction units."

"I'm Wing Commander General Franklin Scott of the First Tactical Bomber Wing," another officer said, while shaking Brenton's hand. "My pilots and crews are at your disposal, to help any way we can."

Breton smiled. "We're going to keep your crews very busy."

"General, I'd like to introduce Peter Berry," Powers said. "Mister Berry is the Chief Executive Officer of Pacific Gas and Electric. The company operates this power generation plant."

Berry brushed back his long groomed blonde hair. "I'm very happy to meet you General. This is Wilhart Brimler, our Chief Financial Officer. And this is Daniel Corrigan, our Vice-President of Operations."

"The government appreciates your company's cooperation and assistance." Brenton shook the men's hands. He introduced his staff, and then Roger, Steve, and Bonnie.

Berry then introduced various crucial members of his company's technical organization. He explained the men and women supervised plant maintenance, reactor engineering, electrical transmission, engineering, finance, and human resources.

"We're relying on all of you for ideas to improve our plan to kill Osiris," Steve said. "Thank you all for helping us stop the killer bacteria."

Berry motioned another man forward to meet the group. "I'd like to introduce William Mason. He's our company's chief reactor operator."

"Howdy." A tall man wearing a long sleeve plaid flannel shirt and khaki pants stepped forward. Long graying black hair rested on his shoulders. A long graying beard covered his chin.

"It's a pleasure to meet you." Steve frowned while shaking the man's hand. He thought, *'We may have a problem. I've watched people that look and talk like this guy dying from drug overdoses in the emergency room. He's six feet tall and weighs ninety pounds, so he may be using some heavy drugs.'*

"I'm ready to take on that killer cloud alongside you." Mason shook the men's hands. He turned away to cough.

Steve studied him again, frowning. *I'm guessing he's in his mid-forties. He looks like he's sixty. I think he's burned out on drugs.*

"Thank you for offering to help us," Roger said.

"I'm really looking forward to it, man." Mason rubbed his nose, to ensure none of the people would suspect he inhaled cocaine several minutes earlier.

"Did you review our plan to destroy Osiris with radiation?" Roger was puzzled by the man's wide grin.

"Yeah, man. Colonel Powers told us about your radical ideas yesterday."

"Are you aware of the risks? What we're asking you to do is very dangerous."

Mason rubbed his nose again. Then he laughed. "I ain't afraid of a flipping cloud."

Steve thought, *'Does this man know what drugs are doing to his heart? I can't say anything to him. If we can't find another volunteer to stay here with us at this plant to release radiation, we're screwed, and so is our plan to destroy Osiris.'*

"My staff would like to hear the details of your plan to attack Osiris using our reactor," Berry said. "We have photographs of the plant to use as reference."

During the next four hours, Roger and Steve presented an overview of the researcher's use of radiation to destroy the Osiris cells, and the overall plan to destroy the bacteria cloud, to company officials and their employees. They answered questions to ensure every person understood how they planned to destroy Osiris cloud with radiation.

Berry stood before he said, "Thank you for your presentation and detailed explanation. We realize the importance of this situation, and your vigorous

231

plan. My company and employees are prepared and ready to help in any way we can."

Brenton stood before he said, "Let's get a quick status from the military commanders in the room. General Grocey, are your California Air National Guard units retrieving tires from the twenty-six landfills my Intelligence people identified?"

"Yes, Sir. That activity is under way. My teams are extracting tires from those landfills. They'll begin transporting them to this location within several hours, using our Chinook and Blackhawk helicopters."

"Excellent." Brenton nodded, as he briefly looked at Steve and Roger. "Do we have Army and Marine resources readied to offload those tires and position them around this power plant?"

"Yes we do, General. Our assets are on standby here at the plant, waiting for the helicopters to arrive."

Colonel Powers opened a map, before placing the long and wide document on a table. He pointed at clusters of red triangles on the green and brown topographical map. "We need the tires stacked in these six exact locations around this plant."

"My Engineering battalion resources are out there now, using surveying equipment to mark the exact locations with stakes and markers, and paint on the grass and dirt, where those tires need to be piled around the plant."

"Those piles of tires will look like huge black pyramids when they're built, and each of them must be at least three hundred feet high."

"We're working from your specifications, Colonel. We'll give you what you need." General Grocey studied his notes on a pad, and compared them to information on the map, while speaking to his aides.

"We'll also need those pyramids of tires laced with incendiary explosives, so they can be set on fire to attract Osiris."

"My explosive experts are putting those incendiary devices together in an area far from this plant. We don't want any mishaps to compromise the timeline for getting this job completed!" Grocey wrote notes on his pad. "What other tasks do you have for us on your priority list?"

"We'll need additional tires stacked inside the reactor containment buildings, if our resources have time to do it."

"I understand. We'll get that job done too, before we evacuate our teams." Grocey motioned a thumbs up signal to his staff. Then he led them from the table to discuss the timeline, and to determine if additional troops were required to work at the plan to meet the timelines.

Brenton said, "Wing Commander Scott, your assignment isn't going to make the Air Force popular with the local residents."

"We can deal with a little bad publicity, General." Scott laughed. "My men and women will do whatever it takes to make your operation a success."

Brenton pointed at the light brown shaded area of another large map, depicting southern California. "I

233

need this designated area totally destroyed before Osiris reaches it."

Scott frowned while intently studying the map. He listened to questions asked by his aides. "Are you saying you want my bombers to flatten that land mass?"

"That's affirmative. Your crews will bomb the area, after the Army and Marine's send in their Blackhawk, Apache, and Cobra helicopters to strafe the area. They'll destroy high profile targets such as gas stations, to ignite fires."

"I want to ensure I understand the nature of this assignment, General. You want to ignite fires, which will consume the adjacent buildings and structures, to reduce them to rubble and ashes? That will deprive Osiris of that needed nourishment?"

"That's correct. After the helicopters create fires to destroy as many buildings as possible, you'll roll in your aircraft to bomb the area."

"I understand. I'll order my crews to begin arming my bombers with high incendiary munitions."

"Can we use explosives to destroy the buildings south of here?" Steve said, while pointing to an area of the map. "We don't want falling bombs getting close to this plant."

Brenton pointed at Colonel Hudson before he said, "I'll give you that assignment Colonel. I want your teams to place incendiaries in the buildings within a five mile radius of the plant."

"Yes, Sir." Hudson nodded, and briefly smiled, while remembering similar planning sessions while serving under Brenton in Iraq and Afghanistan.

Colonel Powers began displaying pictures on monitors in the room. He said, "We'll need the Navy Seals and Seabees to open the reactor containment buildings here at the plant."

"How do we accomplish that?" Admiral Garity sounded apprehensive.

"We have a plan to cut through the walls of the buildings."

"Mister Berry, can you explain how the containment buildings at this plant were constructed?" Steve said. "So our military partners know what to expect?"

Berry motioned to one of this staff. "Jim Winthrop is our Senior Design Engineer. He can explain the process."

Winthrop, an older man, began drawing on a white board. "The outer walls of the containment buildings are, ah, constructed of concrete fifteen inches thick. That concrete is poured over a steel shell made of three inch thick, ah, steel. The concrete is, ah, strengthened with steel reinforcing rods. Each rod is two inches in diameter."

"That's a lot of material to get through, in a limited amount of time." Roger looked at Steve, conveying his concern.

"That's only the, ah, outer wall," Winthrop said, as he continued drawing on the white board. "There's a five foot wide air space between the inner and outer walls. On the other side of the air space, ah, is the building's inner wall. It's made up of, ah, two layers. The first layer is reinforced concrete, that's, ah, four and a half feet thick. A three-eighths inch thick steel liner protects the concrete wall inside the building."

"What's inside those containment buildings?" Roger said.

Winthrop began drawing another diagram. "A reactor core is located in the floor, in the center of each building. There's, ah, equipment for repairs, cranes, and small carts in the buildings. There's also, ah, equipment for refueling the reactor, and ah, safety equipment."

"Where do we need to be to release the radiation?" Steve said.

"All of that activity can be accomplished from the control room," Berry said. "It's the nerve center of the plant set back from the containment buildings."

The meeting continued and ended late that night. As Steve and Bonnie sat together, eating food brought into the room, she looked into his eyes. "I want to be in that control room with you."

Steve frowned. "While we release the radiation?"

"Yeah. I want to be there with you. I want to be by your side."

"I can't let you do that."

"Why can't I be there with you? I can document what happens in the control room with a video camera."

"If radiation doesn't stop Osiris, I'll be in a struggle to stay alive. I won't put you into that situation."

"Then don't do it." Tears began filling her eyes. "Tell them you changed your mind, and it's too dangerous."

"I don't understand. Why are you saying this now?"

"Find someone to take your place in that control room."

"I can't do that. Roger may need me."

"I need you more than he does!" She wrapped her arms around his neck. "I'm selfish, and I don't want to lose you!"

He gently touched her hair as she sat back. "This is something I have to do."

"Why does it always have to be you?"

"I thought I could make a difference in Iraq, but I didn't. Soldiers kept dying on me in the operating room."

"You tried to help them. I wasn't there, but I know you and I know you did everything you could to save men that couldn't be saved! I'm sorry!"

Steve swallowed hard. "When I came home, I chose cancer research because I thought I could make a difference while I help people, but I didn't. My patients are still dying while I try to save them."

"You're trying, and you're comforting people. You're making a difference in so many lives, but you don't see it."

"I guess my mind is telling me I need to do more."

"Why do you have to put yourself in danger in that control room?"

"Because, I want to spend the rest of my life with you. But to do it, I need to destroy Osiris."

She nodded while wiping away the tears streaming down her cheeks. "I understand. Now I remember why I love you so much. I'll be waiting for you after you kill Osiris."

He smiled, before kissing her. "I wonder where we're staying tonight."

"That Colonel Powers had his men set up cots for us in a room down the hall. We can sleep in there."

Steve stood before he took her hand. "Let's get some rest."

The next morning Bonnie and Steve met the others for breakfast in a large military kitchen tent. The tent was crowded with hungry military personnel already working around the plant.

Brenton said, "Intelligence reports Osiris is moving north. They estimate we have eighty hours to prepare this plant to ambush the cloud."

"We have a lot of tasks to complete," Roger said, as he looked at his watch. "It's going to be tight."

"We're going to give you and your men and women a tour of the control room, and a containment building," Berry said. "We want to show you where you'll be working."

He led them to a white single story building where armed security guards opened the doors. "This is the control room building. There are no windows, and the building is bomb proof, and virtually impregnable."

"It won't stop Osiris," Roger said, remembering the destruction he witnessed in the cities.

"Nothing will get into this building! We'll see how tough your bacteria is, after I hit it with radiation." Mason adjusted the sleeve of his flannel

238

shirt while laughing almost comically after Roger's comments. He entered a code into a keypad fastened to the wall. Two black steel doors slid apart. He led the group into the well-lighted control room where multi-colored electronic instruments covered the walls. Fifteen employees worked at computer consoles.

"We control the reactors and electrical power generation from this central location," Berry said. He stood back and listened as his engineering staff explained the functions of the control room equipment.

"I'll show you where the magic happens!" Mason led the group through another locked electronic door and down an inclined walkway. It opened into a tunnel made of concrete, nine feet high, and fifteen feet wide. Rows of fluorescent ceiling lights extended the length of the tunnel. It felt cold and smelled musty in the underground passage.

"This underground tunnel provides emergency access to the containment buildings," Berry said. "It's buried twelve feet below the surface of the ground. The large gray metal conduits you see attached to the walls enclose the wires that send signals to the reactor controls in the containment buildings."

Barry led the group forward while explaining all of the safety measures built into the plant. He explained the need for primary and secondary mechanical safety features, and the need for redundant systems to prevent nuclear catastrophes, and the accidental release of radiation into the atmosphere. Several minutes later, he stopped beside a set of orange metal doors set into the tunnel wall.

"This is the access point to the first reactor." Mason entered a code into another electronic keypad, and the doors slowly opened. He led the group into the towering containment building.

"I had no idea the interior of these buildings is so enormous," Roger said, as he appeared shocked by the immense size. Wide silver pipes snaked their way through the entire building.

Mason stepped forward before pointing at a huge circular structure in the floor of the building. "That's the reactor pool. It's one hundred fifty feet in diameter. The water in the pool keeps the fuel rods cool, and prevents a possible meltdown."

Roger stepped to the yellow safety railing around the reactor pool. He stared at the steel reactor structures submerged deep under the clear water. Underwater floodlights illuminated the submerged black reactor. "Where do we get the radiation?"

Mason pointed upward, at an enormous overhead crane. "Radiation will fill this building after that crane lifts the fuel rods out of the reactor." He spent forty minutes explaining the details of the reactor, the building, and the equipment contained in it.

"What is that device used for?" Brenton pointed at a large clear glass cube approximately twelve feet wide, mounted on a trailer. Water filled the cube to the top.

"That's used for moving depleted fuel rods from the reactor, to the storage pool. The water in it keeps the rods cool as we move them."

"When do you use diving equipment in here?" Steve saw black diving suits, air regulators and silver air tanks, and masks, hanging beside maintenance lockers.

"We keep that equipment handy if we have problems in the storage pool."

After the tour in the containment building concluded, Barry led the group back to the control room. As they walked, he explained he would have his entire staff on stand-by, to assist with work at the plant whenever necessary.

Steve thought about the situation. "General Brenton, can you move our key people here from your command center. We'll need their help coordinating preparations at this plant, to ensure we'll be prepared to attack Osiris, before it gets here."

"What should I do with the rest of the researchers?"

"I'll tell them to continue looking for methods to destroy Osiris. They'll need an alternate plan if radiation doesn't stop the cloud."

"I'll fly back and bring back the people we need to help us," Roger said.

"That works. I'll stay here to answer questions, and help out."

"I'm going back to the camp to do a live newscast from that location," Bonnie said. "If people know you're here trying to destroy Osiris, it may help them cope with their own fears."

"That's a great idea." Steve smiled at her, as he took her hand. Twenty minutes later, he waved at the helicopter carrying Bonnie, as it flew over the plant.

"This is for you, Doctor." Straley smiled while handing Steve a portable radio. "Now I can find you when I need to talk to you."

Both men became concerned when a speeding Hummer skidded to a halt nearby. A soldier inside said, shouting, "There's a problem at Brenton's base camp."

Steve immediately ran to the vehicle. "What type of problem?"

"Someone named Feltault needs to talk to you immediately, Doctor." A soldier handed him a microphone.

The feel and smell of the military microphone were familiar. They instantly conjured up horrifying images of Iraq and Afghanistan in his mind. "This is McClellan."

"Steven, this is Doctor Feltault on the radio."

"What's going on, Doctor? What's the emergency?"

"There was a tremendous explosion here a few hours ago."

"How did it happen? What exploded?" Steve began to panic. "Did anyone get hurt?"

Feltault paused as he rested his head on his hand. "I'm sorry to say it killed more than one hundred of our people."

"How could this have happened? Those people were volunteering their time and talents to save the world, and they died because of it!" Steve felt a sickening sensation in his stomach. The same feeling he experienced in Iraq and Afghanistan, when soldiers died on the operating room table.

"We've just finished transporting more than three hundred gravely injured people to military hospitals."

"What caused the explosion?"

"It may have been a gas leak from the propane tanks. Someone saw a man running from those tanks in the moments before the powerful explosion. We'll never know what happened."

"What man? Do you know who it was? Can anyone identify him?"

"No, everything happened too fast."

"Damn it! How can all of those people be dead?" Steve closed his eyes while taking a deep breath. "How can this have happened?"

"I fear a major discovery may have died with those poor people."

"What does that mean?" Steve lowered the microphone, as he looked at Straley questioningly.

"The group reported being on the verge of a breakthrough minutes before the explosion."

"What kind of breakthrough?"

"I'm assuming they found a way to stop Osiris, without the need to use radiation."

"They made a discovery, and then they suddenly died?" Steve frowned at Straley.

"Yes, that's what happened! I don't know how! I don't know why. I don't know if they made a fatal mistake. I'm not sure of anything at the moment!"

"Calm down, Samuel." Steve took a deep breath in a futile attempt to calm himself. "How's everyone else reacting to the accident?"

"Things are not good here. Many of our research teams are packing up to go home. They're defeated, and have given up, and want to return to their families."

"You can't let them do that. You've got to speak to them and stop them. We need them to continue working to find a way to stop Osiris." Steve paused. "Do you want me to fly back there to be with you?"

"No, you're needed at that power generating plant. My people will tend to things here."

"Thank you, Samuel. If you need to talk, reach out to me at any time. I'll be here."

"I know you will, Son." Samuel wiped away the tear running down his cheek before anyone noticed it. "Thank you for everything you're doing for us."

During the next hour, Steve felt strangely helpless and ineffective as he wandered around the plant, watching the military preparation activities. He questioned the explosion, and mourned those who lost their lives while researching ways to stop Osiris. He could not justify the loss of life, where volunteers died in a horrible fiery inferno.

Straley found him sitting on a sidewalk in a parking lot a short time later. "Steve, I want to introduce Major Tony Cavanna. I've known this guy for years. His teams are preparing to cut through the containment building walls."

"It's a pleasure to meet you." Steve stood to shake the man's hand.

"I'm sorry to hear about the accident that took the lives of your people, Doctor."

"Thank you." Steve nodded. "What are your men doing?"

Cavanna shaded his eyes from the sun, before pointing at the containment buildings in the distance. "They're assembling metal scaffolding and staging inside and outside the three containment buildings."

"I want to help them." Steve stared at the two surprised men. "If that's possible."

"Doctor McClellan was stationed in Iraq and Afghanistan for some time," Straley told Cavanna, 'and I think he wants to be in the action around the plant."

"I understand." Cavanna smiled. "You're part of the team, Doctor. Let's get over to those containment buildings, and I'll introduce you to the men and women that comprise my teams."

Forty minutes later, as they helped to assemble scaffolding outside a containment building, Straley handed Steve a bottle of water. "Slow down, Doc. You'll burn yourself out in this heat."

"I'm good. I'm trying to pay back for getting those people killed in that propane explosion at the camp." He wiped perspiration from his face with a shirtsleeve.

"You can't look at it that way. You didn't kill those people. It was simply an unfortunate accident."

"They're all dead because of me. I pushed them too hard." In his mind, Steve saw the faces of people he befriended at the camp. He panicked as he mentally questioned if they were now alive or dead.

"No, you didn't. You did what you thought was right. We're all doing a dirty job here."

"That's not how I see it. I'm responsible for their deaths." Steve stopped speaking when he heard a familiar loud rumbling sound in the distance. He smiled when he saw approximately sixty Marine, Air Force, National Guard, and Coast Guard helicopters approaching.

"Let's get this plant ready and kill Osiris, as a tribute to those people who died. They deserve it!"

Steve nodded, and then smiled. "Let's do it, Colonel." He shook Straley's hand.

As the helicopters circled the plant, large rope slings filled with tires dangled under each aircraft. When the pilots released the slings, the tires fell to the ground at predetermined locations. Some of the tires bounced wildly on the ground, before rolling away. Five hundred military personnel immediately began stacking them in the designated locations around the plant.

Late that afternoon a large group of helicopters carrying the researchers landed at the plant. Roger led the group into a building, as they carried documentation and research equipment.

"This is a long walk from the helicopters!" Troxell made it appear he was struggling to carry a box of books. He looked around, making mental notes of ways to hinder the activity at the plant, so Osiris would not be harmed or destroyed with radiation.

Roger eventually found Steve stacking tires with soldiers in a field near a containment building. He handed him a cold bottle of water. "Hey, we need to talk."

246

"My back is breaking." Perspiration saturated Steve's clothing. Black marks from the rubber tires covered his arms. His throat hurt from the dust. "How bad are things back at the camp?"

Roger took a deep breath. "It's worse than I expected after the gas explosion tragedy. People are already leaving for home."

"What will they do at home? They're going to wait for Osiris to kill them?" He became angry, then frustrated. "They're just giving up, and running?"

"I don't know what they're thinking. I tried talking to them, but they wouldn't listen to me."

"Do you know who died in the explosion?"

"I have a list of names for you in my pocket."

Steve took a piece of paper from Roger. He became horrified while reading the names on it. Then he angrily crushed the paper in his hands. "This is terrible! Absolutely terrible! She came her to help me, and she should not have died in a god damn inferno!"

"What did you see? What did I miss?"

"Kirsten Rusnak died in the explosion!" Steve felt tears welling in his eyes. "She was an excellent Oncology nurse who worked closely with me, taking care of patients in the hospital."

"I'm sorry. I didn't connect the name to you."

Steve's hands clenched with anger. He suddenly felt the need to scream at Roger. He thought, '*Osiris just killed one of my best friends! You may not have killed her yourself, but this bacteria situation did! It's your fault she's dead! This is all your fault!*"

"There's nothing I can say, other than I'm sorry." Roger began pacing as he watched low flying and

247

loud helicopters nearby, while blaming himself for the accident.

"None of this is your fault." Steve slowly regained his composure. "What else is going on?"

"Radio and television stations are warning people living around here to evacuate the area immediately. The President is giving hourly news conferences. He's telling people about our plan and work here to destroy Osiris."

"Maybe that will help calm people, after they know there's a possibility we can stop Osiris. I don't know how to help them any other way." Steve shook his head, while suddenly feeling defeated. "Which research people did you bring back here to the plant?"

"Doctors Feltault, Lancone, Louth, Reglovic, Colonel Caraster, and sixty other volunteers who asked to make the trip here."

"Why did so many people want to put themselves in danger?"

"They all want to help. They told me they felt helpless back at the camp."

"I can understand why they feel that way."

"We can use all of the help they can provide." Roger looked around. "We need everyone to end this."

Chapter 11

The sun felt scorching hot, and it was ninety-seven degrees, when Steve checked on the progress of the soldiers assembling scaffolding beside the containment buildings. He was soon struggling to lift long and heavy metal struts in the oppressive heat with the soldiers. Thirty minutes later, he noticed hundreds of soldiers lying on the ground, suffering from heat exhaustion. "We're burning out our men with this manual effort."

"We need a better way to do this," Major Cavanna said. "This is backbreaking heavy work."

Several minutes later Steve heard someone calling his name on the portable radio. "This is McClellan."

"This is Colonel Ragare. I command the Military Police at the plant's main gate."

"What's up?" Steve wiped away the small streams of perspiration running down his arms.

"I've got some civilians here at the gate. They want to speak to you, and only you."

"I don't have time to talk to reporters. Tell them to contact Bonnie Saunders if they want an interview, or information about what's happening here at the plant."

"They're not reporters." Ragare studied the vehicles parked near the gate. "They're truck drivers."

"They're what?" Steve laughed with nearby soldiers. "I'll be right there."

Cavanna flagged down a passing Hummer. Then he and Steve climbed into it. When they arrived at the main gate, they were surprised to see a large number of tractor-trailers and flatbed vehicles idling on the plant's access road.

Colonel Ragare ran to the Hummer. "Those guys will only talk to you, Doctor McClellan. They won't tell me why they're here or what they want."

"Open the gates." Steve studied the male and female truck drivers of all ages, nationalities, and races, while walking toward them. "How are all of you? I'm Doctor McClellan."

"I'm Jack Peterson." An older driver, the group's apparent spokesperson shook Steve's hand. "I'm one proud American to meet you, Sir."

"Thank you." The compliment surprised Steve. "The military police are saying you asked for me. How can I help you?"

"We're from the Firestone Tire plant about twenty miles north of here, as the crow flies. We saw what you heroes are doing here to save our nation on the news."

"Wait a minute." Steve raised his hands to stop the conversation. "Don't you know you're all supposed to be evacuating this area before Osiris gets here?"

"We're union. We ain't running from anything, Doc. We gotta protect our families, our pets, and our homes!" The comment brought cheers from all of the truck drivers.

Steve smiled, and nodded. "Why are all of you here?"

"We're carrying thousands of tires in our trucks. Can you use them to kill that damn cloud?"

"We sure can. They'll be the bait we use to get Osiris here so we can kill the bastard." Steve smiled after the elated drivers began cheering and whistling.

Peterson lit a cigarette before he said, "We'll keep hauling in tires from our plant as long as we can."

"That'll be perfect. I may not get a chance to thank any of you later. I want to take the time to do it now." Steve walked through the group, speaking to each of the men and women, while shaking hands.

Two hours later, while assembling scaffolding with soldiers again, Steve overheard a peculiar radio conversation. He heard a soldier report, "No sir Captain, I don't know why they're here. I'd estimate there are two to three hundred of them."

"Lock those damn gates. Don't let them into the plant. Move up some armed reinforcements to back up the Military Police, before we have a riot on our hands. We have to know what they want," someone said, screaming into a radio.

"This is McClellan," Steve said, after lifting his radio. "Everyone calm down. What's going on?"

"We got construction workers stopped outside the plant's main gate," a panicking soldier said. "They want to get in. They're threatening to pull down the security fence if we don't let them in now!"

"Did you say construction workers?" Steve opened a bottle of water and took a drink. "What're they doing here?"

"They want to help us."

"Help us do what?" Steve smiled at Roger.

"We don't know. They don't look happy, and this could get ugly in the next few minutes, where we'll need to shoot some of these people if they continue to threaten us."

"Keep your fingers off the trigger and relax. I'll be right there."

"I'll go with you," Roger said. "I don't want you doing anything dangerous alone."

When he climbed from a Hummer at the main gate several minutes later, Roger saw construction company trucks lining both sides of the access road. "Who are these people?"

"Whoever they are, they brought a lot of equipment." Steve studied the large group of construction workers standing silently on the other side of the security fence. He noticed the heavily armed Military Police and Marines silently watching the men and women warily.

"They brought cranes too." Roger shaded his eyes from the sun, while pointing down the access road.

"Open the gates!" Brenton stepped beside Steve as a group of Firestone Tire trucks sped past them. "I'm not sure what to expect with this group."

"Let's find out why they're here, when they should be evacuating this area." Steve led the General and Roger forward.

252

An older man with an unshaven graying beard waited impatiently in front of hundreds of construction workers. He spit tobacco juice onto the road, while his hands rested on his hips. He wore faded jeans and a green shirt. "You're Doctor McClellan, aren't you?"

"That's right." Steve watched as the men and women moved to huddle around him, Roger, and Brenton, ominously. "Who are you?"

"I'm Ed Mallory. I own Mallory Construction." He pointed at the plant. "My company built a lot of that power plant."

"What's your reason for being here?" Brenton said. "Everyone was told to evacuate this area."

"We're here because my workers are as stubborn as me, and they want to volunteer to help you get this plant ready to kill Osiris."

Steve smiled as he immediately felt a sense of relief. "Mr. Mallory, we can use your help, but we don't want to put any of your people in danger."

"We'll be fine. We can take this plant apart for you a lot faster working together, military and civilians."

"Thank you." Steve shook Mallory's hand. Then he began talking to each of the construction workers, to thank them personally.

"I want to thank you and your staff, for stepping forward to provide us with this assistance." Brenton extended his hand, while smiling.

"It's our pleasure. It's our way to help the country." Mallory motioned to his workers, who ran to their trucks. He climbed into a rusting pickup truck overloaded with equipment. Then he drove through the gate. A convoy of company trucks followed with horns blaring, and drivers shouting enthusiastically.

Troxell became angry while watching the activity. *'I have to stop this work. I'll kill off small groups of these fool construction geeks. That'll slow things down. They'll never finish the work if they're worried they're going to die doing it.'*

Late that afternoon, Ed Mallory found Steve discussing plans with Doctor Reglovic outside, near rapidly growing pyramid of black tires. "We're moving into a much better position, Doc."

"Ed Mallory, I'd like you to meet Doctor Reglovic. He's my mentor."

"Don't listen to this young man, Mister Mallory. He's giving all of us old timers new insight into the world around us." Reglovic shook Mallory's hand. "It's a pleasure to meet you."

"I'm sure he is. He doesn't stop working." Mallory pointed at the top of a huge scaffolding structure secured to the side of a containment building. "My men just secured the floor at the top."

"What's next?"

"We move our equipment up there, and start cutting through the concrete."

"We could not have accomplished this on our own. Thanks for your help." Steve watched tall cranes lift floodlights, cutting torches, jackhammers, and other tools three hundred feet, to the top of the scaffolding. He saw another crane lifting soldiers and construction workers in a wooden enclosure.

Forty minutes later, everyone working around the plant heard the loud sound of air driven jackhammers, as workers began chipping away concrete from the outside of the containment building at the top of the scaffolding. Men and women, civilians and military, began cheering, when they realized they were making progress.

Steve drank from a water bottle while watching the activity around the plant. As streams of perspiration saturated his clothing, he felt a great sense of pride and accomplishment. He smiled while thinking, '*Nice. Very nice everyone.*'

Bonnie stopped to talk to him, while her camera crews recorded the activity. "I've been interviewing soldiers working around the plant. I want to get their personal stories."

"That's a great idea. These people deserve the recognition for trying to save our nation." He kissed her.

Moments later, the powerful concussion of a nearby explosion violently knocked them to the ground. The accompanying noise was deafening. Steve shaded his face from searing heat with a hand, as an enormous fireball thirty feet away billowed into the sky. The boiling hot flames sucked the oxygen from his lungs. He gasped for air while crawling forward to protect Bonnie with his body.

While gasping for air, Steve watched raging flames destroying approximately sixty military vehicles. The intense heat shattered windshields, and blistered the camouflaged paint off the vehicles. Hundreds of soldiers screamed in agony as flames consumed their clothing and skin. Large groups of soldiers lay dead on the ground. The flames blackened their skin.

Steve stood on shaky legs. He staggered to a fallen soldier. The explosion tore away the man's arms and legs. He was already dead.

He heard a woman screaming. He turned to see her running in circles wildly, while flames burned her clothing and hair. He pushed her to the ground before pulling off his shirt, which he used to smother the flames. When he noticed a growing red stain on the front of her uniform, he tore it open. He stared at a jagged piece of metal embedded in her abdomen. His fists clenched with rage when blood suddenly flooded from her mouth, in the moments before she died.

Troxell stood beside a truck, watching the chaos and pandemonium he orchestrated. He hummed while listening to dying soldiers screaming. He smiled as Brenton walked aimlessly through the debris and wounded. *'This is what I wanted General, dead bodies, and mass confusion. This was much better than the tents I blew up at your command center. Everyone thinks that was a propane gas explosion, but I know my bombs killed a few hundred of those geeks, and now the survivors want to run home because they're afraid little puppies. I see at least four hundred military people dead, and another two to three hundred dying. This'll shut down things here at the plant for hours. I'm not going to let you fools destroy Osiris!'* Troxell walked away, while listening to men and women screaming in agony.

At eight o'clock that night, Brenton called Ed Mallory, Peter Berry, Roger, and Steve to the conference room. He appeared exhausted while studying notes on a pad. "I lost more than three hundred personnel in that explosion today. They were good people! They were too good to die senselessly!"

"I'm sorry, General," Steve said, compassionately. "You do everything you can to protect your men, but they still end up dying, even after all of the precautions."

"Thanks Steve." Brenton nodded. "We've evacuated almost three hundred burn victims, along with another two hundred seriously injured people. I know a many of those men and woman won't make it."

Mallory said, "What caused the explosion, General?"

"I'm embarrassed to say we can't determine the cause of that deadly explosion." He paused, to take a deep breath. "Should we slow down the pace of work to reduce the chance of another accident?"

"We won't make our deadline and be ready to attack Osiris, if we slow down," Mallory said, while he peeled one of two bananas. "We need to push harder to get all of the work completed."

"Ok, we keep going. Tell all of our people to watch their damn asses out there, so no one else gets hurt! How is work proceeding on the containment buildings?"

"We finished assembling the scaffolding beside the second and third buildings an hour ago."

"Our men, and Ed's construction supervisors, are already working together to cut through the concrete of those two containment buildings," Straley said. He sat back to stretch out his legs.

Brenton notice the rip in the leg of his camouflaged pants. It exposed skin, covered with a large amount of dried blood. "I told you to have the medics look at that leg hours ago, Colonel!"

"It's nothing, General." Straley sat upright. "Really, sir."

"Ask the medics to clean up that wound now, Son! I'm determined to take everyone else out of here alive and uninjured."

"Yes sir."

Roger said, "Are we making any progress stacking tires?"

"Military, and now various civilian helicopters, are transporting tires to the plant. We'll be stacking them all night."

Steve said, "Where's Osiris currently located?"

"It's currently moving across the city of Los Angeles." Brenton paused, before he continued. "We've captured some disturbing reconnaissance satellite images as it did."

Steve frowned. "Satellite images of what?"

"We've identified large crowds of people fleeing from Osiris in specific locations. When the satellite passes over the same area again several hours later, we see thousands of clothed skeletons on the ground. Those were people Osiris killed as it devoured their flesh."

"I should rerun our calculations, to ensure our timing forecast for when Osiris will get to this plant,

258

is still accurate." Steve bit the inside of his jaw while thinking. "We need to understand the window of time for when we can expect to see Osiris."

"You should get some sleep Doctor. Colonel Straley told me you've been working nonstop all day."

"I'll be fine." Steve buried his face in his hands.

"The last thing I need is you in a hospital suffering from exhaustion!" Brenton studied Steve's dirty yellow shirt, and brown shorts.

"I'll stop for a few hours." Steve nodded. "I'll wash my clothes in a sink, before I sleep."

"That's all I have for tonight," Brenton said. "You all need sleep. Let's plan to meet at six tomorrow morning, so I can provide you with an updated status."

At ten o'clock that night, after showering in the plant's employee locker room which was reserved only for women, Bonnie walked into the office she and Steve used for sleeping. She saw him lying on a cot looking at several pictures, before she closed the door. "I got some snacks for us."

"Thank you." He studied her face and damp hair. "You look beautiful."

"Really? I look like hell!" She laughed while handing him a bag of potato chips. "What are those?"

"Reconnaissance satellite images of Osiris moving across Los Angeles."

She lifted several pictures off the cot, before she sat beside him. "How big is the cloud?"

"Its five miles wide, and seven miles long. The cloud has become a thirty-five square mile killing machine."

She frowned while flipping through the pictures. "It looks like the leading edge of the cloud, and these cloud tentacles, are zigzagging across the city. Why would it be doing that?"

"I think it's searching for large groups of people."

"People? Now it's hunting people?" She swallowed hard. "Why isn't it feeding on the plastic in the city?"

"The bacteria may have learned human flesh provides it with more nutrients than plastic or foam."

She pulled two donuts from a bag, before handing one to him. "Why doesn't the bacteria destroy an entire city, before it moves on to the next food source?"

"I think the primitive intelligence Goldberg gave the bacteria has something to do with it."

"In what way?"

"It may mark the cities it passes over, so it can find them later when it needs food."

"Like a squirrel burying acorns for the winter?"

"Yeah, that's a great analogy." He stood. "I need a shower."

"I'll take a walk with you."

As they walked around the plant, they saw thousands of military personnel working feverously. Bright floodlights lighted the buildings. They walked past tents where soldiers and construction workers waited in lines for food. They saw tents

260

where exhausted men and women slept, despite the loud noises of passing trucks, helicopters, and people shouting instructions nearby.

Bonnie noticed Steve staring into the glow of a floodlight. "What are you thinking about?"

"The people in the cars we saw on the highways, as we flew over them."

"What about them?" She looked up at the loud, low flying helicopters overhead. "You couldn't help all of those people."

"If we can't stop Osiris here, I don't think they'll ever stop running."

"You're a brilliant doctor." She smiled before kissing his cheek. "I know you can do it."

"I don't know that." He frowned at her ominously. "I'm afraid of the bacteria. I'm very afraid of it!"

"Your bedside manner is slipping, Doc. You sound as if you're telling the patient she's going to die." Bonnie felt body trembling after his comments. If Steve doubted he could destroy Osiris, she realized she would be forced to deal with the death of the man she loved, and her own eventual horrible death as the bacteria consumed her flesh.

While Steve was in the shower tent, she paced nervously outside while waiting for him. She became frantic as she thought, '*Osiris will knock out electricity across the country. We'll have no lights, no refrigeration, and no food. There won't be radio or television to warn the people which way Osiris is moving. We'll be forced back into the Stone Age. Without modern medical technology to stop it, Osiris will kill everyone. Steve has to stop the bacteria here. He has to kill it, or we're all going to die!'*

Shortly after midnight, the sounds of several loud explosions startled Steve from a deep sleep. He was dazed and confused, and briefly thought he was hearing bombs in Iraq. Seeing Bonnie on the cot beside him brought him back to reality. He ran out of the building wearing only underwear. Then he began running toward the flames behind the plant with hundreds of military personnel.

He soon saw twisted burning wreckage spread across a large field. He panicked when he saw soldiers spraying fire extinguishers onto burning wreckage, and bodies. "What happened out there?"

"Three helicopters crashed," a soldier said. "One exploded for no reason, and that brought down the other two aircraft."

Brenton ran to the area, with several officers following him. "What happened to those aircraft? I want to know now."

"They refueled and were taking off," a soldier explained. "Mechanical failure may be the cause."

"We didn't need this." Brenton watched soldiers pulling dead bodies from the mangled wreckage. "How many people did we lose?"

"I'd estimate there were twenty-four crew members in those aircraft, Sir."

"Damn it!"

Troxell hid in the shadows, behind several large vehicles. He was angry with himself. *'The bomb I put on that helicopter should have exploded over this plant. I had my chance to destroy this power plant, and I screwed up the opportunity! This*

262

reminds me of when I tried to kill the Libyan ambassador and my bullet killed his young daughter. I'll have to do something drastic so they won't have this plant ready.'

When Steve walked back to the administration building, he found Bonnie crying while sitting on the steps. "Hey baby, what's going on? Why are you so upset?"

"I know more soldiers just died needlessly out there." She wiped the tears from her cheeks.

"Yes they did." He sat beside her, upset by the deaths. "The one thing you can't forget is those men and women wanted to be in those helicopters. They were helping to make a difference, and they wanted to serve the nation. All of those people are heroes!"

"Was it like this in Iraq and Afghanistan? Were people dying all the time?"

"It was worse." He remembered red blood on operating room floors, after struggling to save wounded soldiers lives.

"This is how I imagined it."

"In combat, things are happening all around you and you don't understand why. The enemy tries to kill you when you think you're safe. Your own people mistakenly shoot at you when situations become insanely confusing. People are always shouting. You're never safe, and death is always with you. Combat was an inferno, and this plant is close to it."

"I don't want to see any more people die." She rested her head on his shoulder."

"Neither do I. I want all of the people working here to be safe." Steve sighed as he looked at the people working around the brightly lighted buildings, while loud helicopters flew low overhead.

At six the following morning, Brenton met the group for breakfast, outside a kitchen tent. Steve studied the mountains in the distance, and the sunlight shining on them. It was a calm and serene setting. The noise of trucks, helicopters, and people faded away, for several brief and precious seconds.

Brenton said, "How is work progressing on the containment buildings?"

Mallory flipped through his notes while eating a bagel. "We're jack hammering concrete away from the walls of the three buildings."

"Do you have any issues where I can help, or provide assistance?" Brenton sipped coffee from a paper cup.

"The steel reinforcing rods in the concrete have become the biggest obstacle. It's taking longer than we expected to cut through them with torches and carbide wheels, and that's slowing us down."

"Can we stay on schedule?"

"My men know this work is critical." Mallory nodded, affirming his workers perseverance. "They're working to save their families and friends from that killer cloud, so they're all motivated to succeed!"

"What is the status of our tire stacking efforts?"

"We're having some problems and the work is taking longer than we planned," Straley said.

"What can hold up stacking tires?" Roger frowned at Steve.

"The higher we build the piles, the longer it takes our men to lift tires to the top. That manual effort is taking longer than we planned, and exhausting our men."

"Problem solved." Mallory pulled a radio from his belt. "I'll contact my men and move some of our heavy cranes over to those work areas. The cranes will lift large numbers of tires on pallets for your men, so they only need to stack them."

"That will definitely help us. Thank you." Straley motioned a thumbs up signal to the group.

Berry said, "General, was anyone else hurt while people were working overnight?"

"Eighteen of my people died in an accident early this morning."

"How did that happen?"

"A tractor trailer crashed into a bus moving troops from a containment building to a mess facility, so those people could eat and get some down time."

"Did you ask the truck driver how it happened?"

"We can't find the damn driver, which makes no sense! Witnesses to the accident report he was a man with a shaved head, that jumped from the truck before the crash, and ran from the accident scene. The Military Police are investigating, and looking for that guy."

Berry seemed confused. "Why would he run?"

"Maybe he's afraid to come forward!" Brenton sounded frustrated. He could not imagine Troxell was responsible for another deadly accident, as he attempted to stop the preparation activities at the plant. "But we're going to find that driver."

Steve shook his head, upset by the news of more deaths he considered unnecessary. "Where's Osiris this morning?"

"The bacteria cloud is located over Los Angeles."

"Are portions of the cloud still reaching out in somewhat zigzag patterns?"

"Yes they are." Brenton paused, looking at his aides questioningly. "How did you know that?"

"I believe the bacteria are sending out feelers, to hunt for humans for nourishment. Were you able to evacuate the majority of the people from the city?"

"No, we could not make that happen. That proved to be impossible."

"People are still in the city?" Steve's sudden panic became apparent immediately. "You didn't get everyone out?"

"The highways were too congested and traffic stopped. We couldn't complete the evacuation."

"Why didn't you fly them out? When we left Afghanistan, we evacuated people on military aircraft! Why didn't you fly them out?"

"We attempted to use aircraft. But that attempt proved to be futile."

"Why couldn't you make that work? You have the entire Air Force at your disposal."

"We received numerous confirmed reports of gunfire, and people killing others to get onto helicopters and airplanes. I couldn't ensure the safety of the aircraft or flight crews. I suspended that evacuation operation."

"What's your estimate of the number of people that died in the city?"

"I'm sorry to say, hundreds of thousands of innocent people lost their lives."

"That news, that fear of death, must be tearing the rest of this country apart mentally and socially."

"That's exactly what's happening. The number of daily suicides as people look for a way out of this situation is unimaginable."

"That's not what I wanted to hear!"

"Panic and hysteria are spreading across the nation, and impacting almost everyone."

"In what way?"

"We're seeing widespread looting and insurrection across the nation. People are killing others to steal property, food, and gasoline."

"This is terrible." Steve rubbed his forehead with his fingers, while feeling frustrated and helpless.

"The President has mobilized the National Guard nationwide to restore order. However, the majority of those soldiers did not respond to the call up."

"I'm thinking those civilian soldiers are more concerned about caring for and protecting their families, then they are about keeping looters out of buildings."

"I agree, Doctor. This situation is unique, and military leaders do not know how to get those missing National Guard troops engaged in the action to stop looting, robberies, and murder."

"What else is causing people to panic?"

"The President ordered the New York Stock Exchange to close indefinitely, and that created sudden chaos."

"That chaos is because people can't sell their stocks, and don't know how they're going to get money to buy food and supplies during this crisis?"

Brenton nodded. "Depositors are also overwhelming banks to demand their savings."

"Those people don't understand banks invested their money in projects like this power plant, as a way to make money for their customers," Berry said.

"Banks don't have the cash to give out," Brenton said, "and that's causing more widespread rioting, and the murder of bank workers, when people become furious they can't withdraw their life savings."

"I never imagined a deteriorating social situation would become this severe." Steve stared at the group while imagining the chaos in city streets.

"We've got to stop Osiris before it destroys our nation, and the people destroy themselves," Roger said.

"I'm also hearing reports of mass suicides across the nation," Brenton said.

Roger was not prepared for that devastating news. "What are you talking about? Groups of people are killing themselves?"

"Huge groups of people are gathering in locations outsides cities and towns, in somewhat of a ritual death ceremony where they read their religious documents. Tens of thousands are killing themselves and their children, to avoid being killed by Osiris."

"Oh my God, this is a nightmare! People are killing children!"

"How much more time do we need to get the plant ready?" Steve became angry, while thinking about the irrational behavior of people. "We've got to kill Osiris, to stop people from killing family members, and themselves, because they're terrified!"

"We need thirty hours to complete the work," Mallory said, after reviewing his notes.

Roger checked his watch. "I'm going up on that scaffolding to help out the workers chipping away the concrete."

Brenton said, "Steve, I'd like to get you up in a Blackhawk helicopter as an observer later today."

"I'll do whatever is needed? What activity will I be watching from the helicopter?"

"I want you airborne to watch the activity when the military begins destroying cities and towns south of this plant."

"I can do that."

"Okay, let's get back to work gentlemen," Brenton said. "The clock is ticking."

At ten o'clock that morning Mallory found Steve stacking tires with hundreds of soldiers in the hot sun. "We just finished cutting through the wall of the first containment building Doc. Do you want to see the hole?"

"Sure." Steve smiled, visibly relieved. He sensed the difficult work was finally beginning to show results.

Mallory led him to his truck, where a young woman with long black hair stood beside it. "Doc, this is my daughter Wendy. She's my construction supervisor."

"It's a pleasure to meet you." Steve shook the smiling woman's hand. "How are you holding up?"

"I'm a little tired, but nothing more than that." Wendy adjusted a radio headset, before she spoke into a microphone, talking to the workers at the top of the scaffolding. "Let's give the Doctor a tour, Daddy."

Ed Mallory spit black tobacco juice onto the ground. He pointed at a monitor in the rear of the truck. "We have a camera up on the scaffolding. That's your hole in the concrete, Doc. It's ten feet high, and thirty feet wide. Do you think that will do the job?"

Steve smiled at the image on the monitor. "I'm sure that will allow for the release of radiation to kill Osiris. Nice job." He shook Ed Mallory's hand.

Wendy smiled before she spoke into the microphone, "The Doctor is happy with your work at the top of that scaffolding, gentlemen. Congratulations."

"Please give those men my personal thanks." Steve smiled several seconds later, after air horns on construction vehicles around the plant began sounding to celebrate the first construction success. Workers on the scaffolding lifted a long metal pipe before clamping it in place. An American flag attached to it began waving in the breeze.

"That flag looks terrific." Steve choked back his emotions.

"I'm going to check on our men fixing the broken air compressor," Mallory told his daughter. "They gotta get that equipment fixed, because we need air to power tools on the scaffolding!"

270

"I knew we could break through the wall of that building, Daddy." Wendy hugged her father tightly.

"Shouldn't you get your daughter out of here while it's still safe?" Steve said, as he and Ed walked toward a group of Mallory's trucks hauling air compressors and generators.

Mallory laughed while pulling a cigar from a pocket. "She won't go, Doc. She's thirty years old, and says she wants to be here with me. She's not leaving until the job is done!"

"You must be very proud of her."

"I'm proud of all these kids. My workers, and Brenton's soldiers. They could have run, but they decided to stay and fight."

"We owe them a lot of thanks."

"The way these kids think is a mystery to me. But I wouldn't trade them for anyone else."

Steve looked around after he heard someone shouting his name. "Who wants me?"

Mallory pointed at the wooden enclosure a crane slowly lifted toward the top of the scaffolding. "Your friend Roger is going for a ride."

"Watch yourself up there!" Steve said shouting, as he waved to Roger and the construction workers accompanying him.

'Your friend Roger.' Steve thought about Mallory's remark. 'Yeah, he's become a very good friend.'

At two o'clock that afternoon Brenton called Roger and Steve to the plant's conference room. He studied the gray concrete dust covering Roger's skin and hair. He saw the perspiration saturating the man's clothing. Then he noticed Steve's arms and

271

face were black with rubber dust. "I see you two have been busy."

Bonnie walked into the conference room several minutes later. She wore white shorts and a blue blouse, while preparing to interview additional soldiers working around the plant. "What are we doing in here?"

"I want you to see this new story." Brenton turned on a television monitor. "It aired several hours ago."

A male reporter in disheveled clothes said, "Reports suggest Osiris may have killed almost two million people in the Los Angeles area. Many areas of the city are burning out of control. The governor ordered firefighters not to extinguish fires. This comes after Osiris killed thousands of volunteer firefighters who travelled into the city earlier in the day to battle fires."

The reporter paused to review his notes. "In a related story, scientists report smoke and ash from the massive fires have been carried around the world by the upper jet stream winds. They predict catastrophic effects, and the possible onset of a nuclear winter if Osiris is not stopped soon."

"Osiris killed two million people?" Roger's face became pale, and anguished. "The situation is much worse than I imagined!"

"General, we need to forcibly evacuate the people ahead of the cloud," Steve said. "You need to use armed soldiers to maintain order, as you force people to evacuate their homes and businesses!"

"We're attempting to do that, Doctor." Brenton switched off the television. "However."

"However nothing! There can't be any screw ups. Force the people to leave, or they're going to die."

"That's our plan." Brenton paused, concerned by Steve's outburst. "The governor asked me to delay the bombing of the area ahead of Osiris until eight o'clock tonight. The people in that area need more time to evacuate."

"They had plenty of notice to get out. Why didn't they leave already?"

"The dense black smoke from fires is making roads impassable. It's turning daytime into the complete darkness of nighttime."

"Will this delay our timeline General?" Roger looked at his watch.

"We'll have that area leveled ahead of Osiris. The cloud will come here to you."

Steve remembered his previous deadly encounter with Osiris, when they captured a sample of the bacteria. He began trembling. "How do we burn those piles of tires when we want to get Osiris' here to the plant?"

"We buried drums of napalm in the piles. You'll ignite them with remote detonators in the control room."

Roger studied a large map. "Where is the cloud?"

"It's stationary." Brenton touched an area of the map. "It's currently located north of Los Angeles."

"The damn cloud is multiplying and expanding." Roger nodded to Steve. "It's preparing to move on to the next food source."

Steve smiled, nervously. "We're beginning to understand how it thinks."

After the meeting, Steve led Bonnie out of the building, and into the oppressive heat. He watched the chaotic work around the plant, before he said, "Hey beautiful, I need you to do something for me."

She smiled as she took his hand. "Anything for you, handsome. What's up?"

He looked around apprehensively, while suddenly appearing nervous. "If things go bad here at the plant, Brenton has agreed to fly you and your family to Australia on a military transport plane."

She frowned, while confused. "I don't understand."

"I did some calculations. Osiris can't reach Australia. That land mass is too isolated from other continents for Osiris to reach."

"What're you talking about?"

"You and your family will be safe there, because Osiris cannot reach that land mass. It's surrounded by too much ocean water."

She suddenly understood what he was suggesting, and she became horrified. "Do you think you're going to die here?" She pointed at the control room building.

"I'm not sure what's going to happen." He hugged her. "I love you, and I need to take care of you."

"Oh my God, I can't believe what you're saying!" Tears began running down Bonnie's cheeks while she cried on his shoulder. Her hand trembled while touching his short dark hair. "If

274

something happens to you, I won't be able to make it alone. I need you in my life!"

He stepped back, to stare into her eyes. "You'll need to go on, and lead the fight to destroy Osiris if I can't do it here"

"I can't do that without you! Leave Roger here to fight Osiris! Let's leave for Australia today and say the hell with the rest of the world! Let someone else figure it out! I need you, and I want you!"

"I can't leave, Baby."

"Why not?" She became angry, and defiant. "Why do you have to be the one to stay and fight Osiris alone?"

"It's difficult to explain." He struggled for the correct words. "I've always believed combat changed me. I hope it made me a better person."

"If you weren't a caring and understanding and compassionate person, you wouldn't be here."

"That's not why I'm here."

"What are you saying?" She became angry. She ignored the gathering crowd watching and listening to them. "Why did you come here?"

"I went out with one of our patrols to help find a group of soldiers that were wounded outside of Baghdad. An insurgent tried to shoot me in the head, but his weapon jammed for some reason. He was killed by one of our men, before he could kill me."

"What does that have to do with us?" Bonnie was unconcerned she was now screaming at him.

"Maybe God saved me that night, so I could be here today to stop Osiris."

"God saved you from the flipping hell of combat, so you could die here alone? I don't think that's how he works!"

"I don't know what's going to happen? But I need to know you'll be safe if things don't go as we planned."

"How can you do this to me? How can you push me away, when you tell me you love me?" Bonnie turned and walked away, ignoring his pleas for her to stop and talk.

He shook his head, mentally blaming himself for her angry reaction. "I should have explained I love her very much, and I want her to be safe, no matter what happens here. I screwed up that conversation." He began walking toward the area where soldiers were stacking tires, to help them again.

At seven o'clock that evening, Steve felt exhausted and realized he was scheduled to fly in a helicopter as an observer within the hour. He studied the ten towering piles of black tires strategically positioned around the plant. The towering structures resembled huge black pyramids. While walking toward the administration building, he saw Brenton speaking to several of his aides. "How are we doing General?"

"Mallory's men finished cutting through the wall of the second containment building. We have everyone working on the third building. That hole will be finished before we evacuate everyone from this area."

"Where's Osiris located?"

"The cloud is forty miles north of Los Angeles. It's moving north, fast."

"It's almost time to begin the next battle." Steve watched soldiers struggling to push a large air compressor across a parking lot. Their teamwork seemed to motivate him mentally. "I know what I've got to do here."

"You're in a difficult position Doctor. I don't envy you."

"I'm getting that same strange feeling I had in Iraq and Afghanistan." He took a deep breath. "I'm beginning to think I may die here."

"Doctor." Brenton paused, while searching for the correct words to make the message more personal. "Steve, I've had that same feeling many times in combat. You need to push it out of your mind, and get the job done. You'll fail if you allow your fears to dictate your actions!"

"Now I know what my patients think and feel when I tell them they're terminally ill with cancer, and they're not going to survive to see their kids get married and have kids."

"Everyone thinks about dying differently."

"I met a wonderful woman in this pandemonium, and I want to spend many years with Bonnie." Steve looked into Brenton's eyes, before he confessed. "I'm afraid to have my life end here."

"We're all afraid of dying, Steve. That fear has many faces and aspects, and impacts our lives, and our need to succeed before we do die."

"I'm afraid of the unknown."

"We all are." Brenton took a report from a soldier.

"I'm afraid of what comes after death, if anything." He looked away, pushing back his own emotions. "It's confusing, and I didn't expect this would be so difficult for me."

"You need to be on the flight line in twenty minutes, Doctor." Brenton watched him walk away silently. He understood the man's fears. "Take care of yourself."

Steve walked into a locker room in the building. He stripped down to underwear. Then he began washing the black dust from his face, arms, hands, and short black hair. He smiled after Bonnie unexpectedly walked in several minutes later. "Hi. How are you? I'm sorry I upset you, when I tried to explain what's on my mind."

"Please stop, you don't need to apologize for anything. I'm sorry for what I said to you. I over reacted."

"Why are you sorry?"

"I shouldn't be telling you what to do." She nervously played with her long hair.

"You're part of my life, and I love you. You should be sharing your thoughts and ideas with me."

"Well, I'm upset with myself. I need to trust the decisions you make to keep people safe."

"My decisions are not always correct, and I need you to tell me when you think I'm wrong." He kissed her. "You keep me sane."

She put her hands on his shoulders, and then stared into his eyes. "I want you to come back to me when this is over. Do you understand me? I want you back by my side, so we can build a future together!"

He smiled and then kissed her. "I'll be back in your arms before you know it."

278

"That's where I want you, and in my bed." She smiled seductively.

"There's a helicopter crew waiting impatiently to give me a ride." Steve began pulling on green aviation flight suit.

"I'll let you get ready. Please me careful. I love you." She kissed him, before walking from the locker room while wiping away the tears streaming down her cheeks.

Steve thought about Bonnie's comments while walking out of the building. Outside, he found Feltault, Harrison, Meridian, and Troxell talking. "How are we doing, gentlemen?"

"The military, and the construction workers, will have the plant ready for you to attack Osiris," Feltault said. "Brenton just reported the work is on schedule."

"That's excellent news. I'm going flying with the Army."

Troxell rubbed a painful scar on his thigh while watching Steve walk toward the area where a helicopter crew waited for him. *'This bloody leg wound I got from that struggling British diplomat bitch I killed last month still hurts. As I strangled the damn bitch, she smashed that glass and cut me. She paid for it. I slashed her breasts and legs with that glass, before I cut her damn throat. You should be dead right now too McClellan. I thought you were in the bus I hit with that tractor-trailer. All I did was kill some worthless soldiers. But now, I finally know how to kill you, to ensure you can't hurt Osiris.'*

At one of the helicopter landing areas, Brenton's executive officer introduced Steve to the flight crew of a Blackhawk helicopter. "This is Colonel Tom Jacoby. And this is Major Cynthia Connelly, the Colonel's co-pilot. Their Crew Chief is Sergeant Jeffrey Marcowski."

"It's a pleasure to meet all of you." Steve climbed into the helicopter. He heard the familiar sound of the turbine whining to life, before the aircraft lifted off several minutes later. He watched as they began flying over densely populated residential areas.

"What are the helicopter pilots doing in this area?" Steve said, using the helicopter's intercom system.

"They're attacking high profile targets in various areas," Colonel Tom Jacoby said.

Steve frowned, questioningly. "What is considered a high profile target?"

"Any facility that will explode, such as gas stations, gasoline and oil storage facilities, and large buildings. Structures that will burn, and ignite other buildings nearby. We want everything burned to the ground."

"That should deprive Osiris of nourishment." Steve nervously grasped his seat moment later, when the helicopter banked sharply to the left.

"The heavy bombers will destroy everything that's still standing later tonight."

During the first hour of the flight, Steve saw numerous buildings explode violently, after missiles fired from attack helicopters struck them. The structures became infernos, spewing black smoke and glowing red embers into the darkening evening sky. Fires began consuming entire city blocks and residential neighborhoods. The dense black smoke soon obscured the setting sun.

Shortly after dark, Jacoby flew toward Santa Barbara to inspect the area. There he saw raging flames consuming almost every building in the city. In residential areas, red flames leaped from houses. Every building in the commercial business areas was burning. The heat from fires buckled metal building supports, allowing roofs to collapse into the infernos below.

Steve watched the shimmering orange glow of fires extending to the horizon in the darkness. '*How will we ever rebuild this area? This plan didn't bother me when we put it together on paper. Now that I'm seeing the destruction I recommended, I feel very guilty about what we're doing.*'

Chapter 12

The helicopter carrying Steve arrived back at the plant several hours later. As it circled the power plant to land, he watched the men working at the top of the scaffolding in bright lights, frantically attempting to complete the hole in the wall of the third containment building. Below, on the ground, he saw thousands of soldiers working in the lights around the plant. Lights positioned around the huge piles of tires lighted the soldiers who climbed to the top of the pyramid shaped piles. There they stacked a few hundred additional tires, hoping the added effort would ensure Osiris would find the plant tempting.

After landing, Steve told the researchers huge firestorms were destroying every city and town south of the plant. Brenton reported the Air Force began the bombing operation to destroy the areas ahead of Osiris as planned.

Steve changed into clean shorts and a tee shirt in the administration building. Outside, in stifling heat and humidity, he devoured a dinner of cold milk and chocolate chip cookies. He did this while reviewing the plan to attack Osiris, with a large group of senior military strategists.

At eleven o'clock, he and Roger met with the researchers in a large lighted parking lot. Parked camouflaged military vehicles were scattered around the lot. Roger climbed onto the bumper of a large truck to speak to the group. "We want all of you to be ready to evacuate this area in two hours."

"Where are we going?" Reglovic said, shouting to be heard over the noise of nearby military electrical generators.

"Brenton is flying you to a command center seventy miles east of here." The noise of the jackhammers and loud passing trucks distracted him. "Does everyone understand? You've got to leave tonight!"

"I wish you'd reconsider and allow some of us to remain here to help you," Feltault said. He looked around at the others who nodded their heads in agreement.

"We feel like we're deserting you," Doctor Satriano said. "We don't agree leaving you here alone is the correct course of action."

"We don't want to go," Doctor Rocco said. He smiled after his comments brought enthusiastic clapping, cheers, and whistles from others.

Steve shook his head before he climbed onto the truck bumper beside Roger. "We need all of you, and the knowledge you carry in your heads, to be safe."

"We want to help you fight Osiris." The remark brought additional shouts of support, and cheers.

"We don't want you here," Roger said. He began laughing with Steve.

"Why don't you want us here?"

Roger raised his hands, asking for quiet. "You're all family now! This is what Steve and I have to do to keep our family safe. You're all leaving here tonight."

"We don't like the idea of you two putting yourself in jeopardy to protect us," Doctor Rocco said.

"We're leaving you with the most dangerous piece of work," Reglovic said.

"This is what Roger and I have to do," Steve said.

"Why are you the only two doing this?"

"There's no other way to conduct this experiment," Roger said.

"What does that mean?"

"If we can't stop Osiris with radiation here at this site, you'll have to continue searching for a way to kill the bacteria. That's why we need to keep all of you safe."

Reglovic stepped forward. "If something unfortunate does happen here, you two can be assured we will carry on the battle." He smiled at Roger and Steve after all of the researchers behind him began cheering and whistling.

Doctor Satriano glanced at his watch. "When do you expect Osiris will reach this plant?"

"We're estimating the cloud will be here at approximately ten o'clock tomorrow morning," Roger said. He watched as the researchers suddenly became silent, while thinking about the death and destruction caused by Osiris. He realized some people were silently questioning how he and Steve would survive at the power plant.

Feltault studied the researcher's somber faces. "This isn't a funeral! We proved radiation will destroy Osiris. We'll be back here reveling with

Steven and Roger later tomorrow, after they destroy the cloud."

"Bring back a case of champagne so we can celebrate." Steve began shaking the hand of each researcher while thanking them for their ideas and tireless efforts. He paused, before hugging Doctor Cindy Licitra and several others tightly.

Troxell smiled while watching Steve and Roger. He thought, *'You'll both be dead before you can stop Osiris. I want you to know it's me killing you McClellan. I want to watch your face while you die slowly and painfully, because you're a pain in my ass!'*

Steve noticed Bonnie standing beside her crew, while they recorded the meeting from a nearby grassy hill. He smiled while walking to them. "I don't want any of you staying behind to record what happens when Osiris gets here. Do you all understand me?"

"We don't have any heroes in this group," Bonnie said. She kissed his cheek gently. "They've already assigned us to an evacuation helicopter."

"If I know you're safe and away from here, I'll be good." Steve turned and walked back to the group of researchers.

"Are things okay between you and Bonnie?" Roger said, after Steve returned to the parking lot.

"Yeah, we're good." Steve turned to look at her. "We want to take care of each other, and be sure the other is safe, and that's difficult."

"You should be getting out of here with her when she's evacuated. Watch over her, and let me coordinate the activities we have planned at this plant!"

"I can't do that." He smiled while shaking the hands of researchers offering their best wishes.

"There's no reason to intentionally put yourself in danger here. I can do this alone."

"This battle is now personal for me." Steve shook the hands of several plant workers while cordially thanking them for their assistance. "I'm going to stay with you, to help you."

"Why? Why do you want to do that?"

"That bacterium tried to kill me. Now, I want to have a direct role in killing the bastard."

Roger fought back a smile. "You want revenge?"

"Yeah, something like that." Steve smiled, feeling somewhat embarrassed after his confession. "I need to know I can make a difference, and stop the death and destruction, by stopping that cloud."

"You could die here! You're a great doctor, and that would be the loss of a great medical mind, that might find a cure for cancer."

"I took an oath to help people whenever and wherever I can."

"But that oath doesn't say you need to die while you're doing it."

"I have an amazing opportunity here at this facility, to help all people by destroying Osiris. If it means I may die during that attempt to stop the cloud, then that's an outcome I need to accept. In my mind and heart, I need to be here at this time to help you!"

Roger understood. He smiled while extending his hand to Steve. "Thank you for being an amazing doctor, and friend. It's a pleasure knowing you, and working beside you, Doc."

Several hours later, as workers completed final preparations around the plant, air horns and sirens began wailing a warning. That signal indicated the evacuation of all personnel was beginning. Large groups of helicopters began circling the plant in the darkness, waiting for military air-traffic controllers to give them permission to land. The pilots and crews realized they needed to evacuate thousands of personnel.

As Steve and Roger, along with Straley, Brenton and Mallory, walked to the now brightly lighted helicopter landing zone, they watched large groups of soldiers and workers running past them. Then they saw long lines of people waiting to climb aboard landing helicopters, as they watched others flying from the power plant.

Steve watched soldiers and construction workers scrambling onto helicopters immediately after they landed. Most of the men and women appeared exhausted and dirty. Some looked around ominously for the approaching Osiris cloud in the darkness while appearing terrified. The scene reminded him of combat soldiers in Iraq. "General, we couldn't have done any of this without their help. I hope each and every one of them understands the important part they played while preparing this plant to battle Osiris."

"I'll relay your thoughts to them, Doctor. They'll appreciate knowing you value their efforts."

"Thank you." Steve smiled, before he began looking around for Bonnie.

"Let's go! Move out and get to a helicopter!" Brenton said, while shouting at groups of soldiers running from the communications and radar trailers. He then turned to Steve and Roger, while taking a deep breath. "This plant is now your only weapon, gentlemen. Use it wisely to defeat the bacteria monster ravaging our nation, and killing our citizens."

"Good luck guys." Mallory shook both men's hands. He ran to a helicopter while dragging his daughter forward by her wrist.

Straley said, "Steve, Roger, I'm honored to have served with you." He unexpectedly saluted both men.

Roger appeared shocked. "Thank you, Colonel."

Steve returned the salute. He stepped forward to shake Straley's hand. "We couldn't have done this without you. Take care of yourself, Charles."

"I will do that, sir. Good luck to you." Straley led his men toward the landing helicopters.

Steve watched a large group of helicopters landing on the grassy fields beside the power plant's administration and maintenance buildings. He noticed Bonnie and her crew filming the soldiers boarding the aircraft. He frantically pushed his way through a crowd of soldiers and workers running toward the landing zone, before he gently grasped her arm. "I'm glad I found you. I have to hold you one more time, and tell you I love you."

"Oh my God, I looked everywhere for you and I couldn't find you." She hugged him tightly. "I was worried they'd force me to leave without seeing you."

"I'm here now, and we're okay." He felt her soft hair pressed against his face as he hugged her. The familiar scent of her perfume made him smile, while holding the woman he loved.

She began crying. "Please promise me you'll be careful here without me."

He kissed her gently, before wiping away her tears while smiling. "I want to start a life with you after we stop Osiris." He hugged her again.

"I love you." She kissed him as tears flowed from her eyes.

"Let's move and get another group onto this helicopter now," a crew chief said, shouting to people. "Time is limited and we need to leave!"

"I love you and I need you to be safe tonight." Steve kissed her, before helping her climb into the helicopter. The rotors created a blinding, deafening downdraft. He squeezed her hand one final time. "I love you."

"I love you!" She tried to lean out and kiss him, but a member of the helicopter crew pulled her back.

Troxell watched them, while running toward the helicopter with researchers. He thought, *I'll get rid of your girlfriend with this bomb I made. Then I'll kill you McClellan. You're going to die tonight.'* He frantically fumbled with the silver metal case he carried, after a nearby soldier's knee struck it, almost knocking it from his hand. He took a deep sigh of relief while sliding the case into the helicopter beside Bonnie.

Troxell climbed into the helicopter and sat on the floor beside her. He silently stared at the case, concentrating as people screamed information to each other around him, while gently squeezing the handle. He felt the familiar click. He realized he armed the bomb, and the timer was counting down. He unexpectedly stood before pointing at the helicopter crew chief. "I have to get out of here so I can talk to Doctor McClellan before I leave!"

"There's no time," the crew chief said.

"I'll be right back." Troxell jumped from the helicopter before he disappeared in the crowd of people waiting for additional helicopters to land.

As Steve and Brenton concluded a discussion of their mutual concerns forty minutes later, they watched the last of the soldiers boarded helicopters. Brenton's Executive Officer ran to him. "It's time for us to leave General. We're running late."

"I understand. We're almost done here." Brenton looked at his watch. "Steve and Roger, use the radio my communications team set up in the control room to stay in touch. We have surveillance cameras located everywhere around the plant, but I need to know from you what's happening here in real time."

"We'll keep you informed as long as we can," Steve said.

"My men left a flare gun for you to use as a backup signal." Brenton shouted over the deafening sounds of departing helicopters.

"Your men explained how to use it. If you see a green flare, it's safe to return," Roger said.

Brenton watched the last of the helicopters lift off, and fly away. "We've been working together for only a few days gentlemen. I can say it has been a great pleasure collaborating with you."

290

"It's been fun, General." Steve smiled with a boyish grin. He shook Brenton's hand.

"Thank you, General," Roger said. He shook the man's hand. "Take care of yourself."

Brenton walked to a waiting helicopter. He realized he was reluctant to leave. He turned to Steve and Roger, before saluting them. Then he climbed into the helicopter and displayed a thumbs-up signal to both men.

"The General is on-board the aircraft," the Executive officer told the pilots. "Let's get him to the alternate command center as soon as possible."

Brenton studied Steve and Roger as the helicopter lifted off the ground. He mumbled, "I should be staying here with those two boys."

"What was that, Sir?" His Executive Officer said.

"It was nothing important. I was just talking to myself." Brenton began reading a document developed by senior officials at the Pentagon, in the glow of red overhead lights in the helicopter.

Several long minutes later Roger and Steve watched the red, white, and green lights on the exterior of the departing helicopters disappear into the blackness of night. As the engine and rotor sounds faded away, they heard faint explosions. They turned to see the distant night sky shimmering with a bright red glow. They immediately realized the raging fires created the glow, south of the plant. The large bombs falling from the Air Force bombers and then detonating, created the sounds and concussions.

"Who could have imagined we'd be bombing our own country?" Steve shook his head.

"All of this destruction is being caused by my brother's need to be famous, and Goldberg's need for revenge." Roger suddenly noticed the stillness now surrounding the plant. The only noise came from whining electrical generators, lighting the exterior of buildings. He watched flying insects swarming around the large bright floodlights. He also noticed it suddenly felt oppressively hot and humid. "It's too quiet and spooky out here with no one around."

"Let's find Mason, and see what he's doing. I want to make sure he's preparing those reactors to attack Osiris."

Brenton cursed after unexpected turbulence buffeted the helicopter, as he attempted to read the attack plan transmitted from the Pentagon. He became angry, as he fully understood the details. "I don't approve of this damn attack strategy, or the outcome we're hoping for, to save our people and nation. This plan is a piece of crap! It was developed by people who don't have an accurate assessment of our situation."

"We have a visual on your command center, General." The co-pilot pointed forward. "It's directly ahead."

Brenton squinted through the helicopter windshield. His teeth clenched while staring at a dimly lighted area ahead in the darkness. Moments later he instinctively shaded his face with a hand, after a brilliant flash of light directly ahead of the helicopter blinded him. He felt the enormous concussion from an explosion violently buffeting the helicopter. Brenton was shocked to see red burning remains of a destroyed aircraft plummeting downward in the darkness. "What just happened? What was that?"

"One of the aircraft flying ahead of us just exploded. The helicopter exploded in flight!" The pilot sounded shocked and confused. He would never understand the bomb that Troxell placed into the helicopter carrying Bonnie Saunders to safety, exploded violently.

"Did I see other explosions?"

"Yes you did, Sir. The explosion took down several of the other helicopters flying near it." The co-pilot looked down to study the burning remains of the aircraft on the ground below.

"Radio the Alert One Rescue pilots. Tell them to scout that area where the helicopters went down, and look for survivors."

"Alert One Rescue?" The pilot said, confused after the General's order. "I don't recall a rescue team being part of our evacuation plan, General."

"They're an undocumented component of my personal plan to ensure we got everyone out of that power plant safely, Son. I brought in extra helicopters, so if any of our aircraft could not make it out of the plant because of mechanical issues, they would evacuate stranded people and pilots! Get them on the radio, tell them what just happened, and give them the coordinates."

The pilot nodded while smiling after hearing the previously undisclosed details of Brenton's plan to keep everyone safe. "Yes, Sir. Where are those rescue helicopters located?"

"They're flying two minutes behind us," the Executive Officer said. "They were told to pick up stragglers who may be forced to land due to engine or mechanical problems. We're not leaving any of our heroes behind."

"Give that rescue team the coordinates of the crash site," Brenton said. "They have thirty minutes to search for survivors. They cannot stay in the area any longer than that, because they may be bombed by our Air Force operation."

"Yes, Sir." The co-pilot began supplying information to the airborne rescue team.

Thirty minutes later Brenton's helicopter circled his temporary command center. It was located on a huge rocky plateau high in the mountains. The full moon cast a glow that dimly lighted the towering rocky peaks above the plateau, when the helicopter landed. Large bright floodlights lighted twelve large camouflaged military tents. The sounds of electrical generators disturbed the tranquility of the remote mountain base.

Other helicopters began landing at the mountain base. Thousands of military personnel and construction workers soon stood together in the humid night air. They talked in groups while staring at the red glow in the distant sky, created by the exploding Air Force bombs.

"Is everything in order here?" Brenton said, after several aides rushed to greet him, as he walked toward a large tent guarded by heavily armed soldiers.

"Yes sir, we're good to go here!"

"What the hell is that sound?" Brenton suddenly stopped, and frowned while looking south from the plateau. The sky made an eerie hissing crackling sound, while glowing with a bright orange hue. It was a phenomenon created by the raging firestorms after falling bombs ignited huge areas of buildings and homes. He continued walking into his command center tent, while troubled by what he saw happening in the distance.

Twenty minutes later, Brenton's Executive officer stepped out of the tent. Soldiers accompanying him walked through the crowd of people shouting Doctors Feltault, Meridian, and Reglovic's names. When they stepped forward, the Executive Officer led them away from the others. "Gentlemen, the General would like you to join him in his command center tent."

"Why does he want us in his command center?" Feltault said. "We prefer to watch events unfolding in the distance, out here with the other researchers so we can discuss what we see."

"He needs to discuss a rapidly escalating situation with you. Your input is imperative to the success of our operation."

"Of course we'll do everything we can to help," Meridian said. He nodded to the others.

Armed soldiers escorted them into the darkened tent. Small lights illuminated computer keyboards, communications equipment, and notebooks, around the tent. Dim red lights illuminated monitors. Lighted buttons on electronic equipment dotted the ten with red, orange, blue, and green points of light.

Soldiers talked on radios, while others stared intently at computer monitors.

The soldiers led the men to large monitors located at the front of the tent. One monitor displayed the radar image and position of Osiris over California. Another monitor displayed the computer-enhanced infrared image of the swirling bacteria cloud, captured by a reconnaissance satellite and airborne Air Force radar planes. Another monitor displayed the entire border of the state of California. A green square depicted the location of the power plant, with Osiris depicted as a large orange mass now slowly advancing toward it.

"Have a seat, gentlemen," Brenton said, after he looked up while reading a status report displayed on his laptop computer. "Do you have any questions before we get started?"

"I heard some rumors and talk outside about a helicopter crash, General," Feltault said. "Is there any validity to that rumor?"

"Unfortunately, six of our aircraft went down while making their way to this location."

"Went down? Are you saying they landed for some reason while flying here?"

"No Doctor, those helicopters crashed for some unknown reason."

"They crashed while flying people away from the plant, to safety here?"

"That's correct Doctor, at this location." Brenton pointed at a monitor with red boxes marking a specific area of a map. "I watched as the aircraft appeared to disintegrate and fall to the ground as flaming debris."

"What happened to the people on those helicopters? Are they alive? Did they die?"

"My rescue teams reported there are no survivors on the ground. They found mangled burned bodies in the area."

"This cannot be happening," Meridian said. "Not now. Everything was going so well."

"The situation is terrible!" Feltault began shuddering from sudden anxiety. "Do we know who died in the crash?"

"A preliminary assessment indicates the helicopters were carrying members of the news organizations."

"Reporters?" Meridian looked at the others, before turning back to the General. "Is Ms. Saunders safe?"

"My men have been unable to locate her, or her film crew, in the people we evacuated to this site. We can't find them, or account for any of them."

"There must be some mistake." Feltault felt himself begin to panic. "They must have been overlooked during your initial search. Send your men to walk through the group again, shouting their names. They must be here, alive and safe!"

"You've got to face the hard facts, Doctor." Brenton pointed at his computer. "This preliminary assessment I'm reading indicates she and her film crew perished during the crash."

Feltault was shocked. He grasped a chair to support himself as his body trembled. "Did you tell Steven what happened?"

"No. Not yet." Brenton took a deep breath while studying the radar image of the steadily advancing Osiris cloud. "This is not the time to relay this information to him."

"Why didn't you tell him? He should know what happened to Bonnie. He appears to be in love with that woman."

"That information may jeopardize the plan to destroy Osiris, and eventually get him killed."

"How can being truthful jeopardize our plan to destroy Osiris? I don't see that happening?"

"The revelation that Ms. Saunders was unexpectedly killed in the crash may devastate him. Steve may make a fatal mistake while he's grieving for his lost love."

"I don't agree with this approach of withholding information from him."

"I'll tell him about her death, when I feel the time is appropriate! And you will not say anything to him! Am I making myself perfectly clear, Doctor?"

"Yes, General."

"Excuse me, Sir." A soldier interrupted, to hand Brenton a printed message. "This is the latest update from the Pentagon."

"What are the desk experts in Washington telling us to do now?" He read the message, before angrily crushing the paper in his hands. Brenton turned to the soldiers in the tent, and said, "I want to see the present location of our bomber wing."

The bright blue outlines of twenty-five airplanes appeared on a large monitor in the tent. An Intelligence officer said, "Those are aircraft from

298

the One-Hundred-Tenth Bomber Group, dropping bombs. The next six airborne wings are moving up and into position behind them, to continue the bombing operation when those bombers return to their base to be refueled, and to take on additional armaments."

"Very good. Where are the components of Operation Blue Eclipse?"

The yellow outline of six aircraft appeared on the monitor, depicting them over the Pacific Ocean. "They're two hundred twenty-five nautical miles west of the power plant, and flying in a holding pattern."

"We have a secured communications link established with each of those flight crews," the communications officer said. "We want to ensure there are no issues if those teams are needed."

"What's their current status?"

"They're waiting for the transmission of the Presidential authentication code."

"Very good." Brenton looked over the shoulder of a soldier, to study a computer monitor. "Show me the location of our Navy Aegis destroyer group."

The bright amber outlines of ten ships appeared on the monitor. "That's Surface Group Seven. They're two hundred nautical miles west of the California coastline."

"Do we have constant communications established with that battle group commander?"

"Yes, Sir."

"General, the President is asking to speak with you," a communications officer said.

"Put this conversation on the speakers. I want these doctors to hear it." Brenton waited for an Army communications specialist to point at him, indicating it was time to speak. "This is General Brenton."

President Stillman sounded impatient as he said, "Did you complete all planned preparations at that nuclear power plant, General?"

"We're good to go. That facility is readied to attack Osiris with radiation."

"Have you completed the destruction of the buildings and structures ahead of the advancing bacteria cloud?" The President studied a topographical map displayed on a large monitor. Other monitors displayed real time images from spy satellites and high-flying reconnaissance aircraft, showing huge areas of burning buildings. "So the cloud will travel to the plant, as planned?"

"That operation is in progress, and the heavy bombers are leveling the area ahead of Osiris at this time."

"Are Doctor McClellan and Mr. Samulson in position at the plant?"

"Yes, they are. The fate of our nation, and that of the entire world, is in their hands."

"Did you review the updated attack plan my advisors created, which was sent to your command center?"

"I did read it." Brenton paused. "If I may, Mister President. I do have reservations about some of the details."

"Your only concern should be the successful execution of that plan if it is required and implemented, General," President Stillman said tersely. "Your job is to make it happen. Do you understand your role?"

"Yes sir, I do."

"Have we overlooked anything?" The President nervously looked at his watch. He sat back, before pulling down his tie, while clenching a cigarette in his fingers. He looked around at the hundreds of civilian and military advisors surrounding him.

"Are you prepared to issue the nuclear weapons authentication codes if they are needed, Mister President?"

"I will do whatever is necessary to safeguard the lives of our citizens, and their property." The President glanced at a military officer seated in the room. He saw the silver handcuff around the man's wrist, and the chain extending to a black leather attaché case on the desk. "Colonel Bennetterri is sitting beside the encryption device which will enable me to utilize our full nuclear arsenal if necessary."

"I'm sure you realize you cannot hesitate if our people at the plant are unable to stop Osiris."

"I know my job General. I understand what I need to do. I don't need to be reminded of my crucial role in this scenario by you!"

"Yes, Sir."

"How long will it take to launch the missiles after I transmit the nuclear release code?"

"The first Cruise missile will be airborne within five minutes."

President Stillman looked around the room, studying the somber faces of his advisors. He searched for several particular individuals. "General, I want you to contact to me when Osiris is twenty miles south of the nuclear power plant."

"I will do that, Sir." Brenton pointed to an officer, silently assigning him that task.

"That's all I have for now. Contact me immediately if something we didn't anticipate becomes an issue." A long tone sounded, indicating the call ended.

Meridian immediately said, "Please explain your discussion with the President? What are you planning to do with Cruise missiles?"

Feltault said, "Why will the President need to send codes to arm nuclear weapons? What is the purpose of using those weapons?"

Brenton sighed, realizing he owed the confused men an explanation. "The President's scientific cabinet members cautioned him we cannot destroy only a small or minimal portion of Osiris at the plant. The entire bacteria cloud must be completely obliterated with radiation during this attempt. There will be no second opportunity to attack and destroy the cloud."

"Our intention is to subject the cloud to radiation," Meridian said, interrupting Brenton. "We're confident we can destroy the entire bacteria mass with the exposure to radiation."

"If your controlled release of radiation doesn't end this situation," Brenton said, "the President plans to expose the remaining bacteria to a massive amount of radiation."

"How does he plan to do that?" Feltault said angrily, after the startling revelation.

302

"He's going to use Cruise missiles to attack the cloud if Steve and Roger fail," Meridian said. He shook his head disgustedly.

"That's correct, Doctor." Brenton gestured toward the outlines of airplanes on a monitor. "Each of these Stealth Bombers is carrying two Cruise missiles equipped with nuclear warheads."

"Nuclear warheads?" Feltault appeared shocked as he glanced at the others, before looking at Brenton again.

"This is a very foolish and dangerous plan! You cannot detonate nuclear weapons in the continental United States," Meridian said. "The land mass contaminated with radiation will be uninhabitable for thousands of years!"

"I share your concerns Doctor, but no one in Washington is listening to me." Brenton pointed at the outlines of ships on the monitor. "This is the U.S.S. Ticonderoga and she's carrying thirty Cruise missiles armed with nuclear warheads. Those missiles will be utilized if additional firepower and radiation is required to obliterate Osiris."

"Why weren't we told about this ridiculous alternate plan before now?" Anger suddenly made the veins in Reglovic's neck appear as if they were about to burst. "You can't explode a nuclear bomb in California."

Meridian said, "Doesn't anyone in Washington realize nuclear radiation will make that crucial American land mass uninhabitable for possibly thousands of years?"

"This wasn't an easy decision for the President to make after meeting with and listening to his

303

advisor's recommendations. He approved the plan less than an hour ago." Brenton took a status report from an aide.

"You're telling us President Stillman has his own agenda, and we weren't informed of it?"

"I was informed of this plan during the flight here, Doctor. This is breaking news that I'm sharing with you."

"What if Osiris doesn't kill Roger and Steve? You'll kill them when you drop a bomb on the plant."

"Those men were well aware of the risks when they chose to stay and confront Osiris."

"They never imagined their own government would come up with a secret plot to kill them," Reglovic said.

Feltault sat forward on the chair. "Are you going to tell them about this Plan B?"

"Will that information help those men to do their jobs more efficiently?" Brenton became frustrated after the question. "Tell me Doctor! Will that knowledge help them to do a better job, or will it put fear in their minds, and compromise their already deadly situation?"

"I, I'm not sure." Feltault looked to his colleagues for their opinions or guidance.

"Will adding more tension to this situation improve their chances for survival?"

"I guess not."

"That's my thinking exactly. I'll allow them to attack the cloud, and hope they can destroy it."

"The President's plan is the epitome of insanity," Meridian said. He began pacing between the tables cluttered with maps and laptop computers.

"What is our part in this blindsided scheme?" Reglovic said, sarcastically.

Feltault said, "Why are we so privileged to know the details of this ridiculous scenario to destroy our own nation?"

Brenton pointed at the men. "Because I need all of you to talk and decide if and when a nuclear strike is a feasible option to terminate the bacteria cloud formation."

"What will you do with that information?"

"I'll relay your opinion to the President, who will make the final decision."

"Oh my God," Meridian said. "You want all of us to play a crucial role in this insanity?"

"You are no longer observers, doctors. Now you're combatants along with us, in this attack on the monster which is decimating our nation." Brenton began a meeting with his staff, where he introduced the doctors and explained their new roles in the pending conflict.

Roger and Steve walked into the reactor control room at the plant, expecting to see Mason working at a computer. They were surprised to discover he was not in the room.

Roger appeared surprised. "Mason should already be working to prepare the reactors."

Steve said, "I hope his own growing fears didn't make him climb onto one of those evacuation helicopters, and fly out of here."

"I don't like this." Roger looked at his watch. "We're running out of time. We should split up and look for him."

Steve agreed and as he walked toward a locker room he realized it was so quiet in the building, he could hear his heart pounding in his ears. He began frantically running from room to room in the building, while searching for Mason.

He suddenly stopped running after he heard the faint sounds of a man gasping for air, while choking. He rushed into a nearby room, thinking Mason needed medical assistance. There, rage immediately overwhelmed his concern when he saw something unexpected. "What the hell are you doing in here?"

"Jesus man, what the hell are you doing! What the freak do you think you're doing, shouting at me that way?" Mason appeared terrified as he stood upright, dropping a small black plastic straw onto the floor. He held his nose while backing toward a wall. He quickly wiped the white powder from it. His face became red from the embarrassment after being startled. "I'm not doing anything. Nothing at all that concerns you!"

Steve saw several short rows of white powder arranged on top of a black laptop computer case. He slid a finger through them. Then he carefully placed some of the powder on his tongue. He immediately recognized the unique taste of sweet and sour vinegar and salt. "You're snorting god damn cocaine before you're going to operate the reactors? What the hell is wrong with you? Are you stupid, or you just don't give a damn about staying alive!"

"This is nothing." Mason briefly pointed at the powder, before brushing it off the computer. "See, it's gone! I was just having some fun, while I was killing time waiting for you. No damage done!"

"You're doing drugs, hours before we attack a killer cloud that's intent on eating your god damn body?"

"I needed something, to help me relieve the tension. The pressure you're all putting on my mind is starting to get to me, Doc."

"What is wrong with you?"

"Nothing man! What's your damn problem! Calm down! Relax! A hit of cocaine will help me think more clearly when your cloud gets here."

"Are you stupid? You believe cocaine helps you think clearly?" Steve pushed Mason backward until his body pressed against the wall behind him. "Do you know what that shit is doing to your mind and body?"

"It's not doing anything." Mason unexpectedly appeared annoyed. His tone changed. "Open your ears. It'll make me more alert for whatever is going to happen. It may keep you alive, Doc."

"You're using drugs, and justifying it by saying it will help you keep me alive?" Steve's hands clenched tightly from growing anger. "You're a fool if you think cocaine will help you get through this battle."

"What's going on in here?" Roger said, after rushing into the room. "I heard you two shouting down the hall."

"I found this fool pushing cocaine up his nose!" Steve pointed at Mason. He realized his hand trembled from anger, and he needed to quickly regain control of his emotions.

"You're doing drugs, when you should be working at those reactor controls?" Roger appeared horrified. "What are you thinking?"

"I told you're partner, it's nothing! I've been doing this for years at work, when I need to relax and think clearly."

"Do you think he's in any shape to do his part when we attack Osiris, Steve?" Roger stared at Mason while the tall skinny man's hands trembled uncontrollably.

"He's got to do the job for us!" Steve slid a hand over his short dark hair. "We can't get anyone else in here to help us now!"

"Let's go!" Roger firmly grasped Mason's arm. He dragged him toward the control room. "It's time to start doing your job."

"Hey, take it easy, man." The tall thin man stumbled several times. Inside the control room, he sat at a computer console, before he began entering instructions while watching television monitors showing the interiors of the three containment buildings.

"Can we still destroy Osiris with him high on drugs?" Roger watched, as Mason appeared exhausted while resting his head on a hand, as he read a reactor operation manual.

"If we keep him away from the damn drugs, and keep pushing him hard, I think we can get him to release the radiation when it's needed to destroy Osiris." Steve began to relax. He felt guilty about manhandling the only person who volunteered to remain at the plant. He suddenly felt an overwhelming sense of compassion for the man, and said, "Mason, how are you doing?"

The man rubbed his nose with the back of a hand. He inhaled loudly before looking up. "I'm going over the notes I wrote during our meetings the past couple of days. This whole show of killing the cloud is a no brainer, man. This will all be over in a few minutes, after I start the process."

The man's response immediately concerned Steve. "You think this operation is a no brainer? I heard that same expression many times in Iraq before unpretentious situations got unexpectedly crazy, chaotic, and very deadly."

"That's because I wasn't there to save your ass, man!" Mason laughed. "I always say everything I do is a no brainer. I'm smarter than most other people are. I can do things other people can't comprehend, or even imagine."

Steve remembered Osiris destroying the fleeing Hummers when they attempted to capture a sample of the bacteria. "Don't underestimate Osiris! It's a living organism that thinks, it's a cunning hunter, and it's very dangerous!"

"I'm not afraid of anything." Mason grinned while sitting back on the chair with hands behind his head.

"That's too bad." Steve thought about mistakes and ill-conceived missions in Iraq and Afghanistan, where soldiers died needlessly. "Being afraid can keep you alive if situations get hot."

"What are you saying?" Mason did not understand the ominous warning message. He frowned, skeptically. "I should be afraid to be here? Come on man, you can't be serious! Nothing can get into this building. It's a fortress!"

"You'll keep us alive, and you'll stay alive a lot longer, if you're as afraid of Osiris as we are." Steve felt his anger growing as he attempted to explain the severity of the planned deadly encounter with Osiris.

"I'm not afraid of too many things, Doc. Maybe you need to take a pill and chill, so you relax while you watch me kill the cloud!"

"Take it easy, Steve," Roger said. "Getting upset again isn't going to help the situation."

"I'm fine." Steve unexpectedly felt himself trembling from the fear and apprehension of what was to come.

"Shouldn't you two be doing something more constructive than watching and harassing me?" Mason smiled at the men.

"There's nothing else for us to do," Roger said. "We'll wait for Osiris to get here with you."

"Fine. Do whatever." Mason rolled his chair to a control panel. He rubbed his nose while pushing red, orange, green, and blue buttons.

"What are you doing now?"

"Are you checking up on me to make sure I'm doing my job?" Mason laughed sarcastically. "I'm moving the cranes into position in the containment buildings to lift the covers off the three reactor shells."

"How long will that work take to complete?"

310

"It'll take me about two hours to move the overhead cranes and equipment into position, and an hour to do the heavy lift."

"After the reactors are uncovered, what do we do next to get ready for Osiris?"

"I'll prepare the equipment and get it into position to lift the fuel rod assembly out of the cooling pool, whenever we need them."

"How will that allow you to attack the cloud?" Roger asked. He watched a crane moving in one of the containment buildings, on a television monitor.

"Lifting the fuel rods will release radiation into the atmosphere, to kill your Osiris buddy."

"When you're done, and we're ready for Osiris, we'll contact Brenton and ask for a status from his end." Steve stepped behind Mason while watching him work. He thought, *This guy is in his fifties. Why is he risking his life in here with us? I don't understand why he's doing something that can potentially kill him.*

Mason sensed he was being watched. "Don't worry Doc. The cocaine isn't going to affect my work!"

Steve sat on a nearby table. He took a deep breath to relax. "How long have you been using drugs?"

"About twenty years."

"Are you joking with me?" Steve was shocked and became more alarmed, while considering the medical risks associated with Mason being in the reactor control room.

"I've used marijuana, PCP, animal tranquilizer, cocaine, fentanyl, and a few other more potent

311

drugs. I've even crushed prescription pain killer pills into powder so I could inhale them to make me feel good."

"You may have heart and lung problems you're not aware of yet. Problems that can lead to strokes, and heart attacks."

"Don't try to scare me, Doc! I'm fine! I think that medical problem hype is something started by our government, so people don't buy and use drugs."

"You really believe that conspiracy theory?" Steve stared at him.

"Yes I do! It's a pathetic government attempt started to stop people from using drugs by frightening them."

Steve looked at the floor while slowly shaking his head in disbelief after listening to Mason's comments. "I can't tell you how many people I've watch die in the hospital emergency department, from heart failure and heart attacks, induced by their use of illegal drugs. It's not a pleasant way to die!"

"Believe me, drugs don't hurt you."

"How do you know that?"

"I started smoking marijuana. Then I dropped acid for ten years. After that, I switched to cocaine and the stronger drugs to keep me mentally sharp, and superior to my co-workers."

"Doesn't your company have a drug testing program?"

"It does." He laughed. "I think they know I use drugs almost on a daily basis!"

"Why would they keep you employed here knowing you're stoned or baked or whatever, in

312

such a high risk job where one mistake can trigger a disastrous and deadly nuclear accident?"

"They know I'm too valuable a guy to lose off their organizational chart." He nodded, reinforcing his idea of his importance within the company.

"What does your family think about you being here with us, and this deadly encounter we have planned with Osiris?"

"I don't have a family."

"I'm sorry, no one told me." Steve realized his question was out of place.

"My wife died in a commuter plane crash a few years back. I never remarried."

Steve felt worse after the shocking revelation. "Do you have any kids?"

"No. We didn't want the responsibility that goes with raising them. It actually worked out better for me."

"In what way?" Steve looked at his watch. He wondered where Osiris was located.

"I don't have the interruption of a family life. I'm able to concentrate on my technical manuals at night after work."

"How does that help you?"

"Everyone considers me the intellectual member of the control room staff."

"Is that right?" Steve's jaw tightened as he became concerned.

"I'm the most experienced member of the team. Everyone comes to me for help."

Steve watched Mason as he continued working at the control panel. He thought, '*No family, an avid drug user, and considers himself an intellectual.*

313

Not the kind of person I'd want in combat, or in this control room when things get hot. He has nothing to live for. The cocaine has weakened his heart, and if he suffers a heart attack while he's panicking, we're dead!'

Roger walked across the room, and said in a whisper, "Let's not leave him alone."

Steve nodded. "One of us should always be with him. That'll prevent him from using any more drugs."

"What're you going to do now?" Roger studied a television set, carrying a newscast.

"I've got to write a couple of notes to my family, and some people at the hospital."

Roger sighed. "I've got to write my will. I'm leaving my company to charity if I die here, so they can use the money to help people."

"That's a great idea." Steve smiled while shaking friend's hand. "Have a seat. I have a pad and pens we can use to write notes."

Chapter 13

'This sterile white control room reminds me of an operating room.' Steve sat at a desk, after suddenly remembering several upsetting events during his time in Iraq and Afghanistan. His hands clenched tightly while remembering speeding through narrow, dark, and deserted city streets in Hummers at night with other soldiers, while insurgents shot at the vehicles from rooftops.

He remembered one particular medical rescue mission, where he futilely struggled to save the lives of two American soldiers ambushed by insurgents. Both soldiers were shot and stabbed repeatedly during the unexpected and brutal encounter. He felt his body trembling while remembering the overwhelming sense of helplessness, while he frantically worked to save their lives, and their subsequent tragic deaths several moments apart. The frustration and failure made him curse, before he quietly prayed over the bodies of the two fallen heroes. He remembered staring at the warm red blood from the two soldier's wounds staining his uniform and hands, and his sense of personal failure when he could not save their lives.

He looked up at the television set to watch a news report to clear his mind, but then Steve shuddered while remembering and reliving the ambush that almost took his life. It was a scorching hot day in Iraq when powerful improvised explosive devices destroyed several Hummers and trucks carrying doctors and medical supplies to care for children and the elderly in villages. After the blinding and deafening explosions, he remembered being dazed and disoriented, as insurgents shot at him, and other survivors. Army and Marine helicopter gunships soon intervened to kill the insurgents, and save the survivors of the ambush. *'I survived every one of those deadly encounters, but never understood the reason why I didn't die. Now, I finally understand my mission in life is to destroy Osiris. God spared my life in combat, to have me fight my greatest battle here at home. I hope God, or his angels, are here to help and guide me tonight.'*

He sat back, twisting a pen nervously in his fingers. *'I may die here tonight. I was always upset with myself for not telling people how much I cared about them before I shipped out to Iraq. I'm not going to make that mistake tonight. I have to write a will. Then I'll write a letter to Bonnie. I want her to know how much she means to me. I want her to understand I love her very much.'*

Steve's eyes filled with tears while writing his will, as he documented leaving his possessions to his family. As he stuffed the written document into an envelope, he mentally relived the horrifying encounter when he and Bonnie fled from Osiris in the Hummer. It seemed as if it was years ago, instead of only days. Another scene filled his mind. He smiled, almost feeling the sensations while he and Bonnie made love passionately in the hotel room.

Roger felt restless and nervous as he changed the television channels, while taking a short break as he struggled to compose his will. He noticed every channel carried a news report describing the horrific deaths and destruction caused by Osiris. The graphic videos of raging fires and clothed skeletons covering the roads, sidewalks, and lawns began to overwhelm him with grief.

He became angry after a television network aired an in-depth story of his family, and childhood. He felt the tears welling in his eyes while staring at pictures of his parents, and the horrific car crash that took both of their lives. When the story became focused on his father's obsessive drinking and alcoholism he changed the channel, but found a similar story on another network.

One hour later Steve slipped the long and detailed letter he wrote to Bonnie, into an envelope. He was satisfied his written words conveyed his true feelings and love for her. He noticed Roger staring at the television. "Are those reporters saying anything we haven't heard before?"

"Their so-called experts are predicting what Osiris will do when it gets to this power plant." He laughed. "It's not pretty."

Steve began laughing. "Experts? What do they see for our future in their crystal balls?"

"They say we're going to die."

Mason said, "Those reporters are dumb as shit! Never listen to those fools. They're always lying to the public to get you to do what the government wants! They treat us like cattle being taken to the slaughter!"

"What they're predicting, will happen."

"What are you talking about?" Mason frowned questioningly as he became alarmed.

"We are going to die." Steve smiled. "But it's not going to be today!"

"That's not funny, man! You're playing with me!" Mason went back to work. "Keep your deranged morbid thoughts to yourself!"

Roger said, "Some of the reporters are saying Osiris is unstoppable."

"No, it's not! It's vulnerable and we know its weak spot, like any other living organism. Radiation will kill it."

"A lot of the reporters are predicting the end of the world after we fail here."

"Believe me, I won't let that happen." Steve became defiant, mentally pushing aside his personal fears.

"Roger, Steve, are you there?" Brenton's voice blared from the military radio on a table in the control room, startling the men.

Roger lifted the microphone. "Yes we're here, General. We're sitting with Mason while he prepares the reactors."

"I urgently need to speak to Steve." Brenton's voice sounded strained, and unusual. "It's imperative we talk now. This cannot wait."

Steve took the microphone. "What's going on now, General?"

Brenton paused, as if the normally self-assured senior military commander was searching for the correct words. "I have some bad news to relay to you, Son."

"Did Osiris change direction? Is it moving away from the plant and we're not going to have an opportunity to attack the cloud?"

"Stop talking, and listen to me!" Brenton paused, after realizing he was shouting into the microphone while his staff watched him. "This has nothing to do with Osiris."

"I don't understand." Steve became more concerned. "What's going on?"

Brenton studied the faces of his staff. The men and women appeared somber, almost defeated. "I don't know how to tell you this."

"Is it my family?" He began to panic. "Did something happen to them?"

"No, they're safe. This is about Bonnie."

"Bonnie?" Steve frowned at Roger. "What about her?"

"I'm sorry to have to tell you this. She was killed in a helicopter crash during the evacuation of people from the power plant."

"What? What the hell are you saying?" Steve appeared confused. He sat on a chair, his strong legs suddenly unsteady. He suddenly felt dizzy, and unbalanced. "This can't be right. It can't be."

"I'm sorry to report I do have confirmation the helicopter she was riding in, went down after it exploded. We assume the aircraft suffered an in-flight mechanical failure." Brenton rested his arm on the radio, then his head on his hand. He suddenly and inexplicably felt exhausted.

"I'm so sorry this happened," Roger said, while at a loss for more compassionate words. "I don't know what to say."

"What am I going to do with her?" Steve sat on a chair before burying his face in his hands.

"Are you still there?" Brenton said. "Someone talk to me."

Roger lifted the radio microphone. "Give us some time, General. This news is a shock."

"I'm glad I wasn't on that egg beater," Mason said. "I'd be dead and rotting right now."

"Shut your god damn mouth, now," Roger said. "You're not helping the situation with those remarks."

"I need a few minutes to be alone, so I can think." Steve stood. His legs felt weak while he stumbled forward. His heart raced while images of Bonnie smiling and laughing overwhelmed his mind. The sudden shocking loss paralyzed him both mentally, and physically. "I don't understand how this could have happened?"

"I'll wait here for you." Roger looked at Mason, remembering his drug addiction. "I can't leave."

"Yeah, no problem. Just need a few minutes to think this through." Steve mumbled incoherently while walking out of the control room.

"You don't have to be alone," Roger said, shouting toward the door. "We can talk this out together."

Steve stepped into the humid night air outside the building. He walked aimlessly between the abandoned military and construction vehicles scattered across large parking lots. Tears flowed from his eyes before they ran down his cheeks. *'How can Bonnie be dead? She just left. I just saw her. I just kissed her a few minutes ago.'*

320

He walked across a grassy area, oblivious to the deafening sounds of the large nearby electrical generators used to light the exteriors of the containment buildings. *'I love you Bonnie. I wanted you to be my wife, but I didn't find the time to ask you. I should have asked you to marry me today. Why didn't I ask you to marry me, before you climbed onto that helicopter? You died, not knowing I wanted you to be my wife!'*

His grieving was interrupted unexpectedly in the darkness and solitude moments later, when he heard something cutting through the air behind him. Moments later, a wide steel construction shovel struck the back of his head. The impact jerked his head forward violently. He stumbled forward, hurting and dazed.

'What's going on? What just hit me?' Steve reached for the terrible throbbing pain behind his head, as he stumbled to the side. He felt warm blood flowing onto his hands from a deep open wound. Moments later the shovel struck his head again. The terrible pain forced a loud cry from his mouth. He collapsed to his knees, stunned, seemingly paralyzed from the pain. The shovel struck the side of his head again. That painful blow forced him to fall onto the grass on his stomach.

'What, what just happened?' Bright multi-colored flashes of light in his eyes blinded Steve. Thinking was impossible as he fought back the pain, and rapidly approaching unconsciousness. He struggled to lift himself to his hands and knees. As he gasped for air, the shovel struck the right side of his body. The impact forced the air out of his lungs.

It propelled him onto his back. Painful spasms began cramping damaged muscles. He squinted at the brightly lighted plant, but his vision became blurred. The sounds of the generators became deafening as he slipped closer to unconsciousness.

"Who, who are, are you? What's going, going on? What do you want?" Steve struggled to speak after he saw the tall person standing beside him. He was unsure if the person was real, or his imagination was playing tricks. Moments later, a sharp stabbing pain blinded him and caused him to cry out, after the shovel struck his head again. It bruised his jaw and the side of his face. Blood began running from his mouth, ear, and eye.

"The famous Doctor isn't a superman after all," the person said, before laughing. "You're such a fool! You trust everyone, you dumb shit!"

Steve thought he recognized a woman's voice. His body convulsed from the unbearable pain. "Why are you doing this to me?"

"I led you on all this time! You never knew why I wanted to get close to you!"

"Bonnie, why are you doing this to me?" Steve believed the woman he loved was abusing and punishing him, for a reason he could not understand or comprehend. He looked for her in the shadows around the vehicles while calling out her name. As he did, someone kicked his head with a shoe, blurring his vision again. He rolled to the side, with dirt on his hands and clothing.

"What do you want?" Steve took several deep breaths, attempting to relieve the almost debilitating pain in his chest. He slowly raised his head. "I love you!"

"There's no love involved in this." The person laughed. "It's strictly business and revenge, where I stop you from hurting our nation and government."

"You told me you loved me! How can you do this to me?" The ringing in Steve's ears began subsiding as his head cleared, and his eyes began to focus on the surroundings. He rolled onto his stomach before spitting salty warm blood onto the grass. As he looked around, he realized he made a terrible mistake while dazed and confused. He was relieved to see it was not Bonnie attacking him, as he watched Troxell laughing beside him. "Why are you here, fighting with me?"

"I can't allow you to hurt Osiris, until my team of medical experts located several miles from here, secures samples of the bacteria." Troxell smiled while waving away the bugs swarming around his shaved head, as he pointed a handgun at Steve. "Osiris will become our military's ultimate biological weapon!"

"I don't understand anything you're saying!" Steve slowly raised himself to a kneeling position on his hands and knees, before spitting out more warm blood. The spasms of chest pains forced him to take long and slow breaths.

"You only need to understand my job is to ensure you're not a threat to Osiris, ass hole." Troxell stared transfixed at the injured man like a predator surveying wounded prey, before the kill. He checked his watch. "Get up, and start walking! I'm wasting time talking to you!"

"I can't walk!" Steve gasped for air, while fighting off the spasms of pain causing his body to shudder. "I hurt too much."

"Get up off the god damn ground, ass hole!" Troxell grasped Steve's wrist, before violently pulling him to his feet. He enjoyed listening to the injured man's cries of pain. He began violently pushing him forward while punching the injured man's back to continue the punishment. He smiled while feeling triumphant, while watching Steve stagger toward the control room.

"What're you going to do to us?" Steve held his aching ribs with one hand. He rubbed his badly bruised face with the other, as spasms of pain brought tears to his eyes.

"I'll tell you before I shoot you. Keep walking."

"What're you doing here?" Steve leaned against the exterior wall of the building housing the control room, as the pain became overwhelming.

"We're going inside so I can tell your ass hole buddy Roger why I need to kill all of you!" Troxell laughed while violently pushing him through the entrance doors, and into the building.

Roger heard a loud and frightening commotion in a hallway, before he watched Steve's body crash through the access doors of the control room. He was shocked to see Steve collapse onto the floor. He became alarmed after noticing the black and red bruises marking the side of his face. "My God, what happened to you out there? Are you okay?"

"He'll be fine, until I kill the ass hole." Troxell said, after stepping into the brightly lighted control room. He laughed, while pointing the handgun at

324

the men. "If you don't do anything stupid, you'll get to live a few minutes longer!"

"What are you doing here, Troxell? You were supposed to go out on an evacuation helicopter." Roger frowned at the handgun. "That weapon won't stop Osiris."

Mason stood at a computer console, while staring transfixed at the handgun. "What's up with that gun, man? You're not flaking out cause of the pressure, are you?"

"Shut up, you drug induced waste of a human life!" Troxell's eyes opened wide as he spoke. He looked maniacal, and seemingly insane. "I'm going to do the world a favor when I kill you!"

"Kill me?" Mason became terrified. He felt his body tremble from sudden and uncontrollable fear. "What are you talking about, man? You're looney and you need some help or some drugs to calm that inner rage!"

"Shut the hell up, ass hole! No one will miss a burned out hippie fool, after I put a bullet in your goddamn head! I should get a medal for helping to end the drug crisis when I kill you!

"Are you crazy?" Mason trembled while briefly looking at Roger questioningly, before he stared at Troxell's handgun. "We can do a deal here. Do you want my drugs? Is that why you're here? Take them. I have a huge stash in my locker, and I manufacture PCP in my garage at home. You can have all of it. You don't need to kill us. Why do you want to kill us, man?"

"I need to ensure you're all dead, so you can't do anything to harm Osiris."

"Are you insane?" Roger began to panic. "We need to kill Osiris today! If we don't stop the bacteria here, it'll move on to kill millions of innocent men, women, and children."

"I don't care about those dying fools. They can all die in agony. They're not important."

"We're the good guys, trying to help, man!" Mason said, shouting almost incoherently while frantically pointing at Troxell. "Why do you want to kill the good guys trying to help people stay alive?"

"You three are the government's biggest problems right now, and need to be stopped." Troxell's eyes became wide with enthusiasm, while imagining watching the men suffer and die, after he shot them. "I'm going to kill all of you ass holes, so you're no longer a problem!"

Steve slowly stood as his body ached, before unsteadily leaning against a wall. He wiped the blood from his face with a sleeve of his shirt. "Which deranged person in our government sees us as a problem?"

"When your bacteria destroyed that military laboratory, it triggered the creation of a new and unexpected life form."

"A new life form based on what?" Steve looked at Roger, who shrugged questioningly.

"Osiris combined or mutated, or whatever the hell it did, with Frostfire in that laboratory."

"Frostfire?" Steve frowned. "What is that?"

"A hybrid biological weapon the government is developing. That's what turned Osiris into a lethal flesh eating machine."

326

"The government inadvertently turned Osiris into a killing machine!" Roger said. "And killing us will ensure no one knows the truth about what happened."

"You're not as dumb as you look, Samulson!" Troxell looked at his watch. "My biological team of doctors is securing a sample of the bacteria from the cloud right now. A sample we'll turn into a deadly weapon that we'll use to intimidate all of our enemies and allies into submission!"

"You can't control the bacteria. It's a killing machine," Steve said. "It thinks and has intelligence, but you can't communicate with it. It's useless as a weapon."

"Our government doesn't have to control it or talk to it, ass hole. Just having the bacteria in our arsenal will keep our enemies in line for the next five hundred years."

"You would release an unstoppable bacterium onto the world, to attack another nation?"

"I would do it, if it meant saving our great nation from attack!"

"You need a flipping psychiatrist, because you have some serious personal issues." Steve shook his head. "Who sent you here to kill us?"

"The White House sent me here to stop you."

Steve's mouth fell open after the startling and shocking revelation. "The President knows you came here to stop us from destroying Osiris?"

"That fool doesn't know what's going on inside his own government agencies, and military. His highest ranking civilian and military advisors sent me here to clean up this mess."

327

"You're an assassin?" Mason said. "You're a government killer!"

"I'm the best at eliminating people who become problems for our government." Troxell laughed. "Killing you will take no skill at all."

Steve squinted at the man's handgun, while thinking. He said, "Did you kill the people at our research camp in Arizona?"

"Of course I did." Troxell laughed comically, while enjoying the sensation of power over the frightened men. "I also helped to kill Powell in his jet."

"Why kill a messenger doing everything he could to protect the government?"

"He knew too much about Frostfire. His knowledge posed a risk to our nation's leaders."

An image of Kirsten Rusnak appeared in his mind. Steve remembered the sun shining on her red hair during their lunchtime walks around the hospital in Miami. Moments later a horrific image flooded into his mind. He watched the flesh burning and peeling from her skull, before scorching red flames consumed her entire body, when Troxell murdered her and other researchers with the gas explosion. He shuddered while imagining her screaming hysterically from the burning searing pain in the last moments of her life. He pushed the gruesome scene from his mind as his anger became uncontrollable. "You're the hero that's been killing people since you got here!"

Troxell nodded while smiling. "I ensured no one found a way to stop Osiris. I killed your scientist

328

geeks, the military, and your slut girlfriend. I enjoyed killing every one of them."

"Why did you kill Bonnie?" Steve felt his heart racing, as his anger and a need for revenge rapidly intensified. "She wasn't a threat to you!"

"The reporter bitch might have figured out I was killing people. She had to die to protect our government, so I put a bomb on her evacuation helicopter to eliminate that threat."

That admission enraged Steve. "You're a God damn animal!" He stepped forward to attack the killer, ignoring the almost debilitating pain causing his body to shudder, while craving revenge.

"Don't do anything stupid." Troxell pointed the handgun at him. "Enjoy the few minutes you have left to live."

"Someone will realize you murdered us, and those other people." Roger defiantly crossed his arms. "They'll be an investigation, and it will all come back to you."

"No one will care about the deaths of some geeks." Troxell took a deep breath to control his growing excitement, knowing he was about to kill helpless people again. "Osiris will destroy your bodies. Your own bacteria will eliminate the evidence of your murders."

"The bacteria will continue killing people if we don't stop it here! Please don't do this. Let us continue with our work here to save innocent people!"

"The government scientists who are much smarter than you, say Osiris will burn itself out north of here. We'll see what happens."

"What about the people it continues to kill? You can't let them die without trying to help them. Work with us to save them!"

"I don't give a shit about anyone." Troxell laughed, almost hysterically. "My only concern is protecting my government. I'm guaranteeing our leaders come out of this mess you created, untouched and looking like heroes."

A screeching high-pitched sound suddenly blared from a portable radio in Troxell's pocket, signaling an incoming message. Someone on the radio said, "Black Horse, this is Tango Zero Zero."

Troxell pulled out the radio. "This is Black Horse. What's your status, Zero Zero?"

"We're in position, but the bacteria cloud is acting strange," a government medical technician said. The technician looked around, at the twenty-five confident medical personnel readied to capture a sample of the bacteria in a deserted residential area of a town. He watched a large group of heavily armed soldiers shouting as they moved into defensive positions around the technicians.

"What the hell are you talking about?" Troxell nervously tightened his grip on the handgun. "How can a cloud act strange?"

"The cloud somehow appears to know we're here." The technician watched the swirling cloud lighted by several large floodlights mounted on military vehicles. "The cloud is moving around, as if the bacteria are preparing to hunt us."

"Get the sample of the bacteria, and get the hell out of there, now!"

"Wait, wait, something is happening!"

"What's going on? Don't screw this up! Our government needs that bacteria sample to manufacture a new biologic weapon!"

"This can't be happening! The cloud just blocked off the roads we used to drive to this position. We can't get out of here!"

"I don't give a shit if you use the Hummers and trucks to drive cross country to get out of there with the bacteria sample. Do your jobs!

"The cloud is surrounding us," the terrified technician said while staring at the swirling silver mass. "It's closing in on us! It's all around us!"

"Get the sample and evacuate the area, god damn it! We need that sample!"

Everyone in the room appeared startled when they heard the hysterical screams of men and women blaring from the radio. Gunshots accompanied the screams moments later as the terrified soldiers attempted to stop the advancing Osiris cloud. The screams became louder as the bacteria devoured people's flesh, before there was silence on the radio.

"Things aren't going as you planned?" Steve stared coldly at Troxell. "You're nothing more than an expendable fool, sent here to do a job, and you just failed!"

"Shut the hell up, ass hole!" Troxell bit his lip while thinking. "I'll kill you ass holes, and then I'll find another medical team to get a sample of the bacteria. It's time for you heroes to die!"

"Can you say that again, but this time a little louder, Troxell! I'm not sure I got the part about you killing these heroes!" The shouted request startled everyone. They immediately looked toward the control room door.

"Bonnie!" Steve smiled when he saw her standing in the doorway filming the group with a small video camera. He began laughing after realizing she was alive, and safe.

"What the hell are you doing here, bitch?" Troxell became confused and disoriented while staring at the woman.

Bonnie said, "Is there anything else you want to add to your confession? I recorded everything else you said so far, since you walked into this room."

The experienced killer mumbled incoherently while confused, as he stared at the woman he boasted about murdering minutes earlier. "You can't be alive! My bomb destroyed your god damn helicopter!"

"You're not as good as you think." She focused the camera on his face. "Actually, you're an amateur, if you ask me."

Troxell pointed the handgun at her. "I can correct any of my mistakes, permanently."

Steve suddenly realized his experiences in combat might now save his life, and those of the others. He made a tight fist while pulling back his arm. Then he lunged forward, ignoring the pain, to violently strike Troxell's wrist. "I'm putting an end to this insanity, now!"

The impact knocked the handgun from the assassin's hand. Troxell was shocked, but quickly regained his composure. "You're no hero, ass hole. I'll kill you first!"

"Everyone, get down!" Steve punched Troxell's jaw with a fist, knocking the large man with the shaved head backward.

"You need to be a lot better than that." Troxell unexpectedly stepped behind Steve to wrap an arm around his attacker's neck. Then he began pulling back his arm with the other hand, to break Steve's neck.

The rapidly growing pain terrified Steve. He frantically clawed at Troxell's arms, but could not break his grip. He panicked and began struggling frantically when he realized he could not breathe. He knew it was only a matter of seconds before the viselike pressure broke his neck.

"You're nothing more than an annoyance to be crushed!" Troxell tightened his grip, by violently pulling back his arm several times to choke his victim. "You're an insect I'm going to kill."

Steve's lungs began burning, feeling as if they were about to burst from a lack of oxygen. His anger suddenly flared out of control as images of the burned soldiers Troxell murdered at the power plant flooded into his mind. He pulled an arm forward as unconsciousness began darkening his vision. Then he jammed his elbow backward into Troxell's stomach several times. Struggling wildly, he struck Troxell's groin with a fist. He struck the area again with all of his remaining strength.

"Ugh!" Troxell's body reacted to the unexpected and painful blows. He released his grip, before the shocked and hurting man staggered backward.

Steve gasped for air while turning toward his attacker. He unexpectedly reached out to grasp the front of Troxell's trousers, and the testicles under it. He squeezed as hard as he could. "These are small balls for a freaking tough guy like you. How does it feel to be the ass hole?"

"No! Stop!" Troxell grasped his violent attacker's wrists. The unexpected and overwhelming groin pain clouded his reasoning. He could not react. The pain quickly became unbearable, causing him to cry out.

"I'm just getting started!" Steve pushed the large man backward against a desk, while tightening his grip to apply more pressure. "I'm going to yank on this like a pull starter, until I rip it off!"

"What're you doing, man? Are you crazy?" Mason appeared terrified and frozen from fear while watching the men struggling. "Don't make him madder at us! It won't help our situation. Talk to him, man!"

"I don't know how to help, Steve!" Roger panicked. He ran forward. Stumbling, he inadvertently tackled both men to the floor.

"Get off me!" Troxell pushed Roger off his chest, before kicking his face.

"My nose is broken!" Roger began rolling on the floor holding his nose, while in agony.

"You're not going to stop me from killing you!" Troxell appeared to be angry and out of control while violently punching Steve's chest with a fist, before wrapping his hands around the man's throat to choke him.

Bonnie shuddered from almost paralyzing fear while she frantically ran across the control room, to lift the large black handgun off the floor. She pointed the weapon at Troxell while her hands shook uncontrollably. When she pulled the trigger, the recoil almost knocked the weapon from her hands. The deafening gunshot startled her, and the others. The bullet struck an overhead fluorescent light mounted in the ceiling. Shattered glass rained down into the room, before the fixture and ceiling tiles around it crashed onto the floor with a loud noise. A large amount of bright white electrical sparks began showering down into the control room.

Troxell dove onto the floor, after a second bullet ripped through a metal desk beside him. He looked up to see Bonnie pointing the handgun at him with violently trembling hands. He studied the expression on the frightened woman's face. He immediately realized the terrified amateur was unpredictable and dangerous. That realization frightened the killer who was normally in charge of every situation. "Stop shooting before someone gets hurt!"

"Stay, stay where you are," Bonnie said shouting as she struggled to hold the handgun steady. "Don't move, or I swear I'll pull the trigger again, and this time I won't miss!"

"Please, don't shoot me!" Troxell stood with hands raised. He brushed broken light fixture glass from his hair, while thinking, *This bitch is so scared she'll pull the trigger if I rush her. I may get shot four or five times. I'll be dead before I cross the*

335

twelve feet between us. Why didn't I bring my knife? This bitch would already be dead if I had a knife.'

"If that bastard moves, kill him!" Steve slowly stood. He used a shirt sleeve to wipe the blood from his face.

'I've got to get out of here, and find another way to kill all these fools, so I can get that video the bitch made of me.' Troxell unexpectedly began running wildly across the control room, toward the door. He screamed and shrieked hysterically with his arms flailing, to frighten and unnerve everyone in the room. Moments later, he disappeared into the hallway.

"Get back here, damn it!" Bonnie fired the handgun again. The bullet struck a wall near the door.

"I'll put out the fires!" Mason began frantically spraying the burning electrical wires dangling from the ceiling with a fire extinguisher.

Steve hobbled to where Bonnie continued pointing the handgun at the door with trembling hands. "I'll take this. You can relax. It's over, and you did fine." He carefully pulled the weapon from her hands, and placed it on a desk.

She looked at him, with eyes wide as if in shock. "I'm sorry I let him get away! I tried to stop him!"

"I don't care about him right now, baby. I need a long tight hug!" He wrapped his arms around her body, while enjoying the feeling of her long hair pressing against his face. He kissed her neck, then looked into her eyes before he kissed her lips passionately. "I thought I lost you!"

"No, you're stuck with me for a very long time." Bonnie smiled as she slid her fingers across the bruises on his face. Then she pressed her body tighter against him, before she kissed him passionately.

"I'm sorry to interrupt you two," Roger said, "but we still have some problems to discuss." He smiled as both Steve and Bonnie laughed after his remark.

"You're right." Steve could not stop staring into Bonnie's eyes. He kissed her again, while grasping her hand tightly to ensure she would not leave his side.

Bonnie studied the blood that flowed down Roger's face from his nose. "Your nose looks terrible. What can we do to help you?

"I think I'm good." He wiped the blood from his face with paper towels. "I'm still shocked knowing that damn Troxell killed the researchers and military people who were working to help us."

"He did whatever his government handlers told him to do," Steve said, "and those are the people who need to pay for trying to stop us!"

"We've got to find that murderer so we can turn him over to the police." Roger began walking toward the door.

"That's what he wants us to do." Steve grasped his arm to stop him. "There's a hundred places for him to ambush us out there in the dark."

"You're going to let that killer escape?" Roger became confused and frowned. "We've got to find him and hold him for the police."

"He'll kill us one at a time if we go after him. I know how he thinks. I've been there in combat in Iraq and Afghanistan. I know what to do in this situation, because the military taught me well." Steve paused, while thinking. "Mason, seal the control room doors so Troxell can't get in here again. We don't know if he has an arsenal of weapons out there he can use to kill us."

"Why do you want to do something so stupid, man?" The tall upset man trembled from fear. "You want to lock us in here with that killer cloud coming this way? Go out there and talk to that killer guy, and make a deal so we can get out of here!"

"Close and lock the control room doors, now!" Steve pointed at him, reinforcing his order. "We're safe in here, and you need to finish preparations to release the radiation to kill the damn cloud!"

"Troxell will die out there in the open when Osiris gets here," Roger said.

"I'd pay to watch him, suffer before he dies." Steve slipped the handgun into his pocket. "He'll probably give Osiris indigestion."

"We need to keep this safe." Bonnie pulled a compact disc from the video camera she used to record the action in the control room. She pushed it into the pocket of her tight shorts. "This is Troxell's confession."

"You're right, we need that as evidence." Steve kissed her, before he frowned as his mind attempted to comprehend everything he heard and experienced during the past several hours. "Brenton told me you died in a helicopter crash. How did you get here? How did you not die in that crash?"

"I'm alive because I noticed something suspicious during the evacuation."

"What was that?"

"I got onto that evacuation helicopter. Just as it was about to take off, Troxell suddenly jumped out, and that made me suspicious. He didn't see me get off the helicopter a few moments later. That's when I began following him to see what he was doing."

"I'm so glad you did that, baby." He stared into her eyes, while smiling.

"Oh really?" She took his hand. "Why is that?"

"You saved our lives by being here." He kissed her.

"I guess you owe me, Doc." She smiled. "You owe me big time."

Steve glanced at his watch. The reality of the deadly situation made him stop to think. "Damn, I've got to get you out of here, and we're running out of time! Osiris is still headed for this plant!"

"I don't want to go. Don't make me leave! I want to stay here with you."

"It's too dangerous." He looked at Roger. "Let's find a car or truck in the parking lot with the keys in it. She can drive out of here."

Roger frowned after the seemingly irrational statement. "That's not an option."

"She's got to leave now! It's too dangerous for her to stay here."

"She can't drive away! Not with the abandoned cars blocking the roads out of here. You can watch over her if she stays with you. She doesn't have a chance out there alone. She'll die."

"I don't want to go, Steve. I need to be here with you," Bonnie said.

"I have an idea." He lifted the radio microphone. "General Brenton? Talk to me."

"Yes Steve. What is it?"

"We've got a problem here at the plant. Bonnie is here with us."

Brenton frowned at his executive officer. He saw other members of his staff stand at their consoles, while staring at one another questioningly. "My men reported she was on a helicopter that crashed."

"They were wrong! She's alive!" He hugged her with one arm. "You've got to send an evacuation helicopter for her!"

Brenton looked at his staff as they shook their heads. "I can't do anything to help you."

"Why the hell not?" Steve became suspicious. "Why can't you help us? What's going on?"

"There's not enough time."

"Of course there is! Osiris won't be here for hours."

"She'll have to ride it out with you at that plant."

"Send a helicopter to pick her up now!" Steve frowned, growing upset with each passing second.

"Wait one. I have a high priority transmission coming in from our radar surveillance aircraft."

Steve clenched his teeth while staring at Bonnie. He admired her beauty after she whispered an emotional love message in his ear. He remembered how she intrigued him when she first burst into the convention center in Arizona. He said, "I wanted to die after Brenton told me you were dead. Now I want to strangle you because you put yourself in danger for me."

She briefly smiled. "I'd do it again too!"

He laughed. "I love you."

Bonnie brushed back her long hair. She noticed her name written on an envelope laying on a desk. "What's that?"

"A letter I wrote to you while I was sitting here thinking about how much I missed you."

"What did you put into a letter at a time like this?"

"Read it. I want you to know how I feel before anything else happens."

"Doctor, its Brenton. The AWACs radar operators, and Military Intelligence Artificial Intelligence satellite imaging, agree. Osiris is moving north rapidly in your direction."

"We didn't expect it to start moving for another eight hours." He frowned at Roger

"We have confirmation the cloud is advancing toward your position. We'll tell you when you should start lighting up the piles of tires with the incendiary explosive devices."

"We can't burn the tires while Bonnie is here! The smoke will bring the damn cloud to us!"

"If you don't burn those tires, you'll jeopardize the entire operation we planned.

"The General is right," Roger said. "You know what we have to do."

"I'll get back to you General." Steve grasped Bonnie's wrist, startling her as she read the letter. "Here's the way it's got to be. You're stuck here with me."

She smiled. "I'm where I want to be, with you."

"No matter what happens, I want you to stay by my side."

"I will do that." She smiled, as if suddenly calm and at peace. "This letter is something very special."

"I put my thoughts in writing, because I may not have told you everything on my mind during the confusion and chaos of the past week." He looked at his watch nervously. "That letter says it all."

"I love you." She wrapped an arm around his neck. "I really do."

"And there's one more thing that's not in that letter." He looked into her eyes. "When I thought you were dead I hated myself for not asking you a question earlier today when we were alone."

"What's that?" She smiled, while intrigued.

He gently took her hand. "Will you marry me when this is over? I want to spend my life with you."

She stared into his eyes, while a smile slowly formed on her lips. "I'd enjoy being your wife very much, forever. I love you."

"I love you too." He kissed her passionately, before he whispered into her ear.

She laughed, while hugging him tightly. "Let's do it."

"Very nice." Roger began clapping. "Congratulations!"

Chapter 14

"Roger? Steve? Someone talk to me!" Brenton's frantic voice unexpectedly blared from the radio, startling everyone.

Roger lifted the microphone. "We're here General." He gently rubbed his injured nose.

"Our airborne surveillance radar aircraft report the leading edge of Osiris is already ten miles north of Los Angeles!"

"How can the cloud be moving forward so fast?" Roger became tense after the ominous report.

"We may have pissed off the bacteria when my attack helicopters and bombers destroyed its food source. I'll get back to you, after my radar aircraft relay more information to my command center."

Roger appeared apprehensive while staring at Steve. "We have to set off the explosives in the buildings south of here. We don't want the Osiris to find any nourishment in that area."

"I agree." Steve motioned to a dozen green camouflaged detonators lying on a desk in the control room. "You should ensure the bacteria are starving, and bring the cloud to us."

Roger placed his fingers on the buttons of one detonator. "It's time to call Osiris, the Destroyer." He pushed the buttons, before he pushed similar buttons on all of the other detonators. Those simple actions detonated tens of thousands of explosives strategically placed into buildings. The floor vibrated as the explosions began destroying structures.

Steve heard Brenton calling him on the radio. He lifted the microphone. "What's going on General?"

"The World Health Organization estimates Osiris may have killed one million people in Los Angeles."

"One third of the city is dead?" Steve sighed, shocked by the news.

Brenton studied a topographical map. "You've got to stop the bacteria at that plant, or our entire nation is at risk of being destroyed."

"We're trying to do the job, but we're getting outside interference."

"Interference of what type?" Brenton frowned questioningly at his staff. "Explain that statement."

"When you talk to the President, ask him for an explanation of Frostfire." Steve's fist clenched with anger, while thinking about Troxell attacking him.

"Frostfire? I've never heard of it." Brenton scribbled notes on a pad. His aides shook their heads, indicating they did not recognize the cryptic word. "What is that?"

"It's the name of a new," Steve said, as he began explaining what he knew.

Brenton unexpectedly interrupted him. "Wait one Steve! I'm getting an urgent updated report from our radar aircraft."

"What is it telling you?"

"Osiris is now moving north rapidly."

"When can we expect it to be here?" Steve stared at the radio, waiting for the response he dreaded.

"Based on Intelligence projections and radar simulations, Osiris will be at your location in two hours."

344

"Are you still bombing the areas ahead of the advancing cloud?"

"We're burning everything in its path to the ground."

"Depriving it will ensure the bacteria is hungry and needs nourishment. It will have to come to us for food."

"I'll have to get back to you, Steve. Pentagon Intelligence wants to discuss this rapidly escalating situation."

"We'll be here. Keep us updated."

"You didn't have a chance to tell him about Frostfire, or Troxell." Bonnie said, as she appeared disappointed.

"I have an idea." Steve smiled. "Write down everything we know about Troxell and Frostfire on pads. We'll leave a record of what we know."

Thirty tense minutes later Brenton contacted Steve. "Osiris now appears to be racing toward your location. The cloud is immense."

"That's perfect." Steve shuddered, attempting to conceal his growing apprehension. "An immense, killer cloud."

"Wait one! Wait one!" Benton turned toward his radar technicians after they began shouting in the tent, startling soldiers working around them.

"What's going on? I hear someone screaming!" Steve placed a hand on Bonnie's shoulder as she documented Troxell's involvement in the government cover up. He smiled as he gently slid his fingers through her soft hair.

Brenton's voice blared from the radio. "The cloud's forward movement has stopped! Osiris is now stationary! It's not moving, gentlemen! What are your thoughts?"

"It never stopped moving before now." Steve frowned while thinking. "Why now?"

"Multiple radar images from the ground and surveillance aircraft confirm the cloud is at a standstill."

"Maybe it's confused," Roger said, after thinking about the scenario. "Maybe it can't sense a food source, as it grows weaker from a lack of nourishment."

"What are you talking about, man?" Mason's facial expression conveyed his confusion. "Are you saying it's looking for a supermarket to get food?"

"In a way, you're correct Mason." Steve nodded, agreeing. "It doesn't know which way to move to find food."

"We should burn the tires so it knows nourishment is here." Roger looked at another group of detonators on a desk.

"It's still a hundred miles south of here. Do you think it will sense the rubber is here?"

"The bacteria knew there was food in San Diego, when it was in Las Vegas. That's four hundred miles away."

Steve nodded. "Ok, let's light up the tires."

Roger began pushing buttons on the detonators. "Come to your last supper, Osiris." He heard the sounds, when drums of incendiary explosives buried in all the piles of tires began exploding. Huge streaks of red searing flames erupted outward from the barrels in the darkness, to cover the large piles of tires with burning liquid.

"I want to see what's going on outside. Mason, open the control room doors." Steve pulled the handgun out of his pocket before he cautiously led everyone to the building's front doors, and then onto the exterior steps. They stood in winds created by the growing tire fires around the plant, now lighting up the night sky.

"Those fires are burning hot! They're creating a huge updraft, and generating these winds." Roger said, shouting so he could be heard. He pointed at the orange flames destroying the tires, now shooting hundreds of feet into the night sky.

"We're going to fry out here." Mason shaded his face from the searing heat of burning tires with his hands.

Acrid dense black smoke began blanketing the area around the power plant. The smoke occasionally reduced visibility to ten feet, and soon made breathing difficult.

"All of the piles of tires are burning." Steve stared through the smoke, at the flames. The growing infernos illuminated wide black rivers of molten rubber flowing across the ground, and on the streets and parking lots.

Bonnie grasped Steve's arm after she noticed him staring transfixed at the fires. She wiped away the tears created by the dense smoke causing her eyes to burn. "Are you all right?"

"I'm good." He turned to her while unexpectedly feeling relaxed and calm, after watching the infernos around the building.

The wind violently blew her hair into her face, forcing her to pull it back with a hand. "What do you see out there?"

"The enemy who tried to kill me." His jaw tightened.

"The enemy in Iraq?" She rubbed her smoke irritated burning eyes, as tears streamed down her cheeks. "I don't understand what you're telling me."

He nodded. "Now I'm going to attack another enemy, and I don't know if it can be killed." He shouted over the sounds of the howling fire driven winds, which were dramatically increasing in intensity.

"You promised you wouldn't let anything happen to me! I know you can kill Osiris." She remembered filming a story about the post-traumatic stress experienced by combat veterans. *What will I do if Steve can't deal with the pressure when Osiris gets here? We'll die, if this fight reminds him of Iraq, and he can't deal with it.'*

"I'll keep you safe. I promise." He smiled as he grasped her hand firmly. Then he led everyone back into the building.

Inside the control room, they heard Brenton's voice blaring from the radio. "Steve? Roger? Are you there?"

"This is Steve. We were outside checking on conditions. We're looking good here. All of the piles of tires are burning."

"Wait one, Doctor." Brenton took a report from his Executive Officer. "Lighting up those tires appears to have worked."

"In what way?"

"Radar images confirm Osiris is now moving toward your location."

"The burning rubber is the bait we needed to bring Osiris to us."

"You should also know the cloud's forward speed has increased significantly."

Roger tapped Steve's shoulder. "Tell him about Troxell."

Steve nodded. "General, I want to tell you how we were attacked here tonight. You have to know the details."

Brenton interrupted him. "The cloud is now two-thirds of the way to the plant."

"I'll have to get back to you General. I want to ensure we're ready on our end." Steve looked at Mason.

"Do you want me to pull the fuel rods out of the reactors?" His growing apprehension, and an overwhelming need for cocaine, caused his hands to tremble uncontrollably. His arms began flapping wildly at his sides.

Roger frowned while watching Mason's animated gestures. "Osiris has to be on top of this power plant before you release that radiation. Do you understand me?"

"No way, man! We can't wait that long. You never told me we'd have to wait that long. This is no good! No good at all, man!"

"We're not releasing radiation until Osiris is close to us," Steve said, verbally reinforcing the plan.

"You may want to die here, but I don't!" Mason rushed toward a control panel. "I'm releasing radiation now. It'll protect us from those bacteria."

Roger grasped Mason's shirt. He pulled him backward, and away from the controls. "We spent too much time putting this plan together to let you screw it up! Settle down and wait for us to tell you what to do, damn it!"

"We're going to die here! I'm not staying in this coffin control room! I've got to get out of here before it's too late!"

"There's no way to get out now. Do what we tell you and you'll walk out of here with us in a few hours."

"I can't get through this without some of my stash. I need to unwind and some of my big flakes will help me do it." Mason looked at his trembling hands. "This stress is killing me and I need some smack, now!"

"Forget it! I'm not going to let you push cocaine up your flipping nose," Steve said, with an unimpassioned tone in his voice. "Get some candy out of a vending machine."

"I need something to calm me down! Don't you understand?"

"I'm not letting you snort cocaine." Steve looked at Roger, who was shaking his head.

"I have some amyl nitrate in my office. I need a small hit to calm my nerves."

"You've got to be kidding me," Bonnie said, disgustedly. "You're a drug user working at a nuclear power plant? Should I feel safe with you at the controls?"

"Calm down, Mason!" Steve realized he was shouting, and he lowered his voice. "Sit down! I can't think while you're begging for drugs!"

"But, I need something to take the edge off, man."

"Sit down, and stop talking!" Steve pointed at a chair, signaling the end of the conversation.

Brenton's voice blared from the radio. "Steve, I'm watching Osiris on radar. This is amazing."

"What are you seeing, General? What's going on out there?"

"The bacteria cloud will be at your location in less than thirty minutes, son."

Steve pointed at the television monitors mounted on a wall in the control room. "Mason, can we see outside with those?"

"Yes, we can. I can link into the plant's security system and show you views outside this building, and around the containment buildings." The trembling man rushed to a control panel, where he powered on the monitors. "We use these knobs to control the position of the cameras on the roof of this building, and the containment buildings."

"I've used similar systems while filming and editing my stories for network television." Bonnie stepped to the controls. Images on the color monitors changed, as she repositioned cameras around the plant. She focused them on the raging smoky infernos consuming the huge piles of tires, and the exterior of the three containment buildings. "We can see everything going on outside on these monitors."

"Steve, Roger," Brenton's said, his excited voice blaring from the radio. "Radar echoes confirm Osiris has started moving toward you at an incredible speed!"

"Let's get a look at the buildings you blew up south of this plant." Bonnie repositioned several cameras, and then focused them. She studied the flames destroying buildings in the distance. "The entire horizon is red with flames. Buildings, warehouses, homes, and even trees and shrubs, must be burning in that area."

"Wow, look at that, man!" Mason squinted at the monitors. "It looks like you brought hell to earth out there. Imagine how many drug factories you just destroyed! I bought some of my stuff from a few of them."

"We destroyed everything," Roger said. "Everything people spent their entire lives building."

"You had to do it," Bonnie said, while attempting to console him.

"What is going on out there?" Steve stepped forward several minutes later, while studying several monitors after the images became blurred and seemingly fuzzy. The brightness of distant fires began to diminish slowly in intensity.

Bonnie raised a hand to her mouth while shocked, as she pointed at the monitors. "Is that Osiris obscuring our view? Is the bacteria cloud that close to us?"

"The silver cloud looks orange when it's lighted by the flames in the darkness. It's like a ghost moving toward us." Roger watched the indiscernible orange mass swirling on several monitors. "A specter of death is rolling forward toward us in the darkness."

Brenton's voice blaring from the radio startled everyone. "Steve, are you there? Are you okay?"

"We're good here. We can see Osiris is maybe twenty miles from the plant."

"Yes, yes, I see that on radar." Brenton felt his heart racing before the battle began. "Are you ready to attack the bastard?"

"We're ready here at the power plant." Steve paused to look into Bonnie's eyes, before he smiled. "Australia with you, is looking really good right now, baby."

"Australia? What does that mean?" Brenton frowned while shaking his head after the unexpected statement.

"It's a personal message, General." Steve leaned forward to kiss Bonnie.

"I'm confident God is with all of you, son." Brenton felt his hand trembling while imagining the mental state of people at the power plant, while they watched Osiris moving toward them. "Good luck."

"Take care of everyone if the battle goes on beyond today General."

"Maybe we can see which way the cloud is moving." Bonnie focused a camera on the leading edge of Osiris in the distance. She took a deep breath while watching the others stare silently and intently at the advancing swirling mass on the monitors.

"That freaking cloud is huge, man!" Mason pointed wildly at the monitors while jumping nervously on his tiptoes. "You didn't tell me it would get that big!"

"Relax, and don't panic." Steve inexplicably felt compassion for the now terrified man. He remembered seeing the same reaction in frightened young soldiers in Iraq, when situations became horrific and deadly. "Listen to us, and we'll keep you safe."

"We will do that." Roger smiled at Mason, hoping to ease the man's fears. "We'll tell you what to do."

"The enemy is about to over-run our perimeter," Steve said coldly while staring at the monitors five nerve-wracking minutes later. "The leading edge of Osiris is rolling over the plant's outer most security fences."

Mason's face became ashen from fear. "That means its only three miles from this control room!"

Brenton's voice blared from the radio. "Roger and Steve, our radar estimates indicate the bacteria cloud is now twenty-one miles in diameter."

"What the hell is that?" Steve looked up at the control room ceiling, after he felt a strange vibration.

"What did you hear?" Bonnie became alarmed when he did not immediately respond.

"It sounds like a Blackhawk helicopter." Steve listened to the distinctive sounds of the low flying aircraft. He smiled as he became excited. "Brenton must have sent in an evacuation helicopter for you."

"I'm not leaving you here alone!" She became defiant. "Use the radio. Tell them I'm staying with you."

354

Steve frowned while frantically scanning the monitors, searching for the landing aircraft. "It isn't landing near the plant. It sounds like its hovering somewhere out there."

"It may be a news helicopter," Roger said.

An excited radar operator in Brenton's command center stood, before shouting across the tent. "General, you need to see this now!"

"What is it?" He motioned to the members of his staff who were shouting instructions, indicating he wanted quiet.

"I have two unidentified airborne targets circling the plant. They're danger close to the cloud."

"Where the hell did two targets come from?" Brenton paused, while thinking about the land mass around the power plant. "Can you be seeing the leading edge of the cloud as it approaches the plant on that flat terrain?"

"Negative." The radar operator studied his screen. "I've got hard targets airborne, beside the plant, Sir."

"Give me your best assessment, Son. What are they?"

"Judging by the speed and maneuverability, they appear to be helicopters."

"What are helicopters doing in there?" Colonel John Powers looked at a monitor showing the radar images. "The area for one hundred miles around the plant is a designated no fly zone."

"Those reporters will jeopardize our mission, to be the first to get a story," Brenton said. "Radio them, and wave them off."

"I can't confirm it Sir, but they don't appear to be news helicopters," the radar operator said.

"What makes you think that? I don't have any aircraft in the area."

"They're moving too fast, and banking hard over the plant while making tight turns. They resemble military attack gunships, maybe Blackhawks or Cobras."

"I need to talk to you, now." Brenton immediately gathered his staff officers together, away from the other soldiers.

While hiding in the back of a large military truck parked near the control room, Troxell heard the sounds of two approaching Blackhawk helicopters. He pulled the radio from his pocket while scanning the sky lighted by the raging fires. Dense smoke blown by the strong winds obscured his view. He wiped away the tears flowing from his burning eyes. "Native Dawn, this is Black Horse. I'm on the ground near the control room. Where are you?"

"This is Native Dawn Zero Zero. Native Dawn Zero One has my back." The pilot struggled to identify buildings in the power plant complex, while smoke obstructed his view. "Visibility is poor. What's our primary target? I can't see anything, and these winds are more than we expected. Over."

Troxell looked around questioningly, after hurricane force winds began howling, and shaking the large heavy truck. He felt the winds blowing toward the plant from all directions as the massive piles of burning tires created violent updrafts. "Take out the control room. They're running the reactors from in there. Destroy the building and kill those people, and we'll save Osiris."

The pilots struggled with their controls as the winds increased in intensity, while they slowly circled the plant. A pilot radioed, "Black Horse, the smoke and the winds are making seeing and sighting impossible. We cannot identify the primary target. Give us a secondary target."

"Hit the damn containment buildings!" Troxell jumped out of the truck before pointing wildly into the smoke and wind. "Destroy the reactors so they can't release radiation. Use your heads! Get creative!"

"Roger that. We're moving into position to attack the containment buildings." The pilots flew away from the plant while buffeted by the increasing winds. Both aircraft turned to attack. "Get out of that area, Black Horse. We're going to make a mess of this power plant!"

"Fox One!" A pilot radioed as he fired a radar guided missile at a containment building. The smoke obscured his view, while the winds buffeted the missile. It misguidedly exploded at the base of the construction scaffolding. The towering steel structure swayed, before toppling to the side, accompanied by the deafening sounds of twisting metal. It crashed down onto trucks parked nearby. The damaged vehicles began exploding with loud and violent concussions.

"Your missile didn't hit the containment building," Troxell radioed, screaming as he became angry. "Are you blind? You can't do anything right!"

"Let's burn down this entire complex." The other pilot fired the helicopter's machine guns into military trucks parked beside buildings. Many of those vehicles began exploding in huge fireballs. Those fires spread to the plant's maintenance building.

"What're you doing?" Troxell said, screaming into his radio. "I told you to hit the containment buildings! If you destroy the reactors, they can't release radiation!"

"The fires we can ignite will spread to the plant buildings," the pilot said. He turned to his co-pilot. "This guy is crazy!"

"Hit the buildings with your damn missiles! Kill everyone inside them!" Troxell pointed furiously at the control room.

"That sounded like an explosion outside," Roger said, after hearing a helicopter fly over the building. "I felt the vibration."

Steve frowned. "Troxell must have called in a helicopter to stop us."

"That insane guy you pissed off when you attacked him, and that helicopter, want to kill us?" Mason panicked, as his fear became debilitating. He began wetting his jeans. "They're trying to kill us?"

"Maybe Osiris will rescue us when it destroys that helicopter." Roger smiled.

"Imagine that." Steve laughed. "The cloud kills Troxell and his companions, and saves us?"

"That's not funny," Mason said. "Because that means it's coming after us next."

The leading edge of the bacteria cloud silently engulfed the sprawling employee parking lot, inside the outermost security fence of the plant. The bright overhead lights on towering poles began sparking and exploding after the bacteria devoured the plastic insulation on electrical wiring. The ravenous bacteria consumed the plastic and rubber it found in a fleet of power company utility trucks. Its intelligence realized the plant was a huge food source. The ravenous bacteria deprived of nourishment, now became determined to survive.

A helicopter pilot flew his aircraft through the dense smoke, while buffeted by winds increasing in intensity. He smiled after his co-pilot fired a missile into a building housing the electrical generation turbines. The powerful explosion collapsed the immense roof of the building, and ignited fires. "Now we're cooking! Let's put missiles into those other buildings and burn this place to the ground."

"What the freak is going on?" The pilot looked down at his controls after they unexpectedly became sluggish. Moments later, they failed to respond. The tail section of the aircraft began turning to the right.

"The navigational computers went down," the co-pilot said after he watched the instrument panel darken unexpectedly. "We lost all of our damn instrumentation."

"We've navigated into the cloud, and didn't know it!" The pilot said, screaming moments later. "We're in the bacteria cloud! I've got to get us out of it!"

The pilot and co-pilot became terrified moments later, when a sudden blast of air pushed them back into their seats after Osiris devoured the plastic windshield of the helicopter. In the darkness, and while concentrating during the attack, neither man realized they inadvertently flew into the bacteria cloud. Osiris silently attacked the entire aircraft, biodegrading plastic, rubber, and flesh. The last thing the screaming men saw in the dying glow of the raging fires below was the skin bubbling away from their hands. No one heard their loud agonized screams as Osiris devoured their bodies, leaving only white skeletal remains.

Troxell looked overhead into the sky lighted by raging red flames leaping from the piles of tires, after he heard an unusual sound. He could not know it was the sounds of a helicopter engine failing with metal ripping apart, after Osiris destroyed crucial components. He fell to the ground warily when the disabled helicopter swooped low over his head, before it crash violently into a nearby parking lot. A powerful explosion hurled metal fragments and rotor blades outward like shrapnel.

As vehicles damaged by the crash began exploding nearby, Troxell surveyed the devastation as he stood. His concern was not for the dead pilots or destroyed aircraft, but for their failed mission. He radioed the other helicopter crew. "You're the last hope. Wipe this plant off the map. Put a missile into every building."

"Wilco, we're moving into attack position to hit the plant in force. We will extract you after our mission is accomplished." As the pilot flew through the dense smoke, something unexplainably buffeted his aircraft. He attributed the turbulence to the winds. Several seconds later, the pilot reached to his face, when a strange numbing sensation spread across the skin. He pulled back his fingers in shock after feeling the exposed bones of his jaw and teeth.

Neither pilot realized Osiris was already devouring their flesh after the cloud reached out to surround their aircraft. The two men screamed as the bacteria invaded the interior of the helicopter, to strip the flesh from their bones.

'This cannot be happening to me!' Troxell watched the second helicopter explode violently after crashing into a field west of the power plant. He began running toward the containment buildings. *'Incompetent fools! I'll have to kill McClellan and those others myself!'*

"Should we tell Brenton about that helicopter?" Roger watched the wreckage burning on a monitor.

"We don't have time." Steve intently studied another monitor. "Osiris is almost on top of us."

"The cloud is moving toward a pile of burning tires!" Bonnie nervously pointed at a monitor with a trembling hand.

Twenty seconds later, the swirling cloud unexpectedly stopped advancing. The glow of the raging fires, and the military floodlights, lighted the swirling silver mass.

Bonnie squinted at the monitor. "What is it doing? Why did the cloud suddenly stop?"

Everyone apprehensively watched a huge finger like area of the cloud advance to cover a portion of the burning pile of tires. Steve frowned before he said, "It's studying the flames before it moves into them."

Roger shook his head as if shocked by the bacteria's intelligence. "It's comparing them to the

361

flames it's already been exposed to, while it destroyed cities on its way here."

"It learned how to recognize potential danger. We may have underestimated its thought process."

Moments later the cloud lurched forward to surround the pile of burning tires. It began devouring the rubber to quench its hunger, and its rapidly growing need to survive.

"The bacteria is smothering the fires to get at the rubber." Roger watched the action on a monitor. "We're watching it learn to put out fires."

"The cloud formed that tunnel shaped cone to surround the smoke." Bonnie focused a camera on the raging orange flames, and the smoke rising off them.

"Why's it doing that?" Mason's body trembled from his growing terror. He did not understand anything the cloud was doing outside the control room. "Is it playing with the smoke like a child?"

Roger realized his mouth was dry from nervousness, and he found it difficult to speak. "The bacteria is sucking the burned rubber particles out of the smoke for nourishment."

Several minutes later Osiris began devouring the unburned tires in the pile, after it completely smothered the raging flames. A wide section of the cloud slid across nearby roads and parking lots, biodegrading the long and wide rivers of molten black rubber. The hot flowing rubber appeared to evaporate into the air as the bacteria consumed the liquid for nourishment.

"The bacteria is reaching out and going after another pile of burning tires!" Bonnie felt her anxiety increasing while watching a tentacle like portion of the cloud slide across a parking lot.

Osiris silently slid from one pile of burning tires to another. At every pile, it methodically extinguished the flames. Then it consumed the tires for life sustaining nourishment.

"It's moving toward the containment building furthest from us!" Bonnie held her breath while watching the cloud slide across a parking lot, where it destroyed trucks, and the equipment on them. Many of the vehicles began burning, before the equipment and supplies loaded on them, and their fuel tanks, violently exploded with deafening sounds and powerful concussions.

"The bacteria are eating the thousands of tires we stacked beside that containment building," Steve said. "Osiris took the bait."

"It looks like your bacteria is scoping out the cooling towers," Mason said. "But why would it do that, man? That doesn't make any sense!"

"The bacteria thinks there's food inside them," Steve said, before he laughed and turned to look at Roger. "They look like bowls, in a kitchen!"

"That's a rat's thought process," Roger said. "The bacteria has a rat's intelligence."

The cloud surrounded the three immense cooling towers. It began rotating around each tower in a counter clockwise direction, as it slowly rose upward to engulf the top of each structure. There, the cloud fell into each cooling tower and descended to the bottom, while searching for additional nourishment.

At the same time, eight long finger-like sections

of the silver cloud slid up the rough gray concrete exterior of the containment building. They slowly wrapped themselves around the top of the domed structure like a hand while studying the building. Moments later, a larger section of the cloud surged forward to envelop the entire building. The floodlights lighted the swirling mist in the surrounding darkness.

Roger became confused while watching the action on several monitors. "Osiris didn't move into the containment building through the hole we cut in the concrete. Why did it stop?"

"The bastard is thinking about what to do next." Steve thought about what he was watching, while studying the cloud's cautious and deliberate movements. "I'm wondering if Goldberg unknowingly gave the bacteria a cognitive intelligence."

"Cognitive intelligence?" Bonnie frowned at him. "What does that mean, and how could it be influencing the cloud's movements?"

"Osiris is a single cell organism. It shouldn't be capable of logic or reasoning." Steve pointed at a monitor. "It shouldn't be doing what we're watching here."

"It looks like Osiris is studying that hole!"

"That's what I'm thinking too. But a single cell organism wouldn't have the brain power or intelligence to make its way up to that hole, and then inspect it."

Roger became excited. "You're thinking the billions of cells in that cloud are somehow linked

364

together, and thinking like a huge mass intelligence?"

"That could be what we're seeing right now. Each cell has an infinitely miniscule amount of logic. But when combined together in that cloud formation, all of the cells are processing and storing information faster than one of our leading edge super computers."

"Then the Osiris cloud is actually a huge collective and expanding intelligence." Roger's own words frightened him.

"The bacteria has been learning since the day it was released at the landfill. I'm assuming it acquired new intelligence capabilities after if destroyed that military laboratory. That may be why it began hunting for humans as a food source."

"We never realized Osiris was learning and making decisions as it moved across the country destroying cities!"

"The bacteria cloud is moving toward that hole in the concrete!" Bonnie felt her body trembling from fear while pointing at a monitor showing the silver cloud sliding through the hole, and into the containment building.

"We need radiation released inside that building to kill the bacteria," Roger said, as he felt his excitement and apprehension growing. "Mason, release that radiation now!"

"Okay! Okay! I just hope we're not too late to stop that thing!" After Steve and Roger prevented him from using additional cocaine and other illegal drugs, the man's hands trembled uncontrollably, while he struggled to concentrate on the computer screen and the reactor controls. His eyesight began to blur as his head throbbed while suffering from a pounding headache. Multi-colored lighted buttons on consoles began to merge to form a distorted mass of colors, as he attempted to work and control the cranes in the containment building. Moments later, he groaned when he felt his heart racing in his chest.

Bonnie pushed several buttons to activate the security cameras mounted to the walls inside the containment building. She pointed the cameras toward the ceiling. "I want to watch Osiris die when you hit it with radiation! It killed my news crew and I want it to die! If the bacteria has intelligence it will feel pain as it dies! I want to hear it scream, like my friends did when they died!"

"Take it easy baby." Steve placed a hand on her shoulder. "You'll get your wish in a few minutes."

"I'm using a crane to lift the fuel rod assembly now!" Mason squinted at multicolored buttons on a control panel while attempting to read the lettering on each one, to ensure he was depressing the correct switches.

Everyone stared at the monitors as four huge winches slowly lifted the fuel rod assembly out of the reactor cooling pool. The fuel rod assembly resembled a huge black steel cage one hundred feet high, and fifty feet square. A deluge of water cascaded from the structure, splashing onto the concrete floor, and into the cooling pool. The assembly contained thousands of slender black fuel rods. Thick black cables carrying electricity, and computer signals, dangled from the fuel rod assembly. The winches stopped when the fuel rod assembly dangled fifty feet above the cooling pool.

Other monitors showed the silver bacteria violently swirling around in a counter clockwise direction at the top of the domed containment building. A dozen wispy silver fingers began sliding down the walls, toward thousands of tires stacked around the reactor. The ceiling lights darkened and began showering sparks onto the floor, after Osiris destroyed the electrical wiring in conduits along the walls. Showers of white and red sparks erupted from the other electrical systems in the darkness, after those high voltage wires began shorting as Osiris devoured the insulation.

"It's getting too dark to see what's going on in that containment building," Roger said. "Mason, are there other lights you can turn on?"

"We've got emergency lights in there." He flipped the switches to power on floodlights set into the concrete floor of the building. They glared upward, illuminating the silver metal liner fastened to the walls. They also lighted the cloud swirling around the top of the building.

"How much more time do you need, until you release radiation in the building?" Roger was growing impatient, wanting to destroy the killer bacteria he helped to create. "We need that radiation now."

"I, I need twenty seconds." Mason hands trembled violently from fear and drug withdrawal as he turned knobs frantically, while stumbling from one console to another. "I can't go any faster. I'm doing all I can, man!"

"Settle down, Mason," Steve said. "Relax and do your job, and we're going to win this battle."

"I'm releasing radiation now." Mason rubbed his aching eyes while studying the graphics on three monitors, before pushing several additional buttons. Motors in the assembly opened lead covers along the length of the long fuel rods. Deadly radiation immediately began flooding into the building.

Moments later, several unique sounding wailing alarms began screeching in the control room. The sudden blaring noises startled everyone, as they stared intently at the monitors.

"What the hell is that?" Steve said, shouting over the alarm.

"The sensors located in the containment building detected the radiation we just released." Mason winced as the shrieking sound of the alarms hurt his ears. He nervously clasped his hands together and rested them on his head, after a third screeching alarm began sounding.

"Steve, I don't think radiation is affecting Osiris," Roger said, shouting to be heard over the alarms. He pointed at a monitor. "The radiation isn't killing the bacteria."

"Our assumptions based on laboratory experiments may be incorrect." Steve studied the monitor. "It looks as if radiation will not kill the bacteria as we thought it would."

"Why won't radiation stop the cloud?" Bonnie was confused after the ominous statement. "Is the bacteria cloud too big to be killed by the reactors at this plant?"

"Don't tell me your idea won't work now!" Mason crossed his arms tightly as if protecting his chest. "You told me radiation would kill the cloud, man!"

"Damn it!" Steve lifted the radio microphone as adrenaline surged through his system. He felt mentally and physically prepared for the deadly confrontation with the enemy he planned to destroy. "General, we have an issue here. It appears radiation is not stopping Osiris."

Brenton looked at Meridian, Feltault, and Reglovic. He uncharacteristically felt frightened and apprehensive after he saw the sudden concern on the men's faces. "Do I understand you correctly? Radiation will not kill the bacteria?"

"Yes, yes, that's what I'm telling you!" Steve watched the unaffected swirling bacteria cloud on a monitor. "Radiation isn't doing anything to it."

Meridian placed his elbows on his knees, before burying his face in his hands. "We'll never stop Osiris now. This was our last hope! Humanity is now on the brink of extinction!"

Reglovic pulled a small computer from his pocket. He began reviewing mathematical equations. "I don't understand how the bacteria mutated again. What suddenly made it impervious to radiation?"

"What's that noise?" Brenton became concerned after hearing the alarms blaring from the radio speaker.

"Steve, put him on hold and step over here," Roger said, as he became excited. "You need to see this."

"See what? What are you watching?"

Roger pointed excitedly at a monitor. "Look at what's happening to the cloud!"

"I'll have to get back to you General. Something is going on here." Steve dropped the microphone.

"No, don't leave! Stay on the radio," Brenton said, shouting. "Tell me what's happening at that damn plant!"

"We need to know what's taking place at this very moment," Reglovic said.

"I need Steve on the radio talking to me, and he walks away, damn it," Brenton looked at his staff while shaking his head.

His Executive Officer said, "How do we proceed from this point forward, General?"

"I don't know what to do at this moment. I can't make any valid assumptions or decisions to proceed forward, without additional real time intelligence information from Steve."

"What if he's dead already, and can't report a status? He may have been killed by the bacteria in those last few seconds of his radio transmission."

Brenton studied a monitor showing a radar image of the bacteria cloud surrounding the power plant. "Let's not assume that happened yet, until we're sure we can no longer reach him on the radio."

"We've got bombers and the Ticonderoga prepared and readied to attack the plant, and we don't know if radiation will destroy the bacteria."

"Shouldn't you tell the President his plan is falling apart," Meridian said. He looked at his companions who appeared confused, and frightened.

"Shut off those alarms so we can think," Steve said, shouting to Mason.

"All right man, I'm getting to it." Mason stumbled to a console in the control room while feeling exhausted from the growing stress and apprehension. "If we all shared a joint right now, the stress wouldn't be killing us!"

"Look at this monitor," Roger said after the alarms stopped blaring in the room. He frowned moments later after the screen mysteriously darkened, eventually fading completely to black. Moments later he shaded his face, after a brilliant flash of light, brighter than the sun, momentarily lighted the monitor.

"What was that?" Bonnie became concerned after another sudden and momentary bright flash of light blinded her. A few seconds later, another brilliant flash of light forced her to turn away from the monitor. "What is going on now? Is something exploding in the containment building to create those flashes of light?"

"This equipment must be failing." Roger rubbed his aching eyes, after watching several more bright flashes.

Mason squinted at the flashing monitors. "The short circuiting electrical wire in that containment building must be causing those flashes."

"The flashes of light are too bright to be shorting electrical wires," Steve said.

Mason became upset after Steve disregarded his explanation. "So what do you think it is?"

"I don't have any idea. I have to see what's going on." Steve grasped Bonnie's hand and began leading her across the control room. "Mason, open the door so we can check out the conditions outside the building."

"You want to go outside now?" Roger frowned at Bonnie skeptically. "The cloud is knocking on the door to get in!"

"We've got to see the situation out there, so we can give Brenton an accurate assessment of what's happening."

Several minutes later, the group stepped out of the building. Deafening hurricane force winds howled around them, buffeting them. They grasped onto the railing of the stairs leading to the control room building for support, when the winds made standing upright impossible. Construction materials, construction blueprints, pieces of paper, smoke, military tents, vegetation, foliage, and tree branches, flew past them in the wind.

"This is a scene out of a horror movie," Steve said, shouting so the others could hear him over the noise of the flame driven winds.

"Look over there," Roger said, while pointing excitedly and shouting. Large military floodlights located around the containment buildings began eerily flickering and shutting down, as Osiris destroyed their electrical wiring. Raging orange fires covered two huge piles of tires. The orange and red flames darted high into the night sky as the winds blew dense acrid smoke around the plant.

Eventually, only the piles of burning tires and a few remaining floodlights lighted the huge swirling silver mass. In that dim light, the leading edge of the silver bacteria cloud appeared to be attached to the containment building, while the remainder of the cloud extended for miles to the south.

"I can't see the top of the bacteria cloud!" Steve studied the flat bottom of the silver bacteria mass, now several hundred feet above the ground. It glowed orange, lighted by the fires below. Large areas of bacteria fell through the cloud. At the same time, other areas rose upward violently through the swirling formation. "The cloud could be several miles high over this power plant."

"This is amazing." Roger appeared fascinated while staring at the cloud seemingly attacking the containment building. The towering building appeared insignificant, dwarfed by the unnatural cloud formation.

"We gotta get inside, man! It's scary and dangerous out here!" Mason looked around nervously after screaming his warning, while watching the wind blow construction tools across the driveway, as the violent winds buffeted his body. "It's crazy to be out here! This is a really bad trip!"

"Why doesn't Osiris roll forward over all of this power plant?" Bonnie appeared terrified by the cloud mass trailing to the south, after screaming her question. "What's it waiting for? Why doesn't it kill us?"

"This leading edge of the cloud must be exploring the plant and that first containment

373

building for possible danger." Roger speculated, while shouting. "Before the rest of it moves forward to devour everything."

"Look at that hole in the wall!" Bonnie said screaming, while pointing frantically at the containment building. "I can see flashes of bright light inside the building. Something must have exploded in there!"

"Those are the same flashes we saw on the monitor," Roger said, shouting over the increasing howling winds.

'What the hell is happening now?' Steve was shocked and confused after a long brilliant streak of orange and white light arced from the hole in the containment building. The colored mass of light resembled a bolt of lightning traveling horizontally through the cloud, several thousand feet above the ground. The light rapidly traveled in a southerly direction inside the bacteria cloud, after unexpectedly departing from the plant. It caused the bacteria to glow with a metallic silver hue while passing through it, until the mass of light disappeared in the distance. *'What are those lights? Where are they coming from?'*

Roger shaded his eyes with a hand, while watching another fast moving streak of bright white light after it flew from the hole in the containment building. The light traveled through the cloud before it unexplainably burst apart inside the mass of bacteria, creating a huge blinding flash several miles above the ground. "I don't understand what's happening," Roger said, shouting.

374

"What are those things?" Mason pointed at several long brilliant streaks of light after they raced through the cloud from the containment building. They traveled erratically several thousand feet above the ground before disappearing. The blinding streaks appeared surreal inside the swirling silver mass of bacteria.

Bonnie shaded her eyes, after another brilliant streak arced from the containment building. "Those lights are so bright, they hurt my eyes."

"The cloud looks like its evaporating when those streaks passed through it!" Roger became excited. He frowned and looked around for a reason why the howling winds suddenly and mysteriously increased in intensity.

Long tentacle like streaks of light began arcing from the hole in the wall of the containment building, to mysteriously form a circular mass of brilliant white light approximately one hundred yards in diameter. The glowing sphere began tumbling through the cloud, as it slowly moved away from the power plant in a southerly direction. Twenty seconds later, when the circular mass of light was several miles from the plant, it mysteriously split into five thick long streaks of brilliant white light. Those streaks quickly traveled outward through the bacteria cloud in different directions, before disappearing in the distance.

"I don't understand anything we're seeing!" The expression on Roger's face mirrored his amazement, as he shouted so the others could hear him over the winds. "I don't understand what's happening to create those streaks of light!"

Steve remembered the testing in the NASA trailer. He said, shouting, "They look like the flashes of light we saw when we bombarded Osiris with radiation. They may be the result of radiation destroying billions of the Osiris cells."

"We can't confirm the radiation is destroying the bacteria! It could be some phenomenon where those white streaks are electrical charges coming from the reactor fuel rods, and they're lighter in density than the bacteria, and that's why they float through the cloud!" Roger looked up to study areas of the cloud after bright white streaks of light travelled erratically through it.

"When those white streaks rocket through the cloud, it looks like its leaving a void in the cloud mass," Steve said, " and more bacteria moves in to fill the void."

"Maybe the cells destroyed by those flashes of light off the fuel rods, don't have time to warn the others of danger." Roger rubbed his burning eyes as the dense smoke blowing in hurricane force winds caused them to tear.

"Or the bacteria doesn't understand dying. Nothing has harmed it before today." Steve watched streaks of bright blue light suddenly radiate from the containment building, before they began travelling through the cloud. The streaks of light brightly illuminated the lower areas of the silver bacteria cloud, the power plant buildings below it, and the land around the plant.

"The cloud is spreading out," Bonnie said, screaming while pointing frantically to the left. She covered her mouth with her fingers as she became horrified while watching the silver mass surround the remaining piles of tires to smother the fires.

"It needs those tires for nourishment." Steve grasped Mason's arm, as the hurricane force winds pushed the tall slender man backward. "The bacteria is starving!"

"Osiris may need food to regenerate the cells destroyed by the radiation." Roger watched the bacteria biodegrading the tires, and the black molten rubber flowing on the roads and grass.

"It started moving this way! The cloud is moving toward us!" Mason pointed wildly at the swirling silver bacteria cloud now advancing forward on the ground toward the control room, before he began screaming incoherently.

A large section of the cloud began sliding forward, across the one thousand yards separating the first containment building it attacked, from the second reactor containment building. The bacteria rolled over thousands of tires piled on the ground, biodegrading them for nourishment as it slowly and cautiously moved forward. It eventually surrounded the second containment building. The bacteria swirled around the structure in a counter clockwise direction, before entering that building through the hole cut in the wall.

"We need you to release more radiation," Steve said shouting, while pushing Mason toward the doors of the building housing the control room, in the strong winds. "We need more radiation to kill the damn bacteria!"

"After Osiris finds, and searches through that third containment building for food, it'll be coming after us," Roger said, shouting. "You've got to do your job Mason, and release the radiation."

Steve could not understand the source of the long slender blue and white streaks of white light arcing outward through the cloud, from the first containment building Osiris surrounded. Several of the bright blinding streaks traveled vertically and erratically through the cloud, rising thousands of feet above the ground. Other streaks travelled outward horizontally through the cloud, until they disappeared from sight over the horizon. Several streaks exploded violently in brilliant blinding balls of white light, several thousand yards in diameter, inside the bacteria cloud.

The strong howling winds caused the trunk of a tall tree near the building housing the control room to splinter with a thunderous noise, before the upper section toppled over onto military and construction vehicles. The winds increased in intensity and caused other nearby trees to fall over onto vehicles. The sound of cracking tree trunks, and falling trees, became unnerving.

"We've got to get inside the building where it's safe!" Steve grasped Bonnie's hand, before he led her to the control room with the others following closely behind.

"You don't have time to rest! Pull the fuel rods out of that second reactor and release as much radiation as you can," Roger said, after he watched Mason fall against a desk, while seemingly exhausted from fear. "The Osiris cloud is already inside that building."

"We're not going to stop that monster killer cloud with radiation!" Mason's body began trembling as he panicked, while overcome with fear and anxiety. "The cloud is too big for us to stop! We gotta get away from this plant before it kills us!"

"This isn't the time for you to be giving us advice," Steve said, coldly. "Calm down. If you panic and can't do your job, we're all going to die, along with millions of innocent people Osiris will kill after it moves past this plant!"

"Can't you see what's happening out there, man?" Mason pointed frantically at the monitors showing the activity around the power plant. "Radiation isn't harming that cloud. There's no way to stop it! It'll kill all of us if we stay here!"

"We have to assume radiation may be killing the bacteria!" Steve placed his hands on his hips as he became frustrated during the verbal confrontation. "It's too early to tell what affect the radiation is having on the cloud."

Mason inhaled loudly, as if suddenly enlightened. "Maybe we can get out of here in a car or military truck out there in the parking lot. You were in the military. You can drive one of the military trucks and get us out of here, man! Let's leave while that cloud is eating this plant!"

"We're here to a do a job! We're not running because you're frightened!"

"You're crazy, man!" Mason frantically pointed at Steve. Then he gasped for air as he turned to Roger. "You said the cloud needs food! Let it eat the tires and destroy the plant while we drive away in a car! We've got to go man, before it's too late and we can't leave!"

Roger could no longer control his growing anger. "Sit your ass down at that terminal, and do your god damn job, Mason! We stayed here to do a job, and we're going to destroy that cloud, or dying trying to do it!"

"Are you blind or stupid, man? We can't stop that cloud!"

Steve's fists tightened as his anger increased, fueled by Mason's hysteria. He grabbed the man's arm, before dragging him to a control panel. "We're not going to let that bacteria win! Do you understand me? It's not going to win and defeat us! Get to work, and release the radiation!"

"We can't stop the cloud! It's too big! We're all going to die when it comes for us, after it has us trapped in this control room!"

"Pull the fuel rods out of the damn reactor or you won't have to worry about Osiris killing you, after I'm done with you! I'll kill you myself if you don't do your damn job!"

Roger was not expecting Steve's threatening statement. He smiled after Mason began talking to himself as he worked at the controls. "You convinced Mason to do his job."

"He just needed some motivation!" Steve laughed.

Several minutes later three alarms each with a unique sound began blaring in the control room, signaling the release of radiation in the second containment building. The sudden shrieking alarms shocked everyone.

380

"Those noises are killing my ears!" Mason rushed to a console to flip several switches that silenced the alarms.

"Okay, okay, I released the radiation," Mason said, while nervously rubbing his hands together. He took a deep breath while swallowing hard, during a futile attempt to relax. "How do we know if that radiation is killing the bacteria? It's gotta kill that cloud!"

Roger said, "Can you turn on the cameras inside that second containment building, so we can see if the radiation is affecting Osiris?"

"Check out monitors twelve through seventeen." Mason rushed to the video camera control panel, before turning several switches to activate cameras in the containment building. Then he switched on additional bright lights inside the building.

The lights illuminated wide columns of the swirling bacteria, as they attempted to descend and consume the tires piled around the inside of the building. The silver misty cloud appeared to dive toward the tires below, before suddenly and unexplainably retreating upward, to the ceiling of the building.

"Did you see the flash of light inside the building on that monitor?" Bonnie said, screaming as her excitement increased while she pointed frantically at a monitor. "Did you see it?"

Several moments later, everyone watched as bright white and blue thick masses of light began appearing in the bacteria cloud inside the building. They turned and twisted randomly in the cloud while becoming slender and elongated. Then the streaks mysteriously arced across the interior of the building, before they traveled outward through the hole in the building wall.

Steve looked at Roger and said, "I'm going to speculate and say those flashes of light occur as the radiation is destroying the bacteria."

"That's a real possibility. As millions or billions of cells are destroyed by the radiation, the nucleus of each cell might burst and somehow create those bright flashes of light."

Steve nodded. "We need more radiation."

"Do you see what's happening inside that building?" Roger stared into the blinding flashes of bright light on a monitor.

"I don't see a thing going on, man!" Mason appeared confused and now more frightened after Roger's statement. "Is the cloud coming after us? Do we need to run?"

Roger pointed at several monitors. "The bacteria hasn't biodegraded the tires in either containment building. It's trying to reach out for the tires for nourishment, but it can't get down to them."

Everyone was suddenly startled, after another alarm began wailing in the control room. Brilliant red warning lights suspended from the ceiling began flashing.

"What is that alarm telling you?" Steve said while looking around questioningly, as the screeching alarm forced him to shout. "What's going on?"

"I can't deal with all of this pressure!" Mason squeezed his head between his hands as if overwhelmed. "That's the high radiation alarm.

When an excessive amount of radiation is released into any of the three containment buildings, it warns us of the imminent danger."

Bonnie focused several cameras mounted on the roof of the building, on the three reactor containment buildings. "The bacteria is still swirling around those first two buildings. The streaks of light are shooting through the cloud from both holes in the walls of those buildings."

"Then the radiation is destroying Osiris," Roger said, before he smiled at Steve. "Maybe the end is near!"

Bonnie squinted at a monitor. She studied it carefully. "The cloud changed direction, Steve! Osiris is moving toward the third containment building, and toward this building. It's coming after us!"

Chapter 15

Bonnie's hands trembled from fear while she adjusted the controls, to point a camera toward the third containment building. She watched a monitor as the billowing silver bacteria cloud lighted by military floodlights, rapidly rolled forward while resembling a cresting ocean wave. She held her breath and moaned fearfully, after the cloud enveloped the third towering containment building, along with the military and construction vehicles it found in nearby parking lots.

She became alarmed while watching as Osiris biodegraded the plastic insulation covering the electrical wiring of the floodlights. They began sparking and shutting down one after another, to plunge the plant into ominous darkness. Several moments later, she became terrified after a large group of floodlights exploded violently, propelling metal debris, and raging red-yellow flames high into the sky.

Steve became alarmed while writing notes on a pad. "What caused those explosions?"

"The bacteria is spreading out on the ground to surround more of the plant. Its destroying everything as it moves forward!"

"Pull the fuel rods out of that third reactor to release radiation into that building," Steve said. He paused to add additional notes to Bonnie's written description of Troxell's activities. "We need all the radiation we can squeeze out of those reactors, to destroy the entire cloud."

384

Mason collapsed onto a chair as if exhausted. His arms fell to his sides. Then his head slumped forward onto his chest, an indication of his overwhelming sense of desperation. "We can't stop that bacteria. We're all going to die!" He suddenly stood while appearing panic-stricken, before he looked around the control room frantically as if waiting for an invisible enemy to attack.

"What are you talking about?" Steve frowned while confused by the man's sudden and unexplained outburst. "Sit down at those reactor controls, and do your job!"

"Look at the size of that killer cloud, man!" Mason's arm trembled from fear while pointing at the monitors. "It's already too big to stop! You're stupid to think we can destroy it with just a little radiation! We need a nuclear bomb to stop it! And that will kill us too!"

"We're going to destroy that cloud, so the damn bacteria can't kill anyone else! Get back to work and do your job!"

"This is an insane waste of effort! We should be driving away from here right now, instead of screwing around with these reactors and radiation!" Mason began talking to himself, while turning switches on his control panels. They started the winches that lifted the third fuel rod assembly out of the cooling pool. Alarms blared in the control room after deadly radiation began filling the containment building. "This won't work. Your plan won't work! It's going to fail! The small amount of radiation I can release will not stop that huge dwarf killer cloud!"

Roger and Steve intently studied the monitors, watching for subtle changes in the billowing cloud after exposure to radiation. They studied the brilliant streaks of white and blue lights now racing through the bacteria after they arced from the three containment buildings. The streaks appeared to be growing in length and brightness as they traveled through the bacteria, lighting all areas of the darkened plant below the cloud.

"I hope Osiris doesn't move away from here before we destroy all of it." Roger watched hundreds of long brilliant streaks seemingly racing through the cloud mass.

"The bacteria may be too weak to move after we exposed it to radiation." Steve bit his lip while thinking. "Maybe we have it trapped here!"

Bonnie's eyes slowly widened with terror, while she stared at a monitor. "Oh my God!"

Steve said, "What's wrong? What're you seeing?"

"Osiris is moving toward this building!" She immediately felt paralyzed from an overwhelming sense of fear and futility, while watching the silver cloud billowing forward on the monitor.

"She's right." Roger studied the monitor with growing apprehension.

"The bacteria is moving straight toward us!" Bonnie looked to Steve for consolation, and became upset when he remained silent as she watched him staring at a monitor.

"Your bacteria knows we're in here, man!" Mason stood, his body trembling as he became hysterical. "It knows we're in here trying to kill it. It wants to kill us first, to protect itself! Your bacteria wants to kill us!"

"Is what he's saying correct? Can Mason be right?" Bonnie's eyes were wide with terror, while staring at the monitor showing the steadily advancing bacteria cloud, lighted by the brilliant flashes of blue and white streaks travelling through it. "Is Osiris looking for us, to stop us from killing it?"

"I don't know what the hell Osiris is doing now! We're not going to wait here to find out what it's thinking, damn it!" Steve looked around the room, as he became angry while realizing the bacteria may have outmaneuvered him. The piercing sound of another shrieking alarm startled him, causing him to shudder as he became distracted. "We need a way out of this damn control room."

"There's nowhere for us to run or hide." Roger apprehensively watched the monitor, as Osiris moved toward the building housing the control room. "We're trapped in this building."

"I told you heroes we couldn't stop that cloud, man! I told you, but you ignored me!" Mason said, screaming hysterically. "We should've left here a long time ago, but you were too stubborn to leave! Now we're going to die because of you!"

"I don't want to hear anything else out of your damn mouth!" Steve became annoyed by both the man's remarks, and the screeching sounds of various alarms. He began contemplating ways to save the group. He realized Mason's words might accurately describe his own determination to destroy the cloud. '*Did I put these people in harm's way because I was over confident and wanted to kill Osiris myself?'*

"Steve, do you think Osiris knows we're controlling the reactors from in this room?" Roger shuddered after another set of warning alarms unexpectedly began shrieking with deafening wailing tones. "Is it trying to destroy this control room to stop us from killing it?"

Steve frowned while thinking. "Maybe it knows about this control room, after studying the wiring it found and destroyed inside those damn containment buildings."

"I'm thinking the bacteria is much more intelligent than we originally assumed."

"We can thank that bastard Goldberg for giving it a brain! We definitely need to kill Osiris at this damn power plant, so it can't take away the knowledge it gathers here to avoid future attempts to kill it!"

"Why do we have to kill it here?" Mason said, shouting. "Why can't we run away from this place and save our own lives? We still have time to run and hide from your cloud!"

"Brenton won't get a second chance to lure Osiris to another power plant, because of what it's learning here!"

"We should tell Brenton we're thinking the radiation is destroying the bacteria," Roger said.

"We don't have time." Steve studied the monitors. "Osiris will eat its way into this control room, before we radio that information to him."

"Look at those monitors, man! Your cloud is destroying everything outside this building!"

Mason's body trembled from anxiety and terror as he watched floodlights, vehicles, and some of the power plant's buildings, explode in huge violent fireballs. He felt the building housing the control room shake after some huge nearby explosions destroyed electrical transformers. "We're trapped in here and that bacteria is going to kill us, because you two want to be heroes."

"Steve, what can we do?" Bonnie said. Her shrill voice emphasized her growing terror. "Are we going to die in this place?"

Steve became angry with himself. He realized he allowed Osiris to gain the advantage. Now a single-cell bacteria with intelligence was hunting him. "We're not waiting here for that bacteria to kill us. If Osiris wants us it has to find us, damn it!"

"Where can we go?" Bonnie began screaming hysterically as her arms shook uncontrollably, after her mind became overwhelmed while imagining her imminent agonizing death.

"We can't go outside into the open. We'll never outrun Osiris on foot."

"The cloud is still moving this way," Roger appeared frightened as more of the floodlights around the power plant continued shutting down, before some of them exploded. The monitors began to darken as the bacteria destroyed cameras mounted on the roofs of nearby buildings. "The cloud is going to surround this control room building in a few seconds. Then the bacteria will eat its way in here to get to us! What are we going to do?"

Steve looked at the control room doors. Then he turned and noticed the silver metal doors at the far end of the control room. "Mason, are those the doors that open into the access tunnel that leads to the containment buildings?"

Mason was confused and mentally overwhelmed by the question, as his body shuddered from traumatic fear. He turned, staring blindly across the room. "What, what tunnel, man?"

Steve grabbed the man's arm in an attempt to make him focus on the surroundings. He pointed across the room. "Do those silver doors open into the access tunnel that leads to the three containment buildings?"

"Yeah, yeah, man! But the cloud is already inside all three of the containment buildings. There's nowhere to go in there. The cloud will kill us when it sees us in those buildings."

"Maybe there's a place to hide." Steve stared at the doors while contemplating his limited options.

"I told you heroes we should have left long ago, but you had to stay. You had to stay and put all of us in danger with your lousy plan!"

Steve's fists clenched tightly from anger after the derogatory remark. He immediately restrained himself. "Open those silver access doors for us, now! We need to get into that tunnel!"

Mason shook his head while staring wide-eyed at Steve. "The bacteria will kill us in that tunnel, man! There's no place for us to run! Osiris is everywhere, man! You killed us!"

"Listen to me, damn it!" Steve grasped the terrified man's arm. He violently dragged Mason across the room. "Open those god damn doors!"

"Ok, ok, man! Jesus Christ, calm down so I can think!" Mason fumbled with his security badge, before pushing it into an electronic scanner. After he entered his personal access code into a keypad, the thick steel doors silently slid apart.

"We've got to get out of this control room now!" Roger's anxiety rapidly increased while watching the approaching Osiris cloud on the monitors. "We, we, gotta go before it's too late!"

"We have to go, baby!" Steve ran across the control room to grasp Bonnie's wrist. He realized she was trembling uncontrollably from unbearable fear and could not move, while staring at a monitor showing Osiris engulfing the building housing the control room. The monitor suddenly darkened after the advancing bacteria destroyed the camera. "We're leaving. Let Osiris eat this damn place!"

Roger took a deep breath while watching the monitor showing the lobby of the building. "Osiris is coming in through the front doors. It'll be in this control room in a few seconds!" He was shocked after the monitor suddenly darkened, knowing Osiris biodegraded the insulation on the electrical wires as the bacteria filled the building.

Steve warily looked quickly into the access tunnel brightly lighted by electrical fixtures attached to the walls and ceiling. He estimated the tunnel to be fifteen feet wide, with a ceiling twelve feet in height. Bright white paint covered the rough cement floor, walls, and ceiling. He studied the numerous wide steel conduits attached to the walls and ceiling which contained electrical wires. They extended the entire length of the tunnel, each color-coded with a distinctive red, blue, yellow, green, and purple paint. "We're good! It's clear in here. Osiris is not in this tunnel."

"But it's coming after us," Mason said, shouting. "Osiris is hunting us now, man!"

"I'm not giving up! We're not going to wait here." Steve led the group into the tunnel. They began running away from the control room. "We've got to get to the far end of this tunnel."

Twenty seconds later as he ran awkwardly, Mason unexpectedly raised his hands over his head. He slowed before staggering forward and falling against a wall, while gasping for air. He struggled to speak. "I have to catch my breath. I can't run! You're killing me with this physical crap stuff!"

"That's where we need to be." Steve pointed toward the end of the tunnel. "It's only a few hundred yards to the doors that open into the third containment building. We've got to get in there, and find a place to hide."

"Have you lost your mind? Your bacteria is already inside that building, man," Mason said, while gasping for air. "And we already released radiation in that building. If the bacteria doesn't kill us, the radiation will fry us!"

"That may happen, but we're dead if Osiris finds us in this tunnel!" Steve looked around at the ceiling and walls, while searching for options to save the group.

Bonnie trembled while pressing a shoulder against the tunnel wall as she stared at the floor, thinking about her impending agonizing death while Osiris devoured her flesh. She attempted to control her breathing and growing sense of terror as she imagined screaming hysterically while watching her flesh bubble away into the cloud as the bacteria consumed her body.

Bonnie unexpectedly noticed a slight movement in her peripheral vision while gasping for air. She turned her head and squinted, looking toward the end of the tunnel, near the control room entrance. Her eyes opened wide after a sudden and shocking realization. She watched the silver bacteria cloud billowing forward violently into the tunnel, while searching for nourishment. She said, screaming, "Osiris is in here with us! The bacteria is in this tunnel and its moving toward us!"

"How did it find us so fast?" Roger said, after he turned to stare at the silver cloud flooding into the far end of the access tunnel. He watched the bright lights attached to the walls and ceiling explode after sparking violently, to darken areas of the tunnel as Osiris destroyed the wiring while rolling forward.

"Osiris is searching every area of the damn plant for food," Steve said. "We have to keep moving, now!"

Debilitating terror suddenly numbed Bonnie's mind. She could not speak while her body trembled violently and uncontrollably. She visualized the skeletal remains of her co-workers killed by Osiris, during the attempt to capture samples of the bacteria. She pictured their remains lying on the ground in Arizona in her mind. She remembered the jaw of every skeleton frozen open during screams of agony in the last moments of life. She watched the advancing silver cloud filling the access tunnel from floor to ceiling. "There's no way out! We're going to die in here!"

"I'm not going to let that happen!" Steve became more determined to survive, while dragging Bonnie forward by a wrist as he began running. "We've got to keep going!"

"Go! Go!" Roger frantically pushed Mason forward. "Get moving Mason, before the cloud catches us!"

Ninety seconds later Steve led the group to the end of the long tunnel, still lighted by the ceiling and wall lights. He pointed at the silver steel doors that blocked the group's access to the third containment building, while watching the silver bacteria cloud advancing toward them in the tunnel. "Mason, open these damn doors! We need to get out of this tunnel!"

"I can't do this! I can't handle this pressure, man!" Mason fumbled with his security badge with hands trembling violently from fear. As he attempted to push it into the badge scanner, he dropped it onto the floor while watching the advancing cloud in the tunnel. He stared down at the thin plastic card while physically and mentally paralyzed from fear. "I give up! My heart can't take this pressure! I'm going to die in here! This tunnel will be my grave!"

Roger picked up the badge. He placed it into Mason's hand, before forcibly closing the man's fingers around it. "Open those doors before Osiris strips the skin from our bones! I'm not ready to give up, or die!"

Mason pushed his badge into the scanner with trembling hands. He closed his eyes while attempting to remember his access code. The loud crackling sound of shorting high voltage electrical wires inside the tunnel terrified and distracted him. He wrapped the fingers of his left hand around his violently trembling right hand. Then he slowly entered his access code into the keypad with one finger. He stepped back and frowned at the silver steel doors when they remained tightly sealed. "They're not opening! What's going on? The doors won't open! I entered my code, and they should be opening!"

"What the hell is going on?" Steve stepped beside him. "Are you sure you entered the correct code?"

"My code is simple. Its 1, 2, 3, 4, 5!" Mason looked at him questioningly. "The doors aren't opening. They should be open!"

"Why aren't they opening? Think! You're the expert. How do we get them open?"

"I don't know what's going on, man! They should be open right now!" Mason trembled while watching the silver cloud moving forward, plunging sections of the tunnel into darkness as it shut down the lights.

"Enter the code again," Roger said, shouting. "You have to do it now."

Mason reentered his access code several times, but the doors remained sealed. "I don't know why they're not opening. I don't know, man! I can't think!"

Roger wiped the beads of nervous perspiration from his face with the sleeve of his shirt. "I'm thinking Osiris must have destroyed the electrical wiring in the containment building, carrying power to these doors. We'll never get them open."

"There's no way to get out of here!" Mason began screaming hysterically, while clawing frantically and futilely at the steel doors. "We're trapped in this coffin tunnel with Osiris! It's going to kill us!"

"Do something to stop Osiris, Steve!" Bonnie grasped his arm with both hands, seeking comfort, while watching the approaching bacteria cloud. The woman's eyes were wide from both shock and the terror ravaging her mind. "The bacteria is almost here! Do something to help us get out of this tunnel, before Osiris gets us!"

Steve watched sections of the tunnel lights darkening, after Osiris destroyed the electrical wiring while swirling forward. He turned to Mason. "What's the backup system for getting through these doors?"

"What are you asking me?" Mason appeared confused. He stared at the approaching silver bacteria cloud. "I, I don't understand what you want from me?"

"You told us there's a redundant system for every process in this plant." Steve grabbed the man's shirt with two hands, to ensure he had his full attention. "What's the manual system for opening these god damn doors when the power is out?"

396

"You don't have time to open them, you fool! We're trapped in here like animals!" Mason pointed frantically at the silver bacteria cloud moving toward the group. "We're going to die when the bacteria fills this tunnel and eats our skin!"

"How do we open these damn doors?" Steve became furious after the man's response indicated he was mentally defeated. He pointed at the solid metal barrier blocking his retreat. "Tell me how to open these doors!"

"Even if you open them, there's nowhere to run in there. The bacteria is already inside the containment building, waiting to kill us!"

"I'm not ready to die, damn it! Tell me the backup system!"

"That! That's it!" Mason's arm trembled violently from fear while pointing at a long silver metal bar suspended from the wall by hooks.

"What do we do with it?" Steve briefly looked at the approaching silver cloud.

"You put the bar onto that fitting sticking out of the wall. Then you turn it."

"What does that do?"

"The backup hydraulic system will open the doors." Mason collapsed backward against the white cement wall. Overwhelmed by fear, his legs gave way until he eventually sat on the floor. There, he buried his face in his hands in desperation, before he began crying.

"Let's do this, Roger." Steve violently pulled the metal bar from the hooks. It was four feet long, but surprisingly heavy. He pushed a square fitting in the middle of the bar over a steel knob protruding from the wall. Then he began turning the bar with Roger, as if it were an airplane propeller.

"They're opening! You're doing it! The doors are opening!" Bonnie said, screaming moments later, after a small space appeared between the two doors as they slowly moved apart. "Hurry, please, hurry! Osiris is getting closer! It's almost here!"

'What's that sound?' As Roger helped Steve turn the bar to open the doors, he heard loud and unusual noises coming from inside the containment building. They reminded him of the crackling, reverberating thunder, heard during violent summer storms. He frowned as the unusual and unexpected sounds confused him. As the doors continued to slowly slide apart, brilliant flashes of light inside the containment building began briefly lighting the tunnel floor and walls.

'I can't stop! I've got to keep going! Don't stop!' Steve struggled for breath while frantically turning the metal bar. His shoulders and arm muscles burned from the strenuous physical exertion. *'I've got to get these doors open so we can get out of this tunnel and find a place to hide from Osiris! Keep going, don't stop!'*

"The bacteria is getting closer!" Bonnie said, screaming hysterically as she grasped Steve's arm. She watched more lights in the tunnel darken, as Osiris began moving toward the group faster. "It knows we're here! It's coming closer! Hurry, the cloud is moving closer!"

A section of tunnel lights fifty feet from the group suddenly darkened after Osiris biodegraded the insulation on the electrical wiring. Large and loud explosions, accompanied by blinding multicolored sparks spraying from the shorting lighting electrical fixtures, served to light the darkened tunnel. The sparks lighted the billowing silver bacteria cloud as it steadily advanced toward the group, while it sensed nourishment several yards ahead. Clouds of smoke created by the shorting electrical wires mixed with the advancing swirling silver bacteria.

"Bonnie, get over here! Get over here now!" Steve said shouting after the doors were fourteen inches apart.

"Where am I going?" She appeared terrified while watching the brilliant flashes of light inside the now dark interior of the containment building. Her body trembled uncontrollably. "I don't want to go in that building alone! I don't know what's going on in there! I'm afraid!"

"I'll be in there with you!" Steve briefly looked at the approaching Osiris cloud, before he pushed Bonnie through the narrow opening between the doors. He frowned as she stumbled and fell to the floor while screaming. "Mason, you're next!"

"It's too late to run away from the cloud!" Mason stared at Osiris silently billowing toward the group. His fears became incapacitating, when ceiling lights twenty feet from the group shut down, after the bacteria destroyed the wiring. "The bacteria found us! We can't get away from it."

"Do something to save yourself!" Roger pulled Mason to his feet. He violently pushed him between the doors. Then he followed him into the containment building.

'What the hell is going on in here?' Steve shaded his eyes from the blinding overhead flashes of light, after squeezing between the doors. The brilliant white, blue, and now orange flashes blinded him, causing him to stumble forward while shading his eyes with his hands.

The unexplainable streaks of light traveling through the bacteria cloud lighted the interior of the containment building, after Osiris destroyed all of the interior lighting systems. He squinted at a dozen bright long and thick streaks of light traveling through the swirling silver bacteria cloud, now filling the upper two thirds of the huge building. He watched brilliant streaks of orange, white, blue, and green lights arcing outward from the fuel rods hanging in the center of the building. They traveled erratically inside the translucent cloud before escaping from the containment building through the hole cut in the thick concrete wall.

'I don't know where those noises are coming from, but they're deafening!' The thunder like sounds accompanying the brilliant flashes of light vibrated deep inside Roger's chest. *'Those sounds are louder than thunder!"*

"I'm so scared," Bonnie said, shouting to Steve. The loud reverberating thunder muffled her cries. "Please help me! Please, please, help me! Don't let me die! I don't want to die!"

Roger squinted while staring at the brilliant long slender streaks of light, as more of them appeared to shoot from the radioactive fuel rods. They began appearing with such frequency, he realized they resembled brilliant blinding strobe lights inside the

400

building. He watched the silver bacteria cloud descend to within twenty feet of the floor several times. Then it rapidly retreated upward to the ceiling of the building, as the streaks of bright light unexplainably appeared to frighten it. *'I don't understand what's preventing Osiris from moving down to the floor to biodegrade those tires, and us.'*

Steve prepared for a tremendous explosion after several bright streaks collided with overhead cranes, and other pieces of machinery in the containment building. He was shocked when the streaks mysteriously wrapped themselves around the equipment, while resembling pulsing lighted cords. The streaks became brighter as they separated from the equipment with a thunderous noise, before traveling through the bacteria cloud and eventually escaping through the hole in the wall.

"The cloud! The cloud followed us in here!" Bonnie screamed a warning that startled everyone, while pointing frantically at the open tunnel doors behind the group.

"What're we going to do?" Roger watched the silver cloud violently billowing into the lower area of the building, through the open silver access doors.

"Do something, Steve! Please, help us!" Bonnie pressed her hands tightly over her ears as the mysterious sounds of thunder in the building intensified and became deafening. "Don't let me die!"

"This way! Follow me!" Steve grabbed her wrist while leading the group further into the containment building. As they walked forward in the pulsing flashes, while the sounds of thunder caused the floor to vibrate, he looked around warily. *'Is this the end? There's nothing here I can use to stop Osiris, or protect us from the bacteria! I didn't die in Iraq, but now I'm going to die here.'*

He unexpectedly stopped while staring ahead, as he released Bonnie's hand. A strange expression appeared on his face as he squinted, while mentally improvising a plan. "Can it be that simple?"

"Osiris is still coming after us! It's not stopping!" Bonnie trembled uncontrollably from fear while watching the silver cloud billowing into the containment building from the access tunnel. She pressed her hands together as if praying, while looking around the building lighted by the blinding flashes of light. "Why are we stopping? Why are we standing here? We've got to run and hide somewhere!"

"I've got a flipping idea." Steve smiled confidently while leading the group around the reactor cooling pool, and the fuel rod assembly dangling above it. He motioned the group forward while ensuring Mason was still following him, as he led them beyond the spent fuel rod storage pool. "Follow me!"

"Where are we going?" Mason squinted, while frightened by the brilliant streaks he watched mysteriously emanating from the radioactive fuel rods. "What are we going to do in here? There's no place for us to go! The radiation in this building is already killing us!"

After leading the group between rows of towering gray electrical panels, Steve pointed at the glass cube twelve feet square mounted on a large steel trailer, which he first noticed during his tour of the building several days earlier. "That's the glass cube and trailer they use to move fuel rods inside this containment building. It's filled with thousands of gallons of water that will protect us from Osiris."

"Protect us how?" Roger looked around questioningly, as the thunderous noises in the building increased in intensity, as did the flashes of brilliant light that appeared to jump off the fuel rod assembly before streaking through the bacteria cloud. "How can this trailer save our lives?"

"What are you talking about?" Bonnie appeared confused while staring at the water filled clear glass cube. That confusion added to the terror that clouded her mind and mired her reasoning. "This idea is completely insane! It won't work! How can it work with Osiris in this building?"

"This is the best idea you can come up with, man?" Mason said, screaming hysterically while frantically pointing at the trailer with two hands. The overhead brilliant flashes lighted his face, showing him to be enraged. "You're stupid to think you can use that trailer for anything!"

"What's your idea to use that trailer?" Roger appeared startled and ducked after the loud sounds that resembled thunder frightened him.

"Come with me. I need your help." Steve began running toward another area of the containment building.

"Wait for me," Roger said, shouting before chasing him.

"No! No! Don't leave me here alone!" Bonnie said, screaming after she watched Steve and Roger run from her side. She turned to watch the approaching bacteria cloud rolling across the containment building floor toward her from the tunnel entrance. Her legs suddenly felt weak before she stumbled forward, as breathing became extremely difficult, while her body trembled violently from fear.

"Those two are leaving us here to die alone, while they save themselves!" Mason watched the silver Osiris cloud billowing as it slowly moved toward him, lighted by the overhead brilliant flashes of light, as terror numbed his mind. His body shuddered, after the thunderous sounds frightened him. "They abandoned us! They're cowards who only want to save themselves!"

"Steve, don't leave me here alone," Bonnie said, before she screamed hysterically while staring at the approaching bacteria.

"What're you looking for?" Roger became confused, while watching Steve frantically opening black steel supply cabinets.

"Where the hell is their equipment?" Steve violently opened the doors of more metal equipment lockers. Then he smiled triumphantly. "I saw this diving equipment during the tour of the plant."

"What're we going to do with this stuff?" Roger stared at the multicolored red, green, and blue diving air tanks. He remembered seeing divers wearing similar air tanks on the beaches in Florida.

"These tanks will save our lives." He handed Roger four diving masks. Then he frantically pulled four air tanks from the cabinet. He began dragging them across the concrete floor by their red harnesses.

"What are you doing with those?" Bonnie was shocked and confused while watching Steve dragging the equipment toward her. Tears flowed down her cheeks from her eyes after she began crying. "Do something, anything, to save us, please!"

"We'll use this diving equipment, to get away from Osiris," Steve said, shouting over the thunderous noises that continued to become louder. "The bacteria won't be able to reach us if my plan works!"

"What is this thing, man?" Mason stared at an orange diving mask Roger handed him. The increasing intensity of the thunder reverberating inside the building terrified him. "What am I doing with this thing?"

"We'll put on the masks and hook them to these air tanks." Steve straightened the yellow air hoses attached to the diving air tanks. "Then we'll get into that cube filled with water. Osiris won't be able to get to us when we're underwater."

"I can't wear this thing!" Mason fumbled with the mask as his hands trembled.

"I don't know what to do!" Bonnie began crying while staring at the purple diving mask Roger handed to her. "I'm going to die here!"

"This mask will cover your entire face." Steve took the mask from her hands. He turned it, to show her how it functioned. "Each mask has a radio so we can talk to each other under the water."

"I can't." Bonnie shook her head before she screamed, "I can't do it!"

"You have to do it. I'm not going to let you die. We'll climb into the water in that trailer. It should protect us from Osiris, because the bacteria won't be able to get to us."

"This is a great idea." Roger watched the approaching bacteria cloud, as it slowly slid across the floor of the containment building toward the group. "We don't have any other options!"

"I don't know how to use this thing!" Bonnie said, screaming while staring at the yellow rubber diving mask she held. She dropped it to the floor before stomping her feet in frustration. "I'm going to die in here! I know I'm going to die!"

"No, you're not." Steve was becoming excited, after realizing he could save the group. "None of us are going to die."

"Yes, I am!"

"I do a lot of diving. I know how to use this equipment."

"I can't do this!" Tears flowed down Bonnie's cheeks while she momentarily glanced at the approaching bacteria cloud.

"You pull on that mask and then breathe normally. It's nothing more than that."

"I can't!" Bonnie's face mirrored her sense of hopelessness. "I can't do it!"

The terror incapacitating Mason's mind became overwhelming. He watched the brilliant streaks of light racing through the translucent silver cloud above his head. He covered his ears, as the deafening sounds similar to thunder increased in intensity and loudness. His heart pounded wildly, while imagining a grisly death while drowning as he suffocated underwater. "I can't go in that water! I, I have a drowning phobia! I'll drown under that water!"

"You'll have to deal with your phobia and control it, if you want to live." Steve said, screaming over the thunder like sounds above his head, as white, blue, green, and now orange streaks seemed to jump off the fuel rod assembly before racing through the bacteria cloud. "You'll only need to kneel underwater for a few minutes."

"I, I, I can't stay under that water! I can't do that!"

"We'll only need to be in that cube until the radiation destroys Osiris. Then we'll climb out!"

"I'll take my chances out here." Mason watched Roger helping Bonnie pull the straps of an air tank onto her shoulders.

"What do you mean, out here?" Steve frowned questioningly, while unsure what Mason was saying. "There's nowhere to hide from Osiris! It will find you and kill you, damn it!"

"The radiation may kill the bacteria before it can find me, if I hide in the electrical room. I'm staying out here, until this is over."

"You'll die! It's either get in that water, or Osiris will kill you!"

Mason began warily backing away from him. "I'm staying out here!" He suddenly ran from the group.

Steve realized he had to stop the confused and terrified man. "Come back here." He dropped the air tank he was pulling onto his shoulders on the floor, and prepared to chase him.

Roger grabbed his arm to stop him. "He's on his own, Steve. You've got to get into the water."

Bonnie raised her arm and pointed behind the men, as her mouth fell open from shock. "The cloud is right behind us! Osiris is almost on top of us!"

"Roger, get into the water!" Steve watched him tighten the red straps of the air tank already on his back. "I'll help Bonnie get in with you. I'll climb in after she's safe."

Roger jumped up and grasped the top of the trailer's glass wall, which was six feet high. He threw a leg over the top of the thick glass wall, before pulling himself over the top and falling into the water. He quickly turned and looked at the approaching Osiris cloud. "Hurry up Steve! Lift Bonnie up to me! We've only got a few seconds before the bacteria gets here!"

Chapter 16

Steve heard Bonnie's moans and cries as he quickly lifted her in his arms. "You're going to be safe, baby. I promise you, nothing will happen to you." The scent of her skin and hair triggered a flood of pleasant memories even in the ensuing chaos. He kissed her neck one final time.

Her eyes were wide from terror while watching the swirling silver bacteria cloud. It glided across the floor at the other side of the containment building, at the same time the brilliant overhead flashes illuminated the billowing mass in the eerie darkness. "Hurry Steve! Hurry! I don't want to die!" The startling sounds of thunder added to her fears as they increased in intensity, and became almost deafening.

Roger grasped her wrist before slipping a hand under her knee. "You'll be safe in the water." He carefully pulled her over the top of the clear glass wall, before watching her awkwardly tumble into the water. He immediately grasped her arm and pulled her to the surface.

"This water is cold." She brushed the wet hair from her face while treading water. "We'll freeze in it!"

"It's not that cold. You'll be okay." Roger watched her grasp the top of the glass wall with her hands to keep her head above the water. "Let's get Steve in here with us."

"Watch your heads!" Steve threw a silver air tank over the wall, and into the water. As it sank to the bottom of the cube, he unexpectedly ran from the trailer

"Where are you going?" Roger was shocked while watching Steve unexpectedly running from the trailer. The strobe like brilliant colored flashes of light made it appear as if his friend was running in slow motion. He frowned when Steve disappeared behind the towering gray electrical panels. "Get back here before Osiris kills you!"

"Come back!" Bonnie submerged herself in the water up to her neck after extremely loud thunder like sounds frightened her. She grasped the top of the trailer wall to stare over it in fear, looking for Steve. "Come back before it's too late. Come back now! I love you, damn it!"

'I must be crazy to be doing this!' Steve frantically pulled three full air tanks from a storage locker. He dragged the heavy orange steel tanks back to the trailer, where he threw them into the water in the cube. *'Osiris is fifty feet from me and I'm out here running around. But we may need this air if the radiation doesn't kill Osiris soon. I have to keep Roger and Bonnie safe.'*

"Get in here now!" Roger said screaming, while extending his hand downward, to offer assistance to Steve to pull him into the water. "You don't have time to do anything else!"

Steve noticed the swirling silver cloud was now only thirty feet from the trailer. It was moving directly toward him, as if the hungry killer was hunting its prey. He began shouting, while looking around for the man he now felt obligated to save. "Mason! Mason!"

410

"Hurry Steve! Get in this water with us! Osiris is almost here!" Bonnie watched the leading edge of the silver cloud billowing closer to the trailer, as it destroyed rubber and plastic maintenance equipment on nearby shelves.

"I can't leave Mason out here. I'm leaving him here to die alone." Steve looked around, suddenly feeling unwarranted sympathy and compassion for the man.

"You have no time left," Roger said, screaming. "Get in this water now, or you're going to die!"

When Steve saw the concern on Roger's face, he realized he was now in imminent danger. He reached up to grasp the man's extended hand. "Pull me up."

"Come on, you've only got a few seconds."

Steve quickly looked to the side after noticing a sudden and unexpected movement to his left. Moments later, something violently struck his upper body. The impact knocked him to the cement floor. As he lay on his back in pain, he immediately assumed Mason ran into him while attempting to flee from the bacteria. However, when he raised his head he was shocked to see Troxell smiling as he walked toward him. "I hoped you would be dead by now!"

"You're the ass hole that's going to die now!" Troxell looked around and quickly realized there were no tools nearby to use as a weapon. He fell to his knees before he grasped Steve's head. He lifted it, before he slammed it downward onto the floor with all of his strength. "I'll shatter your skull and spread your brains across the floor for Osiris to eat!

411

You won't live long enough to interfere with the government's plans again."

Steve struggle to lift his arms, as he became dazed during the continued violent attack. He grasped at Troxell's shirt in a futile attempt to defend himself. "Get off me!"

"Your dying will make our government, and the people who sent me here, very happy." Troxell began violently punching Steve's chest, face, and throat.

Steve's inner voice began screaming a warning. '*Do something! Do something to stop him! You'll be dead in a minute!*' He pulled frantically at Troxell's shirt, feeling helpless to stop the ferocious attack.

"You can't do anything to stop me from killing you!" Troxell laughed, while punching Steve's chest. He hoped to break the man's ribs and drive them into his heart to kill his victim. "You're a pathetic looser!"

'*Do something extreme to save your damn life! Improvise, damn it!*' Steve's entire body began aching. He was quickly becoming exhausted and confused. He heard Roger shouting and Bonnie's hysterical screams in the background as they watched the brutal attack while they waited for him in the water. '*Don't give up, or you'll die! Don't give up or he'll kill Roger and Bonnie! Stop this damn fool!!*'

"I should have killed you first, before I killed the other geeks!" Troxell clasped the fingers of both hands tightly around the struggling man's neck. His grip tightened, until he was choking him. He locked his elbows to increase the pressure as he strangled his victim. He bent forward to look into Steve's eyes. "You're dead McClellan! How does it feel to know you're dying like your other people I murdered?"

'I have to break his grip on my neck! He's strangling me! I only have a few seconds left before I die!' Steve's lungs burned from intense pain and spasms caused by a lack of oxygen. He studied the large man kneeling over him, silhouetted in the brilliant overhead streaks of white and orange light. He thought it was strange when pages of a medical anatomy book suddenly began appearing in his mind. When he saw the details on one particular page, he suddenly understood how to defend himself. *'I know how to stop this murdering piece of crap!'*

"You're dead, ass hole!" Troxell screamed, over the loud sounds of the thunderous noises. "I want you to suffer while you die!"

'Now is the time to fight back!' Steve struggled to raise his hands while suffocating. He pressed his fingers against Troxell's face. He slid his left thumb against the man's nose, before pressing the fingers of his right hand into the flesh above Troxell's eyeball. Then he pushed upward with all of his remaining strength, as the darkness of death began numbing his mind.

"You can't stop me from killing you, no matter what you do! You're a maggot that's going to die!" Troxell realized Steve was almost dead, as the skin of his face became blue from a lack of oxygen. "You're a loser that deserves to die for getting in my way!"

413

'If this doesn't work, I'm not getting a second chance to save my life.' Steve savagely pushed his fingers deep into the soft skin of Troxell's face, around his eye.

Troxell screamed in agony, after a sudden and excruciating pain contorted his entire face. Moments later, his right eyeball appeared to burst forward, out of the socket. The eyeball resembled the white veined interior of a grape, squeezed from the protective purple skin. The damaged eyeball swayed violently beneath the man's face, painfully dangling by pink muscles and nerves. Troxell screamed from the pain while releasing his grip on Steve's throat. He fell back to sit on his legs, while reaching for the injured eyeball with both hands. "What the hell did you do to my face?"

"That's textbook anatomy." Steve gasped for air before he savagely kicked Troxell's chest with a foot while lying on his back. He watched the man incapacitated from the searing pain, fall backward onto the floor while in agony.

Troxell shuddered from the burning pain while cupping the damaged eye in his hand! "Help me you god damn fool! Fix this! Fix it, or I'll kill you, you damn bastard!"

"That doesn't look too good." Steve quickly stood while feeling a strange sense of accomplishment. He saw Osiris was only several yards away. "That eye dangling from the socket must hurt like hell!"

"Fix my eye, damn it!" Troxell cradled the injured eyeball in his hand as a large amount of

414

warm red blood began flowing from the damaged socket. He awkwardly stood and began staggering forward while in agony. "Put it back in! Put it in!"

"That's my personal payback for all of the people you hurt, and killed!" Steve watched the silver bacteria cloud advancing toward them. He heard Bonnie and Roger screaming hysterical warnings to him.

"Help me, damn it!" Troxell staggered to the side in pain, as each step and movement caused his injured eye to throb in agony. "Get me some help now, you bastard!"

"I'll help you." Steve studied the large injured man lighted by the overhead flashes. His need for revenge overpowered his need to help the man. "I'll help you into your grave."

"What?" Troxell raised his head to look at Steve, while holding the eyeball. "Help me and I won't kill you and the others!"

"Really? You're pleading for help?" Steve stepped forward, ignoring the dangers of the approaching bacteria cloud, and the warnings screamed by Roger and Bonnie. "You wanted to protect Osiris. You killed my friends doing it."

"Help me! I can't see!" Troxell staggered forward in agony. "I can't see! The pain is too much!"

"It's time for you to meet the monster you wanted to protect! You and Osiris have a lot in common. You're both heartless killers!" Steve violently pushed the large man backward, and into the approaching bacteria cloud. "I'm killing two monsters tonight."

415

Troxell began clawing frantically at the silver cloud swirling around him while in agony, as his eyeball dangled from its socket. "No, no, save me from this bacteria! Help me!"

The bacteria immediately began stinging Troxell's exposed skin while dissolving it. Moments later the man who took pleasure in killing people began screaming hysterically. He fell to his knees while the bacteria stripped the skin from his face to expose underlying muscles. The skin on his hands and wrists bubbled away while he watched in horror, as Osiris devoured it for needed nourishment. The bacteria quickly stripped both hands of flesh while the man screamed, leaving only exposed skeletal bones. The bony appendages fell to his sides after Osiris destroyed his shoulder muscles. Moments later the bacteria stripped the flesh from his neck and throat, silencing the man's agonized screams.

"Nice job," Steve said figuratively, congratulating Osiris as Troxell's clothed skeleton toppled forward onto the concrete floor. "That asshole is going to give you indigestion."

"You've only got a few seconds to get in this water!" Roger said, shouting a warning to Steve.

"That felt so damn good!" Steve ran to the trailer with Osiris chasing him, only several feet behind.

"Take my hand, now!" Roger grasped Steve's hand before pulling him over the top of the trailer wall, and into the water.

Steve took the diving mask from Bonnie's hand. He carefully placed it over her entire face, before pulling the straps behind her head. Then he attached

416

the rubber hose dangling from an air tank strapped to her back, to the mask. "I want you to breathe normally under the water. You'll be fine. I promise!"

She nodded. Her eyes were wide with fearful anticipation while watching the approaching bacteria. "I'm cold!"

Roger handed Steve an air tank after adjusting his own mask. "We need to get under the water now!"

"Let's do it!" Steve frantically pulled a mask over his face while watching the swirling silver cloud, now several feet from the trailer. After nodding to the others, he pulled them under the water, and held their hands as they sank to the bottom of the water in the clear glass cube.

Steve looked at Bonnie's face through the clear plastic of the diving facemask. "Talk to me. How are you doing?"

The sound of his metallic voice blaring from the speakers in the mask startled her. She turned to look at him. "I'm here. I'm ok." The water felt very cold as it saturated her clothing.

"Roger?" Steve said, while adjusting his mask. "How are you doing?"

"This is so strange, but I think I'm good." Roger looked around the trailer, through the clear glass walls.

Bonnie's breathing became strained and more difficult by the strange feeling of the rubber diving mask tightening around her face as she took each breath. She looked around fearfully underwater, as numerous streaks of brilliant light passing through the bacteria cloud, lighted the interior of the darkened building. The shadows cast by the huge equipment inside the building became ominous and foreboding, and frightened her. The thunder like sounds in the containment building vibrated the thick glass walls of the trailer, adding to her fears. Her body began trembling violently after the translucent cloud surged forward to surround the trailer. "Oh my God! The bacteria knows were in this water! It wants us!"

"The monster is here," Steve said. He looked around the trailer. He knew there was no escape. He realized the bacteria trapped them, and was thinking of ways to get at them.

"It's thinking of a way to get into this water!" Bonnie watched the bacteria swirling violently around the trailer as if angry. "It's pissed! It can see us, but it can't do anything more."

Roger gently grasped her arm, while attempting to reassure her. "We're safe in here."

"For how long are we safe? That bacteria really wants us!" Bonnie looked around fearfully as the silver bacteria swirled violently around and under the trailer, as if angry it was denied the human flesh it craved. "Will it figure out how to get in here, to get us?"

"The bacteria can't get to us under the water." Steve stared at the silver cloud billowing into the building through the open tunnel access doors. He slowly slid a hand across the cool glass wall protecting them from the deadly bacteria.

Bonnie became terrified before she screamed moments later, after the trailer unexpectedly tipped to the side, before it almost toppled over. A large amount of water slashed onto the floor after the violent jerking motion. "What's going on?"

Steve looked around frantically for a reason. He frowned while watching the wide and tall trailer tires disappearing in the silver cloud mist as Osiris biodegraded them. "Osiris is eating the tires, and this trailer is falling onto the steel tire rims."

"It's destroying the tires on this side too," Roger said, moments before the trailer crashed down violently to the floor, while the cube remained upright. He looked at the others after more water splashed out of the cube, to ensure they were not injured. "I think we're good now."

Roger frowned while intently staring at the large pile of stacked tires on the floor of the containment building. They mysteriously remained unaffected after the bacteria cloud surrounded them. "I don't understand why Osiris isn't biodegrading those rubber tires for nourishment?"

Moments later, Roger shaded his face with an arm, after an orange streak racing through the bacteria cloud created a brilliant explosion of blinding white light beside the trailer. When he lowered his arm, he noticed a large section of the bacteria cloud beside the trailer unexplainably disappeared in that flash of light. The accompanying thunderous noise caused the trailer to vibrate violently. He grasped Steve's shoulder before pointing in the water, after more areas of the cloud beside the trailer began disappearing in blinding flashes. "Those bright flashes appear to be somehow destroying the bacteria."

"Oh my God! My God!" Bonnie said, startling both Steve and Roger, before she began screaming hysterically. She pushed herself backward frantically in the water. Her arms and legs flailed until her back pressed tightly against a glass wall. She began motioning forward wildly with one arm underwater, pointing at something behind the men, while she continued screaming hysterically in her mask.

Steve quickly turned in the water to understand what frightened Bonnie. He was shocked to see the partially exposed bones of a human hand press against the outside of the trailer's glass wall. "What the hell is going on? I saw Osiris kill Troxell! How can he be alive now?"

Moments later Mason's partially mutilated body fell against the glass, while the bacteria swirled around him. He cried out from the pain as Osiris devoured his flesh, before he said, "Help me! I need your help!" He raised the boney fingers of his other hand to plead for help as he stared at Steve's face through the water, while suffering and in agony.

"What can I do to help him?" Steve watched Mason's face contort from the pain. He felt a strange sense of helplessness while watching the man's skin bubbling on his neck.

"Let me in there! Let me in!" Mason struggled to hit the glass wall with the boney hand as Osiris stripped more of the flesh from his fingers. "The pain is terrible! Help me before it's too late!"

"I can't do anything for him." Steve was fascinated, mesmerized, as he watched the bacteria devouring the man's flesh.

420

"Please, help me!" Mason began screaming in agony. As Osiris destroyed more of his flesh, his screams became one long loud wail. The deafening thunder in the building muffled his hysterical cries. The flesh of both hands completely disappeared before his arms fell to his sides.

Roger moved beside the glass wall while considering his options. "I have to do something to help him. Maybe I can pull him into this water before Osiris hurts me. We can share my mask."

"That won't work," Steve said. "Osiris will destroy your face mask, your air hoses, and your body, if you get out of the water for a second."

"You've got to do something," Bonnie said, screaming in her mask while watching Mason suffering. "You can't let him die out there!"

Roger watched Mason's skin bubbling away for several seconds as the bacteria devoured it. He realized there was not enough time to save the man's life. "There's nothing we can do to help him now."

Steve watched the tortured man's face with a macabre fascination. He studied the flesh as it seemingly formed masses of bubbles before disappearing in the bacteria cloud. "I feel sorry for him."

Mason blindly staggered backward in agony after the bacteria devoured his eyes. It began dissolving the flesh of his neck. His screams soon became inaudible gurgling sounds.

"This is amazing!" The destructive process of the bacteria fascinated Steve as it exposed the bones at the base of the man's skull. Seconds later, it stripped the last of the flesh from the dying man's head. Steve's eyes opened wide from shock when he saw the white skull staring at him, in the moments before the skeleton collapsed onto the floor.

Roger stared at the pile of bones. "I wanted to help people all of my life. The bacteria I helped to create just killed that poor man. What have I done? I've put all of the people on this planet in danger. How could I have done this?"

"Don't worry about anyone else," Steve said coldly. "Our only concern right now is saving our own lives."

As he thought about the destructive capabilities of his horrific creation, Roger noticed the streams of bubbles rising toward the surface of the water from the diving masks. Startling and horrifying images began filling his mind. "Do you remember the fish skeletons we saw in the aquariums in the pet store in Las Vegas?"

Steve frowned. "No, I don't remember going into the pet store. What are you thinking?"

"Osiris somehow traveled downward through the filter air bubbles to kill the fish in every tank."

"You're right!" Steve was shocked, and immediately looked up at the air bubbles escaping from their diving masks when they exhaled, breaking the surface of the water in the glass cube. He saw Osiris swirling above the water. "I forgot Osiris managed to get under the fish tank water!"

"The conditions are the same in here as they were in those aquariums!" Roger reached above their heads and began disrupting the even flow of bubbles making their way to the surface. "I'll break up the streams of bubbles rising to the surface so the bacteria can't get under the water."

Steve nodded, before checking the gauge on Bonnie's air tank. "It's three quarters full. We have the spare tanks. We can stay in this water for about ninety minutes."

'If we run low on air, I'll give my tank to Bonnie. I'll have to climb out of this cube, grab that air tank, and get back in the water, before Osiris hurts me.' Steve shook his head while studying the single green air tank lying on the concrete floor of the containment building beside the trailer. *'That plan is not going to work. I won't make it. If I can throw that air tank into this water to save Bonnie and Roger before Osiris kills me, then I'll be good!'*

Bonnie looked around and soon realized the streaks of colored lights passing through the cloud were becoming more numerous. They appeared to be much closer to the cube, and now much brighter in intensity. She closed her eyes tightly and covered the faceplate of the diving mask with both hands. Even then with her eyes closed, she became terrified when she could still make out brilliant flashes of light. She opened her eyes and slowly lowered her hands to study the colored streaks of light racing through the bacteria cloud from the fuel rods. She struggle for each breath as her chest muscles began to spasm from growing fear. Several moments later, fear suddenly overwhelmed her mind. She began frantically clawing her way toward the surface of the water. "I can't breathe in here! I have to get out of this water."

423

"Where are you going?" Steve was shocked by Bonnie's unexpected actions, and her hysterical screams. He reached out to grasp her ankle just as her wildly flailing arms and hands were about to break the surface of the water. "You'll die out there."

"I don't care if the bacteria hurts me!" She kicked his chest and shoulder with her other foot while attempting to escape from his grip. "I don't care anymore. The bacteria can kill me!"

"The bacteria will kill you!" Steve attempted to grasp her flailing arm, to pull her to the bottom of the water filled cube.

"Let me go! I can't stay in here!" Bonnie kicked at his legs while wildly attempting to free herself. "I have to get out of this water! I'll drown and die in here!"

"Stop struggling and get control of your fears!" Roger lunged forward in the water before wrapping an arm around her waist. He helped to pull her to the bottom of the water in the trailer. "Calm down, and talk to us!"

"Let go of me!" Bonnie struggled violently, before she eventually understood she could not free herself from the men's tight grips. She began fighting back her fears. Her eyes closed while taking several deep breaths to calm herself. Then she nodded, signaling she was again in control. "I'm better now. I really am."

Roger watched Osiris billowing around the trailer while the bright streaks of blue, white, orange and now green lights, coursed through the cloud. "I can't see the other side of the containment building now. Osiris looks like a thickening fog in here, and it's getting denser. I don't understand what's happening."

Steve gently grasped Bonnie's hand while watching the mysterious activities occurring around the trailer. "Osiris may be learning the radiation is destroying its cells. It may be fighting back. Or." He stopped speaking abruptly.

Bonnie looked at his face encased in the tight fitting diving mask, before she said, "Or, what? Tell me, so I know what to expect."

"Or the bacteria is mounting an offensive action, and it's planning to do something to attack the fuel rods."

She looked at the silver cloud swirling around, over, and under the glass cube. "What can it be doing that will allow it to attack the fuel rods? It's only a misty silver cloud!"

"A thinking and living cloud formation. It might think up some way to stop the release of radiation so it can survive."

"If the bacteria survives, we're going to eventually run out of air." Bonnie stared at the cloud swirling around on the other side of the clear glass wall. "I don't want to die this way."

Steve watched her kneeling beside him. Her long hair floated in the water around her head as if it was a halo. *'I can't let Osiris kill her the way it did Mason. I won't allow her to suffer that way.'*

A horrifying scenario began playing in his mind as if it was a video. In it, he watched himself shatter Bonnie's skull with an air tank. He realized the wound would kill her instantly, but save her from

425

the pain of Osiris devouring her flesh. Knowing he might only have minutes to be with the woman he loved, he moved closer to her in the water, until their thighs touched. That brought back more memories, before he grasped her hand. "Hey, did I tell you I love you today?"

She smiled after looking at him. "I love you too!"

"I see trouble," Roger said, startling the others. His words sounded both ominous and terrifying.

Steve said, "What is it?"

Roger pointed downward, toward a corner of the trailer. "I see water leaking out of this cube."

"That's not good." Steve studied the steady thin stream of water spraying onto the floor. He realized the hole was large, and allowing a substantial amount of water to escape.

Bonnie said, "How bad is it?"

"Bad enough. It's eventually going to empty this trailer, and expose us to the bacteria."

"Oh my god, what else can go wrong!" Her eyes closed in defeat. "What else can happen to us? What else?"

"We need to improvise, to survive." Steve frantically pulled off his shorts. Then he stuffed them into the corner of the glass cube to slow the flow of water. "Plugging this leak will give us more time in the water."

Brenton carefully studied live video feeds from the power plant on the monitors in his command center. He turned to Feltault, Reglovic, and Meridian. "We're getting these images from high

426

resolution surveillance cameras my men positioned four miles north of the plant."

"This critical situation is out of control." The night vision equipment allowed Reglovic to see the details of the bacteria cloud as it enveloped the entire power plant.

"Why do you say that?" Brenton was surprised by the remark.

"The radiation should have destroyed the bacteria cloud by now. I don't understand anything I'm seeing on those monitors."

"What are those strange colored streaks of light shooting through the cloud? They appear to be electrical charges!"

"I can't explain them."

"Can you speculate?"

"Maybe the bacteria are somehow channeling the radiation away from the plant in those flashes to protect itself, and that's why the radiation did not destroy the cloud as we predicted."

Brenton studied another monitor that showed an infrared image of the cloud swirling around the buildings of the power plant. "You're saying, utilizing the reactors to destroy Osiris didn't have a chance from the onset?"

"It appears the small amount of radiation released from the reactors will not destroy the mammoth cloud," Meridian said. He looked at the others who nodded their agreement.

"It's also possible Steve could not release a sufficient amount of radiation to kill the bacteria, before Osiris killed him and the others," Reglovic said.

"We need to confirm what's happening at that plant." Brenton pointed at his Communications Officer. "Have we heard anything from Roger or Steve in the last few minutes?"

"Negative. We haven't received any voice communication traffic out of the plant in the past forty minutes."

"What's the status of our transponder?"

"It stopped transmitting data thirty minutes ago."

"The what?" Reglovic looked at the others questioningly. "What is a transponder?"

"My men placed a transmitter in the control room, to monitor conditions in that one area."

"What is it telling you?"

"It stopped sending a signal." Brenton took a cup of coffee from an aide. "That's an indication Osiris destroyed the control room, and all the people in it."

"Steve and Roger must be dead." Meridian slowly rubbed his face nervously. "Those poor souls sacrificed themselves needlessly."

"They were good men on a difficult mission." Brenton shook his head while looking at his staff. "They'll be missed."

"I don't know if it's possible for us to stop Osiris." Feltault visualized the cloud moving through the densely populated areas of the nation unchecked, while it continued destroying buildings and killing millions of innocent people. "I just don't know."

Brenton motioned to his Executive Officer. "Have our Communications people open a secured communications link to the President. It's time we talked."

Reglovic said, "What are you going to tell him? Will you suggest using nuclear weapons during another attempt to destroy Osiris?"

"My job is to destroy Osiris with all of the resources at my disposal, Doctor." Brenton pointed at the bacteria cloud surrounding the now darkened power plant on a monitor. "Unfortunately Steve and Roger died during a futile attempt to destroy the cloud. It's time to bring in more firepower, even if it's nuclear, to kill that damn bacteria!"

Reglovic thought about the hopelessness of the situation. "You're right, General. The nuclear option is the only way to stop Osiris."

The Communications Officer spoke to his team working with satellite communications equipment. He said, "General, we've established communications with the President."

"Put him on the speakers." Brenton paused, waiting for the familiar tone, signaling him it was time to speak. "Mister President, this is Brenton."

"General, what's happening at that nuclear power plant?" President Stillman frowned while studying images of Osiris swirling around buildings at the plant, on large monitors in a bunker deep beneath the Pentagon building in Washington. "I don't understand what I'm seeing."

"The situation is confusing at best, and getting more complicated, Mister President."

"What's your assessment of the situation?" Stillman became angry with Brenton's apparent lack of relevant information. "Tell me what you think. Give me your best guess!"

429

"Based on what you're watching on that live video feed, the situation is rapidly worsening." Brenton read a message handed to him. "The radiation released from the reactors at the power plant is not stopping Osiris."

"Why isn't it working, General? I was told this is a proven method for destroying the bacteria."

"It appears the limited amount of radiation released from the reactors was insufficient to destroy the entire cloud."

Stillman slammed his pen down on a long and wide conference room table, while looking around the huge room filled with hundreds of civilian and military advisors. "What do your analysts and Intelligence people think Osiris will do next?"

"The bacteria cloud will destroy the power plant before it moves north. It will eventually become unstoppable."

The President appeared frightened, and took a deep breath after the ominous prediction. "How should we proceed to ensure the bacteria is eradicated from this plant?"

"I have a drastic recommendation, Mister President."

"I desperately need to hear that recommendation, General. Tell me what we should do?"

"We need to utilize Cruise missiles to deliver nuclear payloads into the Osiris cloud."

"You want to utilize our nuclear arsenal already? There is no way ground based conventional forces can defeat the bacteria cloud?"

"No sir. Tanks, explosives, pesticides, and fire, will have little or no effect on the cloud." Brenton read from a status report his staff hastily pulled together. "We need to determine what adverse effects a larger amount of radiation will have on the bacteria cloud."

"I agree with that approach." The President looked around the room, waiting for comments from his advisors. He was disappointed after none of his most experienced advisors offered recommendations to destroy the bacteria cloud. "How long will it take a Cruise missile fired from the Ticonderoga to reach the power plant?"

"Approximately twenty to thirty minutes, Sir."

Stillman began discussing the situation with his national security advisors. He nervously rubbed his hands together. "General, I haven't yet decided to authorize the use of our nuclear arsenal. I want to be absolutely confident of my decision, before I needlessly destroy a portion of our nation, and kill our people who remained at that plant."

"We're already assuming the people who remained at the plant to destroy Osiris are dead."

"That would be Roger Samulson, Doctor McClellan, and the reactor operator?"

"Yes, Sir. That's correct."

"There deaths are a great loss to the nation." President Stillman sat back in his chair, rubbing his hair as if exhausted. "I'll get back to you in a few minutes, General."

A relieved John Leckowicz, the Director of the Defense Intelligence Agency, smiled while looking down as he flipped through the pages of a notebook. He attempted to conceal the grin on his face with one hand. He appeared relaxed, wearing shorts and a floral print shirt, while men around him wore business suits. He exhaled smoke through his nose, before crushing a cigarette into an overflowing ashtray. Then he leaned to the side to whisper to a female aide. "Have we heard from our secret weapon Troxell?"

"He didn't send his last scheduled hourly status report. He's not answering his cell phone, but he may have lost it while fleeing from the power plant with a sample of the Osiris bacteria."

"Did our helicopter gunship pilots report anything unusual before or after they extracted Troxell from that power plan?"

"We haven't received a status from them yet, Sir. We instructed those pilots not to use their radios, so no one in the military would become suspicious of our operation if they overheard their report. Our assumption is they're safe, and landed far from the power plant to drop off Troxell at that deserted runway. That's where the Air Force transport aircraft was waiting to fly him to Washington with samples of the Osiris bacteria."

"Very good." Leckowicz smiled while sitting back to light another cigarette. "When the pilots check in with a status, tell them to return to the power plant to capture images of the bacteria cloud while they're airborne."

"Why do you want to put those pilots and helicopter crews in danger in the vicinity of that killer cloud?

"We need Osiris to find and destroy those helicopters!"

The woman frowned. "The bacteria will kill our men!"

"That's the outcome I want to see, my dear."

"I don't understand. Why do you want them to die?"

"If they're dead, they can't tell anyone what they did to stop the scientists at the power plant, or what they know about Frostfire and Troxell."

She thought about the explanation, before she smiled. "Now I understand your logic and reasoning. It's perfect, and ensures we're not implicated!"

"My plans are always perfect!"

President Stillman studied the images of the huge Osiris cloud attacking and engulfing the power plant on various monitors in the room, while pacing nervously. He ignored the loud protests of advisors who warned against using nuclear weapons. He did not respond to other men and women offering new and untested suggestions for stopping Osiris.

He suddenly stopped walking, before raising his hands to quiet the group. "I've made my decision. Ask the television and radio networks to broadcast the message I recorded yesterday. That message explains my decision to utilize nuclear weapons to stop Osiris, and the devastating radioactive consequences I'm forcing our future generations to deal with."

General Philip Brage, the Chairman of the Joint Chiefs of Staff, said, "What are your orders, Mister President?"

President Stillman took a deep breath while contemplating the world altering effects of his nuclear attack option. "General Brage, instruct the captain of the Ticonderoga that I have elected to move forward with Operation Hidden Sun. Order that vessel to fire a single Cruise missile carrying a nuclear payload toward the power plant, after I issue the nuclear release code."

"You're ordering the Ticonderoga to launch only one missile, Sir?"

"That's correct. Those are my orders, and they are to be followed!"

"Yes, Sir! Why are you utilizing a single missile attack, and not a salvo of atomic weapons to destroy the bacteria cloud, Mister President?"

"I want to observe what effect the massive amount of radiation released during the single nuclear explosion has on the bacteria. I alone will make the determination if additional missiles must be launched to destroy the cloud."

Brenton's jaw tightened while looking at his shocked staff, as he listened to the President's instructions. "Radiation contamination of our nation should not be a concern at this time Mr. President. If Osiris survives the attack you have planned, it will eventually kill everyone across the country."

"I'm well aware of those facts, General!" The President sat at the table with his advisors, while physically and mentally dejected by his radical decision. "You don't need to tell me what I already know."

"Yes, Mister President."

"Without more information General, I'm not confident utilizing nuclear weapons is the correct course of action."

434

"During Steve's last transmission he mentioned something unusual."

"Is it something that may help us understand the situation?" The President immediately sat forward, waiting for an explanation.

"I can't provide a detailed explanation that will help us, Sir. I don't understand his message."

"What did he say?" The President looked around at his personal advisors questioningly, eager for additional information

"He told me to ask you about something he called Frostfire."

"Frostfire?" Stillman's mouth dropped open in shock. "How does he know about that?"

"Know about what?" Brenton frowned at some of his staff questioningly. "What was Steve talking about?"

"That's not important for you to understand! Forget what Doctor McClellan told you! Do not mention that single word again!" The President became furious, his face red from frustration and embarrassment. "Do you understand me, General?"

"Yes, Sir." Brenton appeared shocked by the President's sudden and angry outburst.

"Your orders are to stop Osiris!" The President felt the beds of nervous perspiration forming on his forehead, and neck. "Do you understand your role, General?"

"Yes, Sir."

John Leckowicz leaned forward to shout into a microphone. "General, this is Leckowicz of Defense Intelligence. Can you hear me?"

435

"Yes Sir, I'm reading you." Brenton motioned his senior staff members forward to listen to the conversation.

"I do not want you discussing the word Frostfire with anyone."

"Say again. I don't understand."

"No one outside your immediate staff is to know about Frostfire." Leckowicz took a deep breath to calm himself, as he felt his heart racing in his chest. "Am I making myself perfectly clear, General? That word is related to our national security policy!"

"I don't understand. Doctors Meridian, Reglovic, and Feltault are in my command center as we speak. They already heard us discussing Frostfire."

"They're listening to our conversation now?" Leckowicz staff immediately huddled around him, whispering recommendations.

"They've heard our entire conversation, while they're in my command center helping me evaluate the situation at the power plant."

"I'm ordering you to kill those men now!" Leckowicz crushed out a cigarette, before he stood and began screaming. "Terminate them immediately, General! Those men are more dangerous than Osiris! Kill the bastards, before you do anything else to stop the bacteria cloud."

"Disregard that order, General," President Stillman said, shouting across the table. "I will decide if and when to utilize deadly force! Do you understand me Leckowicz! Now shut your mouth!"

"We don't have any other options in this current situation! Those men need to be silenced."

"You're out of line!" The President said, shouting as his anger increased.

"You're telling me to murder these doctors only because they heard the word Frostfire?" Brenton frowned. "I don't understand any of this, and I need clarification and confirmation from my Chief of Staff, before I proceed."

"Those doctors risk our very national security by knowing that one word. Kill them now," Leckowicz said, shouting into a microphone. "Shoot them, and kill the bastards now, before it's too late!"

During his fanatic ramblings to maintain the secrecy associated with his project, Leckowicz did not notice the President walking around the table. He appeared shocked when Stillman grasped his shoulder from behind, to pull him backward violently until he fell onto his chair. "What do you think you're doing to me Mister President?"

"I've heard enough out of you. You, and your entire agency, still answer to me!"

"What's going on Mister President?" Brenton now felt very confused by everything he heard from various people.

"General, I want you to disregard everything you were just told about killing people. We need to work together to get that Cruise missile into the air." President Stillman began walking back to his chair.

"I understand Mister President. I'll coordinate final activities with the skipper of the Ticonderoga. Brenton, out."

Leckowicz stood seemingly incensed, while pointing at the President. "Are you stupid? You

437

can't let information related to Frostfire get out to the public! I don't care what it takes or who we have to kill, to protect that information."

The President watched a high-ranking Army officer prepare the computer needed to transmit the encrypted nuclear release codes to the Ticonderoga, to allow the launching of the Cruise missile. "We don't need Frostfire. You never justified the need for that weapon, and you ignored my order when I told you to cancel the project! Your personal efforts to develop the perfect super biological weapon is now threatening all people of our nation, and the entire world!"

"You're a fool sitting in the White House, that doesn't have the stomach to make the difficult decisions! We must safeguard the bacteria so we can use it to trigger an uprising in Iran, and Afghanistan. The public cannot learn we have this new weapon in our stockpile, or they'll know it's us when we use it to topple the governments of other nations!"

"It appears the public is already aware of your super-secret project. Doctor McClellan and others know about it."

"We can correct that mistake with a few well-placed bullets to his head if he's still alive, and you as President showing a backbone and some leadership skills."

The President listened while officials and advisors eagerly huddled around him, as the military officer explained how the computer would transmit the release codes to the Ticonderoga, after

438

Stillman entered his authorization. "How did McClellan know your project's name?"

"How the hell should I know? I'm not a mind reader!" Leckowicz looked at his advisors and laughed with them.

"Frostfire was classified as a black box project. Only a very few people were aware of its existence. Only my staff, and your people, knew the details."

"One of your people at the White House must have discussed it with a reporter. Maybe one of your trusted advisors leaked the flipping details of our bleeding edge project to the press!"

"I'm very confident that did not happen. If that was the case, the press and congress would be banging on the front doors of the White House, demanding an explanation I can't provide to them!"

"Maybe McClellan is a good guesser." Leckowicz looked at the other high-ranking officials who agreed to utilize Troxell, to ensure the Frostfire project remained a secret. He was shocked when they remained silent, and did not come to his aid.

"Did you send one of your representatives to Brenton's command center, to interfere with the work of the researchers attempting to stop Osiris?"

Leckowicz lit another cigarette. He slowly blew out the match. "Of course I did."

President Stillman lowered his pen. "What is the mission of that individual? What instructions did you give that person?"

"He was told to protect Osiris any way necessary. Did you think I was going to leave our

nation's precious security to you, and your staff of
bumbling amateurs?"

Chapter 17

"You violated my executive directive to curtail the Frostfire project!" The President said, shouting. "Now you have the audacity to find fault with me, and the members of my administration?"

"You do nothing to protect our nation!" Leckowicz smiled, suddenly feeling self-righteous during the escalating verbal exchange. "I'm personally taking the drastic measures necessary to protect our nation from external security threats."

"Your unauthorized security measures are unconscionable. You put all of us in danger."

"I put us in danger?" Leckowicz smiled, before his face contorted strangely from growing anger. "Your ridiculous rhetoric with our enemies invites terrorist attacks. We developed Frostfire as an effective deterrent to prevent those attacks!"

"Your actions killed millions of our citizens, Leckowicz!"

"That is unfortunate." He smiled at the others seated around the table. "My bad."

"Your conscious disregard of my instructions caused those people to die!" President Stillman's fists clenched tightly. "You're going to face the consequences alone!"

"This national crisis was not created by my agency alone."

"The press and Congress will put the blame solely on your shoulders! I'll give them all of the information they need to crucify you, and the members of your agency that assisted you! You disregarded government guidelines and broke the law doing so, and you're going to face the consequences!"

"You're going to tell them what actually happened to Osiris? You are a dumb bastard!"

"I may be, but I will personally inform Congress you continued the Frostfire project without my approval!"

"That's not completely true. You're more involved than you understand, Mister President."

"My administration had nothing to do with creating this deadly situation. I will not protect you."

"You're a naive fool. You were misled by your own advisors. The people you trusted betrayed you!"

"Don't attempt to implicate others to diffuse the public focus from you and your agency."

"You're entrenched in this situation deeper than you can imagine."

"What does that mean?"

"Your advisors ordered me to move forward with the Frostfire project eight months ago," Leckowicz said, shouting as he stood. "They didn't forward that critical move-forward information to the Oval Office, did they?"

"That's a ridiculous and very dangerous accusation." President Stillman looked around the room at his personal advisors. He became concerned after all of them avoided eye contact with him. "Did any of you authorize the continuation of the project I personally terminated as being inhumane and barbaric?"

"Open your damn mouths! Tell him how you conspired against our President!" Leckowicz looked at people around the room. "Tell our President the truth, you bunch of damn cowards!"

"What is the truth? Did something take place in my administration I am not aware of?" The President stared at his advisors coldly. "I demand an immediate response from someone in this room!"

Leckowicz laughed. "They won't admit what they did."

"I don't understand any of this, and I'm losing my patience."

"Your advisors are working to keep their jobs when you don't get reelected. They consider you a one-term liability!"

The President sat back while frowning. "You're delusional! Explain to me what my most trusted advisors and friends are doing to save their jobs?"

"They're planning to present Frostfire as the ultimate weapon to your successor. They want to impress him with their creativity."

"That's a damn lie! You're trying to save yourself from being fired and humiliated in the press!"

"I'm not lying! That's the only truthful information you've been told, since this disastrous situation began playing out!"

"Is he telling me the truth?" President Stillman stared at his key advisors. "I demand an answer, now!"

Leckowicz smiled as the men and women remained silent. "They're not going to say you're a terrible leader to your face. They only do that when we're in private meetings, where they berate your stinking performance as leader of our nation!"

"Now I understand. The confidence my advisors exhibit in me is overwhelming." The President sat back, before closing his eyes. "In an attempt to keep your jobs, you, my trusted advisors, have released the apocalypse onto the world. All of you should be arrested and go to prison for negligent homicide!"

"That's how the scenario played out, to get us where we are today, Stillman." Leckowicz said, ignoring the angry stares of others.

"I'm very disappointed to learn of this startling revelation." The President turned to Franklin Perry, his personal senior advisor and closest friend. "Frank, were you aware of these activities taking place in my administration?"

"We're much more experienced in foreign affairs than you, Mister President." The older man with thinning gray hair, who served five terms as senator, sighed heavily. "Your advisors have spent their entire lives in government."

"Making a career of public service does not mean you ignore the President's decisions."

"I understand that. However, the military and all of your advisors unanimously believe Frostfire should be an integral component of our military biological weapons arsenal. It will be required by future administrations to destroy our enemies."

"Why didn't you tell me you gave the green light to develop Frostfire, when this crisis escalated?"

"We did it to ensure you had complete deniability."

President Stillman frowned. "I don't understand. Complete deniability?"

"When foreign leaders asked if your administration was responsible for causing Osiris to mutate and become deadly, you were able to implicitly deny those accusations."

"You hid the truth from me, so I could lie to the world for all of you?" The President appeared shocked.

"You did a very good job being our puppet," Leckowicz said, adding to the escalating tension in the room. "You even read the speeches we composed and edited for you, to protect ourselves."

Stillman gaze fell to the table. "I'm overwhelmed with anguish, now that I understand my administration is responsible for the deaths caused by Osiris. I find this utterly unimaginable, that my administration killed millions. I trusted all of you, and you let me down."

"No one knows this administration is responsible for anything other than attempting to destroy Osiris," said Franklin Perry. "Move forward with your head held high as you end this horrific situation!"

"We have people in the public sector who know the truth. McClellan is aware of Frostfire." The President sat back, before he briefly covered his eyes with his hands. "I, I don't feel comfortable in this position of being a mass murderer."

"We'll deal with those people who know bits and pieces of information related to Frostfire. Those troublesome individuals should not be your concern, as you rebuild the nation after you destroy Osiris."

"How do you propose to deal with those people who have families? Feed those poor individuals to the Osiris monster you helped to create?"

"I can assure you, it's nothing so dramatic."

"What will you do to protect my administration, and advisors? I want to know the details of your plan."

"We'll manufacture character witnesses who will affirm those people are compulsive liars. We've learned that's the most effective deterrent when troublesome people are spreading legitimate claims we need to refute, related to our military or government. After we destroy their lives and reputations with false information, they all become quiet and timid souls, cowering in a corner!"

The President looked at John Leckowicz. "I want you to tell me how McClellan knows about Frostfire? Give me the truth, damn it!"

"I sent a representative to collaborate with the Doctor. They must have talked."

"I'm guessing your representative is responsible for the deadly accidents that plagued Brenton's facility?"

"Again, I don't know what you're talking about. You're babbling like a fool, while everyone watches and laughs at you!"

"Did your representative hinder our leading scientist's efforts, to protect Frostfire for your agency?"

"Those were the exact instructions given to me, by your advisors in this room."

"What did they tell you to do? I want to know, now!"

"If any of the scientists or doctors discovered an effective method for destroying Frostfire, they were to be killed. Executed, so they could not harm the bacteria!"

"My stomach is churning after hearing this disgusting scenario. You murdered our nation's most knowledgeable and valuable scientists!"

"We couldn't let them destroy Osiris until we gathered bacteria samples, which our military scientists will turn into a biological weapon," General Brage said.

"Can someone confirm we have successfully secured those bacteria samples?"

"Yes, we have them in our possession," Leckowicz said. "You can nuke the damn plant to eliminate all of the evidence whenever you're ready to show the world you're a strong leader."

The President looked at John Kump, the Secretary of Defense. "Did you sanction the murders of our scientists?"

Kump looked at the people who agreed to utilize Troxell to maintain the secrecy around Frostfire. "You don't fully understand the implications of this situation, Mister President. We purposely limited your exposure, and direct involvement in the military scenarios, to keep you safe."

"You kept my administration safe with lies, deceit, and murder!" The President's lips pressed together tightly, his uneasiness apparent.

"We're conducting business as usual in Washington, as every administration has done before you."

"I now feel as if I have betrayed the people of our nation, and the Office of the President."

"Nonsense," Kump said, before he laughed. "This is done every day in Washington by congressmen, and the heads of our government agencies."

"What are you saying?"

"We all make mistakes. Then we tailor reality going forward to meet our needs and achieve our goals."

"What options do I have to remedy this situation?" President Stillman noticed groups of his advisors huddling together around the room. They whispered while exchanging ideas.

"We need a plausible, but false, explanation," Shawn Robinson, the Deputy Director of the Central Intelligence Agency said, before he began writing on a yellow lined pad. "I have some ideas I want to socialize with this group."

"You're suggesting utilizing a fabricated story to protect my administration?" The President watched as more of his advisors huddled together. Their conversations became louder.

"Think of it as disseminating misinformation to reduce public anxiety and angina, Mister President."

"We're going to lie about the true nature of the situation?" President Stillman sounded skeptical.

"We'll tell the story with a different perspective."

The advisors began suggesting manufactured scenarios, developed with misinformation, to report to the world. Stories to mislead the public, and ensure the government officials involved in the

Frostfire debacle, could not be discovered or prosecuted.

"I firmly believe we can legitimately explain Osiris was altered by a new medicine," said Byron Groetfield of the National Security Agency.

"Explain that scenario." The President sat forward while interested, his elbows on the table.

Groetfield closed his eyes while thinking. "Researchers in a startup medical research laboratory devastated by Osiris, developed a new cutting edge bacteria to destroy cancer tumors."

"I don't see how new bacteria would affect Osiris."

"Those bacteria combined with Osiris. The tumor destroying capabilities became the catalyst which now allows Osiris to destroy flesh."

"I'm satisfied with that explanation." The President nodded his approval to Franklin Perry. "That's a very plausible scenario. Go with it."

"We'll approach this explanation from the sympathetic viewpoint," Groetfield said.

"How do we do that?" The President frowned questioningly at several of his advisors.

"The company developed the new medicine to eliminate cancer and save lives, but oops, the discovery inadvertently resulted in the deaths of millions. Now move on with your lives, people."

"That story will divert all attention away from my administration." President Stillman nodded to Senior White House Press Secretary, Marjorie Fletcher.

"That scenario is compelling and reasonable, Mister President." Fletcher began entering notes

449

into her laptop computer. "We'll pull together a persuasive speech for you to deliver to the nation, after you destroy Osiris."

"I'll arrange a press conference with all of the major networks for later this morning," James Foster from the White House Public Relations office said. "You can provide the details of that story to the world, along with an explanation of how and why you met with your advisors and made the command decision to utilize nuclear weapons to finally destroy Osiris."

"That's our new reality going forward, Mister President," General Brage said. "We discovered and confirmed Osiris was mutated by a private company's experimental bacteria."

"This is an excellent approach for resolving any questions people may have, Mister President," Byron Groetfield said, before he smiled while looking around the room.

"The National Security Agency will fabricate the paperwork to document the existence of the fictitious medical research laboratory," Robert Thorton said. "We'll report Osiris killed all of the company employees before the facility burned to the ground. We'll have no witnesses, company documentation or records, to refute the misinformation we provide to our nation and the world."

"Excellent! One crisis is resolved." President Stillman smiled, as he became enthusiastic after realizing he could not be criticized for his administration's actions. He watched Osiris swirling around the power plan on monitors. "Now I'll

450

transmit the nuclear launch codes, and our military will finally destroy Osiris."

Inside Brenton's command center, Reglovic still appeared frightened while watching the radar images of Osiris surrounding the power plant on monitors. "Why did someone suggest you kill us several minutes ago, while you spoke to the President, General?"

"I can't answer that question, Doctor." Brenton looked at this staff questioningly. "I don't understand anything we were told."

"We have the captain of the Ticonderoga on a secured communications line, General," the Communications officer said. "He confirmed the President transmitted the release code needed to launch the first Cruise missile."

Brenton lifted a microphone. "Captain, this is General Brenton. How are you?"

"I'm good, General. I'm nervous and apprehensive, and waiting for your instructions, Sir!" Captain Charles Trobowski, the commander of the Ticonderoga, stood in the red glow of overhead lights in the ship's Combat Information Center. Sailors studying computer monitors tracked the location of the Osiris cloud, to identify its location if it began moving from the power plant.

"We're moving forward with the attack plan. I want to verbally confirm Operation Hidden Sun is a go."

"I'm confirming my understanding to move forward with Operation Hidden Sun." Trobowski gave a thumbs-up signal to sailors, silently

451

instructing them to begin preparations to launch missiles.

"The President authorized the launch of one Tomahawk Cruise missile. It will carry a nuclear payload, which will detonate over the power plant as planned. Do you copy, over?"

"Roger that." Trobowski studied a monitor showing an infrared image of Osiris surrounding the power plant. "I'll confirm the launch status, after our missile is airborne."

"Very good. Keep me informed. Brenton, out."

Trobowski stepped to his Combat Assessment Team. "Arm one Tomahawk with a Robust Nuclear Earth Penetrator device. Prepare for immediate launch."

"Yes sir," the Launch Control Officer said.

The Weapons Control Officer began reading instructions to his team from a thick prelaunch checklist manual. "Download the coordinates of the power plant, designated as Echo Hijack Lima, into the missile's onboard computers."

"Target coordinates successfully downloaded and confirmed, Sir," a sailor said. "Terrain guidance maps download to the missile's on-board computer, completed. We're ready to fly."

Another sailor said, "Nuclear warhead programmed for ground impact detonation at the power plant target site."

Loud alarms began wailing in the Combat Information Center, indicating the nuclear warhead aboard the Cruise missile was armed and programmed for detonation.

The Senior Weapon's Control Officer said, "Missile ready for launch, Captain."

Trobowski nodded. "Mark the time, and fire."

The Fire Control Officer shuddered from growing anxiety while watching a large color monitor in the Combat Information Center. He studied the Cruise missile launch area on the deck of the ship to ensure there no visible issues. Several seconds later loud sirens began sounding on the deck, signaling the ship's crew that a launch was imminent.

"Missile launch is imminent!" He squeezed the launch control device, clenched tightly in his hand.

A huge cloud of yellow and red flames erupted from a missile launch tube on the deck of the ship. Flames shot from the end of the long gray Cruise missile, as it flew from the ship with a deafening roar. The missile began a straight vertical ascent into the cloudless sky, before arcing to the east, as it flew toward the coastline of the United States.

"Missile away successfully," the Weapon's Control Officer said.

In Brenton's command center everyone heard Trobowski say, "Our Cruise missile loaded with a nuclear payload was successfully launched from the Ticonderoga. Onboard telemetry, and our radar images, indicates the missile is on course, and flying toward the target as programmed."

"General, the President is asking to speak to you," the Communications Officer said.

Brenton nodded. "This is General Brenton, Mister President."

"What's our status, General? What's going on? I need to understand what's happening!"

"The Ticonderoga just launched the Cruise missile, Mister President. The missile is flying toward the power plant as we speak, Sir."

"Excellent." President Stillman suddenly felt exhilarated by the stressful situation, and the knowledge he had a plan to protect his administration and personal reputation. "My advisors here with me and I will determine if the nuclear device has an effect on Osiris."

"How do we move forward after you determine the impact radiation has on the bacteria, Sir?"

"We'll decide the need to utilize additional nuclear weapons to destroy all of the bacteria cloud."

"Yes, Sir. I want to review the track of that Cruise missile. I'll get back to you in a few minutes with an updated status, Mister President."

Brenton waited for the distinctive tone, signaling the communications link with the President was no longer active. He realized he could talk freely to his staff, without anyone outside his command center hearing him. He studied the anxiety on the faces of his staff. "We still have a few minutes to determine if this is the correct course of action."

Colonel Mark Hudson stepped forward. "What do you need from us, General?"

"Get the ground based radar people, and our airborne radar surveillance teams, to tell us if the Osiris cloud is decreasing in size, after Steve hit the damn thing with radiation. Order our communications people to continue attempting to

454

contact Steve and Roger. I need to talk to them, now!"

"Yes, Sir." Hudson and Straley rushed to different areas of the command center tent to retrieve information.

"Why are you wasting your time trying to contact Steve?" Reglovic shook his head as he stared at the floor, while remembering Steve's laugh and enthusiasm. "If he and Roger are still alive, that missile will kill them when it explodes."

"We can abort the detonation of the nuclear device aboard the Cruise missile, while it's in flight." Brenton frowned after several of his staff began talking loudly. He watched as several soldiers shouted questions, while others responded.

"What does that abort process entail?"

"All Cruise missiles have a fail-safe system built into the technology. The missile can be ordered to self-destruct with an encrypted and coded electronic signal."

Brenton stepped to a table where four soldiers silently studied a topographical map. "Where's my reconnaissance team, and what's there status?"

Colonel Raffalo pointed at a blue triangle. "Savoy Eagle is currently positioned here."

Brenton frowned, questioningly. "Where's that in relationship to the power plant?"

"They're located five miles north of the plant."

"What's he doing five miles from the damn plant? I told Major Baxter I didn't want his ass any closer than ten miles."

Raffalo twisted a pencil nervously in his hands. "After the lights went out at the power plant, Baxter

455

reported he was moving closer with his Hummers, to get a better look."

"He's too damn close to that cloud!" Brenton became concerned about the safety of his men. "Order him to pull back now, and move his team to a safer location. Tell him that's a direct order from me!"

Another officer said, "Yes, Sir. Does Baxter understand we're utilizing a nuclear device to attack the cloud?"

"He's aware of the risks. He and all of his men volunteered for this assignment."

"The nuclear blast will eradicate everything within a thirty mile radius of the plant. Those men are danger close to that detonation point, General."

Brenton studied the map before he motioned to his Communication officer. "Get Baxter's team on the damn radio. Tell him, I'm ordering him to find shelter for his men, immediately!"

Major Anthony Baxter cautiously looked around to ensure he could account for the twenty members of his Special Forces team. He knelt on a highway roadbed to watch Osiris swirling around the plant through powerful night vision binoculars. "Those two scientists were crazy to think they could stop that cloud alone."

A soldier cradling an automatic weapon in his arms laughed, before he said, "They're crazy, Major? We must be the crazy ones, to be this close to that flipping monster."

"Where's your sense of adventure, McNeill? You tell me you enjoy being in the middle of the difficult battles and firefights, or you get bored!"

"This is different! This mission is suicide, Skipper." Sergeant McNeill shuddered while watching the towering deadly cloud swirling a few miles from him as the morning sky began to brighten.

"I thought the same thing when Brenton told me he wanted observers out here in the field." Baxter remembered his meeting with Brenton, and the General's request. '*Tony, I need your recon team in position ten to fifteen miles north of the power plant. I want you to be my eyes on the ground, so you can keep me informed.*'

'*Why do you need my team so close to that cloud, and the power plant?*' Baxter remembered studying a map on a table, while meeting with the General.

'*I need your team in position to tell me exactly what's happening, and how I should react if things go bad.*'

Baxter remembered asking Brenton the difficult question. '*What options do I have for getting my team to safety, if Osiris advances toward our position to attack us? Our weapons won't stop the bacteria.*'

'*You and your team will run like hell and evacuate the area immediately, Major. If that happens, I'll dispatch a team of helicopters to extract you and your men.*'

'*What if we don't have that much time?*'

Baxter remembered Brenton paused, before looking into his eyes. '*I cannot respond to that question, Son. I can only tell you this assignment will be extremely dangerous, and possibly deadly. You can say no based on those factors and concerns. But I'm asking you personally to take on this mission, because I trust and value your judgement.'*

'I'm risking the lives of my men needlessly, General. Why can't you send in an unmanned drone, or Predator to do the reconnaissance work? Those aircraft can transmit live television pictures to your command center.'

'I could do that, but those aircraft will provide me with a one-dimensional view of the battlefield. I won't know if something important is happening just outside of the camera's view.'

'Something? Something such as?' Baxter remembered frowning at Brenton. *'What do you think is going to happen at that power plant?'*

'We're going to be engaged in a deadly battle for the survival of all people on this planet! I can't overlook anything that could drastically change my understanding of the battlefield situation. We can't make any mistakes with this one. Your team will be fine on the ground and out of range of Osiris.'

"Fine? I don't think so," Baxter said mumbling while focusing the binoculars on the upper areas of the silver cloud. Dense smoke rising from the area bombed to the south provided a black backdrop to the swirling silver mist.

"That cloud is the messenger of the devil," Staff Sergeant Miguel Sanchez said, while pointing at the cloud in the distance. "It's evil, released from hell onto the world by the devil himself to destroy all mankind."

"I have to agree with you, Sanchez." Baxter pointed forward with one hand. "I see some strange colored flashes of light moving inside the cloud, but I can't identify them, or make out what they are."

"I see them too, Skipper. They're dazzling colored lights created by the devil," Sanchez said, while staring transfixed at the cloud. "They're shimmering and beautiful globes of light, like jewels luring unsuspecting people to their deaths!"

Baxter frowned while looking at Sanchez, a combat experienced soldier he knew for years. "Hey man, are you okay?"

"I just realized the devil is close by us in that cloud! I know the devil is waiting in that cloud before he steps onto the Earth to destroy it. He's trying to hide, but I can see him, and he can see us. He's tempting us to move closer with those colored lights, so he can kill us."

"Relax. Calm down! We're not getting any closer to the power plant."

"Keep those laser range finders focused on the cloud," Baxter's executive officer, Captain Griswold, told several soldiers. He did not understand why Sanchez appeared to be panicking, but the man's statements alarmed and concerned him. "We want to know the moment Osiris starts moving this way."

"You're not going to believe this traffic I'm receiving from command, Major." A soldier lowered a portable radio handset. "We've got a heavy weapons headed our way."

"Is General Brenton sending in B-52's to saturation bomb this area?" Baxter lowered his binoculars. He appeared confused. "What should we expect?"

"Command reports we have an inbound Tomahawk targeting that Osiris cloud. It's carrying a nuke."

"What the hell? Where's that warhead going to detonate?"

"On the ground directly under the bacteria cloud, and on top of us."

"That wasn't the plan Brenton shared with me, damn it! Confirm that message and authenticate it."

"I confirmed it already, Skipper. We don't have much time to find shelter."

"Where's our extraction helicopters?"

"Command says it'll take too long for them to get here. We're on our own."

Griswold stepped beside a soldier intently studying a topographical map. "Find us a place to dig in, so we can get some cover."

The soldier slid a finger across the map. "I've got a drainage pipe three clicks east of here. It might provide us with some shelter. But I don't know if it can protect us from a nuke."

"Let's find it, now." Baxter led his men to their Hummers. After driving for ten minutes, he saw the large cement pipe extending from an embankment under a roadbed. He was surprised to see a protective wire grate covering the end of the wide pipe, preventing people from entering it.

"Pull that damn wire off the pipe with our Hummers, so we can move our team inside." Griswold checked his watch, before staring at Osiris billowing more than three miles into the sky. "I feel sorry for the people who stayed at the power plant. They're all dead."

"So are we if we don't get into that damn pipe soon," Baxter said.

"Heads up," A soldier said, shouting. "Watch your asses!"

Baxter stepped back to watch two Hummers pull the grate off the pipe using chains. "Everyone get inside that damn pipe. Sanchez, you and the radio are out here with me."

"It's not safe to stay out here in the open, Major?" Miguel Sanchez appeared terrified. "The devil will find us if we're out in the open. He'll make the cloud come for us, like it's a river of death filled with dead souls."

"I want to watch the plant for a few more minutes, before I make my final report to Brenton. Then we'll get into the pipe with the others. Watch our backs."

Chapter 18

Inside the containment building, Steve became more concerned after he realized the thunderous sounds accompanying the brilliant streaks of colored light were becoming louder, and were occurring with greater frequency. The deafening sounds reminded him of roadside bombs exploding in Iraq. Each one startled him. He touched the trailer's thick glass wall as the reverberating sounds caused them to vibrate and throb until the glass became distorted, and appeared to be deformed. He thought, *'If those noises get louder, they may shatter these glass walls. The broken glass will release the water, and Osiris will be on top of us in a second. I thought we would be safe in here, and now I've inadvertently put Bonnie and Roger in danger.'*

Roger noticed that several large sections of the silver cloud beside the trailer disappeared, after four blinding green streaks of light passed through them. He frowned while watching more of the silver cloud violently billowing into the containment building through the hole in the wall, and through the access tunnel, to fill the void. He looked overhead to study the silver cloud now rapidly rotating around the suspended fuel rods in a tornado shaped funnel. "Is Osiris attacking the source of the radiation?"

"How does it know the radiation is coming from the fuel rods?" Bonnie felt her sense of terror increasing again while staring at the silver bacteria cloud swirling around the trailer. "It looks angry because it can't get to us!"

"If it figured out the source of the radiation, this is reasoning well above a rat's understanding," Roger said.

"Maybe it's intelligence developed, so now it's a thinking organism." Steve squinted through the vibrating glass wall. He studied an unusually bright and stationary area of purple light spinning inside the silver cloud. It appeared centered beneath the suspended fuel rods. Several fast moving brilliant green streaks of light blinded him momentarily. "I see a mass of purple light in the bacteria."

"Purple light?" Roger sounded shocked. He looked around. "Where are you seeing that?"

The brilliant streaks traveling through the cloud suddenly became more numerous. The thunderous noises accompanying them startled Steve while he stared into the cloud. He frowned after noticing another mass of purple light, which unexpectedly appeared in the cloud, before it began spinning near the ceiling of the building. "Something's happening inside the cloud mass. I see something tinting the bacteria purple!"

"Oh my God! Look at that! Look over there!" Bonnie startled the men with her excited cries. She began pointing wildly at six small spinning spheres of brilliant yellow light, evenly spaced, and floating stationary within the swirling bacteria cloud. They frightened her when they mysteriously and slowly materialized several feet from the trailer. As they began spinning counterclockwise faster, the spheres became distinct diamond shaped parallelograms of yellow light. The geometrical diamond shaped glowing lights appeared to be four inches high, and two inches in diameter. "What are those lights? Where did they come from? What are they?"

"I see more of those colored shapes behind us." Roger pointed at similar spinning green diamonds of light mysteriously forming inside the bacteria cloud. The center of each diamond shape light glowed with a dark amber hue, while the exterior edges were a bright translucent shade of green.

Steve watched additional diamonds shaped structures forming throughout the silver cloud. "I see red, blue, green, orange, and purple diamonds inside the bacteria."

"Where did they come from? They're beautiful!" Bonnie watched as the color of each diamond shaped mass of light brightened to become vivid and distinct.

"Maybe its escaping natural gas that ignited," Steve said, frowning at the glowing lights.

"The shapes are too uniform to be burning gas," Roger said.

"You're right. If they were gas, they'd burn themselves out in a few seconds. They're something else."

"They're moving! The lighted shapes are beginning to move!" Roger became excited, and confused, after the glowing spheres began unexplainably traveling through the bacteria cloud. Several minutes later, he realized all of the spinning spheres began rotating in a clockwise direction, as they travelled through the bacteria cloud filling the lower area of the containment building.

"Do you have any idea what created them?" Bonnie smiled while watching the colored geometrical diamond shapes slowly and steadily moving through the bacteria cloud. "They appeared out of nowhere."

"They're going to hit the trailer! Get back! Get back!" Roger frantically motioned Steve and Bonnie out of the way, after noticing several diamond shaped lights were about to collide with a glass wall of the trailer.

"If they shatter the glass, run to that reactor pool of water under the fuel rods," Steve said, as his anxiety rapidly increased. "That water will protect us from Osiris.

"How can something so beautiful hurt us?" Bonnie felt a strange calming sensation while her heart pounded in her chest.

"This is amazing!" Roger watched red, blue, and green spinning diamonds of light pass effortlessly through the glass wall of the trailer without damaging or breaking it.

Steve was shocked when he realized he did not have time to move out of the way, to prevent a large number of the glowing orange diamond shaped lights from striking his body, after they passed through another glass wall of the trailer. He looked into Bonnie's eyes before he said, "I love you."

"Steve, no!" Bonnie's eyes widened from shock as she screamed, the moment the spinning glowing lights struck his chest, and disappeared effortlessly into his clothing and body. She frowned while waiting for him to react. Moments later, she was surprised to watch the glowing lights emerge from

465

his body, through his back. "Are you all right? Did they hurt you?"

He smiled, while touching her fingers. "I'm alive, and I don't know why. I'm ok." He quickly turned to watch the glowing colored diamond shapes travel through the water. He pointed at them as they passed through a glass wall, and back into the Osiris cloud.

Roger said, "Are you sure you're not hurt? I thought we lost you."

"I feel great. I don't have any pain. I can't explain any of what's happening in here, but everything is good!" Steve laughed.

Roger motioned upward, toward hundreds of multi-colored diamonds forming in the bacteria cloud above the trailer. After brightening, each individual spinning mass of light began rotating in a clockwise direction inside the cloud. Then the lights slowly rose upward through the Osiris bacteria filling the upper areas of the building.

"We're losing a lot of water." Steve pointed at the stream of water flowing from the corner of the trailer. "The water level in here is falling fast."

Roger looked around. "It's down about four inches. Our protection from Osiris is escaping."

"Don't worry about it," Bonnie said, as she stared into the bacteria cloud.

"Don't worry? Why not?" Roger looked at Bonnie questioningly after her remark.

"These spinning shapes and lights are the most beautiful things I've seen in my life." She smiled, ignoring his concerns. "Relax, and enjoy them with me."

466

Steve immediately became alarmed by her sudden personality change. "Bonnie, are you okay?"

"Yes, I'm perfect." She suddenly felt relaxed while staring at the multicolored diamond shapes that continued mysteriously forming in the deadly bacteria cloud. She pressed her hands against the glass wall of the trailer to study the colors, while ignoring the blinding streaks of light racing through the cloud nearby. She soon became oblivious to the thunderous sounds. "These colors are so vivid and bright. They remind me of the stained glass windows in a church."

"A church?" The observation surprised Steve.

"It looks like the sunlight is shining through stained glass windows. This is a miracle! This is an absolute miracle. I don't know how or why, but I think God has something to do with those colored orbs of light."

Roger frowned at Steve. "Something is wrong. Something is happening in here and it's related to those spinning masses of light."

"I agree. But, I can't explain any of this! Now I see triangle shaped glowing lights forming over the fuel rod cooling pool. " Steve suddenly realized he was now unexplainably ignoring the dangers of his surroundings. The blue, purple, green, and yellow glowing geometrical colored shapes traveling through the water several inches from his body, seemed to mesmerize him.

"Steve, watch out," Roger said while pointing frantically. "I see small circles of red and blue lights moving toward the trailer, headed for your body.

They're perfect circles! Where did they come from? How were they formed?"

"I see them." Steve did not hesitate, before moving a hand directly in their path. He smiled when the colored masses passed painlessly through it. "Are these lights something spiritual, something religious?"

Roger watched a large number of approaching diamond shaped glowing lights, and realized they were about to strike his body. He smiled after watching them pass through his abdomen and legs without injury or pain, before they traveled through a glass wall without damaging it. "This is amazing. Everything we're watching and seeing here is beyond my comprehension!"

"Are we all dying together?" Bonnie experienced a sudden sensation of peace and tranquility while watching thousands of multi-colored spinning diamond shapes traveling through the silver bacteria cloud above the trailer. She no longer felt terrified while underwater. She was no longer afraid of the deadly silver Osiris cloud. "This has to be death. It's so peaceful and comfortable. This is perfect!"

"Is this what it feels like after your die?" Steve smiled while studying more of the glowing colored diamond, circle, and triangle shapes. He felt relaxed and comfortable in the water.

The thunderous sounds accompanying the brilliant streaks of light moving through the cloud grew louder, and vibrated the trailer walls. Numerous streaks of light arcing from the fuel rods and traveling through the bacteria cloud, continued to light the interior of the darkened building like flashes of lightening.

"If I am dying, I never imagined it would be this wonderful." Bonnie felt an unexplainable sense of acceptance. She smiled while watching brilliant red, purple, and green diamonds of spinning light gliding through Osiris in unwavering circles. "I wonder what's going to happen next."

A smile replaced the concern on Steve's face, after a large group of colored lights passed painlessly through his arm. "I don't have an explanation for any of this. It doesn't matter. This is remarkable."

Roger smiled while watching a blue diamond shaped mass of light unexpectedly split apart to become four triangular shaped orange glowing masses. They all appeared to have long white tentacles dangling from their sides. Instead of rotating through Osiris, these colored masses began speeding through the bacteria cloud with tentacles trailing behind. Each mass of light abruptly turned at a right angle and continued traveling through the bacteria cloud, moments after they struck concrete walls, and other objects inside the building.

"Look, look up there!" Bonnie pointed at an area of the cloud directly over the trailer. It appeared unusually brighter than surrounding areas. As she watched, it began glowing with a brilliant white light. Rays of light suddenly radiated from the area, falling on the walls in the building like floodlights. "Do you see them?"

"I don't see anything," Roger said, while look upward.

Bonnie smiled. "I see them now. I see them!"

Steve said, "See what?"

"Those children are playing hide and seek with me, by covering their eyes with their fingers."

"Where are you seeing children" Roger looked upward at the cloud, and the strange glowing area.

"Oh my God!" Bonnie frowned while looking into the brilliant light.

"What do you see?"

"One of those children is telling me he's going to be son!"

Steve frowned after listening to Bonnie's vivid descriptions of something he could not see in the building. He looked at Roger. "She might be hallucinating, caused by oxygen starvation. I'll check the hoses feeding air to her diving mask."

"I'll help you."

"No, stay away from me! Get back!" Bonnie smiled while staring overhead into the lighted area of the bacteria cloud.

"What are you looking at up there?"

"I see five angels!" She pointed wildly overhead. "They're beautiful! The angels are in the bacteria cloud!"

"There's nothing up there."

"A beautiful angel with wings is holding a bird in her hand."

"I'm telling you, there's nothing there."

"I see them, Steve. Another angel is holding flowers. Another is holding a beautiful butterfly in her hands."

"You're hallucinating, Bonnie." Steve checked her air tank and was shocked and confused after he saw it still contained air. "There's nothing up there!"

"You're wrong. I see their wings! They're beautiful. Their faces are so pretty!"

"I don't see anything." Steve looked around, but did not see other people in the containment building.

"They're coming to help us." She looked at him. "They're here to help us. They talked to me."

"They talked to you?" Steve was shocked and more confused after her explanation. "What did they say?"

"They're here to save us."

Steve looked at Roger. "Do you see them? Do you see anything up along the ceiling?"

"I don't see anything!"

Steve became distracted when a group of glowing diamonds moving through the bacteria cloud beside the trailer, began slowly dividing into multiple multicolored glowing circles. Then he saw something he did not understand. Something that frightened him, when he believed he was watching the beginning of a nuclear detonation. He frowned as a group of red, green, and yellow diamonds began slowly losing their individual colors. They quickly became glowing white indiscernible masses of light. "The radiation we released is changing the color composition of those diamond shapes."

"I'm watching something happening on the other side of this trailer. Those glowing shapes are losing their colors over there. Why is the radiation affecting them?"

"I can't explain what I'm seeing." Steve noticed that more of the diamond shaped objects began glowing with a similar brilliant white light. The increasing intensity of the white light in the containment building eventually became so bright, it hurt his eyes. The pain soon forced him to shade his face with a hand, while looking away. The growing blinding light prevented him from seeing the groups of brilliant white spheres, which now appeared to merge in the bacteria cloud. They soon formed large masses of light above the trailer.

"What's happening to those pretty colored lights? Where did they go? Please don't take them away." Bonnie shaded her eyes from the blinding white light. She squinted, struggling to watch a group of glowing masses slowly merging to form a sphere more than ten feet in diameter. "I don't like this. I want the colors back!"

"The white lights are spinning like tops all around this trailer," Steve said, while looking around.

"I wish we knew what was happening in the other containment buildings, to compare it to what we're seeing in here." Roger could not know the same bright light phenomenon was taking place in the other buildings at the same moment.

"They've started moving. The masses of light are moving!" Steve squinted between his fingers, now covering the faceplate of the diving mask to shade his eyes from the bright lights. "They're traveling through the Osiris bacteria, toward the hole in the containment building wall, and the access tunnel door."

"Where can they be going? I don't understand how they're moving!"

"Maybe they're lighting up the world to show everyone a miracle is happening here," Bonnie said, before she smiled while feeling peaceful and content. "I see the angels in those white lights. They're beautiful men, women, and lovely young children."

After escaping from the containment buildings, the huge glowing masses of light began traveling through the sprawling Osiris cloud. They appeared to destroy wide areas of the bacteria after mysteriously spreading out, while racing away from the power plant. They moved so quickly inside the cloud, the masses of white light developed long and brilliant sparkling tails of light. They soon resembled glowing meteors streaking across the night sky.

Steve watched as large numbers of the multicolored geometric diamonds began appearing in the bacteria cloud throughout the building. He pointed toward the hole in the containment building wall. "I see thousands of those colored diamond shapes escaping from this building. Why don't they come back to help us? Why don't they stay with us? We're on our own?"

Major Baxter became confused while watching the bacteria cloud swirling over the power plant through his binoculars. "I'm thinking the computers and controls in those buildings are so screwed up by the bacteria, that the reactors are getting ready to melt down and explode." He frowned while staring at tens of thousands of multicolored glowing diamond shapes of various sizes, which were now traveling in all directions through the Osiris cloud. At the same time, more of the brilliant colored streaks raced from the containment buildings. They began traveling through the cloud resembling colored shooting stars, until they disappeared in the distance.

Baxter became more confused, and then speechless, his reasoning ability suddenly overwhelmed by what he observed. He frowned after realizing vivid purple and blue spheres of light began coming together, until they merged into a mass of bright light more than fifty feet in diameter. At the same time, various green spheres began merging into glowing balls of light more than three hundred feet in diameter. The colored spheres began traveling randomly through the Osiris cloud in various directions. They eventually burst through the sides and top of the bacteria cloud miles from the plant, while creating a deafening roar much louder than thunder. Immediately after they were outside the bacteria cloud, the spheres silently exploded in huge streaking formations of radiant white light filled with silver and gold flashes and streaks, before dissipating completely.

"Something is definitely not going as we planned at that power plant," Doctor Meridian stared at a monitor in Brenton's command center. "I see large areas of brilliant pulsating colors within the Osiris cloud itself. I can't explain where they came from, or their purpose."

"Give me your best guess as to what we're watching, Doctor?" Brenton turned and frowned at

474

the monitor, while watching colors and streaks of shooting light traveling through the enormous bacteria cloud.

"This is not what I expected to see in this situation," Reglovic said. "I expected the bacteria cloud to dematerialize and collapse upon itself as the bacteria died, after exposure to the deadly radiation."

Feltault agreed. "The number of bright streaks radiating from the containment buildings appears to be increasing."

"I have a supposition that exposing Osiris to radiation, may have inadvertently caused the bacteria to mutate into another more deadly species." Reglovic nervously bit his thumbnail while intently studying the monitor.

Brenton became confused. "Tell me what you're thinking, Doctor. Are you saying we're now dealing with a new and deadly version of the Osiris bacteria?"

"It's probably an incorrect assumption, General. But it's my best guess, based on what I'm watching on that monitor."

"Tell me your thoughts, Doctor!

"Well, those fast moving streaks of light, and color phenomenon, may be associated with the creation of a new and different deadly organism, which we did not anticipate in our plan to destroy Osiris. We may be witnessing the birth of an entire new life form."

"How was this new life form created?"

"The exposure to radiation may have mutated the cell structure of the Osiris bacteria."

"The radiation is causing the bacteria to create those streaks of light, and the glowing balls of light?" Brenton frowned at his Executive Officer.

"Yes, General," Reglovic said. "The radiation is the cause of the phenomenon we're watching."

"You're telling me those colors are Osiris evolving into a different form of bacteria?"

"That's my hypothesis. Those colored lights, may be the emergence of a new life form with radioactive properties. As Osiris mutates, the radiation is most likely creating those colored streaks and masses of light, as the bacteria gains new life force properties."

"What properties do you envision in the new form of the bacteria?"

"It appears Osiris can now move much faster from one location to another, after I watched those colored streaks traveling through the cloud on your monitors. I'm assuming the streaks, and the white glow, are generated by the radiation the bacteria absorbed from the reactors at the power plant."

"Based on your assumption, Osiris can now kill people by exposing them to the radiation it carries from the reactors, before it devours the flesh from dead bodies? Do I understand this new situation and scenario correctly, Doctor?"

"Yes, unfortunately you do, General." Reglovic looked to the other scientists for support.

"I agree with this new and more deadly scenario," Doctor Meridian said. "The bacteria cloud must be completely destroyed with the military's nuclear device."

476

Brenton looked at his watch. "The Cruise missile will destroy the damn cloud in sixteen minutes, gentlemen!"

"Look at that cloud now, Major! Look at what's happening!" Sanchez frantically pulled the straps of a military radio off his shoulders, before he let it fall to the ground. The frightened soldier stared at the bright colored streaks passing through Osiris, and the colored masses of light traveling erratically through the bacteria cloud. He pulled a small silver crucifix hanging from the chain with his dog tags, from his shirt. He clenched it tightly while praying, before kissing it. "Jesus, Mary, and Joseph, help us!"

"Settle down Sanchez, damn it!" Baxter lowered his binoculars. He appeared alarmed by the combat hardened soldier's unanticipated emotional reaction.

Sanchez began trembling from growing fear. "It's a miracle, Major. Look at the bright white lights moving through the cloud."

"I don't see anything downrange from here. I scanned the area with thermal and night vision. There's nothing out there!"

Sanchez stumbled forward, pointing into the distance. "I see pure white light. I've never seen anything so beautiful!"

"I don't see it. Where the hell are you looking?"

"Look over the power plant! Is that God? Is God preparing to walk out of that cloud?"

"What do you see?" Baxter felt the hair on his arms rise after the soldier's comments.

"Right there! Right in front of us! I see God in that white glowing mass."

"No, you don't see anything, damn it! You're hallucinating. The stress of this situation is getting to you."

"I see him! I see groups of angels with him. They're floating around him!"

"I can't see a damn thing!" Baxter focused his binoculars and frowned after several huge masses of light appeared to explode inside Osiris. The flashes were so brilliant they hurt his eyes, and forced him to lower the binoculars. "Was that a nuclear explosion inside the bacteria cloud? The damn cloud is glowing, as it becomes radioactive! It looks like the bacteria drained all of the radiation from the three reactors, and its holding that energy inside the cloud!"

"It's not radiation that's causing it to glow, Major! You're wrong!"

"Those are radiation fueled explosions inside the bacteria cloud, Sanchez! I can hear the sounds of those explosions!" Baxter squinted, while studying the brilliant white glowing masses slowly spreading through the cloud. He watched as more of the diamonds traveling through the bacteria cloud slowly lost their individual colors. "Sanchez, get that radio working, now. I have to give Brenton a status. I think this entire cloud is going to explode in the mother of all nuclear detonations!"

The soldier could not move. He felt paralyzed from a growing fear of the unknown, and what was about to happen. He clasped his hands together as he continued praying, while watching the brilliant white glow now rapidly spreading through the

478

bacteria cloud. "Mother of God, pray for us. Mother of God, help us, your children."

"Stand down, Sanchez! I need you to come back to this situation, now! Get your ass in gear, and get that damn radio working for me so I can contact General Brenton! That's a direct order!"

"There are no more rules, or orders, or Generals, or Presidents, or nations, Major. God is coming back to care for all of us!"

"Where the hell do you see God? Tell me! I see a cloud filled with nuclear radiation that's going to detonate in our faces!"

"He's right there! He's floating in the cloud and it's going to touch the ground so he can walk on Earth again. I see him. I need to go to him!"

Baxter tackled Sanchez to the ground after the dazed soldier began running toward the power plant. He shouted to his other team members already huddled in the drainage pipe, "I need some help out here now!"

Four soldiers rushed out of the pipe after hearing the plea for assistance. They were shocked and speechless after they saw the glowing bacteria cloud, and colored streaks of light travelling through it, several miles from their location.

"What's happening out here?" Sargent Cliff said, mumbling almost incoherently while overcome from fear. "What's going on?"

"Get that damn radio working Sergeant, so I can talk to Brenton," Baxter said shouting. "Someone get Sanchez into that pipe and sit on him, so he doesn't hurt himself!"

"What are those colored lights?" Sergeant Cliff stared into the distance, almost transfixed by the shimmering lights and dazzling colors. "Why is the cloud glowing in those areas? Is the bacteria cloud coming this way? Do we need to get the hell out of here in our Hummers?"

"I don't understand anything about this damn situation! Everything keeps changing! I see thousands of lights racing out from the containment buildings. I don't know what they are, but they can't be good!"

Sergeant Cliff watched other soldiers struggling with Sanchez as they dragged him into the pipe. "What do you need, Major?"

"Raise Brenton's command center on that god damn radio! We may have to move back to find a new safe location, before we're exposed to the glowing radiation in that cloud, that Osiris absorbed from the reactors!"

Steve looked around at the thousands of colored diamond shapes rotating through the Osiris bacteria inside the containment building. "The sounds of thunder are becoming louder as more of the bright streaks of light shoot from those fuel rods. Many of the diamond shapes are losing their colors and turning white. It's getting bright in here."

The brilliant white glow spreading through the Osiris cloud inside the building reminded Roger of a conversation with Steve. "Maybe that intense white light inside the cloud has nothing to do with Osiris."

"What do you think it is?"

"Maybe it's the white light people talk about when they die, and then are brought back to life after death, to tell about their experiences."

"I don't think that's it," Steve said before he frowned, "but what the hell do I know!"

"Maybe this light will take me to my mom and dad." Roger smiled.

"Don't assume that white glow is death, damn it!" Steve grasped Roger's arm to shake him, hoping to startle the man.

Roger smiled, and suddenly appeared to be at peace. "I miss them. I want to be with them, and my brother."

"Don't give up," Steve said, shouting. "Don't give up and let this damn bacteria cloud win!"

"I'm not afraid of dying anymore. I want to be with my mom and dad. I want to die!"

"What are you saying?" Steve looked at Bonnie who was staring at the multicolored glowing diamonds moving inside the deadly bacteria cloud. "Bonnie, talk to me!"

"The angels are coming for us. I see beautiful baby girls and boys with wings in the glowing white light."

"I don't know what you're seeing."

"If this is the end of my life, it's a beautiful and wonderful experience. The angels are close. I can almost touch them."

"Listen to me! Your life is not going to end here." He grasped her hand. "I will not lose you now!"

"It doesn't matter anymore, sweetheart. Nothing matters! The battle is over. This is the end of our lives."

"We didn't lose this battle! We need to work together to save the world, and stop Osiris!"

"We'll be together in heaven in a few minutes."

"No! I will not allow this to be the end!" Steve noticed the intense white glow spreading through Osiris was now slowly intensifying.

"I can see the angels. They're beautiful!" Bonnie suddenly began frowning while pointing toward the ceiling of the containment building. "Oh, no! Oh my God, don't do that, please!"

"What is it? What do you see?"

"The angels are crying! They're crying for us! They're reaching out to take my hand. They want me to go with them!"

"Stay with me! Don't leave! Don't go with them!"

The glowing Osiris cloud suddenly became so brilliant it blinded Steve. The intense loud sounds of thunder became deafening, as they vibrated the entire building and the floor. He closed his eyes tightly but the light soon became so brilliant it caused them to throb painfully. "It's getting too bright in here. How can it be getting brighter?"

Roger frantically covered his faceplate with his hands to lessen the painful sensations of the blinding white light. As the glow intensified, so did the painful burning sensation in his eyes. It soon became unbearable. "I can't take too much more of this bright light!"

Several moments later, a strange eerie whining sound began filling the building. In the first moments, the sound was similar to that of an approaching speeding freight train. The mysterious noise became louder with each passing second. Thirty seconds later, the sound became so shrill and loud it shattered the glass and plastic components of instruments and equipment inside the containment building. The thick glass walls of the trailer where Steve, Roger, and Bonnie found shelter from the deadly bacteria, began to twist and bend as they distorted, while the whining sound became a loud shrill screech.

Several moments later, large areas of the swirling silver Osiris bacteria cloud suddenly began collapsing onto the floor inside the containment building. The cloud mysteriously appeared to fall in huge long thick sheets, as prolonged exposure to the radiation began killing the bacteria. The huge amount of dead bacteria cells resembled silver water crashing down onto the containment building floor, as cells continued dying. Dead bacteria cells covered the floor and equipment in the building with a thick silver-gray watery liquid, as massive amounts of dead bacteria cells continued cascading from the cloud.

At the same time, the deadly scenario was being repeated inside the two other containment buildings, as the released radiation killed large amounts of bacteria. The cloud surrounding the power plant began slowly swirling in a counter clockwise direction. As the cells died, huge areas of the bacteria fell from the sky. The dead bacteria cells covered buildings, parking lots, and vehicles, with the gray watery liquid.

Bonnie began experiencing agonizing pain, caused by the brilliant blinding light in the building, combined with the high-pitched whining noise. Her body suddenly tensed and became rigid in the water while she squeezed her head between her hands, as she attempted to cover her ears. As the glow intensified and became more painful, she screamed hysterically in the mask. Images of her mother's house flashed through her mind while she screamed, before drifting into unconsciousness fifteen excruciating seconds later.

Roger's arms and legs thrashed wildly in the water from the painful sensations of the brilliant light, and the deafening noise. *'God help me! Let me die! Take me to my mom, dad, and brother! Please let me die now!'*

Steve screamed in his mask as the pain of the light and noise became overwhelming. He pictured his parents in his mind, and the people he worked with at the hospital. *'I let all of you down. I'm so sorry'*

Sanchez violently pulled away from the soldier pushing him into the drainage pipe. He ran back to Baxter, where he fell to his knees while watching the blinding white glow spreading through the Osiris cloud. The black smoke rising into the sky south of the plant appeared to accentuate the cloud. "The miracle is starting, just like it says in the bible. The Earth is being destroyed by fire."

"Get this soldier into that damn pipe!" Baxter became confused while watching the situation at the

484

power plan. "Sit on him, if that's what it takes to hold him down!"

Sanchez raised his hands to shade his eyes from the glowing cloud. He took a deep relaxing breath, before tears began streaming from his eyes. "Jesus, Mary, and Joseph. That light inside the cloud is brighter than the sun. It's pure white light. I've never seen anything so white."

"I need that damn radio working, now!" Baxter stood and scanned the bacteria cloud that rotated around the power plant, with his binoculars.

"I see the Blessed Virgin." Sanchez became ecstatic. He began pointing wildly toward the power plant. "I see her."

"Where are you looking?" Baxter scanned the entire power plant with his binoculars. "I see the power plant and the damn cloud, and nothing else! There's nothing out there!"

"She's right there. She's coming back to earth, to be with her children. I can see her walking out of the light wearing a veil! She's beautiful!"

Baxter felt his body unexplainably shudder from fear. He shaded his eyes with a hand while watching the glow spreading through the cloud. "I can't see anything. Get this soldier into that damn pipe! Do it now!"

In Brenton's command center, he and his staff, along with Feltault, Meridian, and Reglovic, studied the monitors in awe and silence. None of them understood what they were watching or witnessing. As the brilliant white glow intensified in the bacteria cloud, the cameras documented the phenomenon. The monitors eventually became so

485

bright they flooded the darkened command center with bright white light, preventing soldiers from studying computer monitors.

"Our video feeds from the plant are useless. I can't make out the details of what's happening on the battlefield." Brenton turned to his Communications Officer. "I need a status report from Baxter. Can you contact him on the satellite radio link?"

"We lost contact with him during his last transmission. We can't reestablish communications."

"I assume he was using a secured radio channel that can't be jammed."

"His team has the latest models of communication equipment, Sir. A loss of communications with that team, and not being able to reestablish it, doesn't make any sense, General."

"Sir, we're seeing a widespread communications outage," a soldier reported to the Communications Officer.

"Give me a status," Brenton said. He realized his growing confusion and frustration was becoming obvious to his men. "What's going on?"

"All of our secured and encrypted satellite communications channels just went down. Our communications backbone is down. We can't send voice or data traffic to anyone, and we can't receive voice or data, at this time."

"That cannot happen, based on our current technology! I need you to contact Washington so I can give them a status."

"I can't reach anyone. All of the radios frequencies are dead!"

"All radar systems are going down," another soldier in the command center said, while shouting nervously. "We're blind without radar."

"All of our reconnaissance satellites are dropping offline," another soldier said. "We're blind from the sky down."

"Get me some high resolution images of that power plant, and the bacteria cloud, from the Predator drones circling the area!" Brenton rushed to another set of monitors. "I need to see if the radiation is having any effect on that cloud! I can't make any decisions until I can see the battlefield!"

"We've lost contact with the four Predators circling the power plant," a soldier said. She unexplainably started crying. "They all crashed into the ground. They're down and burning somewhere."

"What the hell is going on?" Brenton appeared shocked while looking at his senior staff for advice. "This can't be happening. Nothing on this planet can shut everything down!"

"Everyone get out of the way!" A senior Weapons Officer violently pushed his way between the people huddled around Brenton. "General, we've lost all telemetry and communications with the Tomahawk Cruise missile, fired from the Ticonderoga."

"How can we lose our encrypted communications link with a Cruise missile?" Brenton appeared shocked. "Is the missile still airborne, or did it crash?"

"I can't definitively confirm anything at this time, Sir. I don't have the telemetry to plot the missile's course and speed."

"So you're telling me we don't know if the missile is still targeting the power plant. We don't know where our missile is headed. And we can't destroy the missile if it's now off course."

"Yes Sir, that's the situation at the present time."

"Listen up," Brenton said while stepping to the center of the command center tent. "Work with your teams to get those communications and telemetry systems back on line. Make that your priority, and get your teams to resolve the issues!"

Brenton suddenly seemed frightened of the unknown. "Did we hear anything from Steve or Roger?"

"Negative," the Communications Officer said while working frantically with his team. "We've been attempting to establish communications with them, but we did not receive a response from anyone at the plant."

"I need a visual of the damn situation." Brenton rushed out of the command center tent, before he began maneuvering his way between the scientists and military personnel staring toward the west. He frowned at the people who appeared transfixed, while watching something in the distance. They were oblivious to his repeated requests for them to move out of his way, and he was soon pushing his way between them.

"What the hell is going on?" When he reached the edge of the plateau, his mouth fell open. He appeared shocked to see the brilliant Osiris cloud glowing white in the distance, while rapidly expanding outward for miles in all directions. The glowing cloud now appeared to be unexplainably brighter than the sun. The blinding white glow soon obscured the entire horizon. "I can't see anything. Osiris looks like the mushroom cloud formed after a nuclear explosion."

Brenton checked at his watch. He motioned to his Executive Officer. "The damn nuclear device onboard the Cruise missile will detonate in a few minutes. I want your security teams to have these people lay on the ground, and look away from the explosion. Do it now!"

When Brenton returned to the command center tent, Reglovic said, "What's going on out there General? Did the reactors at the power plant explode? Is that what's causing that bright light?"

"I don't think the reactors exploded."

"Then where's that light coming from?"

"I don't have any answers. Osiris is glowing like a floodlight. That's the only way I can describe it. That light is coming from the Osiris cloud."

"What can be causing a living bacteria cloud to glow? Is the bacterium becoming unstoppable after exposure to radiation?"

"Our only hope for ending this situation is the nuclear device onboard the Cruise missile. We need the burst of radiation to destroy that cloud."

Inside the containment building, Steve regained consciousness after momentarily passing out from the unbearable pain he experienced, caused by the bright glowing cloud, and the high pitched whining sounds. He slowly opened his aching eyes. *'My eyes are blurred, and I can't see anything. I have a pounding headache from that bright light inside the Osiris bacteria.'*

When his eyes eventually focused, he was surprised to see the silver cloud no longer surrounded the trailer. A white indistinct overhead glow now replaced the blinding light. *'I don't see Osiris down here near the floor. Those sounds of thunder have stopped, but I still hear that whining noise.'*

He looked up to study a large mass of the glowing bacteria cloud filling the upper two thirds of the building. He watched as the silver bacteria violently swirled and billowed beneath the rounded concrete domed ceiling, much like a confused animal searching for a way to escape. He smiled after he saw huge areas of the bacteria cloud fall to the floor of the building, to create more of the watery silver waste. Bright yellow and orange flashes of light, and the streaks resembling lightening, continued racing through the cloud before they escaped through the hole in the containment building wall.

'The radiation is destroying the bacteria in this building, and billions of dead cells are collapsing onto the floor. That area of the bacteria cloud along the ceiling is falling apart and shrinking in size. Maybe we can still get out of this situation alive!'

Steve looked at Roger and Bonnie, and saw them floating motionless in the water. He was relieved to see bubbles rising through the water from their air masks, indicating they were still alive. Roger's body floated at the bottom of the tank. Bonnie's body

490

swayed gently in the water several feet above him. They both appeared uninjured, although they were still unconscious.

"Bonnie, talk to me." Steve gently grasped her arm. He began slowly talking her back to consciousness. "Talk to me, Baby."

"Don't let Osiris kill me," Bonnie said screaming, after she regained consciousness moments later. She began kicking wildly in the water. The tears filling her eyes temporarily blinded her, adding to her confusion. After her eyes focused, she frantically looked around the trailer. "Are we still here? We're not dead?"

"We're not dead, and we're safe, Baby."

"I wanted to die, and go with the angels calling me." She looked around, unsure of her surroundings. "Where is Osiris?"

"I'm thinking the radiation destroyed the bacteria cloud."

"Roger, talk to me." Steve grasped his friend's arm. He became alarmed when he could not immediately revive him. "Come on buddy, it's finally over."

Roger soon opened his eyes. He frowned while looking around the trailer. "Is Osiris still trying to attack us?"

"I think we killed the bacteria with the radiation."

"We did?" Roger smiled when he did not see the glowing bacteria cloud near the trailer.

"Just in time, too." Steve motioned to the water level inside the trailer. "The water is down almost three feet in this trailer, because of the leak. If it was

491

another foot lower, we would have been exposed to the bacteria."

"Look up there!" Bonnie motioned toward the ceiling of the building. She watched the glowing remnants of the Osiris cloud collapse in watery silver sheets, before they fell against the walls of the containment building. As the radiation destroyed the bacteria cloud, the interior of the building began to brighten. Several minutes later, the radiation obliterated the last of the bacteria, leaving a silver gray watery mess on the floor almost seven inches deep.

"Why did Osiris stop attacking this building?" Steve was surprised when he did not see Osiris surging into the building through the hole in the wall. "I wonder what's going on out there."

The bright white light shining into the containment building through the hole in the wall, now came from the glowing Osiris cloud that still surrounded the plant and blanketed the land for miles to the south. The cloud glowed with a brilliant white hue, as the colored streaks that resembled lightening continued traveling through the bacteria, after shooting from the other containment buildings.

The outer regions of the glowing cloud miles from the power plant began contracting and collapsing inward, toward the containment buildings. Portions of the cloud appeared to surge forward, to fill the void created after the radiation continued destroying large areas of the bacteria. Huge sections of the cloud containing dead bacteria cells began falling to the ground in the form of the watery gray liquid.

"What the hell is going on?" Baxter's eyes widened from shock after watching several large areas of the Osiris cloud, which appeared to break away from the large cloud mass. Those bacteria masses began moving rapidly toward the power plant. As they did, they began combining into a huge swirling mass.

Sergeant Cliff frowned while watching as a large growing area of bacteria cloud moved silently overhead, several hundred feet above the team. "The cloud is directly overhead, Major!"

"How did that happen? Get everyone into the drainage pipe and take cover!"

Cliff frowned while watching four long and thick colored streaks of light traveling rapidly through the cloud, toward the group. "We've got multiple incoming threats moving toward our position! Everyone get down!" He and the others watched, as the streaks of light seemed to speed through the overhead bacteria cloud. Moments later, they shot out of the bacteria cloud before silently exploding in huge brilliant balls of light, much like fireworks.

Several moments later, the unexpected fury of violent blowing hurricane force winds knocked the soldiers to the ground, as the sounds of the wind became deafening. Baxter shaded his eyes with a hand as the violent winds blew sand, dirt, and debris, past him and the other soldiers. He shouted so his team members could hear him over the sounds of the violently blowing wind. "A section of the bacteria cloud is moving beyond the plant! It's north of the power plant! The cloud is spreading out. It's spinning like a hurricane with the eye over the plant. The cloud must be thirty miles across, but it's no longer touching the ground."

Several seconds later violent winds normally associated with a tornado began blowing and lifting sand, dirt, and large heavy objects through the air. Baxter shielded his face with a hand. He grasped Sanchez's arm and helped him to stand as the wind violently buffeted their bodies.

After hearing a loud crash and explosion behind him, Baxter turned. The intensifying winds caused several of the Hummers to roll down an embankment where they exploded. The howling winds lifted another vehicle and carried it through the air several feet over Baxter's head, startling him. The violent winds flipped the other Hummers. Some of those vehicles burst into flames, and exploded before the winds carried the vehicles into the air and out of sight. "Everyone get into that pipe now! That's an order!"

"Let's go! Let's go!" Sergeant Cliff began pulling soldiers to their feet in the violent wind. He pushed them toward the pipe. "Get into that pipe where it's safe!"

Baxter turned, covering his eyes with a hand. He squinted between his fingers, as the blowing sand and dirt cut the skin of his face. As the howling winds intensified, he watched the Osiris cloud slowly forming a circular column more than three thousand yards in diameter. It extended approximately five miles into the sky. "What is happening? What is this?"

Baxter watched as the glowing bacteria column began rotating in a counter clockwise direction. The column of brilliantly glowing Osiris bacteria began rising slowly into the cloudless blue morning sky directly over the plant. The higher the bacteria column rose, the brighter the glowing mass became. Two minutes later, the uppermost section of the rotating bacteria column towered approximately seven miles high above the plant.

The bright colored streaks of light continued radiating outward from two of the containment buildings, into the base of the bacteria cloud. The streaks quickly traveled upward through the towering bacteria column. Many of them exploded in blinding flashes of brilliant light after breaking through the sides of the rotating column of bacteria. Other streaks began quickly spiraling upward through the swirling column, destroying the bacteria as they did, before exploding in bright bursts of light.

"Is that god damn radio working? I need to talk to Brenton!" Baxter watched as the towering bacteria column suddenly began collapsing downward onto the buildings of the power plant. As the glowing column collapsed, it spread out over the plant and miles of the surrounding countryside while creating a deafening and violent wind that shattered windows in a thirty-mile radius of the plant. The Osiris cloud began dissipating as the radiation destroyed the last of the bacteria, causing the brilliant white glow to slowly fade away.

Steve pointed upward after bright yellow rays of the morning sun began shining through the hole in the containment building wall. "I hope Osiris didn't move north. Not after everything we've just been through. My body and mind can't do this again."

"You two stay under the water. Let me check out the building." Roger pushed himself upward. His head slowly and cautiously broke the surface of the water. He apprehensively waited for Osiris to attack his skin. *'I wonder if the radiation mutated Osiris into a new bacteria I can't see?'*

"How does it look up there?" Steve's heart pounded in his chest from nervousness while he watched Roger.

Streams of water from his hair ran down Roger's face while he cautiously looked around the outside of the trailer for the deadly bacteria. Several minutes later, he became ecstatic when he realized none of the Osiris bacteria remnants were lurking inside the building. He climbed over the trailer wall and dropped to the floor beside Mason's skeleton. He pulled off the air tank and mask before frantically motioning to Bonnie and Steve to climb out of the tank. "I think it's safe. I don't see any of the bacteria cloud!"

"Oh my God, we're alive!" Bonnie felt overjoyed and exhausted, as Steve gently lowered her into Roger's arms. "We're alive. We're all alive!"

Steve climbed over the trailer wall before slowly, and cautiously, lowering himself to the floor. He was surprised when his feet slipped into the cold silvery slimy liquid more than eighteen inches deep, which now covered the entire floor of the containment building. He frowned while assuming the waste was comprised of dead Osiris bacteria cells, killed by exposure to the radiation. "I'm very happy to see the killer bacteria is lying dead at our feet!"

Bonnie frowned while attempting to tip toe through the silver waste. "What is that disgusting smell?"

"Dead and decaying bacteria cells." Steve frantically pulled off his mask and air tank. "We need to get out of this building."

"Our assumption was correct," Roger said. "The radiation destroyed the bacteria."

"And that radiation is killing us now."

"What do you mean?" Bonnie said, while squeezing water out of her hair.

"Those fuel rods are still releasing radiation. It's killing us."

Roger stared at the fuel rod assembly dangling from the crane. "Let's get as far away from here as we can."

Steve noticed Troxell's skeleton on the floor, submerged in the silver liquid waste of dead cells. "I'm glad that bastard is dead!"

"He deserved to die," Bonnie said. "He was a terrible person, and I hope he suffered like the people he killed before he died!"

"Now we need to expose the people who sent him here to kill us. They wanted him to protect Osiris!" Steve grasped Bonnie's hand. He led her and Roger through the access tunnel doors, and then toward the control room in the darkened tunnel.

"Feltault and the others won't believe what just happened in here," Roger said. "I can't believe what we just saw."

Bonnie felt ecstatic. "I'm so happy to be alive! I'm alive, and I have a second chance!"

Her comments brought back several of Steve's long forgotten memories of Iraq. '*I know how she feels. I felt the same way after I survived bombs and people shooting at me. I have to do something to expose the people who sent Troxell to kill us. We may have stopped Osiris, but I'm not done yet.*'

"Osiris probably destroyed the control room," Roger said, "and the radio Brenton left for us to contact him."

"We've got to get a message to him. We need the power plant's nuclear technicians back here. They have to put the fuel rods back into the reactor cores, before we have a nuclear disaster."

Chapter 19

Steve suddenly felt guilty after remembering Mason's agonizing death. "Mason didn't have to die the way he did. He panicked when he saw Osiris. I should have done more to save him."

"You did everything possible to help him," Roger said. "If you chased after him, your skeleton would be laying on the floor beside his."

"He's right, Steve." Bonnie squeezed his hand, as he cautiously led her through the deep silvery waste on the floor. "I'm proud of you, and everything you did to help him."

Two minutes later Steve cautiously stepped into the darkened control room. The only light came from a large skylight in the corridor outside the open security door. Acrid dense black smoke from burning electrical wires stripped of insulation by Osiris, filled the room. "Osiris destroyed everything in here. The radio Brenton left for us is trashed."

"We'll have to use that flare gun to signal Brenton." Roger lifted it off a table, along with two flares.

"Let's do it now. We need the plant staff back here to stop the release of radiation." Steve led everyone toward the main door of the control room.

"I'm utterly amazed by what I watched!" Meridian carefully studied the monitors inside Brenton's command center. "Can this be real? The Osiris cloud dissipated. It simply faded away!"

Reglovic appeared ecstatic. "The sky is blue again! The radiation destroyed the entire bacteria cloud!"

"Don't become too excited yet, Doctor," Brenton said. "I need my observers on the ground to confirm the bacteria cloud is no longer a threat."

"It appears the radiation destroyed all of the bacteria, General!" Meridian clapped his hands together joyously. "It's unfortunate Steve and Roger will never know their efforts destroyed the cloud!"

"If the radiation already destroyed Osiris," Reglovic said, "you can't allow that missile to destroy the power plant, General."

"What if the bacteria are still alive? I'll lose this opportunity to obliterate the cloud with another blast of radiation, if I bring down that missile."

"You can't trigger a nuclear explosion without first confirming Osiris is still a threat! That action is unconscionable!"

"You can fire another missile later today if you need that radiation to destroy the remains of the bacteria cloud," Meridian said. "But tomorrow, you can't say we shouldn't have let that missile explode because Steve and Roger's efforts had already destroyed all of Osiris."

Brenton turned to his Executive Officer. "How much time do I have until the Tomahawk strikes the plant?"

"Three minutes, fifty seconds."

"All secured satellite communication channels, and the link to the Tomahawk, are back on-line, General," the Communications Officer said shouting ecstatically. He smiled after his

500

announcement brought cheers from other soldiers. "We're requesting a status from all of our teams."

"Allowing that missile to detonate without knowing if Osiris has already been destroyed, is absurd," Meridian said.

"I have my orders from the President, Doctor. I need to follow the instructions given to me!"

"Do your orders make detonating the nuclear warhead the correct course of action? How does the President know what to do? He takes his advice from you, General! Give him your advice and recommendations and call off that nuclear missile, before time runs out!"

Steve pushed open the front doors of the building housing the reactor control room, before cautiously leading the others onto the steps. "Everything is covered with that silver watery waste. All of the plant's buildings and containment buildings, the parking lots and vehicles in them, and even the ground as far as I can see into the distance."

"This waste must be the remains of Osiris cells," Roger said.

"Look around for Osiris. We have to be sure we destroyed it completely, before we fire that flare."

"I don't see the bacteria cloud," Roger said, after scanning the cloudless blue early morning sky. "There's nothing left of the bacteria around the plant."

Bonnie pointed toward the west. "What's that long white line high up in the sky? Is that a part of the Osiris cloud trying to escape?"

"I don't think so." Roger squinted at the horizon. "It's too far out to be Osiris."

501

"It's moving this way." Bonnie frowned, unsure of what she was watching. "Is the bacteria returning to this plant?"

"That doesn't look like Osiris," Steve studied the approaching object far in the distance. It looked familiar, reminding him of Iraq.

"What else can it be?"

"It looks like a missile in flight, moving this way."

"A missile?" Bonnie frowned while staring into the distance.

Roger said, "Why would they fire a missile at this plant?"

"The government must believe Osiris is still a threat. The military probably plans to vaporize this area with a nuclear blast to destroy it."

"We already destroyed the bacteria! There's no need for a missile!"

"They don't know that. And we don't have a radio to contact Brenton."

"Shoot that flare gun," Bonnie said, as she became anxious and terrified. "If Brenton knows we're alive, his soldiers may take a harder look at this plant and realize we destroyed the cloud."

Roger raised the flare gun above his head, before he squeezed the trigger. The flare shot high into the sky trailing a slender tail of white smoke. Several seconds later, a bright glowing green signal began drifting under a white parachute high above the plant. "That's a message to the world. Osiris is dead!"

"They've got to see that flare!" Bonnie stared nervously at the approaching missile. "They've got to know we're still alive."

Major Baxter rolled onto his back, still choking on the dirt and dust in the air after the powerful hurricane force winds subsided. As the overturned Hummers exploded in the distance, he knelt to check his watch. "Everyone get into the pipe! Keep your heads down until after the warhead detonates!"

"The radio is working," a soldier said. "I reported to Brenton's command center, that we're back on-line."

"Get into that pipe now!" Baxter quickly crawled in behind the last soldier.

"Wait one," the soldier dragging the radio said, while listening to messages from Brenton's command center on the handset. "They want you, Major."

Baxter took the handset and listened to the instructions given by Brenton. He said, "Wait one, General. Let me get a visual on that damn power plant."

As Baxter crawled toward the end of the pipe while dragging the radio behind him, Captain Griswold said, "Where the hell are you going? We're close to detonation!"

"Brenton wants a visual on the plant." After Baxter crawled out of the pipe, he appeared shocked by what he saw. "This entire situation is getting confusing as shit! This is bizarre!"

"What's going on out there?" Griswold said, shouting over the excited conversations of his men.

"I see a green flare above the plant." Baxter paused, looking around. "The bacteria cloud disappeared! It's gone! The flipping killer cloud is gone!"

Griswold frantically crawled out of the pipe. "I see that flare too! Someone is alive at that plant. They're signaling for help."

Baxter raised the radio handset to send his status. "I see a green flare over the plant. I say again, I have a visual on a green flare over the power plant!"

"General Brenton!" A radioman in the command center said, shouting excitedly as he stood.

"What is it?"

"Baxter has a visual on a green flare over the plant!"

Brenton frowned, while looking at his staff. "I thought Osiris killed Steve and Roger."

"Baxter also reports he no longer has a visual on the Osiris cloud. It's not in the vicinity of the plant. He believes the radiation destroyed the bacteria cloud!"

"I can confirm Baxter's report." The Executive Officer stood behind a dozen soldiers studying their radar screens. "The last small areas of the cloud approximately seven miles north of the plant just disappeared off radar. We have confirmation from the radar planes in the area. It appears Osiris is completely destroyed!"

Brenton raised his hands to quiet the soldiers in the command center who began cheering and whistling. "How much time until our Tomahawk detonates the warhead?"

"Ninety-eight seconds," a soldier said. "The missile is preparing for the final low flight approach, and detonation."

Brenton turned to Meridian. "I need to know. Can Osiris be hiding? Can it be licking its wounds before it attacks again?"

"That's highly unlikely. I believe we destroyed the bacteria."

Brenton motioned to his Communications Officer. "I need to talk to the President immediately!"

"We've reestablished communications with the President, General. You can speak when you're ready."

"Mister President, Osiris has disappeared off our radar screens. We believe the radiation destroyed the bacteria cloud."

"Can you positively confirm that scenario where Osiris has been destroyed, General?"

"I'm confident we destroyed the bacteria cloud. My radar and reconnaissance teams confirm that supposition."

Loud cheers, whistles, and shouts of relief filled the room. Several of the President's advisors stood and patted him on the back while expressing their congratulations. He smiled and appeared relieved after collapsing back in his chair. "Good work everyone."

"We have two problems that require your immediate attention to resolve, Mister President," Brenton said, immediately ending the celebration.

"Explain what needs to be resolved." The President shook hands with several of his advisors. "I'm sure they're trivial compared to killing Osiris."

"The Cruise missile is still in flight. It's headed directly for the plant."

The President frowned while looking at his advisors. "I want you to stop that missile, General! Shoot down the missile, damn it!"

"We can destroy it in flight, if you concur with the decision to abort the nuclear detonation."

"I'll give you my decision after I hear the details of the second issue, General."

"My hand picked reconnaissance team positioned in the field, reported seeing a green flare in the sky over the plant."

"A green flare in the sky?" The President shook his head questioningly. "What does that signify?"

"It's the device we left for Roger and Steve to signal us, after they destroyed Osiris."

"Those men are still alive at the power plant?" The President was unprepared for the shocking news.

"That appears to be the situation Mister President."

"How much time do we have before the missile detonates?"

"Less than two minutes, Mister President. Do we have your authorization to abort Operation Hidden Sun, and bring down that missile?"

"One minute forty seconds until detonation," someone in Brenton's command center said, shouting to the group. "One minute thirty-nine, and counting."

President Stillman felt the nervous perspiration on his neck, wetting the collar of his shirt. "Let me think."

Steve reached out to grasp Bonnie's hand. He held it tightly as he looked into her eyes. "I'm sorry I got you into this situation."

"I'm where I want to be, and where I should be." She gently kissed his lips. "I'm always by your side, even when things are not going so good."

"That's one of the things I love about you." He brushed back her wet hair. "I don't want your life to end this way."

"It's okay. I'm here with you. I love you." She kissed him again. "This is where I want to be."

"I waited a lifetime for you."

"And I did too. I've wanted someone like you in my life for many years."

"I love you, Bonnie. I wish we had more years to share, to experience life together."

"The past few weeks with you, even in the chaos and death, have been the best time of my life. I wouldn't trade them for anything."

"I love you." He kissed her. "This may be the last time I get to tell you that."

"It won't be the last time, sweetheart."

He looked at her questioningly. "Tell me what you're thinking."

"We'll always be together." She wiped away the tears that began running down her cheeks. "Whether it's on this earth, or somewhere in an afterlife. But we will be together!"

"I hope so. I always want you by my side."

She looked into the distance. "The sunrise is beautiful. If this is the last thing I see, it's perfect."

"I think you're much more beautiful than that sunrise."

Bonnie smiled. "Promise me something, in the time we have left."

"Anything for you."

"After that missile explodes and we die, wait for me." She paused, before squeezing his hand as she began to cry. "Don't go on alone without me."

"After we die?" He suddenly understood.

She nodded. "I'm afraid of what comes next. I want to go with you."

"I will never ever leave your side."

"You take very good care of me, Steve. Thank you."

Tears suddenly began forming in his eyes while he hugged her tightly. "I love you very, very, much."

"I love you too." She hugged him tightly.

Steve looked at Roger, who was watching the approaching missile. "We did it, buddy. We stopped Osiris together."

Roger reached out to shake his friend's hand. "Yes we did. It's been a pleasure knowing you, and working with you Steve."

"I agree. It's been a great experience working with you."

Bonnie turned toward Steve. She kissed him. "I don't want to watch the bomb explode. Don't forget to wait for me." She rested her head on his chest while facing, and hugging him.

President Stillman paused, while closing his eyes. "Maybe we can work out an arrangement with those two men."

"An arrangement?" Leckowicz said, skeptically. "Based on what? What the hell do you have, that they might want?"

"We can possibly buy their silence, by giving them millions of federal dollars to fund their personal research projects."

"Don't be ridiculous! They don't want your goddamn money! They want to crucify you, and us, for developing Frostfire!"

President Stillman appeared to panic. "We'll, we'll, we can convince them it's in the nation's best interest to maintain their silence about Frostfire."

"Mister President, I need a decision now!" Brenton reacted to the hand signals of his staff to escalate the decision process. "We're out of time, and you need to decide how to proceed, now!"

"Destroy that missile, General!" President Stillman's frustration caused his hands to form into tight fists. "Stop that missile any way you can. Terminate Operation Hidden Sun! Do it now!"

"You don't have the flipping balls to be the President." Leckowicz stood, before he began stacking his reports and folders.

Brenton grasped the radio microphone to contact Captain Charles Trobowski, of the Ticonderoga. "This is Brenton. Terminate Operation Hidden Sun immediately! Do not allow that missile to reach the power plant!"

"Say again, General?" Trobowski appeared startled by the unexpected message. "Heads up everyone. Listen to what's being said."

"Terminate Operation Hidden Sun immediately!" Brenton said, shouting into the microphone. "Bring down your missile!"

Trobowski frantically motioned to his Weapons Control Officer. "Transmit the destruct signal to the missile!" Several sailors immediately began entering codes into their computer consoles.

"How much time do we have?" Brenton said.

"Sixteen seconds," someone in the command center said. The soldiers eerily became quiet moments later.

"Come on Trobowski, knock down your damn missile." Brenton looked at a monitor. The green line on it depicted the flight path of the Cruise missile, and its current location. "How much time do we have left?

Seven seconds from the plant, while arming the nuclear warhead, the Cruise missile received an encrypted self-destruct command transmitted from the Ticonderoga. The missile's computer immediately initiated an electrical overload. It caused all of the circuit boards and the wiring harnesses within the warhead to burst into flames. Moments later, the computer initiated its last command, detonating explosive bolts located in the sides of the missile. Several explosive charges detonated, separating the sleek aerodynamic missile into three sections. As those sections tumbled toward the ground, a large explosive charge in each one detonated. The explosions destroyed the

512

sections of the missile, while creating deafening concussions and huge clouds of black smoke in the sky one-half mile from the plant.

"What were those explosions, and those noises?" Bonnie turned to see the clouds of dense black smoke floating in the sky. "What just happened?"

"Brenton must have seen the flare that Roger fired! He blew up the missile!" Steve hugged her tightly, lifting her off the ground while exhilarated.

She hugged him tightly while kissing his cheek, before she said, "We're alive! I love you so much!"

Trobowski watched the image of the missile disappear from a radar screen, as the flight telemetry screens darkened, confirming it was no longer in flight. He took a deep breath before radioing Brenton. "Missile destroyed. I say again, Operation Hidden Sun successfully terminated."

"Message acknowledged. Nice job, Captain!" Brenton wiped the perspiration from his forehead. "Mister President, the Ticonderoga reports they successfully destroyed the missile."

President Stillman smiled as whistles, cheers, and shouts of joy filled the tense strategy room. "I'm greatly relieved to hear that, General. What do we do next?"

"I'm flying to the power plant to check out conditions there. I'm bringing a team of power company reactor technicians to the plant so they can stop the release of radiation. I'll contact you from that location with a status."

"Keep me informed of your progress." The President felt triumphant while watching Leckowicz silently gather his papers. "I want to speak to

Doctor McClellan and Mister Samulson after you establish they are alive."

"I'll see to it Mister President. I'll put you in contact with those two men."

"Mister President, can we allow reporters into this room so they can film our successful efforts to destroy Osiris," Marjorie Fletcher, the Senior White House Press Secretary said.

"Yes, of course. Allow the reporters to interview us. Today is the greatest day in the history of our nation. Let the reporters document it, so it can be shared with all people of our great nation."

Steve smiled while looking at Bonnie's saturated shirt, shorts, shoes, and hair. "We're a little wet, but you look terrific."

"So do you, Doc." She wrapped her arms around his neck. "I love you."

"I love you too." He kissed her.

"You two are beginning to sound very serious!" Roger smiled at the couple.

"I've got to sit down." Steve suddenly doubled over after a painful spasm gripped the muscles of his chest. The pain reminded him of the two strenuous and near fatal encounters with Troxell.

"Can we help you?" Roger grasped Steve's arm to help him stand on the steps of the building housing the control room.

"Thanks. I'm ok. I think Troxell broke a few of my ribs."

"We need to get you to a hospital."

"We all need to be in a hospital getting checked out." Steve rubbed his chest.

"Why?" Bonnie frowned, questioningly. "Roger and I are fine."

"We were exposed to a large amount of radiation in that containment building. We may have been exposed to a deadly amount."

"I totally forgot about that." She ran her fingers through her wet hair, while appearing suddenly frustrated.

Roger began pacing nervously. "Is there any way for us to know if we have radiation poisoning?"

"There's a new test that uses a pin prick of blood to determine if we have Acute Radiation Syndrome. I asked Doctor Reglovic to bring the equipment back here when he returns, so he can run the test on us. That'll give us the information we need to understand if our internal organs have been damaged by the radiation."

Bonnie grasped Steve's hand tightly. "Troxell didn't kill us. Osiris didn't kill us. That missile didn't kill us. Maybe our luck will hold, and we'll all be okay." She smiled before kissing him.

Steve turned to stare into the distance, after he heard the familiar sounds of approaching Blackhawk, Apache, and Chinook helicopters. "Brenton and the others are returning to the plant."

"I see more than fifty helicopters flying this way," Bonnie said, as the noise steadily became louder.

"I see another hundred assorted makes of helicopters coming this way from the north," Roger said.

All of the helicopters appeared to stop and hover approximately three miles from the power plant. A single small helicopter then flew forward, close to the ground. The helicopter rapidly circled the power plant buildings and parking lots several times. Then the pilot flew directly over the reactor containment buildings several times. The pilot signaled a thumbs up sign to Bonnie, Roger, and Steve while hovering low over the control room building. Then he waved to the group, before the aircraft rapidly flew to the south.

Bonnie said, "What was that helicopter doing?"

"I'm guessing they were sampling the air for signs of radioactivity." Steve looked around for other low flying helicopters, but he did not see other aircraft in the area.

Roger appeared confused when all of the hovering helicopters unexpectedly began flying forward, toward the power plant. "Why are they all flying back here, if this area is contaminated with radiation?"

"I don't understand this. They're knowingly flying into a radioactive hot zone? That doesn't make any sense." Steve put his arm around Bonnie's waist.

Large groups of helicopters began landing around the power plant. Reactor technicians dressed in protective white biohazard suits began running toward the containment buildings. They carried equipment needed to force open the doors, to enter the three buildings.

A large helicopter slowly and carefully landed in the parking lot beside the control room. Brenton jumped from the aircraft, before he led Straley and his staff officers toward Steve, Bonnie, and Roger.

He appeared shocked while stepping through the silver watery mixture covering the ground. "I've never been happier to see three individuals. How are you?"

"We're good, General." Roger said, as he shook Brenton's hand

"We're better than good," Steve said while shaking the General's hand, "we're alive."

"Let's get this on you, so you stay warm until we can get you some dry clothes, Doctor." An Army Medic wrapped a thick green blanket around Steve. "Water is dripping from your clothes."

"Thank you." Steve smiled while watching Medics place blankets around Bonnie and Roger, to keep them warm.

Brenton said, "Where did this damn silver goop come from? It's slippery as hell!"

"The green goop as you call it, is comprised of Osiris cells killed by the radiation. You're stepping on the harmless remains of the cloud."

"This is what's left of the cloud?"

"Yes it is. The sun will evaporate this liquid, and it will be gone in a day or two."

Brenton smiled, while sliding his boot through the green liquid. "Victory comes in many forms, gentlemen!"

"Yes it does," Steve said. "And I can tell you, victory feels terrific, General!"

"You all look exhausted after your ordeal." Brenton smiled at Bonnie. "You look very well after being reported dead, Ms. Saunders."

"Thank you, General." Bonnie squeezed water out of her long hair. "When you're ready, I'll give you all of the excruciatingly painful details."

Roger shaded his eyes from the sun while looking at the clear blue sky around the plant. "Did Osiris move north from here, General?"

"You stopped the bacteria cloud at this plant. Your plan was absolutely perfect."

"We changed the plan a few dozen times, but we improvised and made it work." Steve watched another large group of helicopters landing around the plant, in fields outside the security fence. "Is it dangerous for all of these people to be here at the plant?"

Brenton frowned. "No, not at all. Osiris is no longer a threat."

Steve looked around questioningly. He watched researchers and members of the military jump from helicopters after they landed, before the ecstatic people ran forward to congratulate him and Roger. "This entire power plant and the land areas around it, should be contaminated with the radiation we released from the reactors to kill Osiris! These people returning to the plant are being exposed to that deadly residual radiation on the ground and buildings. That radiation will kill them!"

"I share your concerns, but there are other factors that are currently in play, which we don't fully understand at this time." Brenton looked at several of his staff officers talking into radio headsets. "Do we have reports from Colonel Breckmeister, who is commanding the Chemical, Biological, and

Radiation teams, surveying the radiation levels around the power plant and the surrounding areas?"

"I'm in contact with him now, General," one of Brenton's staff officer said. "He's three miles out from the plant, with one of his radiation sensing and detection teams."

"Put him on the speaker, so we can all hear his report."

"Yes, Sir." The officer spoke into a radio. "Colonel Breckmeister, General Brenton wants to speak to you."

"This is Breckmeister." The middle-aged officer stood beside a group of parked military vehicles, while watching soldiers sample the air for radiation. "We're out in the field running tests, General."

"I'm at the power plant with Doctor McClellan. Can you explain the radiation levels your men have found here at the plant?" Brenton looked up, as a large group of fast moving helicopters passed over the plant and adjacent land areas, with radiation detection equipment extending from both sides of each aircraft. "We also need to understand how the surrounding landmasses, and the air, have been contaminated with radiation."

"The radiation sensing and detecting equipment in the helicopters passing over the power plant, and the land around the plant in a one hundred mile radius, are not detecting any radiation whatsoever."

"Are you absolutely sure? We can confirm radiation was released from the reactors, because it did in fact destroy the Osiris bacteria." Brenton look down at the green soupy liquid on the ground.

"My teams can't find any indications radiation was released from the plant, in the land or air in this area. It's as if that release of radiation didn't happen! The instruments in our mobile units are not detecting any amounts of radiation in this area surrounding the power plant. We're not even registering the low-level trace amounts of radiation that are normally found in nature."

"Did you recalibrate your equipment and run the tests again, Colonel?"

"My teams conducted the recalibration exercises several times, to ensure our equipment and readings are precise. There is no radiation anywhere, in this geographical region."

Steve said, "This is McClellan. Do you have any idea why you're not detecting radiation, in an area that should be highly contaminated?"

Colonel Breckmeister looked up at the cloudless blue sky. He felt the warmth of the rising sun on his face. "Something I cannot explain happened at that power plant. Something outside the laws of physics we know today."

"What are you suggesting?" Steve looked at Brenton questioningly.

"There is a distinct possibility the Osiris cloud carried the radiation into the upper levels of the atmosphere, and into the void of space itself, while we watched it spiraling upward. Or, possibly something else happened at the power plant which we don't understand. The physics people will need to review the information we provide to them, and give us their opinion. Whatever happened at that plant, and how the radiation mysteriously dissipated, is well beyond my understanding."

"I want to confirm this area is safe for people to return," Brenton said. "Can I bring our teams back to this location?"

"Yes sir, General. The mobile and airborne units will continue checking the area for radiation, but I'm reporting the area is safe for humans to return."

"Carry on Colonel, and contact me immediately if you become aware of a change in the situation. We don't need our people exposed to high levels of radiation, while they survey the damage to the power plant."

"Yes, Sir. We'll keep you apprised of any changes we detect."

"I still don't understand what happened to the radiation, after it destroyed the Osiris bacteria," Steve said, while sliding his foot through the green liquid covering the ground, comprised of dead bacteria cells. "It could not have simply vanished."

"Let's get an update from the power plant people." Brenton motioned to Berry, as he spoke to a large group of technicians and company executives.

Berry smiled, after speaking to company technicians working in the containment buildings, using his cell phone. He extended his hand to Steve and Roger. "Congratulations gentlemen, you saved our nation, and a countless number of lives, with your actions. You should both be commended for your efforts, and heroism."

"Thank you, but that's not important right now," Roger said. "The military is telling us there's no radioactive contamination on the ground around the plant, or in the air. Can you confirm that?"

"That's something we don't immediately understand." Berry silently read several text messages that displayed on his phone. "My reactor technicians cannot find any radiation inside the three containment buildings, or in the surrounding areas around the buildings. Something literally sucked the radiation out of the reactors."

"How is that possible?" Steve frowned. "What happened to the radiation?"

"We don't have any theories at this time, Doctor. This is a mystery. We need more time to investigate, and evaluate what took place as you worked to destroy Osiris."

"The fuel rod assemblies are hanging in the three containment buildings? Are they still emitting radiation?"

"This is where the situation becomes more of a mystery, Doctor. We can't find any traces of radiation in those fuel rod assemblies. We can't even detect low levels of residual radiation in the old spent fuel pellets, which are kept in the storage pools in each containment building."

"You're telling me something we don't understand, somehow absorbed all of the radiation from this plant, and now it's disappeared?"

"Yes, yes, I realize that does not sound plausible." Berry paused as he became excited, while smiling at company executives now congregating behind him. "I should say, that scenario cannot happen based on our current

522

understanding of radiation and its properties and components."

Bonnie smiled, before she said, "Is it possible the Osiris bacteria cloud drew the radiation out of everything in, and around this plant, and somehow digested it, before it died?"

"And then that radiation inside the cloud was also destroyed as the bacteria died around it, and the cloud collapsed to the ground to form this green slime," Steve said.

Brenton said, "What took place inside those containment buildings, Doctor?"

Roger looked at Steve and Bonnie, as if suddenly enlightened. "Those glowing lights we saw traveling through the Osiris cloud may have something to do with this disappearing radiation mystery."

"Lights?" Berry said. "What lights are you referring to?"

"We saw various phenomenon of glowing colored lights travelling through the bacteria cloud, which we can't explain."

Berry laughed, with his skeptical company officials. "Where could those lights have come from? There's no possible way they could have formed in the containment buildings. You may have been hallucinating, Doctor."

Steve became angry, after listening to Berry's derogatory comments. "Don't downplay what we all saw! We were here in the middle of this battle, while your god damn ass was safe miles away from this damn plant!"

"Don't get upset with him," Bonnie said, as she grasped Steve's hand. "Don't waste your time explaining what we saw. He'll never accept your explanation."

Brenton said, "The lights you're describing must be related to the unexplained light phenomenon my spotters reported. They observed unknown streaks of brilliant light traveling through the interior of the bacteria cloud."

"We also saw those streaks. But we don't have an explanation for them."

Roger said, "There must be a correlation between the unexplained lights, and the missing radiation, that we don't understand. The glowing orbs and streaks of light, may have somehow carried the radiation away from this plant."

"Or possibly," Steve said, "those glowing lights we don't understand somehow neutralized the radiation. I don't know how that can happen, and I can't explain how the radiation seemingly evaporated."

"Maybe it was something as simple as a miracle," Bonnie said, before she hugged Steve tightly. "I can't remember all of the details, but angels came to me, and something miraculous happened in that containment building."

"This conversation is becoming somewhat absurd," Berry said, while watching reporters rushing toward the group. "It really doesn't matter what chain of events took place here. Our power generation facility survived, and you destroyed Osiris. Now I need to give a statement to the press, to explain how my company was instrumental in the destruction of the bacteria cloud."

Steve thought about Mason's personal faults, and fears. He pushed them aside in his mind to ignore them, before he said, "Mason panicked after Osiris surrounded the plant. Unfortunately, he died while helping us in the containment building."

"I did receive a message from my engineering supervisor." Berry read several additional text messages that appeared on his phone. "He reported they found Mason's remains in a containment building."

Steve paused, while briefly looking at Bonnie and Roger, before he said, "He died during a very heroic attempt to destroy Osiris. I'll explain the details, so you can relay them to the reporters."

Berry raised his hands to stop Steve. "Thank you Doctor, but I really don't need to know the gruesome details. What's most important is our plant can be repaired, as we move on from this horrific tragedy."

"I would think the death of a single employee would concern you more, than all the damage Osiris caused at this plant."

Berry appeared flustered after the remark. He realized the reporters were nearby, and listening to the conversation. "Well, I am very troubled by that man's death, but it's a question of priorities."

"Your only priority is your precious image, and your damn company! You don't give a damn about people!"

"That's not the case!" Berry's face became red from embarrassment. "My employees and my stockholders are my only concerns."

"I think you should name this plant after Mason," Roger said. "That will be a lasting tribute to the man who gave his life."

"That's a terrific idea," Steve said, as he shook Roger's hand. "No one will ever forget that man's efforts to save our nation, when Osiris flooded into the containment buildings."

Berry suddenly appeared confused. "Wait one minute. How did you three survive, after the deadly Osiris bacteria cloud surrounded this power generation facility? I want an explanation!"

"We simply kept our heads underwater!" Steve laughed while reaching for Bonnie's hand. "Let's take a walk."

"That is a very good question, Doctor." Brenton laughed while walking beside Steve and Bonnie. "You'll have to give me the details of how you three survived here, when Osiris engulfed this plan."

"We can do that, General. My solution for keeping us alive will make you laugh!"

"I'll tell my staff to schedule debriefing sessions with Pentagon officials, government and state and local agencies, and our intelligence organizations."

"We'll tell everyone what we know, and everything we saw while we destroyed Osiris," Steve said. "But before those meetings, we have an urgent issue we need to resolve."

"I don't understand." Brenton motioned to one of his staff officers, telling him to take notes on a tablet. "Where is this going? Is the issue related to your destroying Osiris?"

"They're going to find another body in the containment building, near Mason's body. A body they can't explain, because it shouldn't be there."

"I wasn't aware there was another person here at the power plant with you?" Brenton appeared shocked and confused. "Was it one of the news reporters?"

"It was that bastard, Troxell."

"Doctor Troxell? What was he doing here?"

"Troxell wasn't a god damn doctor!"

"If I remember correctly, his credentials indicated he was a surgeon."

"He was a government agent. Someone in our government sent him here to kill us."

"Who sent Troxell here? Why would someone want you dead, if they wanted you to destroy Osiris and save our nation?" Brenton remembered the strange conversation and bizarre discussion he had with the President. "Explain what you know, Doctor."

"Troxell tried to kill me too," Bonnie said. "He blew up the helicopter I was supposed to be riding in, trying to kill me. He murdered everyone riding on that helicopter!"

"How do you know that?" Brenton appeared confused. He motioned his staff officers closer, to listen to the details of the confusing conversation.

"Troxell said he wanted to kill me, while he explained the details of his bizarre plan to save Osiris, during a verbal confrontation in the reactor control room while he pointed a gun at us.

Steve said, "Someone in our government sent the bastard to kill our research staff in Arizona, and your men and the construction workers, working here at the plant."

"This doesn't make any sense! Why would they want to do that when they knew we were attempting to stop Osiris?"

"So we wouldn't destroy the bacteria cloud!"

"Why didn't they want us to destroy Osiris?" Brenton's face became red from growing anger.

"The government wanted to use the killer bacteria, as a new biological weapon."

"This is unbelievable, and unacceptable. My men died, or should I say they were murdered, because of our politicians need for power?"

"Troxell brought in attack helicopters in an attempt to destroy the power plant, to stop us from releasing the radiation. They didn't have an opportunity to damage the buildings at this plant."

"How did you stop them?"

"I believe Osiris got to them, and destroyed them. You'll find the wreckage somewhere around this plant."

Brenton turned to his staff officers. "Get some mobile teams out into the field to conduct a search. Find the wreckage of those helicopters. I need to know which military unit authorized them to attack this plant, to kill these people."

"I've got to report this to my superiors immediately. I'll get right back to all of you." Brenton walked away, quietly discussing the shocking revelations with his staff.

Large helicopters began landing around the plant, outside the security fences. Researchers, soldiers, reporters, and construction workers cheered and clapped after climbing from them. Everyone appeared overwhelmed with emotion, knowing their combined efforts and collaboration helped to destroy Osiris. They laughed and joked while walking through the green slimy liquid covering the ground, and roadbeds, after someone explained it was comprised of dead bacteria cells.

The construction workers and military personnel walked around their trucks to inspect their equipment. They shook their heads while studying the damage Osiris created. Many of them walked to the scaffolding that collapsed onto nearby trucks, after missiles fired from Troxell's helicopters damaged the structure.

Reporters and their camera crews began filming the destroyed power plant buildings, and the containment buildings. Bonnie spoke to many of the reporters while still wrapped in the towel, as she provided them with a brief description of events that led to the destruction of Osiris. She declined requests for immediate interviews, while promising to meet with reporters later in the day.

Doctor Reglovic led a large group of jubilant cheering and clapping researchers across a parking lot, while shouting Roger and Steve's names to get their attention. He shook both men's hands as the researchers cheered, while he spoke to Steve and Roger. "I seriously believed we lost you two boys, after Osiris surrounded this facility."

"I thought we were dead at least fifty times last night!" Steve began shaking hands with various researchers, as they congratulated him.

"I can't imagine how you managed to evade the devastating killer bacteria. You'll need to explain the magic you used."

"Whatever you two did in that reactor control room, worked to destroy Osiris! I'm not sure how you did it, but you did a great job Doctor, and you too Roger!" Harrison shook the hands of both men. "I'm sure you also played a great role in this monumental event Ms. Saunders. Congratulations."

"We didn't do this alone, John." Roger smiled while pointing at the large crowd of cheering researchers and military personnel gathering around them. "All of these amazing people working together, allowed us to destroy Osiris!"

Doctor Cindy Licitra pushed her way through the cheering crowd. She motioned to Steve. "We're ready for all of you now, Doctor. This can't wait. You can be media heroes later today!"

Bonnie frowned, before she looked at Steve. "What's going on?"

"Cindy is in charge of decontamination. She needs to ensure we're radiation free, after the time we spent in that containment building with the fuel rods."

"This sounds kinky." Bonnie smiled. "What do we need to do?"

"Follow me, please." Doctor Licitra led them to an area where soldiers held up blankets to form three areas of privacy. "Get inside those blankets, and take off all of your clothes."

"Out here, in the open?" Roger realized they were forty feet from a growing crowd of cheering researchers, while low flying helicopters passed overhead.

"You've been exposed to a lot of radiation. It may have contaminated your clothes, skin, and your hair."

"But they're saying they can't find any traces of radiation in this area."

"But, nothing. I'm not taking any chances with your lives, Roger! You're going to strip down until you're naked, and then you're going to wash up. We brought containers of decontamination fluid, so you can wash your hair and skin."

"Let's do what the doctor is asking." Steve smiled while motioning Bonnie and Roger into the blankets. He stepped into an area where he pulled off his wet clothes. He exposed the red and blue bruises resulting from his near fatal physical encounters with Troxell.

"This is just like camping, with a million people watching your every move at the campsite!" Bonnie laughed while slowly peeling off her wet clothes. She carefully folded her shorts before gently placing them on the ground. Then she began washing herself with the decontamination fluid.

Steve lifted a bucket of decontamination fluid, and poured it over his head to wash his hair. As he washed his body, he smiled while thinking, '*Dear Lord, I don't know how you gave me the idea to use that trailer of water to save everyone's life. I just want to say thank you. Thank you, Lord, for saving all of us.*'

When they finished washing Licitra handed each of them several towels. "That should get most of the radiation off your skin. Brenton made arrangements for a helicopter to fly you to a hospital north of here for a thorough decontamination."

The soldiers passed dry military clothing to each of them. Roger, Bonnie, and Steve pulled on camouflaged shirts and pants, and combat boots. Then they stepped out from between the blankets, as researchers and military personnel cheered and whistled after realizing they were safe, and unharmed.

"Oh, wait a second. I forgot something." Bonnie rushed back between the blankets. She leaned forward for several seconds to lift her shorts carefully off the ground. After fumbling with them, she tossed them onto the ground. Then she stepped out of the blankets. "I'm back."

Steve said, "Is there a problem?"

"Nope, not now. Everything is perfect." She brushed back her long wet hair.

"Let's check each of you out, and ensure there is no residual radiation on your skin or hair." A military doctor carried the sensor of a radiation detector, as he stepped around each person. He frowned when it did not register any radioactivity. "You're completely radiation free. I don't know how. You're all good to go. Congratulations!"

Chapter 20

When Steve noticed several doctors from the University of Texas Medical Center in the jubilant crowd of researchers, he motioned them forward to join him. "Can you take blood samples from Roger, Bonnie, and myself, please."

"Sure, we can do that. Give us a few minutes to find our equipment," Doctor Justin Wellfleet said. "The helicopters are dropping off our containers of medical equipment."

Doctor Eric Simpson said, "What are you doing with those blood samples? Were you injured while destroying Osiris?"

Steve smiled while patting the older man's shoulder. "They're for you to use, Doctor."

"Me? You must be mistaken." Doctor Simpson laughed as he grasped the cane he used for walking with both hands to stand erect. "How can an old man such as I, help you, after what you just accomplished?"

"You're the best hematologist I know, you cranky old man!" Steve laughed. "Can you run your new specialized blood tests to determine how much radiation our bodies absorbed, and if we need to worry about cell damage, or possibly death?"

"It won't be a comprehensive test, such as those you will receive when we get you into a hospital. But the tests will provide you with a preliminary indication if radiation exposure is destroying your blood, cells, and ultimately your body."

"That's exactly what I need to know." Steve paused, before he gently shook the man's hand. "Thank you."

Steve turned after hearing two men shouting his name. He smiled when he saw Straley and Mallory. "I can't tell you how happy I am to see you two are safe."

Straley extended his hand. "I don't know how you're still alive, Doc. I thought Osiris fried your ass, after it surrounded this power plant."

"Panic is sometimes the mother of invention. Fear forced us to find a way to survive."

"Don't listen to him. It was another of Steve's radical ideas that saved us," Roger said, before he laughed while shaking the men's hands.

"Don't let the modest doctor tell you anything different," Bonnie said, before she kissed his lips. "This man is responsible for us being alive right now."

"I wasn't ready to die, and I wasn't going to let Osiris kill us." Steve looked at Bonnie, and appeared infatuated by her smile. "I've got a lot of things I still want to do with my life."

Mallory spit black tobacco juice onto the green slimy liquid covering the ground, while shading his eyes from the sun as he stared at the containment buildings. "I hope my construction people and I helped you in some small way, Doc. I'm sure glad that bacteria monster is dead."

"We couldn't have stopped Osiris without your assistance. Your people and their construction expertise made the difference. I want to thank all of your people personally, and shake their hands."

Steve noticed Doctor Simpson, and several doctors accompanying him, walking in his direction, while they pushed a metal cart covered with medical equipment. He motioned to Roger and Bonnie. "We have to give a sample of blood to these doctors."

"Please sit on the tailgate of this truck, so we can draw blood from each of you," Doctor Justin Wellfleet said. He and other doctors withdrew two vials of blood from Roger, Bonnie, and Steve. They carefully set up the medical equipment, while a portable generator powered it. Then they began conducting the tests.

"What will we do, if the tests come back bad?" Bonnie grasped Steve's hand and pressed it to the cheek of her face.

"We'll spend every minute we have, together. And we'll enjoy life, while we make each other happy." He kissed her.

"I hate to come between you too," Brenton said, after he walked to the truck. "Steve, the President is asking to speak to you and Roger."

"Now that sounds like it's going to be a cluster." Bonnie slid off the tailgate of the truck, after she noticed camera crews recording reporters from national news organizations, speaking to researchers. She ran to speak to them. "Get every reporter and news camera crew you can find, and bring them over here. We have a killer story for you!"

Steve said, "Where are we talking to the President? I'm not flying to Washington."

"We'll conduct the meeting here. My communications team is assembling the video equipment needed for a teleconferencing meeting." Brenton wiped the perspiration from his forehead.

"I don't know what to say to him." Steve rubbed his forehead with his fingers, while deep in thought. "I've been dreading this conversation for hours."

"Tell him exactly what happened here." Brenton stared at him ominously. "Tell him the truth, Son! You may feel guilty or bad about saying it, but it is the truth, and people need to know! Osiris wasn't the only enemy trying to kill you at this plant."

"Thank you for your thoughts, General. I know what I have to do." Steve watched the clouds of black smoke rising from the area burning south of the plant. He contemplated his options and talking points, while staring at the plumes of smoke rising into the blue sky.

Approximately one hour later, Brenton and a team of soldiers, escorted Bonnie, Roger, and Steve across a power plant parking lot. They stopped behind a large construction truck Osiris destroyed. There they studied the military communications equipment on the truck's tailgate. Soldiers completed the work to connect military radios, laptop computers, speakers, and cameras, to the radios. Other soldiers assembled a portable circular satellite communications antenna nearby, pointing it skyward toward an unseen satellite.

As researchers congratulated her, Bonnie spoke to several reporters. "Do you know where I can find a portable video and audio editing unit? The type we use to review and edit our camera disk drives, when we're recording stories in the field?"

"I know where to find one. I saw a news crew working with one of those editing units, after a helicopter dropped them off here at the plant." A reporter ran from the area.

"We're almost prepared to establish communications with the President," Brenton said. "Five minutes, until we contact the Pentagon."

A reporter said, "Do we have your permission to record your conversation with the President, Doctor McClellan? The world will want to hear him congratulate you, and the people who worked together to stop Osiris."

"You can record everything we say." Steve watched silently, while news camera crews positioned their video equipment near the truck. He motioned Roger forward from the crowd of researchers, to stand beside him. He smiled while shaking Roger's hand, while camera crews recorded them.

General Brenton stepped forward after two video monitors brightened to life on the tailgate of the truck. He saw himself with clapping researchers in the background on one monitor. Moments later, he frowned while watching the joyous celebration already in progress, in the Pentagon Strategy Room on the other monitor. Military personnel were serving champagne to celebrating government officials, military officers, and civilian advisors. "This is Brenton, reporting from the nuclear power plant."

The President stepped into the camera's view. "Good morning, General."

"I'm sorry to interrupt your celebration, Mister President."

"Nonsense, you're not interrupting." The President shook the hands of several military officers, while thanking them for their valiant efforts.

"I have Doctor McClellan, and Mr. Samulson, here with me Mister President."

"Excellent." The President accepted a glass of champagne from the Vice President. They toasted one another.

"Ms. Saunders is also here with us, at the power plant." He motioned Bonnie forward, until she stood beside him.

The President appeared surprised by the unexpected news. He studied her on the monitor as she stood with her arms crossed almost defiantly, before he briefly looked at his advisors. Then he turned back to the camera. "I thought Ms. Saunders died in a helicopter crash, during the evacuation of the plant?"

"That was our initial assessment after receiving reports of a crash. However, that information proved to be incorrect. I will determine exactly what happened, Mister President."

"That information is inconsequential now." The President shook the hand of several senators. "The national crisis is resolved, and we can begin rebuilding our nation."

Steve stepped into the camera's view. The morning sunlight radiated on the handsome man's face, and his short dark hair. "Hello, Mister President."

"Doctor McClellan, I'm very relieved to see you are unharmed," The President said. "I don't know how you survived, but you had myself and my advisors very concerned. How are you?"

Steve began laughing, before he motioned Roger and Bonnie forward until they stood beside him. "I'm a little sore, but I can't complain after everything we've been through. We're all alive, and Osiris is no longer a threat to the world."

"I want to extend my heart felt gratitude, and the sincerest thanks our nation can offer, and that of the world, to you and Roger, and all of the dedicated medical professionals and military resources and civilian workers, whose tireless efforts succeeded in destroying Osiris. I know it was a difficult and strenuous task."

Steve's anger slowly increased, fueled by the President's unabashed remarks. He bit the inside of his jaw while thinking, '*Should I accept the President's praise on behalf of everyone who worked so hard, or start a verbal confrontation?*'

"I want you and Mr. Samulson, Ms. Saunders, Mr. Mallory, General Brenton, and the key doctors who assisted you with the destruction of Osiris, to come to the White House for a very special award ceremony." The President's remarked caused the researchers, military personnel, and the construction workers, to clap, cheer, and whistle.

Steve took a deep breath while remembering the images of burned and mutilated bodies of the young dead soldiers Troxell murdered. He looked directly into the camera. "You almost sound convincing Mister President. I assume that's the sign of a true politician. Lie to everyone you're attempting to impress, but make it sound convincing."

The researchers, reporters, and military personnel gathered around the truck immediately became quiet, while looking at one another questioningly. Their shocked expressions mirrored their surprise, after Steve's unanticipated and derogatory remark. Everyone in the Pentagon Strategy Room immediately stopped speaking after hearing Steve's comment.

"I don't understand your last statement, Doctor McClellan." President Stillman briefly frowned at his advisors. Then he nervously glanced at the reporters allowed into the Strategy Room after radiation destroyed Osiris, to observe and document the speech given by the President. They now listened intently to his conversation.

"You know exactly what I'm talking about." Steve remembered the researchers Troxell murdered at Brenton's camp.

The President placed his glass of champagne on a table. He laughed nervously, seemingly shocked by Steve's cryptic response. "I'm afraid I don't understand what you're talking about."

"You're congratulating us for destroying Osiris, yet you did nothing to make our job easier."

"Pardon me?" The President stepped closer to the camera. "I put this nation's entire military at your disposal, Doctor."

540

"I can't disagree with that. We couldn't have stopped Osiris without the help of those brave and heroic men and women."

"What more could I have done?" The President felt his hands becoming damp with nervous perspiration.

Steve stared at the camera. "You could have told us the truth from the beginning."

The President became concerned. He was unsure why Steve appeared upset and angry. "The truth, about what?"

"You lied to us damn it, and you hindered our progress to stop Osiris. You personally may be responsible for the deaths of millions of Americans, because of your deceptive tactics."

"I don't understand anything you're saying. What are you implying?"

Steve was pleased when the news camera operators began recording the reaction of the shocked military personnel, and the researchers. "Maybe I should tell the world what the hell really took place at this god damn power plant."

"Go get him Doc! Turn up the heat and fry his damn ass! " Bonnie smiled at Steve, after grasping his hand. "I'm right beside you, and with you, Baby!"

"Bonnie is right, Steve," Roger said. "She's telling you to do the right thing. Tell the world what really happened to us, and all of these other dedicated people who worked together."

"You must be exhausted after your ordeal, Doctor," the President said. You sound delirious, and may be in need of immediate medical attention."

"The only attention I need, is that of the American people, and the world."

The President saw his advisors huddling together out of the camera's view. He looked at them, as if requesting their suggestions for responding to Steve. "What is troubling you Doctor? Please tell me."

"You should have told us about Frostfire from the very start of this national crisis!"

"Frostfire?" The President looked nervously to his personal advisors for assistance. He frowned when they remained silent, while staring at him from across the room, where they gathered to discuss the escalating situation.

"If you provided information about Frostfire, our nation's new military bacterial weapon, we might have destroyed Osiris weeks ago. That simple action would have saved countless lives!"

"I don't know what you're talking about. What is Frostfire?"

"You're still lying to the American people! You and your advisors know all of the information related to Frostfire, and how it mutated Osiris to transform the bacteria into a flesh eating monster!"

"I don't know what you're referring to, Doctor. Frostfire? Did you sustain a head injury during your ordeal, that is not making you sound delirious?"

"You sent Troxell, a government and military killer, to hinder our progress and stop us from destroying Osiris."

"What? That's a ridiculous and very dangerous accusation!" The President paused to read a note handed to him by an advisor. "You are incorrect. I did no such thing!"

"You're telling me you didn't send Troxell here to murder the dedicated medical people and scientists working diligently, to find a way to destroy Osiris so they could save our nation?"

The President swallowed hard. "Frostfire? Troxell? I don't have any recollection of what you're talking about Doctor."

"You don't know anything?" Steve laughed while glancing at Roger and Bonnie. "You're telling me you have no idea what's happening in your own administration, or the plans of your advisors?"

"I honestly do not know how to respond to these, these, highly unethical accusations."

"Let's say for example, Troxell is a very credible source. He told us Frostfire is a new biological weapon our government scientists are developing for you, Mister President?"

"I'm unaware of that activity, Doctor. However, I will meet with my military leaders this week and ask if they have any information about Frostfire, which they can share with me."

"Let me fast forward the chain of events that led to Osiris becoming deadly, so you understand the situation, Mr. President. Your secret Frostfire bacteria attacked the original Osiris cells. and cause them to mutate! Osiris began to crave human flesh, after it was drastically mutated by a government designed and manufactured bacteria!"

"I'm not aware of those events taking place. As I said, I will meet with my military leaders during the next few days and ask if they are aware of that activity."

"You can stop the charade! You already know Frostfire caused Osiris to devour human flesh, but you won't admit it. You're lying to the American public, after you allowed innocent people to die tragic and horrible deaths!"

"I told you, I don't know what you're talking about! This all sounds highly improbable. You're beginning to sound ridiculous, and I'm growing tired of your accusations, Doctor!"

"Troxell told us everything!" Steve became angry. "We know everything, and we're taking it public!"

President Stillman was shocked by Steve's extensive knowledge of Troxell's mission. He took a note handed to him by Franklin Perry, his most trusted senior advisor. He read the words on the note out loud, "I think it's in the nation's best interest if you refrain from referring to, or disclosing any information related to, Frostfire, or Doctor Troxell."

"Stop calling that murderer Troxell, a damn doctor! That's an insult to the legitimate medical people who sacrificed everything when they put aside their families and friends, and risk their lives to destroy Osiris."

"The behaviors you've described are not consistent with the Doctor Troxell I know. I will meet with him, to review your startling accusations. If we determine Doctor Troxell indeed exceeded his authority in that situation, he will be prosecuted to full extent of the law!"

"You're going to speak to him?" Steve began laughing while he looked at Brenton. His anger suddenly flared while remembering the pain when Troxell attempted to strangle him. "He won't tell you anything, Mr. President."

"Of course he will speak to the President of the United States. He will answer all of my questions. He's a proud member of our nation's military and a high ranking officer."

"I'm positive, Troxell will not speak to you. He will not respond to your questions!"

"Why do you say that?" The President frowned at the camera. "What fantastic insight do you possess, where you can made such an absurd statement, while making yourself look like a fool?"

"I can say Troxell will not speak to you, because I killed the rat bastard a few hours ago! I ensured Osiris ate his god damn flesh!" Steve heard the researchers and military personnel in the background, as they discussed his startling revelation.

"You did what?" The President appeared visibly upset by the news. "You murdered a member of our United States military forces?"

"Troxell attempted to murder us while we were battling Osiris."

"You must be mistaken. Those actions are not consistent with his orders to assist you."

"I have the bruises to prove he attacked me, and Roger and Bonnie." Steve pulled off the military shirt, exposing the red and black bruises covering his upper body. He heard members of the military, and the medical researchers behind him, now talking louder after they saw his bruises.

"Maybe I can help everyone understand what Troxell did, while following your orders Mister President," Bonnie said.

"The circus continues! What do you think you know of the situation, Ms. Saunders?" The President frowned skeptically. "Is this another attempt by the press to fabricate a fake information story based on assumptions, speculation, and misinformation?"

"I have something much more credible to show the world, Mister President. I have the spoken words, and video of a confessed murderer."

"You don't have anything credible!" The President became increasingly alarmed. He motioned to his aides for assistance. "You somehow manufactured misinformation to confuse the public perception of this incident!"

"Bonnie took a portable video editor from a nearby reporter. Then she carefully pulled a silver plastic card from her pocket. "I've been safeguarding this plastic video and audio storage device, all night and all day today in my wet jeans."

"What is your display of disinformation going to show us?"

"This is a scene I recorded in the power plant's control room, earlier this morning with a video camera. This will help the President remember he sent Troxell to kill us. This video will give the public insight into Troxell's mind, and they'll immediately realize he's a cold blooded, psychotic killer!"

"You save the video you recorded when Troxell was about to kill us?" Steve was surprised, and he smiled at Bonnie before kissing her.

"I guarded this all night." She inserted the silver media card into the video editor. Then she pushed buttons, before turning the monitor of the video editor toward the camera on the truck. She laughed before she said, "This video will not make you look good Mister President."

President Stillman suddenly appeared to be confused and disoriented. He frowned questioningly as he struggled to comprehend the rapidly demeaning and embarrassing situation, after he saw Troxell's image appear on the monitor. The video showed Troxell pointing a handgun at Steve, Roger, and Mason. The President was horrified and shocked, almost incapacitated, while listening to the military officer boasting about his mission, and his need to murder innocent people to protect Osiris. Then he implicated the President, his advisors, and military and government officials in the extensive and elaborate cover up to prevent the destruction of Osiris.

The President frightened everyone in the room with him, after he suddenly began screaming instructions. "General Brenton, I'm ordering you to stop that video now! Confiscate the video immediately."

"I believe we have a communications problem, Mister President. I did not hear your last order. Please repeat it!" Brenton stared at the video monitor Bonnie held, while watching Troxell boast and brag about his efforts to murder researchers, while hindering their efforts to destroy Osiris. He became angry while learning more about the situations, and events, which took the lives of both researchers and his military personnel.

John Kump, the Secretary of Defense, rushed to the President's side before he said, "General Brenton, I'm ordering you to arrest Saunders, McClellan, and Samulson immediately. Do not allow them to have contact with any other individuals at your location. Confiscate that video device and ship it to Washington with an armed guard to ensure no one tampers with it! Bring Saunders, McClellan, and Samulson to Washington tonight, for questioning and possible prosecution"

Brenton motioned to a heavily armed security team. "Captain, surround these three individuals, and the video display equipment, with a security perimeter."

"Move up, and assume a defensive position!" The officer immediately led his men forward. Armed soldiers quickly formed a protective circle around Steve, Roger, and Bonnie. They readied their weapons, but did not aim them at the huge crowd of wary onlookers.

"Very good, General," Kump said. "Now stop that video player."

"We no longer understand who is the enemy in this situation. There may be other agents, government assassins, in our midst waiting to strike." Brenton stepped into the circle of soldiers, so he stood beside Steve. "Captain, if anyone approaches these three people, shoot to kill!"

"Understood, General. Security Detail, ready your weapons."

"What do you think you're doing General?" Kump said, shouting. "Those are not the orders I gave you!"

"I'm disobeying your orders to ensure no harm comes to these three civilians struggling to protect our nation, and our constitution, from people in our government who blatantly disregard our laws."

The President watched the monitor Bonnie held as Troxell explained how he murdered innocent individuals. He listened as Troxell explained how he attempted to murder Bonnie by destroying a helicopter she was in, and causing it to crash, killing everyone onboard.

President Stillman said, shouting, "You have been ordered to stop that video, General!" His face became red, and his words slurred, as his body trembled when he began to panic.

"Allow the reporters to review the remainder of your video, Ms. Saunders." Brenton nodded to her. "They deserve to know the truth, so they can report to the American people."

She smiled. "Thank you, General."

As the President and government officials screamed their protests simultaneously, the reporters watched the remainder of the video, and listened to Troxell's remarks. His descriptions and explanations related to following instructions to kill innocent law-abiding people, stunned the onlookers.

"I want that video in the White house tonight, General," the President said, screaming. "I want it in my hand!"

"You can have this media device, Mr. President." Bonnie pulled the plastic device from the video editor, before handing it to Brenton. She looked at the camera. "I already made fifty copies of that media device, and I distributed them to the reporters who are here at this power plant. They're already filing stories with their news organizations. I also transmitted a copy of the video to all of the worldwide news organizations, with a very detailed explanation. You can watch that video on the national news tonight!"

Franklin Perry rushed to stand beside the President, while angrily pointing at a camera. "Your actions can, and will be considered, treasonous, Ms. Saunders! I will recommend the Justice Department prosecute you, to the full extent of the law! You'll spend the rest of your life rotting in a god forsaken prison!"

Bonnie laughed, before she said, "I want to be sure I understand your thinking. You sanctioned the murder of our military personnel and researchers, and you want to prosecute me for revealing the truth. I want to see all of you go to prison for what you did to our nation, and our heroes!"

"Doctor McClellan," the President said, "I'm ordering you to fly to Washington where we can discuss this situation face to face with my advisors. Bring all of the copies of that video with you, so it can be analyzed to determine if it is fraudulent, and as I suspect, manufactured misinformation."

"I can assure you, that video is a very accurate depiction of what took place in the control room, while Troxell pointed a handgun at me, and said he was going to kill me."

"Stop talking, and bring that damn video to Washington immediately, Doctor!"

"You want me to fly to Washington, so you can kill me! I know how you think, after dealing with Troxell." Steve stared at the camera. "That's not going to happen. I'm going to get some breakfast because I'm freaking starving. Then I'm going to sit down and tell the reporters, and General Brenton, and whoever else wants to listen, what actually happened at this god damn plant as we destroyed Osiris!"

"You will do no such thing! I will have you arrested and forcibly transported to Washington, to silence you!" President Stillman pointed at his advisors. "Do something to assist me with this situation!"

"That McClellan, just risked his life to save our nation, and our residents, within the past several hours, Mister President," Robert Thorton, Senior National Security Advisor, said. "We'll look ridiculous if we arrest a national hero, immediately after he successfully saved our nation from disaster."

Franklin Perry smiled coyly while looking at the President. "Doctor McClellan, confessed to murdering a member of our United States military, that being Major Troxell, several minutes ago. You should order the United States Attorney General to arrest him, and charge him with murder."

"Look at my face and body, you god damn senile jackass! Look at the bruises! Troxell was strangling

551

me as he tried to kill me, when I ruptured his eye out of its socket, and kicked the bastard into the Osiris bacteria cloud. The killer cloud he worked so hard to protect for all of you heroes, killed the bastard!" Steve became angry and defiant. "You fools are running our government, and you're trying to protect your jobs, by finding ways to stop me from talking. It's not going to work!"

"That god damn man is intimidating all of you incompetent fools, and this conversation with him is complete bull shit!" John Leckowicz, the Director of the Defense Intelligence Agency, suddenly stood while unable to control his now raging anger. "I told you to kill McClellan weeks ago, so we wouldn't be in this exact situation. Now he's your problem, Stillman. You and your so called advisors can deal with the nuisance doctor!"

"Sit down and shut your mouth, Leckowicz," the President said sternly, while attempting to control the disparaging situation as it quickly escalated, in front of the reporters in the room.

"Don't tell me what to do, you pretentious fool! My advisor Ms. Groody and I are leaving this revolting and demeaning circus! Your pathetic conversation with that meddling doctor is ridiculous. You're the President! Show him you're in charge, and that you've got some balls. Arrest the bastard, as a treasonous threat to national security!" Leckowicz and Groody began walking toward the doors of the Pentagon Strategy Room, while carrying their documents.

"I want you to ensure my contingency plan instructions are carried out immediately, and without incident," John Kump, the Secretary of Defense said, while speaking to two agents from the Space Force Intelligence agency. The men rushed out of the room, and stood, waiting impatiently behind Leckowicz and his aide, while they waited for the doors of an elevator to open. Kump silently nodded to the other government officials and advisors in the room, as if suddenly in charge.

"Stillman isn't qualified to be President!" Leckowicz made a tight fist before angrily punching a nearby cement wall. "He needs me to punch in his god damn face, to beat some sense into that brain dead bastard!"

"He needs a harsh lesson in reality," Groody said, as she read messages on her cell phone. "We have a neophyte sitting in the Oval Office, with no idea of how the government functions, and deals with issues."

Both agents from Space Force Intelligence looked around cautiously before slowly pulling handguns from the holsters under their jackets. As John Leckowicz continued complaining about the President's unprofessional behavior, one agent pointed his weapon at the back of the man's head. A bullet fired moments later shattered Leckowicz's skull. Blood, flesh, and brain matter splattered across the nearby walls, as the lifeless body collapsed onto the floor.

"What have you done to him? You murdered that defenseless man!" Groody dropped her papers and phone on the floor. She screamed hysterically while backing away from the mutilated body, as red blood pooled under the dead man's head. She began struggling wildly after the second agent wrapped a hand around her slender neck, before he pushed her backward until her body crashed against a wall.

"Now you're going to die with him, bitch!" The Space Force Intelligence agent looked into the pleading woman's eyes, before he pressed his handgun against the side of her head. Moments later a single bullet silenced her hysterical screams. The agent pulled another handgun from his jacket pocket and dropped it onto the floor beside the bodies, before he and his companion stepped onto the elevator and closed the doors.

"What was that commotion and noise?" President Stillman appeared shocked, then frightened, as he looked around warily. He was surprised none of the government officials, or his advisors, appeared startled by the noises. "Did I just hear screams, and gunshots?"

John Kump calmly stepped forward. He placed a hand on the President's shoulder, as if consoling him. "Mister Leckowicz was grief stricken, over his possible illegal involvement in this complicated and dreadful Troxell situation, Mister President."

"Where is Leckowicz? Get him back in here so I can speak to him!"

"Unfortunately, moments ago, Mr. Leckowicz murdered his aide Ms. Groody with a handgun, before he turned the weapon on himself, and took his own life."

"He did what? That coward murdered his aide and killed himself? How can something like that happen in the Pentagon?"

"It appears to be the last desperate act of a man obviously overwhelmed by a dreadful situation we will never fully understand, and his involvement in illegal activities that may have violated our constitutional law."

"What the hell is going on there?" Steve said, as he frowned. "What just happened?"

"The Director of the Defense Intelligence Agency just murdered his highest ranking advisor, before he took his own life with a handgun."

"You're telling me he just killed himself?" Steve was shocked. He frowned at Roger and Bonnie.

"Yes, I can confirm he took his own life within the past several minutes! Without Mr. Leckowicz, or Major Troxell's testimony related to their involvement in this deadly situation, we will never determine all of the facts behind this unfortunate series of events."

"This is much too convenient," Roger said. "We killed Troxell while defending ourselves. The man that was directing Troxell's activities, and his aide, die in Washington. All of the witnesses are dead. This sounds like a cover up, that you orchestrated Mr. President!"

"Don't be ridiculous! You don't know what you're talking about!" The President became incensed, and his face appeared red from growing outrage after the accusation. "I am the leader of the free world!"

"You're a true politician! You'll say and do anything to keep your job!"

President Stillman's fists clenched tightly, as he was unable to control his anger. "I'm ordering the

United States Marshalls to arrest you Mister Samulson, along with Doctor McClellen, and Ms. Saunders! I want all of you charged with the murder of a military officer, after you are brought to Washington for questioning!"

"Mister President," General Brenton said, as he stepped forward. "I fought in both Iraq and Afghanistan, defending our nation from external enemies. Now I feel as if I must defend our nation from the enemies within. I will not permit anyone to take Roger, Steve, or Bonnie, from my command center, until I have more information and can determine who is a threat and who is not."

"What're you telling us, General?" Kump said. "You're defying a directive from the President of the United States?"

"Doctor McClellan and the others are now in my protective custody. I want guidance from the Justice Department, before I allow anyone to arrest these three individuals."

"Don't be ridiculous, General," President Stillman said, shouting at the camera. "That action, your defiance, will end your military career!"

"My actions may very well do that, but I have an obligation to the three individuals who worked together to destroy Osiris and save our nation, while murky shadow figures attempted to murder them!"

President Stillman pointed angrily at the camera, with a trembling hand. "You have an obligation to follow the orders of the President!"

"Not in this instance, Mr. President!"

"How can you say that?" President Stillman frowned. He looked at his advisors questioningly and then back at the camera.

"Our founding fathers did not establish the military, to assist with government illegalities!"

"You will surrender those people to federal agents immediately, General!"

"I no longer trust you, or your judgment, or your advisors, Mister President. I no longer consider you the leader of our military, based on your statements and actions!"

"What are you telling me?" President Stillman began to panic. "Have you lost your mind?"

"I instructed my senior staff officers to contact Attorney General Clarkson, and members of the Department of Justice, as we're speaking. The Attorney General is coming here, and the Justice Department is flying teams of investigators to my command center to interview Roger, Bonnie, and Steve."

"That action is unnecessary! We don't need a federal investigation!"

"My staff officers are telling me, members of Congress are watching this news conference play out, and they're already talking about a federal investigation into your administration!"

"I will not tolerate an investigation of that nature! Do you understand what I'm saying? There will be no investigation!"

Steve laughed. "You're already sounding like a guilty politician, attempting to block an investigation of your administration, Mister President. How many of the other people in that room are guilty along with you? This is somewhat reminiscent of the Nixon White House, and how that came collapsing down because of lies and deceit!"

"You are out of line, Doctor McClellan! No one is speaking to you."

"Mister President, I apologize, but I need to interrupt you," Robert Thorton, Senior National Security Advisor said. He frowned while holding a telephone in his hand.

"What is it? Can't it wait?"

Thorton shook his head. "Attorney General Clarkson is on the phone. He's telling you and the Executive Branch to back down, and his Justice Department will begin its own investigation into the incidents Doctor McClellan described during your conversation with him. He also wants to investigate the murder-suicide of Mr. Leckowicz, and Ms. Groody."

"This cannot be happening! We don't need the Justice Department involved in this."

"We don't have a choice, Mr. President. Doctor McClellan and the others will remain with General Brenton, until Justice Department agents transport them to Washington for a series of debriefing meetings, and meetings with the members of Congress."

"That's not what I want damn it! I don't want a damn investigation!"

"The President is a rude bastard when he doesn't get his way," Bonnie said, before she laughed with others.

"This conversation needs to end, now! I'm tired, hungry, and hurting. I don't feel the need to continue a conversation with a President that's going to tell me lies."

"You cannot simply dismiss the President of the United States, while he is speaking to you, Doctor."

"Watch me!" Steve smiled at Bonnie before he took her hand. "Let's find something to eat for breakfast. We need to talk about our future together."

"You are a wonderful person, Doc." Bonnie smiled as the military and civilian volunteers began clapping and cheering.

He raised his hands to quiet the crowd. "Our friends, and our soldiers, died while they were struggling to destroy Osiris. I can't allow our President to dishonor their memory while the government attempts to hide something they did illegally."

The researchers and scientists, reporters, and military personnel, began clapping and cheering. It soon became a thunderous sound of approval. The news camera operators filmed the supportive response.

Ecstatic reporters, military personnel, and researchers immediately surrounded Bonnie, Steve, and Roger. They continued cheering and clapping, and then began asking questions.

Doctor Wellfleet motioned Steve away from the enthusiastic crowd, as he answered questions. "I've got the results of the blood test you requested, to determine if you were exposed to radiation."

"How bad are the test results? I'm not sure I'm ready for this." Steve took a deep breath. "Did Roger, Bonnie, and I, receive a fatal dose of radiation in that reactor containment building?"

"I don't have a plausible explanation for these test results."

"Are you saying we were exposed to a lethal amount of radiation?" Steve swallowed hard. He immediately looked at Bonnie while imagining their lives ending tragically.

"No, no, it's all good! Everything is good! It's perfect! You're all perfect!"

"It's what?" Steve frowned. "Now I'm confused, Doctor. What's going on?"

"You all tested negative for radiation exposure. It's as if you weren't exposed to any radiation at all."

"How can that be? We were only a few yards from the reactor fuel rods."

"I understand that, and that's why I can't explain the test results. This is all very mysterious to me."

"Maybe I shouldn't question it. I should be thankful we're alive, and leave it at that."

"We still need to get you to the hospital for a complete decontamination, and additional blood work."

"Let's make that trip to the hospital now, so we don't wait too long for a thorough decontamination." Steve stepped between the people in the crowd of reporters shouting questions to Roger and Bonnie. He put his arm around Bonnie's waist. "We've got to go to the hospital."

Her eyes widened, as she suddenly became alarmed. "What are the results of that blood test?

Are we going to be all right, or are we going to die soon?"

He kissed her. "We're all going to live to be very old."

"That's perfect, Doc. I want to share my life with you, and grow old beside you."

"Me too!" Steve smiled before kissing her passionately.

A reporter said, "What're you going to do now that the crisis is resolved, Doctor McClellan?"

"I've learned a lot about myself, and the people closest to me, during the past few weeks. I need to spend some time with Ms. Saunders and talk about our future together." He kissed her, before the crowd began cheering loudly.

"You two are going to be very busy during the next four to five months," Bonnie said, before she smiled at Steve and Roger.

"Busy, doing what?" Roger frowned, before he laughed.

"I'm getting requests from all of the major news organizations, asking if we can appear on newscasts and talk shows, to explain how we stopped Osiris."

"Now that sounds interesting," Steve said.

"Newscasters are already talking about us, and calling us national heroes."

"The real heroes are the people who were murdered while they worked to help us. We'll need to remember and mention their sacrifices when we do those interviews," Steve said.

"I wouldn't have it any other way." Roger shook Steve's hand.

General Brenton motioned Steve, Roger, and Bonnie toward a helicopter marked with a red cross. "I'm fly all of you to a hospital north of here, so you can get checked out."

"Where will the researchers be staying, until they leave for home?"

"I'm moving them into hotels in San Jose."

"We'll need to meet to debrief everyone so we understand this entire situation from start to end."

"The press will want to interview the researchers too."

"They deserve the exposure, for the help they provided to save the world."

"You did a great job, Steve." Brenton shook his hand. "I have to congratulate you."

He smiled. "I only facilitated. Everyone else did the work."

"You built a damn great team Doctor, and they delivered."

"I want to personally thank them. Can we arrange it, in a hotel banquet room?"

"I'll arrange a dinner for everyone. You can talk to the researchers and my team before, during, and after dinner."

"I'd like that. I want them to understand I appreciate everything they did! Thank you."

As the helicopter's engine began whining to life, Brenton said, "My pilots will fly you directly to the hospital. The staff has been alerted you're on the way."

After Brenton's executive officer handed him a report, Roger said, "Is that another problem we need to resolve?"

"Not this time. This is an estimate of the number of people killed by Osiris. I need it for a press conference within the hour."

"How many people died?" Roger took a deep breath, as he prepared to hear the horrific news.

"Conservatively, we're estimating eight and a half million individuals perished."

"All of those people died needlessly, because Goldberg wanted to get back at my brother."

"I'm sorry, Roger. Those deaths are not on you personally."

He nodded. "I understand."

"My Army Rangers will accompany you to the hospital, and ensure you're safe. The Justice Department officials, and the Attorney General, will meet you there to take your statements and ask questions."

"We have a lot to tell them, and show them." Bonnie smiled while holding up the silver media card containing the video of Troxell.

"I want to tell the nation about the heroes who sacrificed and struggled, to help us make the last stand at this power plant." Steve smiled while looking around, to study the buildings and cooling towers. "And I want the nation to know you and your staff did one hell of a job, while we battled and destroyed Osiris."

"Thank you Doctor. We made a great team."

After watching news helicopters flying around the plant, Steve turned to Bonnie. "I want you to give interviews to the reporters today at the hospital."

"Why me? You and Roger are the ones they want to interview."

"You saved my life, and Roger's too, when you put yourself in danger while distracting Troxell. It's time for you to take credit for what you did here too."

"I saved your life? Then you owe me big time, Doc." She kissed him. "I want to talk to you while we're in the hospital. We need to get a room for two."

"Talk about what?" He gently slid his fingers through her hair, which was still damp.

"You asked me to marry you, when things were getting insane in that control room last night. Do you still want to marry me, and spend the rest of your life with me by your side?"

"Yes I do. I want you to be my wife." He hugged her tightly, while kissing her passionately.

"Living my life with you as your wife, is now the most important, and precious thing, to me."

"I feel the same way."

"You've become an important and exceptional and amazing person in my life. What you did here to destroy Osiris, has given me back my future with you. I love you, Doctor."

"I have a great idea." He kissed her. "After the government and news interviews are done, let's take some time off and go somewhere for a few weeks."

"I would enjoy that so much with you." Tears began streaming from her eyes.

"It has to be a vacation place with warm water and beaches, great food, and jewelry stores where I can take you shopping for an engagement ring. I want to slip a diamond on your finger, on the beach!"

"That will be so wonderful!" She wiped away the tears of joy running down her cheeks. "And I do need to see your amazing bedside manner again, Doctor! But this time, we'll do it longer and slower, and we won't be rushed!"

"I hate to interrupt you two, but I do need to get you to the hospital," General Brenton said. "The Federal Bureau of Investigation just contacted my command center. They will also have agents meet you at the hospital, to understand what you know about Troxell."

"Thank you for that information." Steve helped Bonnie and Roger climb into a Blackhawk helicopter. Then he climbed in beside them, before he turned to raise his hand to Brenton. "Nice job, General. Congratulations."

Several minutes later Bonnie, Roger, and Steve waved to the cheering volunteers, military men and women, construction workers, and reporters, below as the helicopter flew low over the plant, and then turned north toward the hospital.

"Now we need to begin the cleanup of the nation, as we put people's lives back together," John Harrison said while standing beside Brenton. He smiled while watching a large flock of birds fly over the plant. "That's a beautiful sight."

"It certainly is. We may still have our ecological problems to deal with, but now Osiris is no longer hunting us."

"I think we need to celebrate, General. Let's get a coffee from the kitchen your soldiers put together to feed these people."

"I'll take my coffee in a paper cup, please. I'm staying away from foam cups for the rest of my life!" Brenton laughed along with Harrison, as they walked together.

With the deadly Osiris crisis finally resolved, the people of the nation could mourn for their dead, and begin rebuilding. Both would be monumental tasks, and the greatest to face the people of the United States. Nevertheless, they would see it through together, as they did after all of the other disasters to affect the nation.

The End